Helen MacInnes

"HER NAME HAS BECOME SYNONYMOUS
WITH SUPERIOR THRILLERS
set in exotic and romantic spots around
the globe...In CLOAK OF DARKNESS,
as in most Helen MacInnes exploits, the
action is fast and furious."
John Barkham Reviews

Helen MacInnes

"A GRAND OLD PROFESSIONAL
offers sleekly crafted escape
...in this fast-moving,
colorful adventure."
Cosmopolitan

Helen MacInnes

"DESERVEDLY THE QUEEN
OF THE FEMALE MYSTERY
AND SUSPENSE WRITERS."
West Coast Review of Books

CLOAK OF DARKNESS

"THE ACTION IS FAST,
THE DANGER IS CONSTANT...
If you like thrillers written
for grown-up readers by expert
hands, you'll find it a splendid
evening's entertainment."
Cleveland Plain Dealer

Helen MacInnes

CLOAK OF DARKNESS

FAWCETT CREST • NEW YORK

A Fawcett Crest Book
Published by Ballantine Books
Copyright © 1982 by Helen MacInnes

Library of Congress Catalog Card Number: 82-47667

ISBN 0-449-20115-5

This edition published by arrangement with Harcourt Brace Jovanovich,
Publishers.

Manufactured in the United States of America

First Ballantine Books Edition: September 1983

For Keith and Nancy

with love

CLOAK OF DARKNESS

1

Iᴛ ᴡᴀs ᴛʜᴇ ᴜsᴜᴀʟ Mᴏɴᴅᴀʏ-ᴍᴏʀɴɪɴɢ ғᴇᴠᴇʀ ɪɴ Rᴏʙᴇʀᴛ Renwick's office. After a slow weekend with scarcely a report coming in, there was a deluge of cryptic messages—most by shortwave radio, some by coded cable or Telex, and even two by scrambled phone calls from Berlin and Rome requiring immediate attention.

But now it was five o'clock, the working day drawing to an end, his desk almost free of questions needing answers, of memoranda and suggestions to be considered. The easy replies would go out tonight; the difficult problems would need more computer research and analysis, perhaps further queries to agents in the field, certainly some scrambled phone discussions with agencies in various capitals. The intelligence services, not only of the NATO countries but also of those that had allied themselves with the West, were finding the London headquarters of Interintell a useful clearing house of information.

Interintell—or International Intelligence against Terrorism. It had been Renwick's brain child, conceived in Brussels, set up in London, staffed by ex-NATO intelligence men like Renwick himself. As an American, he would have been pleased to see Washington as Interintell's headquarters for shared information on terrorist conspiracies and connections. But he had

1

decided on London for several valid reasons. Western Europe had been under savage attack by organized terrorism; the United States—so far—hadn't experienced the same intensity. Then there was the matter of co-operation between intelligence services, and that came more willingly from Europeans; they had felt the need. The United States—so far, again—had not.

But then, America had been having its own headaches: the CIA under attack at home, in danger abroad from the exposure of its agents. Small wonder that Washington, overloaded with bureaucrats and competing agencies, had been in a foot-dragging mood when Renwick put forward his tentative idea almost three years ago: the necessity for pro-NATO countries to share intelligence information if terrorism was ever to be challenged successfully.

France, of course, had been interested—it was already establishing its own counter-terrorism department. But even though Paris had its attractions, it also had the headquarters of Interpol, the International Police Organization that tracked the criminals who once thought crossing a frontier would solve their problems. Fair was fair, Renwick had decided, and so London was the choice. In the two years since Interintell had been established, in a quiet house on Grace Street with the modest plate of J. P. Merriman & Co., Consultant Engineers marking its front entrance, it had prospered. Business, alas, was booming: too many damned terrorists, Renwick was thinking as he rearranged three remaining reports on the desk in front of him.

He would read and compare them once more—they were succinct, only a page to each of them—and then go home, still brooding about them, to be ready by tomorrow morning for a conference with Gilman and Claudel. (They were reading the duplicates right now.) He glanced at the clock, looked at Nina's photograph smiling at him across the small room. "Tonight," he told her, "I'll even be home in time for dinner."

And then the telephone rang, the green one, his own private line to the outside world without benefit of the telephone switchboard downstairs. Serious business, he thought with a frown as he picked up the receiver. A man's voice asked, "Renwick?"

"Yes."

"Say a few words, will you?" The voice was strong, confident, American.

Someone who knows me, a careful type, making sure. Renwick said, "'O what a tangled web we weave when first we practice to deceive.'"

There was a pause, then a smothered laugh. "Yes, Colonel, sir. You're Renwick all right."

"And who are you?"

"That doesn't matter. What I know, does. Is this line safe?"

"It should be."

"No other connection? No one listening?" The questions were tense.

"No one." And who the hell was this? Not more than twenty people had Renwick's private number, and the voice didn't belong to any of them.

The man's brief anxiety was over. He spoke more easily now. "I'll take your word for it. Meet me at six o'clock. In your favorite pub."

"Sorry. I'm meeting a friend there for a quick drink this evening. Why not join us?" Renwick would like to see this character who had ferreted out his private number. But not alone. He would get Ronald Gilman or Pierre Claudel to accompany him.

"I'm not joining you there. Just passing by your table. I'll stop to light a cigarette—a red throwaway lighter. You'll see a heavy gold ring on my right hand. Give me five minutes—five exactly—and then follow. Alone. Take a cab. Drive to Paddington Station. I'll be waiting just inside the main entrance. Follow me again. We'll stop at a newsstand, and I'll slip you a ticket. Then trail behind me, and we'll have us a little train ride. An empty compartment is a good place for serious talk."

"If it's empty." A compartment? Did they exist any more? This must be an amateur, and a stranger to Britain, too, who had worked out his own security plans.

"Leave that to me. You just leave your friend sitting in the Red Lion. Got that?"

"Which Red Lion? There must be fifty of them." On Bridle Lane? If so, this man had been watching him. A disquieting thought.

"Come on, Renwick! Your favorite pub. Not too far from the office."

So Bridle Lane it was.

"Six o'clock. Prepare for a short stay. But your friend stays there. No one follows you outside. No one follows me. I've got your word on that?"

"No one follows us into the street."

"And no one waits for us outside, either. Agreed?"

Renwick glanced at the reports in front of him. "Agreed, but I've some work to finish. Make it seven o'clock." And what have I to lose? he thought. If I sense something wrong about this man, I don't have to walk out of the Red Lion after him. He seems to know me. I feel I've heard that voice before, can't quite place it, but if I can see him I may remember where we've met. And was that what he wanted, my recognition? So that I'd follow him, have confidence in him?

"Six o'clock. There's a train to catch. And I hold you to your promise. No one watching the Red Lion. Remember!"

Renwick restrained a surge of annoyance, kept his voice cool. "Why should I go through all these antics? I don't know who you are or your credentials, or even—"

"Three weeks ago, I met a man who had just escaped from a prison in India—sentenced for murder in Bombay, 1979."

Renwick's spine stiffened. That was Erik—it had to be. News of his escape had reached Interintell six weeks ago. Since then, silence. And it had been Interintell (chiefly Renwick and Claudel) who had tracked Erik in 1979 through Europe and the Mideast and Iran, through Pakistan and India to Bombay, where the long chase had ended. Erik, the founder and leader of a West German group of anarchists calling themselves "Direct Action." Erik, or Kurt Leitner, or James Kiley, or a dozen other identities that he had used in his ten years of dedicated terrorism . . . Renwick recovered. "You met him where?"

"I'll tell you when we meet. I'll tell you that and more important things, too." The call ended.

More important than Erik wandering free? Renwick replaced the receiver. He picked up the three sheets of paper, placed them in a folder in his safe and locked it. (Tomorrow he would come into the office before nine, finish his homework on their problem before the meeting with Gilman and Claudel at ten o'clock.) The rest of the litter on his desk was gathered into neat piles, placed methodically in a drawer with a dependable lock: nothing of much importance there. The room was orderly once more.

Antiseptic, Renwick called it. Apart from the large maps

on the walls above the low bookcases, the only decoration was Nina's photograph. The one comfortable item was the black leather armchair with its footrest. Everything else was practical: desk, two chairs, three telephones, good lamps, wall safe, filing cabinet with a radio on top, an electric fire, and windows close to the ceiling with plenty of air and daylight and even more privacy than the room already possessed. Nina had suggested color for the walls, a bright carpet on the floor, but he had kept the room as plain as possible—white walls, wooden floors, nothing to distract or seduce him from the work on hand.

He called Nina on his regular outside line. "Honey—I'll be late tonight. Sorry. Terribly sorry, darling. Don't keep dinner—I'll have a sandwich. And get to bed, will you? Early?"

Nina took it well. She always did. It was as if she could sense some real urgency whenever he was forced to alter their plans. Now, she only said, "Take care, darling. Please?"

"Sure. I love you, don't I?" He was the luckiest guy, he told himself for the thousandth time.

There was no need to call Gilman on the interoffice phone. Their doors were always open to each other. He lifted his Burberry off its hook on the wall, checked his hat in its pocket, and entered the passage that led into the main house. The filing room, vast with its steadily increasing data, was still at work. Next door, the computer room had its two experts busy with their question-and-answer games. And at the end of the corridor was Ronald Gilman's office. He was the director of this establishment, elected by Renwick as much for his diplomatic connections as for his expert knowledge. It was Gilman who had arranged for the lease of this building, for the initial acquiring of equipment, and had managed to attract the unobtrusive support of his own government. The English had a quiet way in such matters.

Gilman, busy comparing the three reports, looked up in surprise. "Finished?" he asked. "Well, it looks as if you were right in your prediction two years ago." He tapped the pages in front of him. "Right-wing terrorism is now as ruthless as left-wing. Joining each other, too, in some cases. An unholy alliance."

"But I didn't foresee any right-wing terrorists being trained in Communist camps." That was what the three reports, each from a different source—France, Turkey, Lebanon—had indicated. "I'll have to finish studying the evidence tomorrow morning. Something else has come up."

Gilman looked at the American's calm face. Nothing there to show any worry or alarm: thoughtful gray eyes, brown hair slightly graying at the temples, even features, a pleasant mouth relaxing into one of his reassuring smiles. Yet Renwick's voice had been too casual, always a small storm signal. "Something interesting?"

"I don't know. It's the damnedest thing." Renwick began pacing the room, no larger than his own and just as sparingly furnished. "I had a call—my green line—" He halted, frowning at the floor, and began an accurate but brief account of that strange conversation.

Gilman was a good listener, silent, expressionless, but as Renwick ended, he said quite flatly. "I don't like it, Bob. It could be a trap."

"It could also be important."

"The man knows you?"

"Seemingly. He certainly knows my phone number. How did he get that? And where did he meet Erik? He didn't just *see* Erik. He met him. Exact word."

"Three weeks ago . . ." Gilman's glasses were off, his hair—blond, thinning on top—was ruffled and smoothed and ruffled again. "Erik will have moved on by this time."

"At least we get a direction. We don't know, now, whether Erik left India, or traveled east or north or west."

"Certainly not south," Gilman said, "unless he was taking a header into the Indian Ocean." Then he looked at his watch, began gathering the pages in front of him. "You go ahead. I'll take my car and join you in the Red Lion."

"I hoped you would. Just as well for two of us to see this man."

"He had no objection to someone meeting you?"

"No. Only to being followed."

From the pub or from the street, Gilman remembered. "He didn't mention anything about being followed at Paddington, did he?"

"No." Renwick raised an eyebrow.

"Start moving, old boy." Gilman locked up the three agents' reports. "I'll see you at six."

Renwick left, still speculating. Why should Ron choose to

delay, then take his car instead of walking the short distance to the Red Lion? Renwick could guess the answer, and felt the better for it. Gilman would now be on the phone to Claudel. And Renwick wouldn't be heading out on a train, as yet unknown, to some benighted part of the country without someone nearby as a backup. Of course, if Gilman's first objections were true, then he could be trapped. A train, to quote the man on the phone, might be a good place for a serious talk, but it was also a useful place for throwing out a body.

Renwick stopped, hurried back to his office, unlocked its door. Quickly, he opened the filing cabinet, found his Biretta and its lightweight holster. Almost two years of marriage and the sweet life had turned him—what? Soft? Careless? Not altogether, he decided as he made sure the Biretta was loaded and slipped it into the holster, now under his tweed jacket. Cigarette case and lighter were in his pocket. All set. He left, using the rear staircase and avoiding the main-floor offices of J. P. Merriman & Co., whose full-time surveyors and practical engineering advice brought in, and legitimately, the profits that kept Interintell expanding.

It was raining hard.

2

TWELVE MINUTES AT A SMART PACE BROUGHT RENWICK IN good time to the lower end of Bridle Lane. It stretched northward for a hundred yards, even less, close-packed on either side by low-storied buildings, before it was obliterated by the blare and bustle of Fleet Street. Up there, as in all the main arteries this evening, the roadway would be jammed with traffic and bad tempers, the sidewalks filled with umbrellas and sodden raincoats. The calendar might say June; today's onslaught of cold wind and rain made it feel like March. But there was no need to approach the Red Lion by an overcrowded highway; there were shortcuts if you knew this part of the city, a loose haphazard web of short and narrow streets that merged and separated and changed their names as unexpectedly as their direction. And Renwick knew this area.

Each day after lunch, usually a sandwich in his office, he seized half an hour for a couple of miles in various directions and got the tension of too much desk-sitting out of his shoulder muscles. This evening he could even take a brief detour once he left Merriman's by its inconspicuous rear exit, and still have six minutes to spare when he reached the pint-sized square where Bridle Lane began. So he slowed his step, making note of everything around him: no one loitering, no one following—

the footsteps behind him hurried on, drew ahead, passed into the lane, kept hurrying. The shops and businesses, all small-scale, were closed, and if people lived up above them, then this was a night to stay indoors. The café at the corner of the square had its usual enticing suggestions on the hand-printed card displayed in its window, chief among them "Hot Peas and Vinegar." That possibly explained the empty taxi, desolate and abandoned, that had been parked in front of the café while its driver enjoyed some sausages and mashed. But it also reminded Renwick that taxis were scarce on a wet evening like this, and he wondered how—in this place, at this time of day—he would find a cab to take him to Paddington. That was one detail forgotten, perhaps not even imagined, by the man who had telephoned with such precise instructions. It was a revealing omission. The man might know the name and location of the Red Lion, but he didn't know this district. So how did he get the address? From someone who had met Renwick there? Someone who also had access to Renwick's private number? If so, decided Renwick, that narrowed down the field: few of his contacts possessed both pieces of information, very few. In grim mood, he entered the Red Lion.

From the outside, it didn't look particularly inviting: it could have used some paint and polish. If that was its method of discouraging tourists in their search for quaint old London pubs, it was highly successful. It had its own clientele, some regular, some—like Renwick—occasional. And that was another point to remember: his visits here had no fixed routine, formed no pattern. Even constant surveillance—and he hadn't seen or sensed any such thing—wouldn't have marked the Red Lion as a special meeting place. No, that information had come from someone who had been here with Renwick. A mole in our group, a real professional sent to infiltrate? Or someone greedy for money, or open to blackmail? Or just a blabbermouth, overflown with wine and insolence?

Renwick resisted a searching look around the long room, seemed to be paying all attention to shaking out his raincoat and the old, narrow-brimmed felt hat he kept for bad weather. As yet, the place was only half filled—it opened at five-thirty—but that would soon be remedied, and the smell of tobacco smoke would be added to the smell of ale that impregnated the dark woodwork of walls and tables. Casually, he noted two groups of men standing near the bar—no high stools here, no chrome or neon lighting, either—and three more groups at the central tables. He chose a high-backed wooden booth, one of a row on the opposite side of the room from the stretch of highly polished counter, hung coat and hat on a nearby hook, and sat down to face the back of the room. It was from somewhere there that the man must come in order to pass this table on his way to the door. I'll make sure of a good look at his face, Renwick thought as he ordered a beer and tried to look totally relaxed, but he felt a tightening in his diaphragm, an expectation of something unexpected, something over which he would have no control.

Even before his beer was brought by a pink-cheeked, red-haired barmaid, the room was beginning to fill: journalists in tweeds, conservatively clothed civil servants interspersed with exactingly dressed barristers, music students in leather jackets, and businessmen in three-piece suits. Renwick smoked a cigarette, seemed normally interested in the growing crowd, wondered if his man was in the group gathered around a dartboard at the far end of the bar.

"Sorry," Ronald Gilman said, ridding himself of coat and umbrella, taking a seat opposite Renwick. "I'm late—this weather." He smoothed down his hair, asked, "Seen any likely prospect?"

"No. But he's here." Renwick could feel he had been observed and studied for the last few minutes. "Where did you park your car?" Gilman hadn't walked—his raincoat was dry, his umbrella rolled.

"I didn't. Claudel dropped me at the door and then drove on."

"Oh?"

Gilman only nodded and ordered a double whiskey with water, no ice. "I'm more nervous than you are, Bob. You know, you needn't follow this blighter out. If you have the least doubt—"

"Here's someone now," Renwick warned. The man didn't pause to light a cigarette. "False alarm," Renwick said with a small laugh.

"Have you managed to place his voice?"

"I've heard it before. I think. I could be wrong." But a

telephone did accentuate the characteristics of a voice—its tone, its inflections.

"Strange that he didn't disguise it. Muffle it. He didn't?"

"No. He wants to be identified, I guess. Hence the double play. There was no need to meet twice, first here and then at Paddington." Another man, could be a student from the school of music near Magpie Alley, passed their table. This one was lighting a cigarette. But no red lighter.

"One meeting with proper signals would be enough," Gilman agreed. "An odd bird. Perhaps—" He heard footsteps slowing down behind his left shoulder, barely turned his head to glimpse the man who was about to light a cigarette, went on speaking. "Perhaps this foul weather will be over before the Wimbledon finals."

"Did you get tickets?" Renwick looked down at his watch. The man continued toward the door. A red lighter, a heavy signet ring . . . And a face that was deeply tanned, fine wrinkles at the side of the brown eyes glancing briefly in Renwick's direction; hard features, thick black hair. His suit was well cut, fitted his broad shoulders, but its fabric was too light in weight for London. Passing through? Certainly the opaque plastic raincoat over one arm was easily packable.

Gilman, with a good view of the man's departure, dropped his voice. "Straight spine, strong back, about six feet tall. Did you get a full view of his face?"

Renwick's voice was now at a murmur, too. "His name is Moore. Albert, Alfred—no, Alvin Moore. He was one of the drivers at NATO—his second enlistment. First one was in Vietnam, saw a lot of action, good record. But in Belgium he got involved with a couple of sergeants who were caught selling stolen supplies to a dealer in Brussels—they drew seven years each. There was no real evidence against Moore. They used his car, that was all. He had a mania for automobiles and speeds of ninety miles an hour." Renwick kept an eye on his watch.

"Did he drive for you?" That couldn't have been very often. Renwick liked to drive himself.

"Occasionally—when I had a meeting and had to be in uniform. Staff car, driver, that kind of thing."

"Then how did you remember him?"

"When he was brought up on charges, he needed me as a character witness."

"And you appeared?"

"He was honest—as far as I knew. One time I carried a briefcase, some sealed folders, an armful of maps. I had a clip of dollars—emergency cash—in my trouser pocket. Belgian francs were in my wallet. The dollar bills slipped out. I didn't notice, didn't even remember where I had lost them. Corporal Moore was my driver that day. He returned the bills intact. Found them slipped down in the back seat of the car."

"Did your testimony clear him?"

"Every little bit helps, doesn't it? But he was transferred stateside, discharged. Joined something more to his taste—the Green Berets, I heard." Renwick glanced at his watch once more. "That was about seven years ago."

"He's the type who needs action, I think."

Renwick agreed. "His trouble at NATO was boredom." Then his voice changed. "On the phone he addressed me as colonel. Just once. Yet I was a captain when he knew me."

"Where did he get that information?" Gilman asked quickly. Renwick's promotion had been kept very quiet indeed; he never used his rank, just as the others in the Interintell group didn't use theirs. Civilians for the duration and the preservation of peace, it was to be hoped.

"That," said Renwick, "needs finding out." There were too many damned questions needing answers. His eyes left his watch. "Time to start trying. It's five minutes to the second." He rose, unhooked his coat and hat. In a voice back to a normal level, he said, "Sorry I have to leave. Be seeing you."

"See you, old boy." Gilman's eyes were troubled, but he gave one of his rare smiles, warm and real. Just hope that Bob has been keeping up his karate sessions, he thought as he watched Renwick pull on his Burberry and jam his rain hat well down on his brow before he stepped out into the cold world of Bridle Lane.

For a moment, Renwick hesitated on the sidewalk. Walk to Fleet Street, try to find a cab there? Or would that taxi parked outside the café still be waiting? He started down Bridle Lane toward the square, then halted. Luck was with him: the driver had finished his sausages and mashed, or was it hot peas and vinegar? The taxi was coming this way. He signaled, and it stopped. He opened the door. A man raised himself from the back seat, held out an arm covered with a thin raincoat. Renwick saw the businesslike nose of a revolver just showing from under the coat's folds. "Hop in, I'll give you a lift," said Alvin Moore.

Renwick got in. "Unnecessary," he said, looking at the pistol. The driver hadn't even noticed; he had had his instructions, for the cab started forward with not a minute lost. A red-necked man, well fed, too, he was only intent on entering Fleet Street and gauging the traffic flow. "And much too noisy," Renwick went on, controlling his anger. Moore was staring back at Bridle Lane.

"Not so noisy." Moore lifted the raincoat's fold to show a silencer was attached. "And not unnecessary. What guarantee did I have that you wouldn't use a gun to make me redirect the cabbie to your office?" He kept looking back.

"No one was there to follow us. As promised." Renwick was watching the direction the taxi was taking. So far, it seemed normal—allowing for one-way streets. They were now out of Fleet Street, driving north and then swinging west. They could be heading for Paddington Station.

Moore took the rebuke with a shrug. He was tense, though.

Preserve me from a jumpy man holding a pistol, Renwick thought. If he releases the safety catch, I'll grasp his wrist, twist it up. I could draw the Biretta in that split second, but I won't: a shoot-out in a cab is faintly ridiculous—would upset my British friends, too. Renwick eased his voice and kept a careful eye on Moore's right hand. "You've got some strange ideas about the way we carry on our business at the office. Forcing people inside is not the way we work."

"You sure don't consult or engineer."

"No?"

Moore stared. "You an engineer?" he asked, unbelieving.

"I was."

"Before the army?"

"And for the first two years of my service."

"As I heard it, you engineer more than dams and bridges now."

"You've heard a lot of things, it seems." Renwick looked pointedly at the driver's red neck. "A friend of yours? Then we can start talking about what you've heard and where you heard it."

Moore shook his head. "Don't know him. Just doing his job. And we'll need more time than we'll have in this cab. There's a lot to talk about." He was no longer on edge.

So Renwick kept the conversation innocuous, nothing to stir up any more tension in Moore. "How did you produce a taxi at the right moment? Quite a triumph."

"Easy. I took a cab to Bridle Lane, found it couldn't park there, so I settled for the square. All thirty feet of it. Some district, this."

"And you paid double the fare, promised double again if it waited for you?"

A grin broke over Moore's face. "With the cost of a hot supper thrown in. Easy." He was back to normal, more like the corporal Renwick remembered from seven years ago. There were interesting changes, though: he carried more weight, but that was muscle, not fat. The deep tan, the leather skin with its creases at the eyes, and the furrows on either side of the tight mouth indicated much time out of doors in strong sun and tropical heat. His suit spelled city, however, some place like New York, where summer needed thin clothing. It looked fairly new, expensive but not custom-made. Not enough time for a tailor to measure and fit? A quick visit to America? The crisp white shirt had a buttoned-down collar, the tie was recognizably from Brooks Brothers. A nice picture of an affluent man. Except for the raincoat—definitely incongruous, probably bought in an emergency this morning when the rain had set in.

Moore noticed the quiet scrutiny. "Well?" he demanded, his eyes defensive.

"Pretty smooth. But you always did like a smart uniform." Renwick touched the sleeve of the plastic coat. "Bought today, thrown away tomorrow. Heading for a drier climate?"

Moore's eyes widened for a moment. Then he laughed. "I came to the right man, that's for sure." He looked long at Renwick. "Engineer!" he said, shook his head. "Never met one yet who noticed anything except stress and strain on a pontoon." He settled back, began watching the streets.

Again, Renwick checked the direction they were taking. It could indeed be Paddington. Fleet Street and the Strand area were well behind them. Piccadilly Circus, as bright and garish as Times Square, lights at full glitter even in daylight, had led them to the curve of Regent Street. But not for long. A quick left turn took them into quieter streets, rich and restrained, where people didn't stand on pavements waiting for double-decker buses. The taxi driver knew his London: a left turn, a right turn, traveling west, then north, then west and north again, through an area of exclusive shops, imposing houses, and most correct hotels. This part of London always seemed to Renwick to be floating on its own cloud nine, far above the dreams of ordinary mortals. But soon the cab would be nearing Oxford Street and touching reality again. Still a long way to travel. Renwick glanced covertly at his watch. Pierre Claudel should be already at Paddington, waiting to track him into the station. "We may miss that train," Renwick said.

It didn't seem to worry Moore. With an eye on a corner sign reading *Park Street*, he stopped lounging. "Nearly forgot about this." With quick, expert touch, he removed the silencer from the revolver, slipped them into separate pockets of the raincoat. "When we leave the cab, you walk ahead. I follow."

"And if I don't walk ahead? Will you reassemble that piece of artillery, use it in front of a hundred people?" Renwick's voice was soft, his eyes hard.

"I can put it together in three seconds flat. But I don't need to use it now."

"Why the reprieve?"

"It did its job. Got you into this cab damn quick."

Renwick remembered Moore's anxiety as they had left Bridle Lane. "You weren't nervous only about one of my friends following us, were you?"

No answer to that. Moore watched the street ahead. "Just do as I say. If you took off, you mightn't live to regret it."

Renwick looked at him sharply, wondering if that negative had crept in by mistake.

"You might not live," Moore repeated. He saw Renwick's glance at the bulge in his plastic raincoat's pocket. "No, not that. I'm no assassin. I'm doing you a favor. I owe you one." Then he looked at the street ahead, raised his voice for the driver. "Is this it? Okay, okay. Stop at the corner. How much?" His wallet was in his hand.

Good God, thought Renwick, we're at Marble Arch.

Moore frowned at the wad of English pound notes, made a guess, began counting them. He spoke to Renwick from the side of his mouth. "Buy a ticket for Tottenham Court Road. We're taking the subway."

"Tube," Renwick corrected quietly as he opened the taxi door.

Moore halted him with another half-whispered command. "When we reach there, reverse positions. I lead. You follow. Room 412."

Renwick nodded and left Moore handing over a clutch of notes; more than enough, judging by the driver's sudden geniality. Marble Arch, he thought again, Marble Arch! Damn me for an idiot. He fooled me. I fell for Paddington. And Claudel hanging around there, watching, worrying? Pierre Claudel would do more than raise a fine French eyebrow when he waited and waited. . . . The French could produce a flow of curses that would outdo anything an Anglo-Saxon tried.

Can't even dodge into a telephone booth and warn Gilman— if I could reach him. Moore would take that as a breach of faith; he'd walk away and leave me flat, and I'd learn nothing in Room 412, wherever it was. In some hotel, obviously. In the neighborhood, again obviously, of Tottenham Court Road: no mention of another tube, or a bus, or a taxi. In Soho, perish the thought? Or in Bloomsbury? Let's hope it's a short distance. Tonight, I'm in no mood for a walk in the rain.

3

THE DISTANCE WAS SHORT, A TWO-MINUTE WALK UP TOTTENham Court Road, which looked even worse than usual by the gray light of a wet evening. Moore set a sharp pace, plunging through the clots of pedestrians seemingly paralyzed by weather and traffic. Although he walked at a quick march through the crowd, Renwick managed to keep Moore's black hair in sight. He almost lost him when a left turn was made into a quiet, narrow street but reached the corner in time to see Moore disappear into the Coronet's doorway. It was one of the new hotels, rising high, a flat-faced block of building with innumerable windows that was attempting to uplift the neighborhood and edge in on the tourist trade of Bloomsbury.

Its lobby was crowded, people discouraged by the weather sitting on fat couches or standing in talkative groups. A plumbers' convention, Renwick noted from the outsize announcement propped on a gilded easel. He crossed the soft mile of carpet—no expense spared—without anyone paying him the least attention and went up to the fifth floor in an elevator filled with jovial Birmingham accents and the smell of wet wool. Then he walked down one flight and in the rear of the building found Room 412.

The door was ajar. Moore turned from pouring Scotch at a

table, gave his first real smile. "Take the load off. Have a drink." The atmosphere has changed, thought Renwick. He's still giving orders, but perhaps that's become natural: certainly, Moore hasn't been following them for a long time. "Later," Renwick said and went into the bathroom, pulling off his raincoat and hat, hung them up where they could drip themselves slightly dry. He glanced around—nothing unpacked here, just gleaming surfaces, cramped but clean; only the two-inch cake of soap and hand towel used, and the two glasses missing from their holders.

The bedroom was small-scale, too. No possessions on a miniature bureau. An air-travel bag, closed, lay on a bed that imitated an armless couch. Curtains were now drawn over the window, the overhead light turned on. Moore was back at the table pouring himself a second drink in one of the bathroom's missing glasses. "Sure you won't?"

"Not at the moment." Renwick chose the chair that had a dwarf table within reach, molded out of white plastic to match the few pieces of furniture; the other held Moore's coat, dripping onto the carpet. "Any music available?"

"Sweet and low. Will that do?" He reached for a knob on the radio on the nightstand. "How loud?" He let "That Old Black Magic" blare out.

"Not so loud that we can't hear each other."

"You boys slay me. Who's to know we're here? They didn't have time to plant a bug." He was confident, assured, his voice—perhaps fueled by two strong drinks—assertive.

"The walls are thin."

Moore shrugged, adjusted the sound to a reasonable level. Then a cough from next door, muted but clear enough, made him stare at Renwick and shake his head. He picked up his glass, empty once more, thought better of it, and put it down. He came over to the couch, sat on its edge to face Renwick. "Not much of a room," he said, speaking more softly. "The best we could get at short notice—a friend booked it from New York. I only got here this morning."

And out tonight, Renwick thought. A friend? But that could wait. "All right, Moore. Let's begin. I have some—"

"Cut out the Moore. Don't use it, now. Al will do," he added just to keep things friendly. He slipped off his jacket, threw it to the other end of the couch, loosened his tie, unbuttoned his collar. "How the hell do you put up with these clothes?" Then he settled back on one elbow, crossed his legs, looked relaxed, but his eyes were alert. "You have some what?"

"Some questions to ask. Then I'll listen to you." Al seemed about to object. "Not questions about you," Renwick went on. "Okay?"

"Any information about me comes from me when I'm damned ready and willing to give it. Understood?"

"Understood." He would be alarmed at how much I've learned about him since we first met, thought Renwick. "First of all, where did you see the man who escaped from an Indian prison?"

Moore, or whatever his new name was to match a false passport, brushed that aside with his hand. "Not important. He won't last long. Forget him."

"I can't."

"Oh, yes—your outfit caught him, he said."

"Tracked him down," Renwick said to keep the record straight. Incredible, he was thinking: Erik the dedicated anarchist, Erik the leader of a ruthless gang of West German terrorists, Erik dismissed as "not important." How naïve could Moore get? "He was recruiting terrorists abroad, and we followed him to India. It was the Bombay police who arrested him."

"Interintell, he called you. That was the first time I heard the name. He was teaching a class. I was standing at the back of the tent, just curious. I wasn't a part of that crowd, see?" Moore wanted to make that clear.

"A class for terrorists? Where?"

"He was giving a couple of lectures on how you dodge arrest, but if you're caught, then how you escape."

"Where did you see him?" Renwick was insistent, firm.

"South Yemen."

"At a training camp for terrorists?"

"Yes, but I wasn't—"

"Part of the scene. Just curious." And why the hell were you there? Renwick wondered. But that would keep. Moore seemed mollified at least, perhaps more ready to talk. "Why won't he last long?"

"He got the Cubans flaming mad. There were two of them—

not terrorists—intelligence agents from Havana, I heard. Sent to Yemen to make sure he got to South America. As ordered."

Casually, Renwick had eased the plastic table closer to his knee, steadied its ashtray, taken out his cigarette case, pressing its hinge to activate it. "Ordered? By whom?"

"By the people who got him out of prison, helped him reach Bombay."

Renwick seemed to have forgotten his cigarette. "He actually chose Bombay?" His disbelief sounded real.

"A cool customer. No one would expect him to enter a city where he had been arrested for killing a cop. So he told the class."

"And after Bombay? Aden?"

"On a freighter as a deck hand."

"Smart customer, too. Unless, of course, he was helped all the way—by the same people who got him out of prison and need him in South America." Renwick abandoned his cigarette case beside the ashtray, shook his head. "Perhaps not so smart, after all—not if he argued with the Cubans."

"There was damn near a fight, words rattling off like a spray of machine-gun bullets. I've picked up some Spanish, other languages, too, but it's just as well not to let others know. That way, you keep your nose clean."

Renwick nodded. "What was the argument about, did you hear?"

"Not much. Too quick. But one thing is certain. He isn't going to South America. A couple of nights later, he vanished. Like that!" Moore snapped his fingers. "The Cubans were fit to be tied."

Yes, thought Renwick, he will head for West Germany, where he will reorganize his Direct Action group. He was their founder. He was their leader. He will get them moving again. To Erik, that is all that matters. "When did he disappear?"

"Ten days ago, just before I got clear of that godforsaken hole. No trace. Not at the airport, not at the docks. But he won't get far. The Cubans have money behind them. He'll never make it." Moore was suddenly restless. "Think I'll have that drink. Questions make me thirsty." He was about to get to his feet. "Keep them short."

Renwick made a fast decision as he lifted his cigarette case— couldn't leave it lying there unused, not all the time, he told himself. "I'll do better than that. I'll postpone them until you've given me your information. Okay?" Moore had been stopped in his tracks. Renwick offered a cigarette, delaying him still more.

"No, thanks. Never use them. That stuff can kill you."

But bullets and whiskey can't? Renwick smiled. So the red lighter and cigarette pack had just been props for the pub scene. Or another subterfuge, like a mustache shaved off—there was a less deep tan over Moore's upper lip—and completely different clothes? "Come on, Al. Begin! I'm listening." He took a cigarette, closed the case, laid it once more on the table top.

Moore glanced over at the bottle of Scotch. "Want me to keep a clear mind?" he asked. "Is that it?"

"That's it," Renwick said brusquely. "Let's get started." He pointed to the corner of the couch. "And keep your voice down." As Moore resumed his seat with a one-finger salute, Renwick flicked his lighter, but it didn't catch.

"Get one thing straight," Moore was saying, leaning forward, elbows on knees, his left hand fingering his heavy signet ring. "I'm no informer."

"Just a reliable source of information," Renwick assured him. The lighter failed again. Renwick dropped it into his pocket and found some matches.

"And I'm no terrorist. I'm a soldier. That's my trade and I'm good at it. That's why Exports Consolidated hired me. Ever hear of them?"

"Yes." A report on Exports Consolidated had been on Renwick's desk for the last month, part of a general survey of armaments sold by Americans and shipped abroad to Third World countries. It was a flourishing business these days, with plenty of competition from European merchants as well as from Soviet Russia and its allies. Renwick's special interest in such trafficking had been roused by one of the simple questions that, as soon as he asked it, demanded an answer: Where did today's international terrorists get their sophisticated weapons, and how? "Exports Consolidated once exported agricultural machinery, then expanded into military hardware. Nothing illegal about that. Unfortunately."

"Nothing illegal?" Moore laughed.

"You tell me," Renwick said softly.

"It began with Vietnam."

What didn't? thought Renwick but restrained himself.

"A buddy of mine—we were in the same outfit—was killed there. When I got back stateside, I went to see his wife. She was an old friend. She had been running her father's business, learning everything she could from him. Built it up, made a go of it. Agricultural machinery, can you beat that? When her father died, she owned the shop. Then Mitchell Brimmer came along—you heard of him?"

Renwick stubbed out his cigarette, compressed his lips. Brimmer was the founder and head of Exports Consolidated. He had been in Vietnam, too. Not as a soldier. Began as an agent, low grade, in the CIA; quit the Agency to become a journalist in Saigon, then businessman. Or perhaps he had been that all along. He made good contacts, helpful friends, but he seemed to have helped them, too. Legitimate business apparently: no drug smuggling, no gems, no official secrets. "Interested in agricultural machinery, wasn't he? Moved back from Saigon to the States, set up a firm there, expanded it and—"

"That he did. Took over several outlets for agricultural machinery. He made an offer to—to my friend. A good deal. She had brains, and he knew it. Paid her a fair price and offered her more money than any she could set aside for herself. So she took the job."

"Doing what?"

"Keeping the books and a chance to rise with his firm. She did, too. But that was during my second tour of duty, when I was at NATO, and after that—well, I was a couple of years with the Green Berets. Then I tried some soldiering abroad—in Africa, mostly." Moore noticed Renwick's expression. He said quickly, defensively, "I wasn't a mercenary. Sure I was paid, but I trained troops to fight. Troops." He shook his head over that memory. "A bunch of slobs when I got them, but I turned out soldiers, all right."

"Guerrillas?"

"Call them what you like, but they damn sure weren't terrorists. They meet the enemy in a fire fight, a fair skirmish. They don't infiltrate a town and pretend they're ordinary folks, and then start plotting where they'll hide the bombs to blow up civilians. That isn't war, kill or be killed. That's bloody murder."

"There's a difference," Renwick agreed, but it was a subtle

one and sometimes fragile. Guerrillas on a rampage could leave a lot of innocent civilians maimed, raped, or dead. "So you're against terrorism. And assassination."

Moore looked at him sharply.

"You told me that. In the taxi," Renwick reminded him. "But you haven't finished about your wars in Africa."

"Two years were enough. In seventy-eight I came back to New York and met—met my friend. She was Brimmer's good right hand by that time. She told me I was just the man that her boss was looking for. Or one of the men—he hired three of us, all with plenty of experience. Exports Consolidated was by then into selling arms to countries that could pay for them— or had rich friends who'd oblige. They wanted the newest and best, and instructors to show them how to use the weapons. Sure, I jumped at the job. It was big money, and travel, and I got respect, too."

Don't rush him, Renwick decided. He has got to justify himself. But even in Moore's self-explanations, the shape of something ominous was beginning to form.

"One thing I made clear to Brimmer from the start. I'd train soldiers. I'd instruct them in weapons. But I wasn't teaching a damn thing to terrorists. I wasn't running a school for assassins, either."

"He agreed to that?" What about South Yemen? Renwick wondered.

"With a joke and a slap on the back. So everything went fine. Big and bigger money. Brimmer can afford it; he's making millions. He's got business contacts everywhere. And three months ago, he joined up with another big outfit that sells arms. It's international, so my friend says. Based in Europe."

That was news to Renwick. "Their name?"

"Brimmer isn't telling. And you won't find the merger in any financial pages. Anyway, when I got back to New York—"

"Your friend"—Renwick cut in quickly—"surely she knows the name of that firm."

"It isn't important."

"Just part of the picture, Al. I must have all of it, as complete as possible, if you want my help. That's why you brought me here, isn't it? You don't need money, that's obvious."

"Wouldn't take it—" Moore began angrily.

"That's right. You are no informer. What's the firm's name?"

"Klingfeld and Sons. They don't sound like much, but she says they're high-powered. Offices in Paris, Geneva, Rome."

"Each firm is keeping its own name?" A strange merger. Stranger yet was the fact that Klingfeld & Sons was not on any list of armament traffickers that Renwick had ever seen.

"They're a silent partner in Exports Consolidated. She says it's funny: Klingfeld is bigger than Brimmer."

"Can't go on calling your girl 'she,' Al. What's her name?" Moore's lips tightened.

Renwick's voice was sharp. "Look—how many personal and invaluable secretaries does Brimmer have? We can trace her. Easily."

"Lorna." The name, incomplete, came unwillingly.

Had dear Lorna instructed Moore not to give her name; not Klingfeld's, either? It had been like pulling teeth to extract these two small items from Moore. "I take it Lorna is a close friend of yours. Very close? Then you can believe what she tells you. You trust her completely?"

"Trust her? Lorna saved me from blowing everything when I got back to New York last week. That son of a bitch Brimmer had sent me out to South Yemen. I didn't object to that. I've been in Libya, Chad, Lebanon, Zaïre, Tanzania, the Sudan. Politics? No interest. I train soldiers, I'm worth my hire. That's that. But in Yemen—" Moore's sudden anger almost choked him. "In Yemen, I wasn't instructing a bunch of camel drivers in how to handle grenades and antitank guns. I was given a bunch of goddamned know-it-all terrorists yapping about ideals with murder in their eyes. Couldn't quit, either, unless I wanted to be found behind cargo containers at the docks with my throat slit—that's happened to one guy I knew who tried to bug out."

Renwick's spine went tense. "Where did the terrorists come from? Who paid their way?"

Moore shrugged his shoulders. "Must have come from ten, twelve, fifteen countries—Europe, South America, the Mideast—you name them, I had them. And the weapons sold by Exports Consolidated didn't come direct. Re-routed through other countries. Rockets, the newest explosives, top-secret detonators and electronic devices, army supplies we don't sell anyone."

"Illegal trafficking in weapons and military equipment," Renwick said softly. Then Brimmer must be using false or cover agreements in sales abroad; falsified accounts, too, in the purchasing of supplies, and bribery. A mess of corruption wherever Brimmer moved. "Get me a sample of one page of his business ledger—"

"That's only the half of it," Moore interrupted, either determined to tell things his way or unwilling to involve Lorna in supplying proof of Brimmer's flourishing conspiracy. He rushed on, and Renwick kept silent. "That super-secret equipment was beyond me or anyone else in Yemen. Brimmer is sending in an expert this week from California—fifty thousand dollars for him out of a two-hundred-thousand fee for Brimmer with compliments of Yemen's big friend in North Africa." Moore paused, well pleased with the effect he was producing. "So I came back from Yemen ready to tell Brimmer to go shove it. Lorna met me at Kennedy, warned me to ease off. For now. That was what she was doing, going along, arousing no suspicion in Brimmer or anyone at the office. But she had had it. Like me. Too dangerous if Brimmer thought we were backing out. We knew too much."

"What changed her? She must have known all along about the sale of illegal arms and secret payoffs. If," Renwick added, "she is as important to Brimmer as you say she is."

"She keeps the records—the private ones. Not the books that are handled by the accountants and shown to the income-tax boys. She's important, all right." He was proud of his Lorna.

"What changed her?"

"A list that Brimmer made. The Klingfeld people insisted on it, passed him some information, too. He didn't like the idea, Lorna said, but he swallowed it. Couldn't refuse his new partners, could he? He might lose more than his business."

"Did Lorna see that list?"

"Yes. Later, she made a copy—photographed it. Took a chance after office hours when Brimmer was in Washington. He has a lot of friends there. Good old Mitch Brimmer, everyone's pal."

"That list—what's it about?" If it jolted Lorna into revolt, it had to be something that scared her. And Lorna didn't sound like a woman who would be easily scared out of an oversized salary and all the comforts of New York.

"Names. Nine names. Men who are dangerous. Too interested in Exports Consolidated. Asking questions, looking for answers. They could blow Brimmer's operation sky-high."

"And what does he plan for them?" Renwick sounded cool, kept his voice detached.

"His Minus List, he calls it. That's his kind of joke. You see, he already had a Plus List—had it for the last five years."

Patience, Renwick warned himself. Moore's evasive, embarrassed. Don't rush him. "A Plus List? Men who are *not* dangerous?"

"More than that. People who help him and get well paid for it. They are hooked and they don't know it. Too busy counting up the dollars deposited for them in numbered bank accounts—the Bahamas, Switzerland, any place where they can dodge the tax man. They've got influence, can persuade a supplier to sell what shouldn't be sold, can introduce Brimmer around, vouch for him."

"So he has a list of them, too?" And that's something I want to see, thought Renwick. "Everything is recorded? An exact accounting?"

"A page to each man. Brimmer needs to know how much he has paid out, when and where. It's kept damn secret, you can bet your life on that."

A page to each man . . . "It's in book form, then. A small ledger or a diary?"

Moore's face went blank. "I didn't say that."

"Just a lot of loose leaves clipped together?" Renwick asked, openly disbelieving; but he got no rise from Moore. "If Lorna has a copy . . ." Renwick left the suggestion floating. No doubt she had, for Moore's strange small smile seemed to confirm it.

"That's not for you," Moore said. "That's for Lorna and me to deal with." He rose, started over to the bottle of Scotch. "The Minus List is yours. You can nail Brimmer with that."

So that's my function, thought Renwick: nail Brimmer and let clever Lorna and her devoted Alvin deal with corruption in high places. With Brimmer out of circulation, they'd feel safe to start a new life—new names, new country—financed, of course, by some of the dirty money now in numbered bank accounts: blackmail barefaced and simple, no matter how they justified it, and they would. Brimmer's friends had been overpaid, could well afford to transfer some of their hidden assets to those who had done the hard work. And if anyone ignored that suggestion? He'd lose more than twenty percent (or was Lorna aiming at thirty?) if Internal Revenue were to receive a copy of his page in Brimmer's little account book. Renwick shook his head. Al, he told the big man's back, you may have survived battles and bullets, but I doubt if you'll survive this.

Moore, coming back with a drink in his hand and a quick one inside him, noticed that head shake. "You're the man to deal with it. But you've got to move soon. And fast."

"We'll need real evidence. Nine names listed for what?"

"Real evidence?" Moore swallowed a gulp of Scotch as he sat down again. "Real? It's in Brimmer's own writing. Just jotted down the names at his last meeting with Klingfeld's men in Mexico—two weeks ago, Lorna said. He wouldn't even allow it out of his hands to be typed."

"Nine names listed for what?" Renwick repeated. Careers ruined, possibly, with the help of Brimmer's powerful friends.

"Assassination."

For a long moment, there was no sound or movement in the room. Then Renwick's eyes narrowed.

"It's true, believe me! You know what he wanted me to do? Pick out ten men I could trust—two squads of five men each—train them to co-ordinate, plan, and execute."

"And how did you handle that suggestion?" A refusal, and Moore would never have reached London with all that money in his pocket. In spite of his protestations—*I'm no assassin*—could I be facing one right now? He's nervous, on edge, increasingly worried. Why?

"I stalled. Told him the job of searching for the right men would take a couple of months, perhaps more. Training and planning needed double that time at least—if he wanted the deaths to look like accidents or suicides."

Renwick put out his hand. "The assassination list. Come on, Al. Give!"

Moore emptied his glass and dropped it on the bed. Reaching for his jacket, his eyes never leaving Renwick, he fumbled with a zipper in an inside pocket. "You'll deal with Brimmer?"

"Yes."

Moore relaxed, pulled out a folded sheet of paper. "Just making sure you'd do the job. Your word on it, that's all we wanted."

"Or else you'd have found someone else?" And I, thought Renwick, would have been the man who had been told too much. Not a happy thought.

Avoiding Renwick's eyes, Moore handed over the folded sheet as he rose and headed quickly for the Scotch, empty glass in hand. He spoke over his shoulder. "Your name is there, sir."

"What?"

"Your name is third on the list."

Renwick stared at him, then unfolded the closely written page. Yes, there it was: Robert Renwick (Col.)—Interintell—cover of Merriman & Co., Consultant Engineers, 7 Grace Street, London. His private number was given; two restaurants he favored on occasion were named; so was the Red Lion, with a cryptic note saying "special meetings." Home telephone was noted as unlisted. Residence changed in April—address to follow . . . Renwick drew a long slow breath, steadied himself.

"Gave me a bit of a shock," Moore said. He looked over at Renwick's grim face, fell silent.

Renwick scanned the list. He recognized six of the names: two inquiring reporters; a crusading editor; a United States senator who kept a sharp eye on sales of armaments abroad; two intelligence men, in Paris and Frankfurt, now investigating terrorists' weapons and their sources of supply. Two names were unknown to him: businessmen, heads of chemical firms. "What's their danger to Brimmer?" he asked, pointing them out on the list as Moore returned, bringing him a drink. This time, he didn't refuse.

"Oh, them! Government contractors. They turned him down when he tried to buy some new type of explosive. Offered big money, talked of national security, hinted at connections with the CIA. He uses that line when he's pressing hard. It has worked. Who's to know it's fourteen years since he's been with the CIA? But these two guys got together: they are making inquiries, stirring things up. It will take time before they get anything out of the CIA. You know these intelligence boys—don't talk, don't tell or explain." Then he looked quickly at Renwick, gave a brief laugh, and covered his gaffe by pointing to the list. "A bunch of unknowns. You wouldn't think they'd be important."

"Not one head of state among us," Renwick said drily.

"Strange how they've got Brimmer so damned scared."

"We're flattered. But this list won't nail Brimmer. It's useless as evidence."

"What?"

"No heading, no indication what it concerns. Brimmer will talk his way out of it. His handwriting, yes. The names? Just people he wanted to meet or entertain. He gives lavish parties, doesn't he?" One of his methods of operation, establishing his credentials with a likely prospect by having credible people around him.

Moore was aghast. The brown eyes hardened, seemed as black as his hair. "You said—"

"I must have evidence, something to stand up in court. Either Lorna or you can testify: she can verify the purpose of that list; you can bear witness about Brimmer's death squads. Or— Lorna gets hold of a record of illegal purchases in the States, of false export declarations, of deliveries abroad."

The idea of testifying, as Renwick had guessed, was rejected. Moore concentrated, as Renwick had hoped, on the record of illegal sales. "She'd have to wait until Brimmer is in Washington. That's early July." He frowned, calculating. "Doesn't give her much time. She's leaving—" He halted abruptly, concealed his lapse by adding, "Okay, okay. She'll get a copy of these records for you. One page enough? Two?"

"Illegal transactions," Renwick emphasized. "Three pages. When she has something to give me, she can send a signal to Merriman's and I'll contact her—"

"No! She can mail the records. No more contacts."

"But if I have to reach you—"

"You don't. Nobody does."

"Traveling far?"

"As far as I can get."

"Lorna, too, of course. But later." Renwick glanced at Moore's bag. Traveling light and all ready to leave. "When you call Lorna from the airport, tell her to include a statement of Brimmer's hidden profits for the last year. The income-tax boys could add fifteen years to his sentence."

"Airport? Who the hell mentioned calling—"

"But you will. She's probably sitting near a telephone right now, waiting for your report." Renwick rose, folding the sheet of paper, slipping it into an inside pocket. He picked up his cigarette case. "Now it's my turn to do you a favor. Avoid any country where there's no extradition. For that's where Brimmer will run, if he skips bail. Also, don't forget Klingfeld and Sons. They will know you have the Plus List as soon as you start making use of it."

Moore's eyes were disbelieving. "They've never seen it. No one has."

"But they'll assume Brimmer had one—just as they must have a list of their own. Don't underestimate their interest in your disappearance. And Lorna's." Especially Lorna's.

Something amused Moore. "We'll make no move for a year. We've got enough money to tide us over until then. And by that time, who knows? You'll have nabbed Klingfeld, too." He pulled on his jacket, buttoned his collar and tie. "I leave first. Room is paid in advance. Take five minutes before you leave."

Renwick tried once more. "That Plus List is as dangerous as any nitro you've ever handled. As soon as Klingfeld starts looking for it, there will be whispers, rumors. There isn't an intelligence agency that wouldn't join the search. You'll have plenty of people on your trail."

Moore, unheeding, was drawing on his raincoat. The allusion to intelligence agencies baffled him. "Why them? Are they into blackmail? Wouldn't be surprised," he said, shaking his head.

"It's a ready-made list of men who could be manipulated or threatened into betraying their countries. They are halfway there already, poor devils."

"What would you do with the Plus List?" Moore was enjoying this moment.

"Destroy it. Saves trouble all around."

"You're crazy."

"Crazy enough to think Lorna didn't need to make a copy of that list. It's in book form, small, easily carried. How many pages, one to each name—thirty, forty? She'll bring the book out with her, complete."

That stopped Moore. Briefly. "That's wild," he said, and lifted his bag.

"It's obvious. If you were Brimmer, how would you plan an escape if you ever had to make a run for it? Destroy the secret accounts with a fire or a bomb, but take the Plus List for future use. So it's a book, small enough to be pocketed, lying right now beside a false passport and a bundle of dollar bills."

Moore had reached the door. "You know all the tricks, don't you? Too smart for your own good."

"For Brimmer's good, I hope," Renwick said, and won a brief nod from Moore. The door closed, and Renwick could safely stow away his cigarette case.

As he turned off the music, he checked the room. The almost empty bottle of Scotch was in keeping with Moore, and so was one glass. The half-smoked English cigarette was not, so he carried it into the bathroom, along with the tumbler he had used, and flushed it down the toilet. His coat was half dry, his hat still sodden. Three minutes had passed. Quite enough, he decided, allowing for his call downstairs from one of the public phones. He wondered, as he closed the door quietly behind him, if Moore had been idiot enough to use that room phone today.

The lobby was less crowded at this hour—it was nine-forty, he saw by his watch—but with enough stragglers to keep him unnoticed. He dialed his number, heard Nina's voice. "Darling," he told her, "I'll be home in an hour. Yes, everything's okay. Are you all right?"

"Ron and Gemma came round to have supper with me, so I wasn't alone. And Pierre has just arrived. We're all having coffee and brandy right now. Have you eaten yet? No? Oh, Bob! I'll put one of Gemma's casseroles in the oven right away. She brought lashings of food in a picnic basket. You know Gemma." Nina's laugh was a happy one, infectious.

He found he was actually relaxed, worry and strain banished for these moments. "No casserole. Can't face it. Make a sandwich—heat up some soup, will you? I love you, darling. Be with you soon."

Outside, the rain had stopped. Wet streets and pools of water reflected the shimmer of lights from never-ending traffic in Tottenham Court Road. Moore might be taking that obvious direction, so Renwick headed into Bloomsbury. There were hotels a short distance away, and his best chance to find a cab would be near one of their doorways. (With regret, he had had to ignore a taxi at the Coronet entrance; just a minimal precaution.) His luck was good. First, a taxi to Euston Station, where he could easily find another cab after a few minutes' delay. Then, sure that no one had been interested in him, he decided to cut down the time spent in his dodging game—it was tedious, and comic, too—and head for home. His heart lifted at the thought. Nina's voice on the phone had brought him back into normal life, blotted out the obscenity of Brimmer's world.

He paid off the cab at Kensington High Street and chose one of the three streets that would lead to Essex Gardens. Once it had been a stretch of Edwardian houses; now there was a block of flats. He looked up at the third floor, saw the lights of his living room, and quickened his pace.

4

Inside Renwick's small flat—it had seemed so much bigger when they had viewed it empty in March—the living room was full of light and warmth. Still better was Nina's welcome, arms around him as they stood in the almost-privacy of the entrance hall, a six-foot-square breathing space inside the front door. He kissed her so vehemently that the breath went out of her body, and her eyes, blue and large, widened in surprise. Then they turned serious as she helped him pull off his raincoat and saw it had been drenched, now only half dry and the hat still sodden. He answered her unspoken question with another kiss and drew her into the room.

"Sandwich and soup," she told him. Very hot soup: his hands had been cold. "Are you sure that's enough?"

"Plenty." They sounded perfect compared to a casserole, his least favorite dish. Thank heaven that Nina hadn't adopted Gemma's art of cooking, a little bit of everything in a heavy sauce with a touch of whatever herbs were in favor at the moment.

Gemma's pretty but indefinite face showed obvious relief. "Now we can all stop pretending not to worry," she told him in a whisper as she dropped a light kiss on his cheek. "I'll help Nina," she said to her husband, and as Gilman gave a thankful nod, she hurried toward the kitchen. Renwick watched her—tall and thin, elegant as usual, her dark hair now showing unabashed gray—until she closed the door behind her. Then he turned to the two men. Gilman, he noticed, had been sitting close to the telephone. Pierre Claudel was pretending unconcern, lounging in the most comfortable chair, but his brown eyes—bright and clever, alive in typically French manner—held a decided question; several questions, in fact.

"I'm sorry," Renwick said. "He fooled me with that Paddington dodge. Sorry."

Gilman deserted the phone to pour a Scotch. "You look as if you needed this."

"I do."

"Well?" asked Claudel, rising to help himself to another brandy, a neat compact figure of medium height, quick in movement.

Renwick glanced at the kitchen door. "Later."

"You got something?" Claudel's English, schooled at Downside, was perfect, with the addition nowadays of American phrases thanks to his years of close friendship with Renwick.

"Plenty. What happened at Paddington?"

"I waited. When you arrived, I was all set to follow you into the station, find what train you were taking. But you didn't arrive."

"He was in a taxi outside the Red Lion, invited me in, with a thirty-eight and silencer pointed at my stomach. Then it was Marble Arch and the Underground to Tottenham Court Road, and then a short walk to a hotel room." Renwick glanced once more at the kitchen door. "Details later, if requested."

Gilman's tall, thin figure drooped into a chair. "We were really quite worried, Bob."

"Worried?" burst out Claudel. "I was practically having fits. Thought I had slipped up, somehow missed you. And then, with almost two hours gone and no show, I went into the station. I had a feeling that we had been tricked. I asked the information desk—a nice girl, pretty, very helpful—if the train to Oxford was modernized. Certainly. All trains from Paddington—"

The kitchen door opened, and Nina carried in a tray.

"They are doing a good job, I hear," Renwick said.

"Who?" asked Nina.

"British Railways. Thanks, darling." Renwick began his supper.

"Still haven't beaten the French records," Claudel said, "but they're on the way. For instance, in every train running out of London—except from Fenchurch Street—all old-style single compartments have had their walls ripped out and central gangways made. No more privacy." He smiled over at Renwick.

"I heard about that," Gemma volunteered. "Privacy is thought to encourage vandalism and attacks on women."

"And it did," said Gilman. "But no more having a quiet compartment to oneself. Frankly, I didn't know that *all* railway carriages had been altered."

"It only proves we don't travel in trains very much," Renwick observed. He was eating soup and sandwich in record time. So we were all misled—even Moore: his idea of British trains had probably come from the movies he had seen. Renwick shook his head.

"We may have to," Gilman said, and led the talk into a possible scarcity of petrol for cars, even with the North Sea oil pouring out by the barrel-load. Rumor had it that it was being used up too quickly: people didn't realize that it couldn't last forever.

"What does?" Claudel asked. "*Carpe diem*—seize the day."

"And seize half an hour before we start heading for bed," Renwick said. "That meeting we have scheduled for tomorrow—I think we'd better discuss its agenda right now and be prepared for any opposition we'll meet from Thomson and Flynn." He rose, the last half of his sandwich in his hand. "No, darling," he told Nina, "you stay here with Gemma. We'll move into the small room." His study, it was supposed to be; but Nina, thinking a year ahead, had been suggesting it would make a wonderful nursery. Not much of anything at the moment, except a dumping ground for the unpacked crates of bibelots and boxes of books which had so far defeated arrangement. Wall space for shelving was limited in this living room with its large windows, its mantelpiece trying to make an electric fire look natural, its radiator that produced more groans than heat, its doorways. "Gemma, you might have some ideas about bookcases. I vote we take down the pictures, except for the two painted by Nina. What do you think?" And with that he could start leading Gilman and Claudel into the temporary box room with no more delay.

In alarm, Nina said, "But there are no chairs, darling."

"Honey, they are the most nicely dusted crates we've ever sat upon."

Nina, bless her, had made curtains and installed them, bright coral stripes on white to brighten the sea-green walls. They were heavy enough to be opaque and, once they were drawn and the light switched on, no curious neighbor from the block of flats across the street could see three men choosing three of the most solid-looking boxes.

"Cozy," Claudel said.

"All eight by twelve feet," Renwick agreed. He looked at his watch. "Here's the gist. The details you'll learn tomorrow from the tape." He took out his cigarette case, laid it beside him. "Two photographs, up close," he said as he produced his lighter and added it to the case. "Moore has changed his hair color since I knew him. It was brown, brindled. Probably got bleached, living in so much strong sun. So, since he is disappearing from sight, he has dyed his hair black, eyebrows, too. These photos will at least show how he now looks."

Gilman asked, "He talked easily?"

"Incessantly. Some of it as a cover-up, a justification for his own role. But it's all informative, more than he realized. The main points are these, in order of importance to us: first, Erik. Moore did meet him. He was in South Yemen about ten days ago. Refused to follow orders from two Cubans who had been sent to meet him there, and took off. Not by the airport and not on a freighter. Disappeared completely. Heading for West Germany, no doubt. By what route?"

Gilman said, "He would scarcely risk crossing the desert into North Yemen. The frontier is watched—an undeclared war going on. Anyone from Communist South Yemen could be shot on sight."

Claudel had a suggestion. "What about bribing his way onto a dhow? Small boats under sail don't use the docks. The dhows sneak over to Djibouti from South Yemen all the time. It's a short distance—the narrow entrance to the Red Sea—a few kilometers." Claudel ought to know: he had two agents in Djibouti, a good listening post as well as a smuggler's delight. Once it had been part—a very small part—of the French Empire in East Africa. Now it was independent, and only recently, but still with the French presence around to guard its port.

"That's an idea," Renwick said. "So why don't you leave for Djibouti tomorrow night—or the next day at latest? Erik may not be there, but your agents could have heard rumors or gossip. They sail in and out of South Yemen, don't they? Besides the news on Erik, we'd like to know if any right-wing terrorists are being trained in left-wing camps."

Claudel nodded, his quick mind already measuring the best means of transportation. "*Mon Dieu*, it will be hot. Djibouti in July?"

Gilman looked at Renwick. "Then you didn't question Moore about right-wing terrorists being trained in South Yemen?"

"Thought it better not to dwell on terrorism at all. I just let him talk about it. He could have been on a fishing expedition, trying to find out how much we have uncovered."

Gilman agreed, but with regret. "Who is he working for? The Soviets? Or other unfriendlies?"

"As far as I could find out, he's now working for himself—or, rather, for Lorna." Then, as eyebrows were raised, Renwick added, "Listen to the tape."

"Did you find out any more details about Erik?"

"Just giving a seminar on how to escape if caught. It's my guess he is trying to reach his old stomping ground. That's where his real support is—the Direct Action group, with their sympathizers and backers. Communists? He tried using them before, but they used him. He will be wary of them, of course, but if he needs their help, he will take it. On *his* terms. It seems the Cubans wanted him on their terms. It didn't work. He probably became more of an anarchist than ever in that Indian prison."

Gilman nodded. "I'll alert Richard Diehl in Frankfurt that Erik could be heading for West Germany. Other friendly intelligence agencies, too. But if somehow he reaches Libya or Algeria—"

"The Communists there don't have enough diplomacy to handle Erik. The quarrel between him and the Cubans was savage. Moore thinks Erik will never make it—the Communists will take care of him. But I wonder."

"I could wish they would," Claudel said frankly. "It would save a thousand lives. If Direct Action has Erik back to mas-

termind operations—they could be on a disaster scale. Like
that wipe-out he planned two years ago for Duisburg." The oil
and propane storage tanks on that huge stretch of docks on the
Rhine would have started a fire storm. Claudel's voice turned
bitter. "Don't underestimate our dear little Erik with his noble,
noble ideals."

Erik's career, until he was caught in Bombay, had been ten
years of violence. Born in Venezuela, educated in Mexico City,
then at Lumumba University, then in a Communist training
camp in North Korea, he had become the founder of Direct
Action in Berlin, an anarchist group that had bombed and
robbed, committed arson and murder and brutal kidnappings.
As for the reason for his appearance in Bombay, he had been
in flight from West Germany after his plans for Duisburg's
waterfront had been discovered, traveling as an innocent American eastward across Europe, through Turkey and Iran and
Pakistan, selecting extreme left-wingers for training and co-
ordination into an international force of terrorists. Dangerous?
He was lethal. We won't underestimate Erik, thought Renwick
grimly. "Now, let's get to the second main point in Moore's
information: Exports Consolidated, founded by Mitchell Brimmer."

Gilman spoke with distaste. "Arms trafficking."

"Illegal arms."

"What?"

"Bought with bribes and lies, shipped with false declarations, sold to foreign countries that send them on to terrorist-
training areas. Brimmer is now supplying instructors to teach
the use of these weapons. Also, Exports Consolidated is expanding, has merged with a European firm—Klingfeld and
Sons."

Gilman and Claudel looked at each other. "Never heard of
it," Gilman said. "New to me," said Claudel.

"Details in here," Renwick reminded them, tapping the cigarette case. "Third main point: Brimmer has a list of names
which his sense of humor calls his 'Plus List.' People with
power or in sensitive places who have been most helpful to
Brimmer and now have the amounts paid to them, *and* the dates
of these payments, all nicely noted under their names."

"Bribery and corruption," Gilman said slowly.

"The whole bloody mess." Claudel shook his head. "Idiots! Did they never think what they were getting into?"

"Fourth main point," Renwick pressed on, glancing at his watch. "There's another list which he calls his 'Minus List.' I was given a copy of that."

"Men who are *not* helpful to Brimmer?" Gilman asked. "Dangerous to him?"

"So he thinks. So Klingfeld and Sons think." Renwick pulled the list out of his pocket. "It's in Brimmer's writing, mostly dictated by Klingfeld. No heading. Just nine names. Men to be eliminated."

"Assassinated?" Claudel asked, lips tightening.

"Apparent accidents or suicides." Renwick passed the list over. Gilman and Claudel seized it, shared its reading. "Four Americans, five Europeans," Renwick went on. "We'll have to warn—"

"Good God!" Claudel burst out, while Gilman raised his eyes from the list to stare at Renwick. "Your name is—"

"Yes. Doesn't get so much space as the other eight. Minimal information. Does that mean only one source?"

Gilman's calm face was furrowed with worry. "Someone inside Interintell?"

"Looks like it. My telephone number was given to Brimmer—or Klingfeld—by someone who has used it. The name of the Red Lion, also given by someone who has met me there. My change of address, by someone who knew my studio, heard that I had moved but—so far—hasn't been invited to our new flat. No mention that I'm married, as yet. But Nina could be added to the list any day." Like the other wives . . . There was a long pause. "I'll get him," Renwick said, too quietly. "But now we concentrate on warning the other names on that death list. Ron—you approach your friends in DI5 here and those in French and Italian Security, get them to offer some protection. I'll handle the American angle. Pierre will have plenty to do in Djibouti. All agreed?"

"Agreed," said Gilman. "We'll sleep on this information, and tomorrow morning we'll have some ideas how to deal with it."

"Without alerting Brimmer. Or else we may not get three pages of his illegal transactions. Assassination and corruption aren't in our particular field of operations. But who supplies the weapons to terrorists, who arranges for expert instructors, who receives them and where and how—that *is* Interintell's business. Let's not cause any flap in Brimmer's office. We need three samples of his secret accounts, photocopied in peace and tranquillity."

Gilman gave a nod of approval. Photocopies made hard evidence.

Claudel broke his silence. And good-bye to my own plans for tonight, he told himself. "I think I'd better take the tube straight to Blackfriars. It's an easy walk from there to Merriman's. Old Bernie never leaves before two or three. He's an owl." And a specialist in dealing with miniature tapes as well as with more sophisticated gadgets. Bernstein found late working hours provided less interruption than normal daytime, and never wandered into his basement laboratory at Merriman's until early evening. "The quicker he makes this ready for Ron's tape player tomorrow"—Claudel picked up the cigarette case— "the sooner we'll hear it. He might even be cajoled into using his back room for us." The lighter was picked up, too. "Okay?"

Renwick nodded. "And while you're there, Pierre, run off some copies of that list."

Gilman looked at the Minus List still in his hand. "Two names for DI5, two for French Security, one for Rome, three for the FBI. Yes, that covers the nationalities. And Pierre— use my car. Safer. This is the pickpocket season." A mild little joke, but it eased the tension.

"We'll move up the meeting tomorrow?" Claudel asked, pocketing all three items. "Eight o'clock?"

"Seven," Renwick suggested. "A lot of discussion, a lot of decisions." Then we start moving.

Gilman said, "I'll call Bernie and tell him to expect you, Pierre. This could be one night he thinks he might knock off early for dinner at midnight. Odd bird."

"Our mad scientist," Claudel said lightly, "but what would we do without him?"

"We'll need special care on this job. Sorry about that, Pierre. Hope you didn't have a prior engagement."

Special care, tightest security. I stay with Bernie until the work is completed, Claudel thought. He will play the minitape, transfer it to a regular tape, filter it to diminish any scratch. And it will all be done behind the closed door of his soundproof closet with both of us on the outside—once he checks the voice level of the first sentence—and not a whit wiser about the words being recorded anew. That over, the two tapes will be placed in separate containers, sealed tight, and locked away in Gilman's ultra-safe safe. Then I stretch out on Gilman's emergency cot. "At seven tomorrow, first order of business, I'll be listening to that recording. So"—he said with a grin—"what's a sleepless night against that? But one thing, Bob—could the Minus List be a fake? This Moore fellow tricked us once today."

"Just another dodge to enlist our help and get Brimmer off his back? Yes, I thought about that. But he talked so damn much, let slip a lot of details that added up to a fairly complete picture. And from that I'd say that the Minus List is the logical development in Brimmer's career. You shuck your moral sense, let greed take over, and one day you are talking murder and excusing it as expedient. That list is for real, Pierre."

"Well, if a man is judged by the enemies he makes, then the list could be taken as a compliment."

"One we could do without," said Gilman. They entered the living room in silence.

It was a scene of concentration. With head bent, note pad on knee, Gemma was writing. Nina, slightly bemused, sat on the couch beside her with three slips of paper in her hand. A fourth was added as Gemma tore off a page. "There—that's the last one. I know Bob will love it." She said to Renwick with one of her ingenuous side glances, "Just giving Nina some of my casserole recipes." Then she noticed her husband waiting by the telephone. "Time to leave? I'd better collect the picnic basket. Coming, Nina?" She was already halfway to the kitchen.

Gemma, thought Renwick, after eighteen years of marriage to Ronald Gilman, had perfected the art of making a tactful retreat. And Nina? An almost imperceptible wink as she passed him, a small flutter of the eyelid, showed she was learning.

Gilman had already dialed Bernie's laboratory, began speaking as the kitchen door closed. "Gilman here. Claudel is bringing your little trinket back for some adjustments. Too delicate for us to handle. Expect him within the hour. Special care," he emphasized and ended his call.

Claudel was amused. "Little trinket?" He would hardly call the cigarette case that.

"Bernie's word for it," Renwick said wryly, remembering

Bernie's disapproval. "Told me it was time to give up these old-fashioned methods, wanted me to experiment with his latest idea of using a micro-bug with a chip that could record and talk back to me, too."

Claudel had picked up his coat and was headed for the kitchen. "I'll use the rear staircase—the car is parked down there, anyway." He paused for a moment. "Did you know Bernie has made a chip to imitate a small sequin on a lady's dress? Now all we need is a girl to wear the damned thing." Then he was into the kitchen, saying, "Good night, fair ladies, good night. What about dinner at my place next week?" And with a kiss for each of them, he made his exit.

The Gilmans' leave-taking was equally short. "Dinner next week?" Gemma asked, and then remembered that if there was one thing that irritated Ron, usually the mildest of men, it was the protracted good-bye. So she didn't sit down for a last five-minute chat, but let Ron drape her coat around her. "Day and time to be arranged, I suppose. Isn't that always the way?" she added lightly to sweeten her small criticism. "But at least we saw you tonight."

"And thank you for that." Renwick's voice said more than his words. A hug and a kiss between the women, an answering nod from Gilman, and he could close the door, lock it securely, and openly look at his watch. Almost twelve.

"You know my trouble?" Nina asked him as he slipped an arm around her waist and led her back into the living room.

"Me."

She laughed and shook her head, her soft blond hair falling over her eyes. She brushed it away. "My trouble is that I never can guess what is really happening."

"I tell you when I can. And as much as I can."

"I know. But only after everything is solved, another case filed away. And not everything is told, either. It can't be, I suppose."

"You suppose right, my love." He folded his arms around her, held her close.

"Sorry," she said quickly. "I shouldn't probe. I really don't mean to, but the questions do rise up and won't lie down."

"Like my problems. They always seem to come in clusters."

Nina broke free, looked at him anxiously. "That kind of

day?" I knew it, she thought; I could sense it over the telephone tonight. "Not just one problem?"

He eased his voice to reassure her. "Don't worry, pet. We'll take them as they come." *New address to follow*—the phrase kept haunting him. Essex Gardens could even now be reported to Brimmer. How did he get Nina safely away until that threat was over? He looked around the room. "Yes, this place is too small. I think we have to face another move, honey."

Nina stared at him. "Bob! We are scarcely settled! And it does get sunshine and fresh air; the windows *are* big. It's so convenient for your office, too—no changing trains, a straight run through. And it's—" She cut that sentence short. The flat was affordable, its rent within their budget. "I thought you loved it," she said, all joy leaving her face. "When we moved here in April, you—Bob, what's wrong?"

Residence changed in April . . . Who the hell gave Klingfeld that information? "I'm all right, honey. Just pooped. Come on, let's go to bed." He pulled her close again, smoothed back a rebellious lock of hair, looked deep into her blue eyes, brought a smile back to her lips as he kissed her chin, her cheeks, her brow, her mouth. "I'm never too tired for that," he told her.

Afterward, he lay beside her, not moving, not wanting to disturb the deep sleep into which Nina usually drifted. His dejection had lifted, his exhaustion, too; perhaps that had only been part of the depression, the feeling of uselessness—so few of us against the hidden threats, the secret intents of a widespread power-force. Not organized crime, he judged, although crimes enough were being committed: if Brimmer or Klingfeld were backed by any kind of Mafia, they wouldn't need to search for assassination squads. They'd have their own hit men already prepared for action. Political backing, then? Klingfeld & Sons could have introduced that note. What else to think of a firm that had so much seeming power and money behind it and yet appeared to be anonymous? Neither Gilman nor Claudel had heard of it, and he was willing to bet that it was unknown, as an illegal business trafficking in forbidden exports of military equipment, to all other intelligence agencies. If its name was recognized, it would be as some family firm in the regular import-export trade.

He looked down at Nina, resting within his arm, her body

soft and warm drawn close to his. Protect and comfort, for better or worse, until death—

She may have heard his small intake of breath. She opened her eyes, saying, "I'm not asleep, either." She turned sideways to face him, drew still closer, slid her arm over his body. "And I thought I had driven away your worries, darling." She laughed, the light small laugh that echoed the affection in her voice. "Bob, you were right. This flat is too small. Look at this room. The bed almost fills it."

He had to smile. King-size was what Nina had wanted. We could have done with a single bed for all the space we take up, he thought.

"But it's storage that really is the problem. Of course, when that carpenter *does* arrive and makes us some closets—I've drawn out all the plans for him, measured everything—we'll have more space. Much more, Bob." He's been so patient about that, she thought. His suits were hung on a rack near the bathroom door. "We could really be settled by July. Or August," she added, thinking of the nonappearing carpenter.

"How about the Fourth of July in Washington?"

She pulled away from him, tried to sit up and look at him in wonder.

"Don't you get homesick, Nina?"

"Yes. As you do. But I thought we were going back in September for two weeks—if you were free then."

"I'm free now. Let's make the trip when we can."

"Leave in a few days?" She was dumbfounded.

"Leave tomorrow—no, day after tomorrow. On Wednesday."

"Bob—how can we? You've got meetings." And problems, she remembered. Even one problem always meant several late nights at the office. "And I'll have to pack, and close up the flat—Why, the Fourth is on Saturday! We'd never make it."

He reached out, took firm hold of her slender waist, pulled her down where she belonged. "Remember the evening in Georgetown when I waited for you in that half-built conservatory behind your father's house, and you came running into my arms?"

"And you swung me up. Told me we were leaving the next morning to get married." Nina was smiling again.

"You didn't find it so hard to pack in a hurry then," he said gently, and kissed her.

"Then," she told him, "I was a foot-loose student. Now, I'm an old married woman."

"The difference," he said in mock wonder, "that nineteen months can make to a twenty-one-year-old!"

"Darling"—her arms were around him, her body yielding—"we'll leave day after tomorrow. I'll pack and write notes to everyone and close the flat up tight."

"No notes," he said quickly, then softened that small command by adding, "A waste of time. We'll just slip away and forget this flat. We'll leave Gemma in charge of the key." And Gemma could start looking for some other place for them. Gemma would love that: no imposition. "We may stay in America for several weeks."

"Can you manage it?" She looked at him. "Or is this a business trip?"

"Now and again," he admitted. "I'll take you to see my—" cut out the word "people"—"my sister who married an ex-Marine and lives in La Jolla." Not to see anyone with the name Renwick, not now at least. And what about the name O'Connell, if Nina's family connection was being traced? "Is your father in Washington, or has he left for the Maryland shore?" Nina's stepmother liked its cooler temperatures in the summer months for her incessant dinner parties.

"He isn't very happy in either place nowadays."

Out of a job, Renwick thought. No longer an economic adviser to the White House or attached to the State Department. A quick and total resignation—the modern way for an honorable man to put a bullet through his brain.

Nina was watching him. "He likes you, Bob."

"That's news." Why should a proud man like Francis O'Connell like anyone who knew about his stupidity? With his high-minded scorn for all security, he had almost walked into a White House meeting with an explosive device planted in his attaché case by someone he had taken on trust.

Nina was suddenly still. She said, "He told me all about it. You saved him. And a president. And all the others in that room."

"He told you?" The words were jolted out of Renwick.

"I'm glad he did. Don't try to shelter me so much, Bob."

"And you never mentioned it—"

"I was waiting for you to tell me. The obedient wife," she said, turning it into a joke.

"How obedient?" he asked, and took her into his arms again.

5

Djibouti was as hot as Claudel had predicted, and more crowded than he remembered from last year's visit. It always had held half the inhabitants of this small and arid land, a sliver of scrub and desert stretching a rough hundred miles in length, even less in breadth, tightly bound both north and west by Ethiopia, in the south by Somalia, freely breathing to its east with an indented coastline that lay on the Gulf of Aden just where the Red Sea began its long stretch northward to the Suez Canal. Facing South Yemen across the Gulf, Djibouti had always been a trader's delight, but with the reopening of Suez it was once again on a major shipping lane—from India and the Far East right up into the Mediterranean. It might be a minuscule republic, a speck on the map of Africa, but it had significance. Today, it seemed to Claudel as if the town would soon hold most of the country's population and its assimilated foreigners.

He poured another cup of coffee, finished the last croissant. He was sitting on the Café-Restaurant's deep-set verandah, shaded almost to the point of darkness against the morning sun. The Café-Restaurant de l'Univers, six modest bedrooms upstairs (one of which was occupied by Claudel), owned by good friend Aristophanes Vasilikis; once of Athens, later of the Su-

49

dan, and for the last ten years a resident in Djibouti, capital of
the Republic of Djibouti. Too bad, thought Claudel, that in-
dependence had ditched the old name: Territory of the Afars
and Issas. That had a sound that few countries could match.

The Afars and Issas were still around, he had been glad to
see, and still predominant; dark-skinned nomads, thin and tall
with hawk-nosed faces, who wandered in from the barren hin-
terland with camels and goats, and lingered indefinitely. Muslims, of course, like the Arab traders who had modernized their
act and no longer exported slaves. There were European set-
tlers, too: venturesome small-businessmen from Greece and
Italy. And, of course, the residue of French who had simply
stayed on. Add to that mix the indefatigable Indian merchants,
the Somali refugees, the Sudanese fishermen, the Ethiopian
laborers, and you had a full house.

Watching the variety of faces and dress out in the street,
people on foot going their own mysterious way, Claudel could
be grateful that they made his visit easier, less noticeable. But
it also meant that the elusive Erik, if he had escaped to Djibouti,
had found a place where he could stay submerged until his
plans were completed for the next stage of his journey toward
West Germany. Yet, once here—if he were here—he would
find it more difficult to leave than to reach. There were only
fifty miles of paved road in the whole country, hundreds of
trails and tracks. And where would they lead him? Into the
desert regions of Ethiopia, or south to Somalia, now filled with
starving refugees from the war with Ethiopia—hardly worth-
while trying to hire a car (scarce and difficult) or a camel (slow
and stately). The railway—one railway only, connecting Addis
Ababa in Ethiopia with the port at Djibouti—hauled mostly
freight: import-export trade, Ethiopia's one direct outlet to the
sea. And Addis Ababa, Communist, had Soviet advisers and
Cuban agents in control. It was unlikely that Erik would find
that an attractive prospect.

So there were two possibilities left to Erik, and Claudel in
the last three days had been checking them both.

First, there was the port for Djibouti, built by the French
some three miles from the town. (Or the other way around,
Claudel reminded himself: the port was begun first; the town
came a few years later.) It had become a complex of instal-
lations: piers, quays, docks, water reservoirs, fuel-storage tanks,

even a refrigeration plant—everything that was needed for the refueling and replenishing of French naval vessels (two destroyers were there now; an aircraft carrier had just sailed). There were many paying customers, too, such as passenger ships that had docked for supplies and oil before they cruised onward, and numerous freighters at the loading and unloading piers. Yes, there was a choice for Erik in that variety of vessels. Except that the French were still in command of the port—its strategic importance higher than ever since the Soviet Union now had its friends established on the other side of the Red Sea's narrow entrance. On Claudel's arrival in Djibouti, he had visited the port to see his friend Georges Duhamel, whom he had known when they were both semi-attached (a diplomatic way of describing their function) as French Intelligence representatives to NATO. It was part of DeGaulle's ambiguity—keeping one French foot inside the Western alliance while withdrawing the other foot. Duhamel was now with French Naval Intelligence and had been sent on special assignment to assist the head of security at the port. He had been delighted to see Claudel again, and there were no false pretenses: Duhamel knew of Interintell and approved. He assured Claudel that there had been no European, no imitation Arab, trying to stow away on any freighter during the last two weeks. So, with the alarm on Erik sounded, Claudel could only return to the town and wait, and rely on Duhamel's eagle eye.

Secondly, there was the airport. Flights were limited, and checking the passenger lists for the last two weeks was fairly simple. Claudel concentrated on the flights to Egypt and France. (The others, to Mombasa and Addis Ababa, were obviously less attractive for Erik: the former because it only led Erik farther afield, farther from Germany; the latter because Ethiopia now had an influx of helpful Cubans.) But there was nothing to discover. No record or sighting of any unknown European, of any unidentified Arab. The French kept tight watch over the airport, a precaution particularly against hijackers. So, again, Claudel could only give a warning about Erik and go back to the town, and wait. And wonder if Erik had ever come to Djibouti in the first place.

But any day now, his two agents should be arriving from Aden. Husayn would sail in, land his cargo of salt and lamp oil and canned tuna at one of the pint-sized harbors some distance from the port. Shaaban would seek another anchorage, equally insignificant, for his cargo of cotton, wheat, and sesame. They would come separately, and Claudel would keep them well apart. Husayn was an Afar; Shaaban an Issa. The nomad Afars wandered in and out of Ethiopia; the Issas in and out of Somalia. That difference was, in these days of war and hate, a possible troublemaker.

Waiting and more waiting, thought Claudel as he finished breakfast. But while he did that, he could turn his attention to some legitimate business as the traveling representative of Merriman & Co., Consultant Engineers. He would visit once more the projected site for a possible hotel—if its backers received any encouragement from Merriman's—to be built on an empty stretch of coastline about two miles from the port and a mile from town. A desolate place, with a gray-sand beach, flat land broken by huge shallow pools where white herons—the only touch of beauty—stood ankle deep and picked fastidiously at the sedge-covered water. He would put in a negative report: drainage problems enormous, costs astronomical, sea view dull, background dismal with gray desert and shrubs, possible objections from the port authorities although their personnel might like a nearby luxury hotel for their families' visits, definite objections from all the sailors and seamen as well as the people in town who couldn't afford the prices charged. Also, Muslims did not drink. Also, swimming near the Red Sea was not comfortable: sharks. Also, fresh-water supply would entail a search for underground streams such as Djibouti and the port were built over. Also, the white herons would leave as the dredging operations began.

His report, of course, would be written as soon as his other business was completed. It made an adequate explanation for his appearance in Djibouti, though. Neither the Police Inspector nor his assistant, both French, had questioned it—not openly, at least, even when he had mentioned the possible need for some of their well-trained native policemen to arrest a murderer and terrorist. Erik... always back to Erik, although Claudel had also taken the opportunity to talk to Georges Duhamel about any freighter unloading crates from Exports Consolidated or a firm called Klingfeld & Sons—both names to be treated as highly sensitive, not to be bruited around the port. Duhamel, good security officer that he was, had promised a few tactful questions. A wild shot, Claudel thought, but every small chance was well worth taking.

"You are thoughtful this morning, my friend." Aristophanes Vasilikis, making his morning tour of the premises, stopped by Claudel's table. He was a blond Greek, now graying, with snub features and blue eyes. Of medium height and girth, he had his clothes carefully fashioned to fit by an Italian tailor: lightweight gabardine trousers that hung without a wrinkle; a cream silk shirt opened at the neck, its sleeves turned back at their broad cuffs. With a reproving frown at the wooden ceiling above him, where a fan had started a slowdown and was threatening a work stoppage, he chose the cane chair opposite Claudel's, sat down as he took out an Egyptian cigarette and fitted it into an ivory holder. He came right to the point, speaking in his fractured French, saying with an increasing frown, "Surely you do not consider giving a favorable report to those idiots who waste good money on building hotels where they are useless."

"They have built many hotels in unlikely places."

"Where?"

"Sardinia, Kota Kinabalu—"

"Oh?" Aristophanes had never heard of it, but that wasn't to be admitted.

"It's in Borneo—the Land below the Winds."

"Headhunters!"

"They've stopped the habit, I hear. In any case, Ari, don't lose sleep over any big hotel being built here. Your place won't suffer at all."

Aristophanes had had a moment of hope, dashed down by Claudel's last sentence. His restaurant was small, with wine for the French and Italians, fruit juices for the wealthier Arabs who liked to adopt European dress. The bar was enormous, with beer and spirits flowing freely for off-duty sailors, seamen from the freighters, the traders who were Christians, the lesser shopkeepers who had forgotten their religion. Both establishments made money, more than his trading post in the Sudan, much more than his hard beginnings in the Plaka of Athens. "They are planning a discothèque, I hear."

"You have better ears than I. And guesses are wild. Rumors rise like dust storms in this part of the world."

Aristophanes shook his handsome head over his friend's

amusement. "Dangerous things, these discothèques. Men and women, half-naked women, dancing together. Have your rich clients forgotten this is Muslim territory? Tell them, Pierre, what happened last year—just after your last visit. Or didn't you hear?"

Claudel shook his head.

"Tourists came off a cruise ship—they come for three hours and then they leave, and tell that to your rich clients, too— and there were some young women, stupid women. They wore short shorts and low-necked blouses and brought cameras to photograph the marketplace." Aristophanes dropped his voice. "They were stoned. They had to run for the taxis that brought them here from their ship. A crowd ran after them, jeering all the way. If the police had not arrived, there would have been a riot." Another rumor? Claudel wondered, but Aristophanes was deadly serious. "Tempers are short. Anger is quick. This place changes like the rest of the world. Ten years ago, when I came here, it was different. Now, politics—" He spat out a vivid oath. To hear a Greek curse politics was quite something, Claudel thought, but he kept silent. "All under the surface," Aristophanes went on when he had recovered. "So far, under the surface." He fell silent.

"What news do you hear from the outside world?" Claudel asked to shift Ari's dark mood away from Djibouti. Ari had, in his very private room on the top floor of his hotel, an excellent shortwave radio, high-powered, which could transmit as well as receive. Provided, no doubt, by Greek Intelligence in Athens; one of Claudel's educated guesses, bolstered by the fact that Interintell and Greek Intelligence had co-operated in defeating a terrorist plan to seize the airport near Athens. Friendly relations had been established, which possibly accounted for Ari's warm welcome on Claudel's visit last year. It was, of course, a guess: Ari, who had a mania for gadgets, might very well have invested some money in a radio that would keep him in touch with Europe. He was an émigré who had become thoroughly attached to East Africa but dreamed back to the West. Neither Ari nor Claudel ever mentioned the word "intelligence." Their conversations were entirely focused on Djibouti or international troubles. But the fact that Ari had shown Claudel his radio was a definite hint: Claudel was welcome to make use of it should there be any urgent need.

Ari's dark mood refused to be shifted. He glared up at the large overhead fan, now motionless, and rose. "So I find a workman who will come, not at once but this evening. He will drive away my customers, fix the fan, and it will break down next week." Then he remembered his manners as host. "Do you need Alexandre and his taxi to drive you out to that godforsaken place?"

"Yes." Claudel glanced at his watch, saw it was ten minutes to nine. The day was half over for most people. By eleven, the streets were emptying; by noon, people were behind closed shutters or lying in the shade of a wall. In the early evening, after the long hot afternoon, life came back to the town. "Ask Alexandre to be here around ten o'clock." Claudel was on his feet. "I'll take my usual stroll to the market, stretch my legs, and buy a newspaper." It was his daily routine, like Alexandre's taxi, and it aroused no comment.

The Café-Restaurant de l'Univers stood at the corner of a broad street, once intended as a boulevard with two rows of trees down its middle. From here branched off some lesser streets, crossing other narrow streets at right angles, all part of neat French planning. After that, things went slightly haywire, but to reach the open marketplace was easy. One walked down a straight street, fairly straight at least, between two continuous rows of houses, mostly white, a few walls painted blue, all a little faded or discolored. Some had brief colonnades, little stretches of curved arches; most were plain-faced, unadorned, rising three stories above the street level, where a few shops had intruded; high-ceilinged stories, to judge by the tall windows, seemingly without glass, whose massive shutters were opened for the morning air.

The road was unpaved but many people walked there, for traffic was light—some neat cars, three small green taxis—and the sidewalks were uneven and raised by knee-high curbs. As if, thought Claudel, the planners of this street had feared torrential monsoon floods. Or, more likely, they had raised the sidewalks high to let people step out of their carriages without a jolt or a jump. What, he wondered, had this quarter been like fifty, thirty, even twenty years ago? Blue and white walls would have looked freshly painted, the shutters would have hung straight—not half off their hinges, comically tilted. Few chips and gashes on the arches, less peeling plaster, no large puddles at the side of the earth-packed road left from the morning's hosing of broken sidewalks. Bless the underground stream that gave the town its water, and pray that it flows forever and ever. Or did Nature's bounty change as men's did? Grow old and weary and tired of giving?

It was a sad thought out of keeping with the people he passed. Intent on their lives, on the immediate present such as the morning's marketing, the cost of buying, the price of selling, the earnest gossip with friends, they brought color and movement to the street. The variety of faces, of languages, of dress, always fascinated Claudel; and, above all, the women. They were young—and where were the older ones? So few to be seen—young and beautiful, very tall, very thin, their faces unveiled but their bodies enveloped by layers of floating muslin in bright flower patterns. Wide skirts fluttered to the ground and hid their ankles. Knee-length tunics, loose and thin, moved with each step. Vivid scarves covered their heads and then wound loosely around necks and shoulders in billowing folds. Their faces were extraordinary: smooth skin, deeply black, tightly drawn over fine-boned faces; profiles that were sculptured to perfection. But the eyes, briefly looking at him, then ignoring, were the hardest eyes he had ever seen, carved out of obsidian. Don't even glance at me, my proud beauties: you'd scare the hell out of me.

Strangely, the tall, thin, black-skinned men, with the same fine features as their women (but they never walked together; it was men with men, women either alone or with another woman), had eyes that seemed more human: clever-quick, deepset, not friendly, but not inimical, either. Some of the younger ones were dressed like Claudel, in trousers and short-sleeved shirts; the rest wore striped ankle-length gowns, drab in color.

He passed the floating dresses that billowed with the slightest touch of warm breeze, made way for a blind old man being led by a young boy, and came to the end of the shops and houses. Ahead of him, on open ground, with flowered muslin and striped nightshirts in mad confusion, was the encircling wall of the uncovered market. Outside the wall were two tethered camels and a few goats under the watchful eyes of eight-year-olds. The main entrance was a jostle of people moving in and out. Claudel took note of the time—five past nine—and removed his watch to the safekeeping of his hand. There was nothing of value in his pockets. The nimblest-fingered thieves were now around. Two pairs of black policemen in starched khaki uniforms were there to discourage the pickpockets if possible, arrest them if necessary. It was all part of the daily scene.

Claudel strolled into the market, rubbing shoulders, ignoring and being ignored. Casually, he looked around for the Old Arab's granddaughter. (But her skin was light brown and less smooth in texture, and her features were neither fine-hewn nor sculpted. Her eyes, however, could dance with delight, and her lips smiled.) If she were here at nine-fifteen, that would be the signal. His agents, one or other of them, had sailed into the bay west of Djibouti. The Old Arab ought to know; he owned both dhows, rented them to Husayn and Shaaban. A man of age, wisdom, and wealth, the Old Arab (his name had three hyphens and was a mouthful in any language) was respected by most, trusted by some, and feared by all. In his house tonight there would be a room set aside for Claudel's meeting.

Claudel's eyes kept searching. Bright dresses floated everywhere, their wearers bargaining shrewdly for the vegetables and fruit lying on the bare earth in the shade of the wall. Following its curve, pressed on all sides by black, brown, and vaguely white faces, he made his determined way. As usual, it was the strange smell that repelled him—a sweet sickly smell that he couldn't identify. A concentration of sesame oil or hashish? Or of aromatic resins from the gum trees in Djibouti, such as frankincense or myrrh? No one around him noticed it, except four seamen with red faces and Hawaiian shirts from some freighter docked over at the port. Their comments, in Dutch and German, were fortunately not understood.

The curving wall brought him to the meat market, a long covered platform with a table matching its length. Behind this counter, strong-armed men hacked away at hunks of goat, while a three-deep crush of women in three-tiered dresses argued and elbowed and pointed as they selected today's dinner. And no sign of the Old Arab's granddaughter. Emilie, she was called—an unlikely name but her own, given her by her half-French Somali father. (Her mother was of mixed origin, too: half-Arab, half-Sudanese. There were always complications in having four wives, as the Old Arab had found out, especially when he had spent earlier years in traveling southward from his native Lebanon, adding to his wives and his wealth.)

No Emilie today. No signal. No meeting at ten o'clock tonight. Tomorrow, he would have to visit the market again.

Behind him, an American said, "Jean! Just look at these black legs of lamb hung up behind the butchers. Coal black! Are they smoked or what? Look!"

Claudel turned his head and saw two women with faces showing horror and fascination. Quietly he said, "Not so loud, ladies. The butcher might throw a hatchet at us." And what the devil were two bewildered women doing here all by themselves? They had enough sense, at least, to clutch their handbags to their bosoms and not to wear short tight pants or low-cut blouses. Perhaps middle age had given them wisdom.

"Oh, thank goodness you speak English," said the older of the two. Her friend, Jean, was still astounded by the black legs of lamb. Suddenly her eyes stared in horror. "It moved—the black skin moved!" A butcher had slapped it with the side of his cleaver, leaving a wide streak of pale flesh.

"Flies," Claudel explained quickly, before any other exclamations would ring out. "Just large black flies." The two women stared in disbelief, but the butcher slapped again and again, ridding the meat of most of the flies before he heaved it off its hook and thumped it down on the table. Then he whacked away at the bone, cutting the leg into the right size for a muslin-draped customer. "And I don't think it's lamb. Goat, more likely." He looked around the market compound once more. No Emilie.

Jean said, "Irene, I think I'll leave. Which way?"

"Best follow the way you came in," Claudel said. "And watch out," he told Irene, who had nearly stepped on a piece of discarded offal, thrown to the dogs who roamed around like the half-naked children.

"At least," Irene said, looking at the children, "they don't suffer from malnutrition. They may be thin, but their stomachs aren't bloated." She took comfort from that, managed to regain some composure. "So very bewildering, so—so foreign!"

"Are you alone?" Incredible, thought Claudel: wandering into this market, two pleasant-faced women with faded blond hair under wide straw hats, the older one thin and fragile, the younger one (younger than he had first guessed) with a hesitant smile that softened her sharp features. Both of them were completely disoriented.

"We did have a sweet old Englishman along with us," Irene said, "but that awful smell—what *is* it?—discouraged him."

Claudel's eyes searched the compound once more. The rear exit ahead of him was closed, blocked by doleful-looking goats. Perhaps they sensed their fate if the butchers ran short of meat. Then, suddenly, he saw her—Emilie stepping carefully down from the chopping table, her white dress with its violent pink roses swirling around her. Briefly, she looked in his direction—she had probably been watching him ever since he arrived at the meat department—and then passed into a group of tall women, her own height now dwarfed.

"Oh, he's not here," Irene said, misinterpreting Claudel's glance. "He's waiting outside the market. We'll meet him at the camels."

If they hadn't moved off, Claudel thought. "I'll lead the way for you." He retraced his steps, the women following closely. Irene, the talkative one, was now mute, with her handkerchief covering nose and mouth. But delicately done, he was glad to see: no criticism made too obvious.

They passed the last of the vegetables, set out one by one. The women who had carried them here sat in the dust beside them in their shapeless dresses of drab gray or brown, their heads covered in coarse cotton. Tired faces, with nondescript features and resigned eyes, thinking of the few francs they had made or of the long journey back to their village. Claudel hurried his charges as much as possible, cutting short exclamations and questions. "The vegetables looked good," Irene was saying with some surprise, as they left the market. "But what *were* they?" Claudel, already regretting his offer to help, just shook his head, looked around for an elderly Englishman.

He wasn't near the camels. He was discovered after a five-minute search, and in some distress. He had lost his camera.

"Nipped off my arm by two small boys," he said indignantly. "And not one policeman around when you need him. Really!" He was a portly, florid-faced man with white hair showing under his rakish, if yellowed, Panama hat. "Anything you can do?" he demanded of Claudel.

"Not a thing," Claudel said cheerfully.

"Now where do we find that taxi?" Jean wanted to know. The heat was making her fretful.

"Wherever you left it."

"We left it somewhere along that broad street with trees," Irene said. "We asked him to wait—at least William did. He speaks French."

The Englishman cleared his throat. "I do my best," he admitted, "but the driver's French was worse than mine. However, he will be there. I paid him for the journey here, promised him more on our return."

"If he doesn't wait," Irene said in alarm, "how do we get back to the ship?" She burst into an explanation of their travels, partly around the world on a freighter; most comfortable, actually, a Dutch ship that could take twelve passengers. William had joined it at Singapore, they had boarded it at Sri Lanka, so much more interesting than traveling on a large cruise, didn't he think?

"Yes, yes," Claudel agreed hurriedly. "If you walk up that street just ahead, you will reach the boulevard with trees."

"There is an antique shop near here," Irene said. "I've got its address somewhere." She started searching in her outsize handbag.

William had other ideas. "After that, we could look in at that leather shop, the one we passed this morning. Attractive place."

This could go on forever, Claudel thought; am I supposed to find their antique and leather shops? "Pleasant journey!" he said with a parting nod, and left Irene searching for that address.

"A bit abrupt, wasn't he?" William said severely.

"Oh, dear!" said Irene. "We forgot to thank him."

It was eight minutes to ten when Claudel returned to the Café-Restaurant de l'Univers. There was no sign of Alexandre and his small green cab—the size and color of all the taxis in town; but no need to worry. "Around ten," Claudel had said, and for Alexandre that could mean eighteen minutes late rather than eight minutes early. He would park, as arranged, along the street, not immediately in front of the Universe, a name that Claudel enjoyed: it made him want to smile every time he heard it, and a good smile these days was hard to find. Apart from his sense of time, Alexandre (half-French, half-Issa) was someone to be trusted, almost as dependable as Aristophanes Vasilikis himself.

There was a message, a note discreetly folded, waiting for Claudel at Madame's desk. She was the Genoese wife of Aristophanes, a red-haired Italian whose ample figure dominated the scene whether it was the kitchen or the accounting office. Outside of them, her manner was genial and her expression amiable, contributing to Aristophanes' pleasure as well as his profits. Above all, she was uncurious about his guests or their business. "My little treasure," Aristophanes called her. Partly true: "little" was a peculiar adjective for five foot nine of solid flesh, all one hundred and sixty pounds of it. With a flash of yellowing teeth, a shake of henna-dyed curls, she sent Claudel on his way upstairs. Such a handsome young man, she thought, so pleasant in manner. Then she turned back to her desk and forgot about him as she corrected the office clerk's list of expenses. People came, people left, but bills went on forever.

It was a telephone message from Georges Duhamel, written down in Madame's fine italic script and uncertain French. *Will drop in for lunch one-thirty.* That was all. Meaning? Anything: it could be news, it could be a friendly visit. Yet, Duhamel wasn't the type to make contact openly unless it was urgent, and a meeting over a lunch table was less remarkable than two men talking on an empty stretch of beach. Claudel washed, changed his shirt, felt cooler—for the next half hour at least. Downstairs, Madame's head was bent over a ledger. Claudel gave a small wave to her briefly upraised face, passed through the deep verandah, ran lightly down its steps into the street.

Alexandre was there, standing beside his taxi, arguing with three people who didn't understand a word he was saying. And he certainly couldn't fathom what Irene's sweet old Englishman was telling him. *"Merde!"* Claudel said softly, and would have halted, turned, retreated, but Jean had seen him and was waving. So he kept on walking. Quick eyes she has, Claudel thought, and she isn't altogether surprised to see me.

"We want to hire this taxi," William announced, "to take us to the dock. Is that so difficult to understand?"

Claudel exchanged a glance with a much-ruffled Alexandre, who prided himself on his French, and soothed his feelings with a kind word. "Thank you for waiting, Alexandre."

"You speak French?" Irene was amazed. "But aren't you English?"

"French is useful here, unless you know Arabic or Swahili. Didn't you go shopping?"

"Jean wanted to get back to the ship." Irene was the fretful one now. "And our cab didn't wait. So would you please tell this young man—"

"I engaged his taxi." It's always the way: he who helps, helps and helps. "Let me give you a lift. No bother. We'll be at the port in no time at all." At Alexandre's rate of driving, three miles could be covered in two minutes.

"Do you know it well?" William asked, and then covered his curiosity by adding. "Fantastic place. Ridiculous, though." He looked as if he were about to take the seat beside the driver—more space than being crammed into the back with two women, certainly much cooler—but Claudel forestalled him. Then his eyes bulged. "Look at that! Foreign Legion, aren't they?" He pointed to two athletic types crisply dressed in khaki, with flat white crowns on their visored caps. They were standing at ease beside a very clean jeep, also white-topped: quietly amused, seemingly impassive. "What nonsense!"

Claudel ignored the disparaging voice. "Where do we take you? What ship?"

"The *Spaarndam*," Jean said. She was relaxed and confident.

Irene was too busy pointing out the Café-Restaurant de l'Univers to pay attention to legionnaires. "Wasn't that the place where you said we'd have lunch—when we drove into town? Jean, you can't have forgotten. Stop the cab!" She spoke quickly to Claudel. "Please tell the driver to stop."

"No!" Jean was definite.

"We could eat and then do some shopping."

"I'm tired, and so are you."

"We've only been here two hours," Irene protested, looking behind her at a vanishing l'Univers.

"Quite enough," said William. "This place is a Turkish bath."

Claudel said, "All shops are closed until late afternoon." And that settled it.

Irene sighed and shook her head: no visit to a foreign country seemed complete without bargains to carry home as trophies.

William's well-worn Panama was off, his brow was mopped, as he shifted uncomfortably on the vinyl seat. "Ridiculous," he repeated as if to cue himself in to the observation he had been about to make when he was entering the taxi. He looked at the last of the town, abruptly ending, changing into a flat gray desert broken only by scrub. "I mean"—he leaned over to Claudel—"maintaining that port—all the money spent—all the enormous trouble. And for what? Why didn't the French let go of the whole place—town, port, everything—when Djibouti became independent?"

Is this, Claudel wondered, a sideways move to discover whether I am French or English? He didn't oblige William's curiosity. Instead of mustering a defense of the obvious—if Djibouti, left to itself, was taken over by a Communist regime as Aden and South Yemen had been, the entrance to the Red Sea would be locked, and what price free movement of shipping?—he merely said, "Haven't the faintest idea."

Irene said, "All these warships—it's madness, just asking for trouble."

Jean said, her voice soft and hesitant, "The Red Sea leads to Suez, doesn't it? I suppose if the Red Sea entrance was closed, the Suez Canal would be useless, wouldn't it?" She looked, ingenuous and appealing, at William.

"Ridiculous, though—all that money being spent," William maintained. "The French have better things to do than hang on to their empire. Say what you will," he told Claudel, "we English had the right idea with Aden. When you get out, stay out." Then, as he noted Claudel's boredom, "You aren't interested in politics, I see. Wise man. What business are you in?"

"I'm with a firm of advisers on construction abroad."

"Constructing what?"

"Hotels, mostly."

"Surely you don't plan a hotel *here*?"

"Our clients were considering the idea."

"Americans?" William was scornful.

"Not this time." Claudel was keeping his good humor without any show of effort. "I believe they are an English-German-

Italian group." With relief he saw they were entering the port area.

There was an easy passage through the checkpoint: Alexandre was known and his passengers were accepted as tourists from the *Spaarndam*. But I slipped through there, Claudel thought worriedly; or did the duty officer recognize me from my visit three days ago? As Alexandre, at slackened speed, drove down the long dock past a Spanish freighter named *Juanita* to reach the *Spaarndam*, Claudel asked, "Is there a check as you board? Passports?"

Irene waved a card at him. "Just this. All signed by the captain and recognized by the authorities. We weren't allowed to take our passports on shore—there's a big trade, the captain said, in stolen passports." She glanced at William, couldn't help saying, "And he did warn us to take no photographs, either."

The allusion to his camera silenced William. He was the first to get out of the cab, his hat jammed down on his perspiring brow, the back of his shirt and trousers soaking wet, his bad temper increasing with the blinding heat that engulfed him.

"Where are the others?" Irene asked, pulling a damp skirt away from her hips as she looked up at a ship deserted of passengers.

"Where we should have stayed," William said. "In an air-conditioned cabin. Good-bye, sir. Thank you for the lift." Without waiting for Claudel's reply, he headed for the gangway.

Irene looked at some crew members who were disembarking, dressed for off-duty sightseeing. "I hope they remember we sail at midnight," she said. "Don't they mind the heat? Oh, Jean, hurry! The sooner we are indoors, the better."

"Not indoors. On board," Jean reminded her. "And the crew has worked hard—all night, all morning."

Irene ignored that, concentrated on her thanks to Claudel, exclaimed once more about the heat, and set out for the ship.

Jean's large handbag suddenly tilted as she stepped from the taxi. "Oh, dear," she said as its contents spilled over the hot asphalt. She knelt to pick them up. Claudel stooped, too, and was startled to see her brush a powder compact sideways, sending it under the cab.

At high speed, her voice low, she began speaking as he bent down to reach for a key ring. "Major Claudel—I received a warning last night by coded cable to pass on to you at the Café de l'Univers, where you are staying."

He had straightened up at her first words, then knelt to reach for a lipstick. "How did you learn that?" Who is she, and what?

"We intercepted a message sent from a business firm in Paris to The Hague." She was picking up a purse that had somehow burst open, gathering the coins as she spoke. "It concerned you. Paris requested full information about your presence here—was it Erik or was it shipments?"

He handed her the lipstick and the comb he had retrieved. Irene's voice called, "Jean! What on earth are you doing?"

"My bag upset. I can't find my powder."

Irene hesitated, looking back at the car in dismay. "Oh, Lord! You would! Forget it—you'll get sunstroke."

"It's the only compact I have." Jean's voice was cross, determined. She stood up along with Claudel, the two of them replacing the remaining items—wallet, mirror, landing and boarding card, traveler's checks, handkerchief—into her shoulder bag.

"It may have rolled under the taxi," Claudel called to Irene. "We'll find it." Irene continued on her way, as William paused almost at the top of the gangway to look and listen.

"He isn't English," Jean said, her head bent to search under the taxi. "Just imitates. A little too much, I think." She raised her voice to reach both Irene and William. "I see it! We'll have the taxi moved. Okay!"

She went on, lips scarcely moving, as Claudel caught Alexandre's attention. He had been leaning against his cab, arms folded, legs crossed, more interested in the unloading of crates from the *Juanita*. "He flew to Singapore from Bombay—hoped to contact Erik, probably." There was a brief smile as Claudel's eyes froze.

Alexandre, following Claudel's quiet instructions, had been having difficulty in starting the engine—enough delay to let her continue. "He made his millions out of greeting cards—was a Communist and one of Erik's early supporters in West Berlin. Lives in England now."

"His name?"

A small but determined shake of the head. "He's our business."

Our? "And who are you?"

The question was ignored. "When we were inside the market, he was meeting a man. Young. Dressed like an Arab. I saw them just after you led us out."

"Erik?"

"I wouldn't know. He's *your* business."

The engine had caught at last. The taxi edged forward.

"And Irene—are you two together?"

"Just another passenger—a schoolteacher—summer is the only time she has to travel. Been saving for this trip for years." She pointed to the small gilded box that was now exposed, and Claudel picked it up, dusted if off.

"And you?" he asked, dropping it into her bag.

"I write travel articles for magazines." Her voice was normal now. "Thank you, thank you so much."

"But who sent me the warning?"

"Friends. We sympathize. We may even join Interintell someday." She was moving away.

"That firm in Paris—whose?" he pleaded urgently.

"Klingfeld and Sons," she said over her shoulder and walked on.

Irene and William were out of sight. But William would be watching. So Claudel spoke a couple of words to Alexandre; they joked and shook their heads over the vagaries of women as they got into the taxi and drove back along the dock.

"Stop, at the entrance," Claudel said suddenly. "Just around the corner." And out of sight from the afterdeck of the good ship *Spaarndam*. "Wait there. About half an hour." His excuse for being at the port was nicely established. He might as well make use of it and see Georges Duhamel right away: there was urgent news to pass on about Erik.

6

IF GEORGES DUHAMEL WAS SURPRISED, HE HID IT WELL. Or perhaps his own excitement about the news he was about to give Claudel made other matters seem unimportant. He rose from his desk, which had several legal-size pages scattered over it. "Couldn't wait for lunch, could you? Just as well. I'd like you to see for yourself what is happening." He gathered the papers and clipped them onto a board. "Hope you had a good excuse for coming to the docks."

"Good enough. I gave three passengers from the *Spaarndam* a lift in Alexandre's cab back to the ship." And Alexandre was certainly describing them, right now, to his friends at the entrance to the pier. Alexandre's imitations were much enjoyed. Including one of me, Claudel thought wryly.

"Adequate," Duhamel conceded. "Now let's have a look at the *Juanita*'s cargo. Destinations: Ethiopia and Djibouti. Ethiopia's consignment consisted of twelve crates—they have already been moved to the railway depot. The freight superintendent, after some persuasion, authorized one of them to be opened. It was described in the manifest as containing typewriters. There were typewriters on top. That, my friend"—Duhamel's face, with its sorrowful dark eyes and long nose, looked sadly at Claudel—"was a bad moment for me. The

67

second row, also typewriters. But the third row—well, it held some highly sensitive communication devices. American. We are checking now with Washington to find out if they are authorized for sale outside of its own military requirements. We"—and there was the Frenchman speaking—"haven't been allowed to buy them, even as America's friends."

"Any more rows in the crate?"

"A fourth one: typewriters."

"Neat. Any other crate examined?"

"The freight superintendent has authorized a full check. It is proceeding right now. Coming?" Duhamel's compact figure took three brisk steps toward the door. "We will have a firsthand view of the operation."

"One moment, Georges. Fill me in completely. Who sent these crates?"

"Didn't you guess? Why did I persuade—with some difficulty—the officer in charge to order a crate to be opened? Because, my dear Pierre, I recognized a name—a name you gave me." He held up the clipboard, riffled through the papers to the third one. "Twelve crates transshipped at Algiers on the *Juanita*, of Barcelona registry, from the initial shipment on a Liberian freighter out of New Orleans to Algiers. The shipping agent who handled this freight, from New Orleans to Algiers to Djibouti, is the representative of—yes, you guessed it!"

"Exports Consolidated," Claudel said, and took a deep breath. "But why the devil didn't you say so right away?"

Duhamel smiled. "Because it wasn't easy tracing all that in the last eighteen hours. I thought you ought to share some of the agony."

Now that Claudel looked closely at his friend, he could see a night without much sleep in the deep circles under Duhamel's eyes: always shaded, but today dark. "Pretty good work, Georges." We've got Brimmer, Claudel thought, we've got him.

"The *Juanita* is now unloading the four crates for Djibouti. Also shipped in the same way."

"Exports Consolidated again?"

"Again. It will be interesting to see what these crates contain. They are listed as office equipment: desk calculators, copying machines, typewriters. Of course"—Duhamel was thoughtful—"we do need these things in Djibouti: the Arab merchants are modernizing their business. And the consignment of crates is going to Asah, a regular dealer—so perhaps this shipment is quite legitimate."

"Asah?" The name tugged at a strand of memory. "Has he a son who trades in a small way—by dhow—called Husayn?"

"Yes. They are Afars, strong Muslims, sharp businessmen, but there is no question mark against Asah's name."

Until today, thought Claudel. And what about Husayn?

"You know him?" Duhamel's question was quick.

"Asah? No. I've met the son."

"He's more of a problem." Duhamel didn't expand that small statement. He went on. "About that other export house you mentioned—Klingfeld and Sons—there is nothing from them on any current unloadings from the four cargo ships now docked here. But the freight superintendent tells me that Klingfeld does export office equipment; we've had several shipments from them in the past. It's a reliable firm, been in business for years. In fact, they supplied us with typewriters—and there's one of them!" He pointed to a machine on a small table near his desk. "So we can cancel out Klingfeld, I think."

And I might be doing just that, Claudel reflected, if I hadn't heard that a message from Klingfeld's Paris office to The Hague had been intercepted. Now its meaning became not only clearer but threatening. Full information requested about Claudel's presence here: Erik or the shipment? "They may be involved. Office equipment is their specialty, you said. I've never heard of Exports Consolidated selling typewriters."

"Concealment of the Klingfeld name?" Duhamel shrugged. "Is that hard information, Pierre, or a guess?"

"A piece of information that might bolster a guess."

"A reliable informant?"

"I'm taking her on trust. But I think she's most reliable."

"She?"

"A professional, Georges," was all Claudel would say. And thinking of Jean, he led into the subject of Erik.

"Hasn't been seen." Duhamel was curt, slightly offended.

"He may be in Djibouti, though. Dressed as an Arab, talking outside the market with an Englishman, so-called, who is said to be a West German and one of Erik's early backers."

Duhamel recovered his usual sang-froid. "You *do* have your sources. Any that I can use?"

"Have you a list of the passengers on the *Spaarndam*? The Englishman is called William. William what?"

Duhamel found a sheet with the full complement of names on board the *Spaarndam*, ran his finger down the brief list of passengers. There was only one William. "William Haversfield." He looked up at Claudel, said with a shrug, "If you wanted him detained for using a false passport, sorry. He's a Dutch problem now. I think that I'll contact the captain of the ship."

"No. He isn't our business. So I was told. Most definitely. But I did need his name to add to details of his weight, height, eye color." That would help Interintell trace him back to his Berlin days, perhaps even lead to Erik if they made other contacts. Then another thought struck Claudel. "How many crew members are at liberty?"

"Day passes have been issued to eleven. Don't worry, Pierre. No one boards that ship without his pass being checked. If your Erik tries to slip in with a crowd of seamen, he won't get far"—the telephone rang and Duhamel picked up the receiver—"I can assure you," he told Claudel, and then began listening.

Claudel seized the chance to read the passenger list, upside down as it was on the desk. It was a trick he had long ago perfected. There were two Jeans. One was Barton from Boston; the other was Zinner from Brooklyn, New York. Which left him not much wiser, but you couldn't win all the time.

Duhamel's call was over. He repeated the report he had just received. A second crate for Ethiopia contained exactly what was stated on the manifest. But a third crate, on its bottom layer, had the latest equipment for long-range detonation of explosives. The entire consignment was being examined.

"Quite a scene at the railway depot," Claudel said. "What about the crates for Djibouti?"

"They are about to be opened. Let's go!"

Claudel hesitated.

"Don't you want to see what's inside them? Possibly nothing—as I said, the trader Asah is a reputable man. But the crates have to be opened; the name Exports Consolidated made sure of that. Come on, my friend."

"I don't think I should be seen—"

"There's no risk—for you. I didn't mention your name in

connection with all this. Took the credit for myself in my usual modest way, said my information came from Algiers ten days ago. What more do you want, Pierre? You will simply be an old friend whom I brought along with me to see what's going on. The innocent bystander—you always were good at that." Duhamel clapped Claudel's shoulder, picked up his clipboard again, and Claudel's silent debate ended. Yes, he wanted to see the contents of these crates. Yes, it was necessary that he should see them if his report to Interintell wasn't to be based on something he had been told. But most of all, it was a very male reaction to a friend's remark: *no risk—for you.*

As they left, Claudel said, "Georges—take care for the next few days. There could be more danger in this than we think."

"Danger? You and I are used to that. Now let's talk about unimportant things, and relax."

They stepped into the bright burning sunshine, found refuge from it in the few minutes' drive to a mountain of cargo stacked on an empty dock. Duhamel was talking about cars—he was proud of his little white Renault that handled so neatly and behaved like something twice its price. "All in the maintenance," he was saying as they left it and found themselves faced by three Somali workmen and a gimlet-eyed Frenchman. One crate was already open. "It purrs along like a Mercedes," Duhamel concluded.

"Why not like a Citroën? Support French industries," Claudel said. "Of course, if we didn't, I'd choose a Jaguar."

"Uses too much petrol. Expensive, my friend."

The supervisor, eyes grimmer than ever at such a casual attitude on an occasion so serious as this, cleared his throat, said nothing, just pointed. .

The top layer of the crate had been removed, a wooden shelf with typewriters in a neat row, each secure in its nest of Styrofoam. Typewriters definitely: their covers slit open showed carriages and keys. The crate's second layer was deep. It held large-sized boxes, each marked with authentic-looking labels, even with printed directions for the use and care of calculators. The boxes had also been slit. Inside, covered by a light packing of Styrofoam bubbles, were thin plastic envelopes showing the glint of metal. Not calculators. Weapons. Handguns, grenades, ammunition.

In the third and fourth layers of the crate, now ripped open, no longer carefully slit, there were M-16 rifles, automatic pistols, and enough ammunition to kill and maim hundreds.

Duhamel's face was white; the shadows under his eyes seemed to deepen. He spoke into his hand-size transceiver. To Claudel he said, "I'll wait here with the superintendent until the guards and other workmen arrive. Take my car to the entrance. I'll get a lift back." He looked at the crate, his lips tight, his jaw set.

Claudel said nothing. Duhamel wouldn't have heard him. He didn't even notice Claudel leaving in his little Renault, heading for the gate where Alexandre's taxi waited.

Trouble, thought Claudel, serious, deadly trouble . . . It was with an effort that he kept his talk with Alexandre away from politics in Djibouti, even produced several small jokes, and spent fifteen minutes looking at white herons grouped on a gray shore.

He left the cab near the Café-Restaurant de l'Univers. "Tonight," he told Alexandre, "I'll need you. Yes, double fare after dark. Around nine-thirty? And, Alexandre, be on time. *Please*. No later than nine-forty. I have an important engagement."

A meeting with a beautiful woman, Alexandre guessed. His smile was dazzling, a sudden burst of brilliant white.

"Wait for me until it's over. Perhaps an hour, or a little more."

So soon? wondered Alexandre. Europeans were strange. "There is no need to hurry. My brother will come to keep me company."

And will be handsomely rewarded, too, thought Claudel. Well, it's all on the expense account: insurance. Alexandre's brother was a policeman. "But not in uniform," he said quickly. No attracting of attention to a waiting taxi, thank you.

Alexandre looked disappointed. A police escort appealed to him, not only from the added status but also from safety. "Is it a quiet district where we wait?"

"Near the Old Arab's house. Tell no one, Alexandre."

"No one." The Old Arab arranged many things, even meetings with beautiful women. A wife of a high official? But one did not talk about the Old Arab's business. He did not like that. "I tell no one," Alexandre said, this time with complete truth.

CLOAK OF DARKNESS

* * *

Claudel left l'Univers one minute before nine-thirty. Its restaurant was beginning to function, its bar already crowded. Some able-bodied seamen, perhaps deciding that if they couldn't have a night on the town, they'd have the drinks they liked among people who talked in recognizable languages, were mixing with the Italians and French and their amiable women. Other hot and bone-weary seamen were about to enter, groups from various ships docked at the port. Outside, the taxis were already in line. What was a couple of hours spent in waiting when a bumper harvest was in sight?

Alexandre was on time, parked discreetly away from the crowd. His brother, in a loose white shirt, was his replica—neat-boned face, large eyes, a small mustache over a wide mouth, dark-skinned—but taller and even thinner. There was a flash of white teeth in greeting, and no word spoken.

The grave silence continued until Claudel gave directions. "Don't drive directly to the house. Let us take the road to the airport for ten minutes. Then come back through various streets." Alexandre's brother nodded his approval. The Frenchman was discreet. "And when we near the Old Arab's house, do not enter its lane. Park the car around the corner."

"The lane is ill-lighted," Alexandre's brother observed. He turned his head to look at Claudel's dark-blue shirt, long-sleeved; dark trousers, too. The Frenchman had come prepared for shadows, he decided, and said no more.

"But safe enough. If I need help, I'll yell," Claudel added lightly.

"Safe enough," Alexandre's brother agreed with some pride. "Only the cars are in danger." There was a plague of small-time thieves: an unattended car, even in daylight, could lose its radio and cassette player.

Was that why Alexandre wanted his brother along? wondered Claudel. No robbery possible when Alexandre was in that candy shop near the corner of street and lane, where a tantalizing variety of sweetmeats was for sale? We've all our own little plans, he thought, and laughed.

"It is," the off-duty policeman said in grave rebuttal to the laugh, "the most serious problem we have in Djibouti."

"Really?"

"Without a doubt." Alexandre's brother plunged into a series

of statistics and examples, which brought them all the way to
the Old Arab's lane.

It was a quiet street, narrow and short. The Old Arab's
doorway was scarcely fifty meters away. All the houses seemed
asleep, a delusion fostered by the blank plaster walls that were
broken only occasionally by barred windows, one here, one
on a floor above, built at random: the outside world, in Arab
tradition, was to be ignored.

But once through an ornate wooden door, large enough for
men on horseback to enter—another tradition remembered from
another era—there was a paved courtyard with windows all
around, and a stone staircase that led to the upper floor of the
Old Arab's house. Instead of horses, there was now a car in
the center of the yard. Claudel followed the venerable servant,
black face looking even darker against his lengthy white shirt,
who had opened the door before Claudel could even knock.
Neither spoke. The man, quite impassive, led the way upstairs,
gestured to him to wait at a low narrow door and disappeared
inside. There were women's voices from other rooms; the smell
of cooking and spices drifting up to the narrow balcony where
Claudel stood, the sound of sad music from an Arab radio
station. Apart from that evidence of life within the house, it
was a cold, bleak place, dimly lighted by meager bulbs. But
above the courtyard, in a square of ink-blue sky, there was a
brilliance of stars to lift one's heart along with one's eyes.

The silent servant beckoned. He could enter. Claudel ducked
his head to pass through the doorway into a small room; into
another very small room; into a third where the Old Arab sat
among rugs and cushions and soft lights. The formalities were
brief, polite: your health, my health, a small cup of coffee
served—and Claudel had to mask his astonishment—by a tall,
thin beauty in a long, loose dress with chunks of gold forming
necklace and bracelets. This couldn't be another wife, Claudel
reflected as he praised the comfort and opulence around them—
the Old Arab had outlived his allotted four. And a girl who
wasn't even half Arab? Originally an Afar nomad, way back
before city lights and city ways had brought her family to town.
Poor little Emilie, he thought, once more an outcast, the quarter-
breed granddaughter tolerated when the old man was completely widowed and needed a companion for his declining
years. Declining? The eyes were shrewd and watchful, the

hawk face ready to strike. Fortunately, he had taken a liking
to Claudel last year. They were wary friends. Fortunately, too,
he had liked Interintell's check discreetly deposited in his Cairo
bank account.

The Old Arab waved a hand. The tall, thin beauty, as hard-
eyed as ever, bowed and floated away. Once the door closed,
he said, "Husayn is here. Shaaban, too."

"They came together?" Surprise mixed with doubt was in
Claudel's voice.

There was a reassuring nod. "Husayn is now in the room
from which you entered. Shaaban waits elsewhere. He will be
brought to speak with you when Husayn leaves."

"With your permission," Claudel said, rising from the un-
comfortable mass of cushions, and, with a small bow, left for
Husayn. The Old Arab will hear everything we say, he reminded himself. There was a certain trick to the construction
of some rich Arabs' houses: voices in an enclosed space could
be heard, even a whisper, by anyone who stood in a certain
corner of an adjacent room. The Old Arab was in that corner
right now, Claudel was willing to bet; if not standing, then
sitting.

Husayn's face was friendly even if its features were hard,
thin, strongly pronounced. There was a welcome on his lips,
but his eyes were uncertain. So were his replies to Claudel's
questions. Yes, he had delivered coffee on his last voyage to
Aden, and taken it right into one of the training camps. Yes,
there were Europeans. Yes, one had escaped from India. Yes,
there were some Cubans, too. No, he hadn't heard of any
quarrel between two Cubans and the European from Bombay.
(How did he know there were two of them? Claudel thought:
I only asked about Cubans in general. And I never mentioned
Bombay). Yes, the European had left camp. He was now dead.
Yes, that was definite.

"Are you certain?" Claudel asked, his voice gentle and un-
challenging. "Could the man not leave in a dhow? Sail to
Africa? The distance is short."

Husayn agreed. The distance was short. But the man had
not traveled it. The man was dead. So Husayn had heard. So
everyone had said.

And so am I to believe. Claudel's face was expressionless.
I've lost a good agent. Who doubled him? Or was it Asah, his

father, who had influenced—commanded—him? Simple people had complex loyalties: complete obedience to the head of their family who was obedient to his sub-tribe, which in turn was obedient to the tribe; and the tribe itself was obedient to the main group which dominated all. The tight hierarchy of these Hamitic peoples was something hard to comprehend, and certainly difficult to deal with. Claudel pitied his friend Georges Duhamel. "One more thing, Husayn. When you visited the South Yemen camp, did you hear that some men there were of very different political beliefs? Men who were of two extremes: one to the right, the other to the left?"

There was visible relief on Husayn's tight face. What had he expected? A question about the weapons he had seen in the camp, or where did they come from? "To the right? To the left?"

He knows damn well what I meant. He's stalling. Afraid to give away his new political sympathies? "Do the men now in the camp all hold the same beliefs as the Cubans and the Yemenis?"

"Some keep apart when they eat and sleep. Very few. Three. No more."

"Thank you, Husayn." Claudel rose, signifying the end of the meeting, and gave a tactful handshake concealing a roll of Djibouti francs. It disappeared into Husayn's ankle-length shirt.

Husayn hesitated. "There was trouble at the port today."

"Oh?"

"None of the laborers have left the docks. That is strange."

So Husayn had heard no details about the actual opening of the crates, but he—and his family—had fears about the delayed delivery to Asah's warehouse. Did Asah's sub-tribe know of his dealings? Or was he acting alone, without their authority? Then who can be backing him? Someone he sees as powerful enough to protect him? Some nation with an eye on the port of Djibouti? Claudel's pulse heightened, but he kept his face disinterested. "Strange? They are working overtime perhaps. Is that unusual when many cargo ships arrive all at once?"

"Many cargo ships? You saw them?"

"I saw their seamen all over town today. Didn't you?"

"They make the Somalis work while they play."

"They unload, but they don't work on the docks. The Somalis wouldn't give up that job. Would they?" Claudel asked gently and added, "Good night, Husayn." Good night and good-bye, he thought as he watched Husayn bow and stalk out of the room. No mention of seeing me again, not even the polite formula for a safe journey home.

Three minutes passed. Then Shaaban arrived—strongly built, short in height, his dark flat-featured face beaming with plea-sure. He could only report what he had seen and heard around Aden's harbor. There was talk of a big search for a man who had murdered and stolen. But the man had been too clever. He had slipped away from soldiers and police. Yes, he had escaped. In a dhow. But no one would even whisper the name of its owner, no one wanted to know where it was sailing.

"The man is alive?" Claudel asked.

"The man is alive."

Claudel studied the wide-set eyes that looked so innocent. Shaaban knew who had brought Erik out of Aden, but Claudel wouldn't embarrass him with a direct question. "Perhaps he sailed to Djibouti."

"Perhaps."

And that, Claudel thought, is as much as Shaaban tells. Yes, he knows; but he is afraid of the man who smuggled Erik into Djibouti. Or is this another case of tribal loyalty?

"To bring him here is a dangerous matter," Claudel said, and by the way Shaaban nodded, his dark eyes large and anx-ious, Claudel knew that it could also be dangerous for Shaaban if he had to answer any more questions. The man's relief was transparent as Claudel thanked him with the usual handshake; his good wishes for a safe journey were long-winded but sin-cere. Next time, he promised, there would be more news to report.

One long minute passed after Shaaban had left. Claudel glanced at his watch: almost eleven o'clock. Would he be summoned to the Old Arab's room for some polite questioning as usual, or had the old boy heard enough from his listening corner? Suddenly, remembering Shaaban's fear—and the man had courage enough—Claudel drew a sharp breath. Had the Old Arab helped Erik? He was most certainly no Communist; a devout Muslim, his hatred for the atheist Yemenis was now intense. Intense enough to let him hide anyone who was hunted by them? If your enemy is my enemy, then we are friends. . . .

Another long minute. The Old Arab won't see me again

tonight, Claudel decided. Now he is caught in a predicament:
I am hunting Erik, who escaped from the Yemenis, a man he
has promised to help. How? With shelter and clothes, obviously. Money, possibly. False papers? To explain to the old
man that Erik's hatred of religion was only equaled by his
loathing for all capitalists, Arabs included, would be futile.
Erik, true to form, would now be the most devout believer of
all Muslims.

The door from the small outer room opened. It was a sad-
faced Emilie who greeted him with stiff politeness. "My grandfather has sent me with his good wishes for a safe return home.
He has retired for the night. Let me lead you downstairs."

Claudel nodded, followed her onto the balcony, said lightly,
"No more jokes, Emilie? No tricks like this morning at the
market? You let me search—"

She touched his arm, drew him quickly past the array of
doors, women's voices, plaintive music. She began to whisper,
her plain little face with its thick features looking up at him
pleadingly. "Please—you must leave Djibouti. There is danger. A talk of kidnapping. My grandfather will have nothing
to do with it. But he remains silent."

He stared at her.

She drew apart, led the way downstairs. Her voice was
raised to normal once more. "I saw you at the market. But you
were so fascinated by two old ladies—"

"Not so old. Just lost." A kidnapping? My God...

"Lost?" Laughter sparkled in her eyes.

"Very lost. They didn't understand a word of French."

"Of course you had to help them!"

"Who else was there?" Kidnapped how? he wondered.

"Where did they come from?"

"America—by their voices." Perhaps drugged and forced
onto a dhow...

"You didn't ask?"

"We never got around to that." Taken to Yemen? Questioned? That would be no bloody joke.

"Will you see them again?"

"No. They aren't my type."

She laughed out loud, almost danced across the paved floor
of the courtyard. The old servant emerged from behind a pillar,

silently opened the heavy door just enough for Claudel to slip through.

He halted on the threshold. "Please give my thanks to your grandfather. I wish him happiness, a long life." *And I hope the old bastard wishes as much for me—if it doesn't inconvenience him.*

Emilie's face had lost its humor, her voice was almost inaudible. "Remember," she said. *Careful,* her eyes warned; *be careful.*

He nodded, kissed her wrist, stepped into the night.

7

IN THE LANE, THE HOUSES SEEMED DEEPER INTO SLEEP. THEIR lights were out. The scattering of windows had become black patches behind iron bars. There was one lamp fixed to a plaster wall halfway to the street, aiming a bright circle on the unpaved ground. Outside of that solitary beam, deep shadows took over. But the distance before Claudel was short: only two doors to pass before he reached the corner.

He set a brisk pace, his eyes watching the first door on the right-hand side of the lane. Suddenly, he felt a warning, just a hint of the sickly sweet odor he remembered so vividly from the marketplace. His eyes switched to his left, to an indentation in the wall of a house, a shallow recess with a door half open, hidden by the shadows as he had approached it. A dark, thin figure leaped out, stick upraised, aiming at Claudel's head.

Claudel whirled around, caught the man's taut wrist, partly diverted the blow's strength and direction. It fell on his shoulder, a moment of intense pain, but he held on to the wrist, twisting it back, tried to loosen the man's grasp on the heavy stick. The door opposite had opened; a second man slipped into the street, a third . . . Claudel saw the glint of a knife and yelled.

For a moment, the three men stood motionless as the yell

shattered the dead silence, reverberated between house wall and house wall. Claudel heard a wrist crack, seized the stick as it fell from the man's limp hand, aimed a blow that sent the thin figure reeling to the ground. The other two came on, two knives now shining. He backed against a wall, tightened his grip on the stick as he faced the two men, watched the glinting blades. One circled around him, avoiding the stick; the other lunged, gashing Claudel's left arm as he fended off the knife from his body.

Running feet. A voice shouting. The knives paused, as the two men turned to glance toward the street. A brief second, scarcely time to draw a breath, and they were gone, vanishing into the doorway opposite, with the third man following at a stumbling run. The door clanged shut as Alexandre reached it, a heavy lock turned.

"You are hurt?" he asked, coming over to Claudel.

"Blood—"

"Could have been worse. Where's your brother?"

"He had to leave." Alexandre looked around him nervously. "No use trying to follow these men. That is a spice warehouse they entered; it has other exits."

Strange, thought Claudel, now that the danger is over, Alexandre's fear of this lane is returning. Completely forgotten when he raced down here to help me. "Let's get out of here," he said, handing over the stick so that he could grasp the slit in his forearm, hold the wound together, staunch the flow of blood. His shoulder hurt like hell.

"They wanted your money?" Alexandre asked as they walked quickly toward the street. Some people had gathered at the corner. Three curious boys had followed Alexandre halfway down the lane.

My life, more like it, thought Claudel. "I guess so."

"Robbers . . . My brother would have arrested them. He will be sorry he missed all this."

"Too bad," Claudel said.

Alexandre looked at him sharply. "There was a call for all police officers to report for duty. An emergency." Then the defensive note left his voice. "It's something big. A special raid. Very important. The military will send units, too." A raid on Asah's warehouse—a search for previous deliveries of weapons that were being hoarded. For what?

"Come on," he urged Alexandre, who was besieged by questions from the curious. They pushed their way through the gathering crowd, the three small boys at their heels telling everyone how they had routed the robbers. Claudel looked at Alexandre's taxi, standing unguarded. "I tell you what—if your radio has been stolen, I'll buy you a new one."

Claudel entered l'Univers by its service door, reached his room by a rear staircase. He was bathing his arm when Aristophanes entered. "Alexandre told me," he said, his alarm growing. "Nasty, nasty," he pronounced as he looked at the wound. "It needs stitches."

"Haven't time." There's a report to be prepared for transmission to London, and I've to encode if first. Not that ciphers aren't easily broken by the new wonder machines, but a code keeps messages safe from the casual eavesdroppers—that new breed of radio buffs who listen to the world's private business with a twist on the dial and hope to make the headlines. Not with my report, thank you.

"The hospital—"

"No. I'll have Interintell's doctors look at it once I get home." No strange hospital for me; no quick injections, no truth serum.

"That may be too late."

"This wasn't any ordinary mugging, Ari. They meant to knock me over the head, kidnap me. When that failed, they tried to shut me up. Permanently."

"Kill you?"

"They weren't playing games." Claudel paused. "Ari, I need your help. Telephone Georges Duhamel. It's urgent. Ask if I can meet him at his office—within the hour."

Aristophanes nodded, his eyes on the blood-soaked towel around Claudel's arm. "I'll send Sophia—she knows about wounds," he said hurriedly as he left.

First, decided Claudel, I'll write out the message, keeping it short but clear. After that I encode it and take it to Duhamel. No one else handles it, and I'll stand beside him. Six items in all. He found his memo pad and pencil near the phone, began noting.

(1) Erik—alive, seen in town, has friends.

(2) Exports Consolidated—U.S. military supplies (illegal)

for Ethiopia, and consignment of U.S. weapons (false decla-
ration) to Djibouti; all crates shipped on S.S. *Juanita* (Barcelona origin) from Algiers.

(3) Klingfeld & Sons—sent message (intercepted) to their
informant in The Hague, asking further details of my mission
here.

(4) Klingfeld, again—may have engineered an attack on
me tonight. (Arm sliced, but not to worry.)

(5) The agent Husayn—can no longer be trusted.

(6) Duhamel—Port Security, co-operating fully, help invaluable.

That about covered it, Claudel thought. The arm had to be
mentioned (all wounds and severe illnesses had to be reported—Bob Renwick insisted on that), but no need to include
the shoulder: not dislocated, not broken, thank God; just a
heavy bruise, a tendon made painful for a week or two. No
need, either, to name William, the sweet old Englishman, not
until Claudel could report in detail when he was back in London
and explain the little he had guessed about Jean. He owed her
that delay.

The door opened. He tore off the page of notes and thrust
it into his pocket. Madame entered, every henna-red curl in
place, with a bottle of peroxide, antiseptic bandages, and a
small first-aid box. "All we have," she said, and set to work.
"This needs stitches."

"Later."

She shook her head. "There is so much infection—"

"I know, I know. I have visited the tropics before. Many
times."

Madame raised a penciled eyebrow but asked no questions.
"So much violence tonight! It comes all at once. A quiet week,
and then nothing but trouble. You are lucky, monsieur. You
are not dead like that poor sailor, all his clothes taken, left
lying in a back street dressed like an Arab. Some Arab! Blue-
eyed and face blistered by the sun."

"Navy or merchant seaman?"

"A sailor," she repeated. "From the *Spaarndam*. But that
took an hour to find out. They say he was in the bar with the
others. Then he left with someone. So many were here, no one
could remember when he left. Or who was with him." She
finished cleaning the wound, began bandaging the arm. "Hold

still, Monsieur Claudel! Perhaps he went out to meet a woman. Men take such chances. But stabbed to death—so silently! No one heard even one small cry for help."

"The other seamen from the *Spaarndam*?"

"Never knew a thing. They left to join their ship before the poor boy was identified."

"Were they together?"

"Why, no—in small groups, some singly." She looked up at him in surprise. What made him interested in sailors who drank so much that they could hardly walk to a taxi?

"When was the body discovered?"

Her surprise increased. "About eleven o'clock."

"Near here?"

"A short distance away. Thank the Lord it wasn't found on our doorstep." She tucked the ends of the bandage neatly in place, said, "You ought to be a lawyer in court, Monsieur Claudel. So many questions."

"Sorry. And thank you. Perhaps you should be a nurse. You have gentle hands."

That won her completely. She even blushed under the circles of rouge on her plump cheeks.

"But you have," he insisted. "One last question, if I may. You said the man's clothes had been taken. Does that mean everything he owned?"

"Everything. Why else was it so hard to identify him?"

Stripped completely. Papers that he might have carried for safety in a belt under his shirt, his boarding pass—Claudel drew a deep breath. "A thorough job."

"A cruel one. So many evil people in the world!" She gathered up the last of her equipment. "I'll have brandy sent up to you, Monsieur Claudel. But the hospital would be the place—"

"Thank you, no. I have some things to do."

Both thin-penciled eyebrows lifted. "At this time of night?" The question had been forced out of her. She didn't wait for a reply, perhaps knew from her experience with Aristophanes that none would be given. With tact and a sympathetic look, she left.

Yes, Claudel verified from his watch, it was almost twelve-thirty. The *Spaarndam* would have sailed. With Erik? In the right clothes he could have slipped on board, mixing with a group of drunks who were hardly capable of noticing anything beyond their own footing. And the officer in charge? Like those at the entrance to the dock, he would be counting heads and passes. And the fake Englishman would be waiting to hide and help the stowaway. I may, thought Claudel, have to rephrase my report.

Angry and frustrated, he reached for the telephone and asked to be connected with the duty officer at the dock where the *Spaarndam* had been berthed. There was a tedious wait, of course, but at last he had his information. The *Spaarndam* had sailed at midnight—no delay.

"Any of the crew left on shore?" He turned quickly as the door opened, but it was Aristophanes with a bottle of brandy and two glasses.

None. Those at liberty had all returned. Earliest arrivals at twenty-three fifteen; the last man at twenty-three fifty.

"Cutting it fine," joked Claudel and thanked the unknown voice. So the correct numbers were accounted for: between quarter past eleven and ten minutes to twelve, all crew members had gone on board. Including a dead man.

Erik . . . "God damn him to everlasting hell," Claudel said, and faced Aristophanes.

A moment for diplomacy, thought Aristophanes, and offered a glass of brandy to Claudel. "You sound more like yourself, my friend. Drink up!"

Hardly the right advice for brandy, thought Claudel, but he did. Aristophanes poured again, along with a glass for himself. Now what deserves two free brandies? Certainly not one small wound on my arm. "So you couldn't reach Duhamel. Or you did, and he couldn't see me tonight. Right?" He cursed softly, steadily.

Aristophanes waited. "He is dead. Duhamel is dead."

There was a long silence. "How?"

"His car went out of control. It crashed, exploded."

"Where? When?"

"Tonight. As he was leaving the port. He had been working late, so his assistant told me, and he was on his way to town— a special meeting."

An official meeting, guessed Claudel. If the raid on Asah's warehouse had uncovered a cache of weapons, then there would be one hell of a discussion. His thoughts broke off, and for a moment his brain seemed to have stopped functioning. He gathered his wits. "His car went out of control?" Georges was an excellent driver, and he babied that little Renault. "There was nothing wrong with it this morning. I drove it."

"I think," Aristophanes said slowly, "you should return to France. Tomorrow."

"Were there witnesses?"

"Yes."

"Which came first—the explosion or the crash?"

Aristophanes studied his glass, dropped his role as innkeeper. "They could have come together. The wheel could have controlled an explosive device. At the first sharp turn—and one is necessary when leaving the docks—there would be an explosion." He finished his drink. "Yes, my friend, you take the first plane to Paris. There is a flight leaving tomorrow."

"First, I must send an urgent message to London. May I use your transmitter, Ari?"

"Very urgent?"

"More urgent than ever."

"Perhaps send it to Athens? London may be too far."

"I'll try for London."

"I'll show you how to—"

"I have to encode it."

"Of course."

"Not because of you, Ari," Claudel said quickly. "But there are unfriendly ears. You understand?"

"Only too well. When will you be ready to send your report?"

"Give me an hour." He'd need all of that. The arm was throbbing, that damned shoulder hurt more than he had expected, and his mind was stunned.

"An hour," Aristophanes said as he left the room.

Claudel drew the scrap of paper from his pocket, lifted the pencil, and began to make the changes.

The first entry now became: Erik—was in Djibouti, most possibly has stowed away on S.S. *Spaarndam* sailing toward Suez, aided by early sympathizer (Berlin origin; false British passport in name William Haversfield) traveling as passenger same ship. Means of escape from Djibouti: murder.

The sixth entry was expanded. Duhamel—Port Security,

co-operated fully, help invaluable, killed tonight in suspicious circumstances.

Claudel began to encode the report for Gilman in London. (Bob Renwick would hear the details in New York.) At the sixth entry, he paused. His eyes blurred. He closed them, passed his hand over his brow. What about Duhamel's wife? She was coming out here in November. In time for Christmas, Georges had said.

Claudel picked up the pencil, finished his task. He added a postscript: Leaving tomorrow.

8

"It's always fantastic," Nina said as she unpacked their traveling clock and set it back five hours before placing it on a night table.

"What is?" Renwick was studying the phone numbers he had copied down from Brimmer's Minus List.

"We left London at one and we were in New York by three." Fantastic, too, that she had managed to pack and close the flat in two days. Not bad for a beginner, she told herself. Bob had managed all these meetings at Merriman's, all the phone calls, all the clearing of his desk in his office, as if he had no more to worry about than keeping a dinner engagement. "How long do we stay at the Stafford?" It was a pleasant hotel, and Ronald Gilman, who used it on his visits to Manhattan, had been able to get them a room. "I mean, do I unpack completely or just for tonight?"

"That depends. Let me put in some phone calls first." It was now four-thirty, he noted. He could catch the Senator and the two businessmen before they left their offices. If not there, then he'd try their home addresses. The Minus List, with deadly efficiency, held both sets of numbers.

"I'll go downstairs and have a cup of coffee."

"No. I'd rather you stay here, honey. Will you? I won't be

too long." He kissed her. "Keep that smile in place. And the door locked." Then he left.

There was a public phone in the lobby. Renwick, weighed down with a load of change, began his calls. The Senator was in Alaska on an ecological study. One businessman was fishing in Nova Scotia but would be home on Tuesday. The other had taken his family for a week in Wyoming.

Duty done, thought Renwick as he ended the three calls. Now he put in a fourth call, but this time it was to a car rental agency. The weekend was his. Relax, he told himself as he returned to their room. There never was any use worrying about something over which he had no control, and three characters wandering through the wilds of Alaska, Nova Scotia, Wyoming were certainly out of reach. Not just his but Brimmer's, thank God.

Nina was in the shower, her dress unpacked and ready for this evening—optimist that she was. "Best of news," he called to her. "We can enjoy the Fourth like everyone else. Keep the water running—I'll have a shower, too."

Nina looked around the bathroom door, her hair bound in a towel. "Couldn't hear you, darling."

He stripped off the last of his clothes. "I said I'll have a shower, too."

"Your telephone calls—"

"All over."

"And everything is all right?"

"Very much all right," he told her, catching her around the waist. "Tonight, the town. Tomorrow, ocean breezes."

All worry banished, she thought, and she hugged him.

He pulled away the towel from her head, let the loose flow of golden hair drop over her shoulders.

"I'm in the middle of my shower," she protested as she kissed him.

"Are you?" he teased. "We'll turn off the water. There's a lot of time to put in before dinner."

Next morning, they drove to the far end of Long Island. The rented car performed well, and an early start from New York helped them avoid much of the holiday traffic on the expressways. "Miles of white beaches," he promised Nina, "and four days of sun. You'll be a beautiful bronze before Monday arrives."

"Or a peeling pink. But how on earth did you get a room at an inn for July Fourth weekend?"

"Friends," Renwick said with a broad smile. He hadn't felt as good as this in months. Four days with Nina and all problems pushed aside until they were back in New York. Communication with Interintell would be easy—again through a friend, Chet Danford, partner in the law firm to which Frank Cooper had belonged. Cooper was gone, killed two years ago, and could never be replaced, but Danford had stepped into that gap and was now a staunch ally of Interintell. He had bought Cooper's place on Sixty-first Street in New York, made use of it when he needed a town house, and—above all—kept Cooper's top-floor room secure. It contained a neat set of communication devices that had always astonished Renwick. (Old Frank had been a radio enthusiast since his days with the OSS when his life in Nazi-occupied territory had depended on it.)

"Friends?" Nina was asking. Bob seemed to know an amazing number of people in America—more than she did.

"One friend in particular. He has also offered us his house in New York. On Sixty-first Street. It's convenient." And safe, Renwick thought as he looked at Nina.

She was wide-eyed with delight. "But how marvelous."

"Just for a week or so. Until we take off for Washington. That all depends, really, on how my arrangements go." Such as the return of three marked men from their July vacations. Such as a visit to the New York office of Exports Consolidated.

"I ought to phone Father and warn him we'll—"

"And have your stepmother start arranging parties for us? No, thank you, darling. Call him when we reach Washington. Time enough." And let's hope Francis O'Connell and his Beryl will be miles away on the Maryland shore. Then, feeling he had been too rough, he added, "I have guilt about not seeing my own people. But that will come later—before we go back to London." And by that time the danger may be over—it will damn well have to be. He glanced at Nina. Horrify her by telling her the truth? Nina, my love, my name is on a death list. All Renwicks are best avoided; all O'Connells, too, until we get a certain matter straightened out. "That's an attractive spot." He pointed to a windmill with a shingled house attached, a garden with roses on a white picket fence, large maples and chestnut trees, and a bright-green lawn.

"It's the third house today I've wanted to buy." This part of the world was new to her. Even New York would be mostly strange: a pass-through visit was all she had so far paid it. "Could we ever, do you think?"

"On second thoughts, too much grass cutting, too much leaf raking in the fall."

"My wandering husband. Travel, travel—"

"Listen to that! From the girl I had to chase from Istanbul to Bombay before she'd even kiss me." He slowed down for the mess of traffic in East Hampton's Main Street, cars parked every inch of the way, trucks of all sizes mixing with the slow stream of automobiles as thick as clotted cream.

Nina looked around her in dismay. "Don't tell me they've let the highway run right through their village."

"Good-bye New England, welcome New York's clutter." Including modern construction, new buildings for old. He shook his head as some real inhabitants—you could tell them by their normal dress and stunned expressions—tried to cross the street, far outnumbered by all the brief pants and yards of bare skin that pressed around them. "We've another village to pass"— and another Main Street gone the way of all flesh—"and then let's hope there are still some farms and woodland around. Can't be shopping centers everywhere."

Twenty minutes later, once they cut away from the highway and took the old road that edged the ocean, they could leave the procession of cars speeding toward the happy hunting ground for shark and swordfish at Montauk, the last tip of the Island's long finger that pointed at Europe. At Portugal, actually. "I always forget how far south New York lies from London. If it weren't for the Gulf Stream, the English Channel could have Labrador's climate."

"What, no playing fields at Eton? No swimming, no tennis, no strawberries and cream?" Then Nina became serious. "Nature's mercies—we don't think of them much, just take them for granted. Which means we're ungrateful. Then Nature blows her top, just to remind us. A mountain explodes or the earth cracks open or—Bob, is this hurricane territory?" She looked out at the Atlantic with its perpetual breakers, high-crested even on this hot summer day of blue sky and little breeze, that sent white surf crashing onto the beach below the dunes.

"Later in the year. Don't worry, my pet. We won't waken tomorrow with tons of salt water dumped on us and winds of a hundred and twenty-five miles an hour behind them." He pointed to the small house that stood just ahead of them, built on top of the dunes. Well beyond it, above some thin but determined trees, he could see the spreading roofs of a hotel. "Yes, this must be it." He drew the car up at the side of the cottage. "Chet Danford said the bed is made up, food is in the refrigerator, and the world is ours. No, to be quite honest, I added that last bit."

Nina stared at the cottage, stared at him, said, "But I thought—"

"Did I ever say we were going to an inn?" he reminded her and kissed her astonished mouth. "And no more thinking for the next four days, honey."

"No work at all? No worries, no—"

"Not even a phone call." He kissed her again, long and hard. "Surprised?"

"By everything," she said happily, her arms around him. "You're always surprising me." From the very beginning— when he had rushed her away from Washington to be married. To London, she had thought, until they were in a plane that was heading for Zurich. And from Zurich to Geneva, where they had first met. "Just an old romantic under this hard-boiled exterior," he had joked. But there was truth in that jest. Her arms tightened, holding him close.

"Why are we kissing in this damned machine as if we hadn't a place of our own? Come on, Nina." He was out of the car, his arm around her waist as she joined him.

"The luggage?"

"Later. No hurry for that."

She looked at the long stretch of white sand below the dunes, at the breaking waves so clean and cool. She glanced at Bob, wondering if he had read her thoughts. Of course he had. "Later," she agreed, "we'll swim later." And after that, lunch; then sleep and— "Oh, it's wonderful!" Four days together, no office, no meetings . . . "I love it."

"Be it ever so humble," he said as the front door stuck, its wood swollen with hot weather and sea air, and he had to

shoulder it before they could enter. Inside, it was neat and
sparkling clean, a simple place for plain living and high thinking: basic wicker furniture and packed bookshelves. But this
is one weekend, he thought, when there will be high living and
no thinking. For a moment there came flickering into his mind
the memory of a list—nine names marked for death. He caught
Nina into a tight embrace, holding her close. The memory
vanished.

The weekend went as they had planned, except for the
weather. Torrents of rain on the Fourth of July. "No fireworks,"
Nina said when they woke up to the sound of heavy drops
sweeping over the roof. No picnic on the shore, watching the
distant display of Catherine wheels and rockets bursting into
the night sky from a village beach. Renwick took one look at
the surge of dark sea and lowered gray clouds. "Back to bed—
it's the warmest place."

"It's four o'clock—we've slept for hours. Aren't you hungry?"

"Aren't you?" he asked, and held out his arms.

She laughed and came away from the window.

On Monday, they drove back to New York. Not even the
snaggled traffic and the waiting for mile-long jams to end could
dampen Nina's high spirits. She would have plenty to do, she
told him: museums and shops and so many things to see, even
two of her old college friends who had come to live in New
York.

"No, not yet, Nina."

Her euphoria vanished. Back to the real world, she thought,
and Bob is already deep into it.

"Wait a little, will you? Plenty of time to see them later."
he promised.

"Are we here incognito?"

"That's one way of describing it."

"When will I see you? In the evenings?"

"As much as possible," he said vaguely and truthfully.

"We'll be sleeping together, won't we?" she asked in alarm.

"That I can promise you," he said. "And this business in
New York may be over quite soon." How to approach the two
businessmen, the government contractors who had become sus-

picious of Mitchell Brimmer and his Exports Consolidated? Phone them, arrange an appointment—yes, that was the first step. But after their experience with Brimmer claiming CIA backing, how would they react to a stranger saying he represented Interintell? Probably wouldn't believe him, wouldn't even listen to a warning about a death list with their names on it. Not until they had checked and double-checked Renwick, and that could take time. As for the Senator—he might believe, just might; but not quickly enough, perhaps.

Nina was saying, "Is this the Queensborough Bridge?"

"This is it. Takes us right where we are going. But first, I think we'd better drop the car at its garage. You stay there with the luggage while I find a cab and leave it around the corner from the garage. Then we'll walk to it. Okay, honey?"

"Really necessary?" She was startled, not so much by the maneuver itself but by what it proved to her: there was danger for Bob in this visit to New York. "Is there trouble ahead?"

"Might be," was all he said. "And I don't want it to reach out and touch you."

"Me?" She laughed that off. "Bob"—she was thoughtful now, blue eyes direct and serious, watching every small expression on his face—"why don't you recruit me? Let me join you."

He shook his head.

"I could help. I know it. Bob—I'm not joking."

"Nor am I, honey. No. And no, again."

"Don't you have women in Interintell?"

He looked at her, almost passed a red traffic light. "Where did you hear that name?"

From Pierre, she thought. Pierre Claudel would tell her almost anything that wasn't a deep and dark secret—if she pleaded with him long enough. And she had. "Partly because," she said, trying to keep to some truth at least, "I saw that report from Holland—it was in the London *Times*—"

"Oh, that!" Yes, there had been a mention of Interintell cooperating with West German authorities and the prevention of a terror-bombing in Greece. How international can one get? he thought. The report had come from Holland, unauthorized but true. That was typically Vroom, now the head of a section of Dutch Intelligence at The Hague and one of Interintell's members. Johan Vroom, a good man in many ways but one who liked to talk about successes once a case was closed. But then, Renwick reflected, I've talked to Nina, too, about cases closed and filed away, only she doesn't go dropping hints to reporters. "Here we are," he said with some relief, swinging the car into the Fifty-sixth Street garage.

"You know, darling, you may keep too many secrets—"

"Not enough, I'm thinking." He reached across the seat and kissed her nose. She never had any answer ready for that.

He went searching for a taxi, his subconscious mind at work. And, as usual, if he just waited trustingly, it came up with the answer. Or at least one that might work. Certainly the surest and quickest way to contact a senator and two government contractors would be through the FBI. His friends there, Bill Wilson and Joe Neill, wouldn't have forgotten him; twenty months ago they had worked with Interintell and saved a president from being blown sky-high. They had been promoted for that: Joe to New York, Bill to Los Angeles. Not a case of passing the buck: he'd go with Joe to talk with the three men wherever that took him. Yes, they might begin to listen then. And keep their mouths shut. If they needed Brimmer nailed and Exports Consolidated out of all business, including assassination, they had better keep their mouths shut. But tight. Myself included, he thought as he caught sight of Nina waiting for him. My dear and beautiful Nina, don't you know how much I want to share everything?

The housekeeping couple at Cooper's one-time residence on Sixty-first Street were quiet and discreet. Breakfast could be brought up on a tray, a sandwich at lunchtime could be provided, but—

"We'll have dinner out," Renwick said quickly and sent them back obviously relieved to their ground-floor apartment. The house was in good order, and Nina explored it from the second floor up. "The top room used to be a study," he told her. "It's possibly shut tight." But the key was in the lock. For cleaning purposes? He only hoped the electronic equipment was safely stored away. Chet Danford had seen to that: a metal cabinet held all the components, with a door securely padlocked. Now Renwick could understand the small key that had come by special messenger in a thick sealed envelope to the Stafford Hotel on Wednesday night.

"Guns," Nina said in surprise, as she stared at their rack. "Mr. Danford's?"

"No. I think they belonged to the previous owner, a friend of his."

"Old, aren't they?"

Most were antiques, but Renwick's eye noted two usable models. He examined the bookcases and then the outsize desk. Paper and pens provided in the drawers.

"Well," said Nina, looking around her with pleasure, "you'll have a study at last, darling, even if it's only for a few days. Don't you like it?" she asked quickly. He was standing so still, a look of sadness on his face.

"Just a memory . . . My last visit here was when Frank Cooper was alive." He took her hand and led her out of the room. "Now what about washing up and unpacking? I'll make some phone calls, and then we'll go out to dinner. How's that?"

"Wonderful. I'll unpack for you and let you start phoning." She gave him a sideways glance, a small mischievous look. "You didn't bring *your* gun with you, did you?"

He stopped, looked at her. "I left it in Gilman's safekeeping. But how the devil did you—"

"I saw it. Hanging on our bedroom chair with your shirt draped over it. Last Monday, when you worked late and came in tired and worried and the Gilmans and Pierre were there."

Tired and careless and too eager to slip into bed. "Damn," he said softly. "Quick eyes, you have."

"I wish you didn't need to carry it around. It worries me, Bob."

"I don't carry it around. Only when there might be trouble."

"Have you had to use it?"

"I've never killed anyone, Nina. Just discouraged some."

"That worries me, too. You wouldn't be discouraging them if you weren't in danger. Oh, Bob—"

He put his arms around her, comforted her. "One hell of a life when you chose to marry me," he said, trying to bring a smile back to her lips.

"It's one hell of a beautiful life." And the smile had returned.

He went up to the study again and made his call to Joe Neill at the FBI office. A meeting in the Drake Room on Fifty-sixth

Street was arranged for tomorrow at noon. A suitable place, cool and dark.

Then he unlocked the cabinet. Yes, all the needed equipment was there, and in good order. He examined it thoroughly, cut in the power to make certain the gear was operative. He was tempted to transmit. But there was a five-hour difference between New York and London. He would contact Gilman early tomorrow morning and set up their schedule for receiving and sending. He padlocked the cabinet and turned to have a look at the covered Telex machine standing near one of the new computer typewriters. These were Danford's additions. Lawyers certainly knew how to make themselves comfortable. He examined the gun rack, too: one of the pistols was his favorite type of Biretta, the other a neat twenty-two; both were clean. Chet Danford, in spite of sixty years and white hair, was as much a perfectionist as the weekend hostess who not only provided the usual soap and towels in your bathroom but toothpaste and new brushes, too.

All set at this end, he thought as he went downstairs. And there was nothing illegal about the communication system; Danford, lawyer that he was, would have registered anything that needed permission for his own private use. And if Renwick used them? His reports, sent and received, would not cause the United States any harm. On the contrary. Very much on the contrary. So let bureaucratic quibbles take care of themselves, he decided. He entered the living room that ran the length of the second floor, with windows at the front looking out at the trees along Sixty-first Street; at the back, two more trees in a small paved garden.

Nina was standing at the rear windows, looking wistfully down at the tubs of bright petunias and pink geraniums. "Out of bounds, I'm afraid." The garden belonged to the ground floor, no doubt. She sighed as she turned away. "Wouldn't it be wonderful—" She interrupted that sentence. Yes, it would be wonderful to have a house like this. But impossible on Bob's salary: it was strictly on the military level. "Wonderful to have so much space," she finished lamely. "How do I look?" She had bathed and perfumed, brushed her hair until it gleamed, applied just enough make-up to accentuate her eyes and lips, and was ready to step out for dinner in her ridiculous high-heeled sandals and soft silk dress.

"Ravishable. Come on, my would-be Mata Hari, let me show you off to the town."

"Darling, I was being serious about Interintell. And you don't have Mata Hari types. I know that. But surely—"

"Nina"—his voice was strained—"four years ago, in Vienna, there was a girl working with me. I recruited her. And she was killed. On a simple assignment."

"Killed?"

"Shot. She was trying to protect someone. She took the bullet meant for him."

"Were you there?"

"No," he said abruptly. "But since then I never recruit any women. Certainly never you, my love. Come on, darling, let's find some place to eat."

Her hand touched his cheek. "I'll never worry you again by bringing up—"

"Subject closed." He pulled her hand to his lips, kissed its palm. "Now, where do we go? French food, Italian, Greek, or a steakhouse? They're all around."

Discussing restaurants, they reached the front door. A key was hooked onto the wall. Renwick lifted it, tried it in the front-door lock, and pocketed it.

"I never thought of that," Nina said in wonder. But then, *it seems I never think of a lot of things. Shot . . . trying to protect someone.* And Bob still feels responsible for her death. She reached up and kissed his cheek. He looked at her in surprise. "I love you," she told him.

Arm in arm, they set off toward Lexington Avenue, just another handsome couple completing their holiday weekend.

9

GILMAN BEAT RENWICK TO THE PUNCH. AT SIX O'CLOCK NEXT morning, New York time, his call came by regular telephone from London. "Sorry to wake you so bright and early. All well? Settled in nicely?"

"Couldn't be better." Renwick kept his voice low.

"I'll be hearing from you?"

"As soon as possible. Good-bye for now."

" 'Bye."

Renwick pulled on his dressing gown, left Nina sleeping undisturbed, found the padlock key, and ran upstairs, two steps at a time. Inside the top-floor study, he locked its door and then opened the cabinet. Now, he thought, as he got the dial set and made contact with Gilman's office at Merriman's, now for some real conversation. They would disguise names in a voice code that he had suggested before he left London. After all, the KGB listening post in New York was as alert as their interception unit in Washington.

Gilman's voice came through clearly. "We've just had a letter from Pete."

Letter meant a report. *Pete* was Pierre Claudel. "How is he? Enjoying himself?"

"Fantastic holiday—lots to see and do. I'll mail his letter on to you, let you read it for yourself."

Mail meant a coded message sent by transmitter. *Holiday* was Claudel's assignment in Djibouti. "I look forward to that. Any talk of Bright Eyes?" Renwick asked.

Bright Eyes was, of course, Erik. "Bright Eyes was passing through. They didn't manage to meet, not this time. Pete fell ill."

"Serious?"

"A nasty cut on his arm. Needs attention, I think. I've told him he'd be better at home with his own doctors."

Home was Interintell's offices in London. "So the holiday is over?"

"Just cut short. He intends to continue it elsewhere. I'll drop round to see him. By the way, some specimens of the Artful Dodger's work were on exhibition—Pete attended the grand opening."

The *Artful Dodger* was Renwick's choice of name for Mitch-ell Brimmer. "Glad Pete managed to see it." Illegal arms shipped to Djibouti . . . Ironic, he thought. We sent Claudel hunting Erik, and he found Exports Consolidated instead. "Impres-sive?"

"Significant. Confirms what your friend Warrior told you."

Warrior, Alvin Moore, that soldier of doubtful fortune. "Don't forget to send me Pete's letter. I'd like to keep in touch."

"I'm just about to mail it, right now."

What about Gilman's efforts with the Europeans on Brim-mer's Minus List? "By the way, how are your five clients taking your advice? Or haven't you persuaded them yet about their future difficulties?"

"Not an easy job. I did make tentative suggestions to two of them, but I eased off when I felt they weren't receptive."

"Perhaps we had better talk with their respective insurance companies—get some reassurances about coverage for their requirements. In fact, that's what I plan to do here."

"Which company is that?"

The FBI, chum. Renwick said, "Federal Insurance."

"That's an idea. Keep me posted. Phone me at the office. I'll be here any day around three o'clock—just after I get back from lunch."

Subtract an hour, as pre-arranged, and Renwick would be

at his transceiver at nine each morning, New York time, to talk with Gilman, courtesy of Telstar. "Okay with me."

"Over and out," Gilman said with a laugh. The phrase always amused him.

It was a cheerful note on which to end. Claudel's report must have held some pleasant surprises as well as the bad news. His arm—what had happened there? An accident? And Erik—elusive as ever, but at least he had been pinpointed in Djibouti. Come on, come on, Renwick urged his radio: the report is all coded and ready to send; give me the signal, dammit.

Two minutes later, it came.

It was in a code he had used before, but he was taking no risk of error. He went downstairs to the bedroom, found the page of ciphers which he had inserted into the copy of Frost's poems lying in his suitcase.

Nina was still asleep, head turned on the pillow, her hair—silken gold, he thought—falling loosely over slender neck and bare shoulders. Gently, he pulled the sheet to partly cover the lithe, tanned body. She stretched and sighed, fell more deeply into sleep with a last flicker of long, dark eyelashes. He left as quietly as he had entered.

Up in the top-floor room, he set to work. The report was startling. Claudel had really produced. But he shouldn't have been there alone. Yet, of the four other Arabic-speaking Interintell agents who could have passed as Frenchmen, two were in Chad, two in Mauretania.

Renwick pushed back his chair from the desk and concentrated on the changes that would now have to be made in his own plans. With the opening of those crates on a Djibouti dock, the whole perspective had been altered. Klingfeld was the important one, the one in command; Brimmer and his Exports Consolidated were secondary—used and manipulated by Klingfeld. But secondary or not, Brimmer had to be dealt with, and soon.

The Djibouti report had been sent early on Tuesday morning—just after the action there on Monday night. With time changes helping London, the report had arrived at Merriman's on Monday evening. Today, Tuesday morning in New York, it was in Renwick's hands. Even Brimmer, alerted to danger by Klingfeld, who in turn had been alerted by an informant in Djibouti, could not have received the warning any earlier than this. Renwick could only hope that Klingfeld didn't trust any informer to have direct contact with its headquarters: not likely, thanks to Klingfeld's obsession with anonymity. That could slow up the news from Djibouti reaching Exports Consolidated, a delay of a few hours possibly—or perhaps a day, with luck? Not more, certainly.

The French were now on the trail of Brimmer. No doubt about that. But by the time they had enlisted the help of the FBI to visit and search the offices of Exports Consolidated, what would they find? Just a set of legitimate business records. Brimmer would have destroyed his secret accounting of illegal dealings, and—with his precious Plus List, false passport, supply of ready cash—be on his way to Brazil.

You'd better make sure of those three pages of illegal transactions, Renwick told himself as he cleared the desk. Claudel's report and his own decoded version were torn up and burned in the metal wastebasket, their ashes flushed down the toilet bowl of the room's adjoining bathroom. All equipment, along with his page of ciphers, was locked behind the cabinet's strong doors. He gave one last check: everything secure, shipshape and Bristol fashion. The caretaking couple would find nothing to fault when they came up to sweep and dust.

Half past eight. He shaved and showered, was dressed before the breakfast tray arrived at the prescribed nine o'clock.

Nina, still dazed with so much sleep, barely roused herself to ask, "Are you going out? So early?"

"Some people to see. I'll be home before dinner."

He drank orange juice and black coffee, anchored them with a slice of toast. With a kiss and a hug and another kiss, he left Nina at her first mouthful of croissant.

At this hour, Sixty-first Street was only half astir, shaded from the sun coming over the East River by the small trees spaced at even distances along its sidewalks. Nearer Lexington Avenue, the shops that had invaded the row of red sandstone town houses were beginning to open. The offices downtown? Not until ten o'clock for the upper echelons. He would have time to walk to the building near Fifty-third Street where the firm Exports Consolidated was headquartered.

Lorna . . . Al Moore's girl, Brimmer's most trusted and very private secretary. It had been no problem for Interintell to discover her full name and particulars before Renwick had left London. He had insisted on it. Margaret Lorna Upwood of Beekman Terrace, a comfortable and expensive address, and merely a few blocks from her place of employment. Originally he had planned to visit her in her apartment tomorrow. But now speed was necessary. He only hoped she would be promptly at her desk, the place fairly quiet, routine just beginning for the day.

He reached the large block of offices, at least eighty firms doing business within this hunk of concrete and glass. The air-conditioned lobby was impressive, a good imitation of marble on its walls and floors, with giant green plants dotted around. He paused at the directory exhibited near a desk where a brown-uniformed guard sat, engrossed in a newspaper. A second guard stopped him as he started toward the elevators, pointed back to the desk. "The tenth floor—offices of Exports Consolidated," Renwick said, and hoped that would be sufficient. But no such luck.

The man at the desk laid aside the newspaper. "Have you an appointment?"

"With Mrs. Upwood."

"One moment." Middle-aged and overweight, he went slowly through the usual motions: telephone picked up; is Mrs. Upwood expecting anyone? A wait, then a reply. The guard looked at Renwick. "Your name?"

Renwick left his study of an inflamed mural, abstract patches of red and violent orange. "Al Moore."

"Mr. Al Moore," the guard reported to the office upstairs, nodded, said to Renwick, "Second bank of elevators to your left." He picked up his newspaper, went on reading about the baseball strike.

On the tenth floor, there were more potted plants, another frenzied mural (wouldn't like to delve into that guy's subconscious, thought Renwick), and a young receptionist. "Mrs. Upwood," he told her, and followed a pointing finger into one of the corridors. There were several open rooms with a drift of voices discussing the holiday weekend; and at last, in pride of place, dominating the end of the corridor were three doors, one narrow, two imposing, and all closed. There was a brass plate on one of them: MR. MITCHELL BRIMMER. The other had a neat name painted in gold: M. L. UPWOOD. The narrow door, beyond Upwood's, proclaimed its inferior status with no name at all.

He knocked, braced himself for any unexpected appearance of Brimmer in his most private secretary's office (I'm here to sell the newest in desk computers, Renwick reminded himself), and entered.

It was a scene of order, meticulous in arrangement, neutral in color: gray carpet, gray tweed curtains, a pale-gray wallpaper with darker roses climbing ceilingward in exact columns. A typewriter and a copying machine were on gray metal stands; a gray filing cabinet. No ornaments, no photographs, no plants. The one light-hearted note was in the gold frame of a painting—a misted river scene—hanging in the center of one wall. (Concealing a safe? There was none in view. Rather obvious, thought Renwick.) Two small neat chairs, chrome and leather, completed the room along with a small neat desk—a closed blotter, a pencil holder, a telephone on its dark-gray surface. Behind it, commanding the doorway, sat a slender woman in a black-and-white silk suit who had tried, quite successfully, to lop ten years from her thirty-five. Smooth white skin, fluffy auburn hair, a tip-tilted nose above vivid red lips, a general feeling of vagueness in a smile that never quite appeared, never vanished either. Just the helpless-looking type to bring out Al Moore's protective instincts. But he had never noticed her eyes in a moment such as this: as gray and hard as any filing cabinet.

Renwick selected a chair in front of the desk, drew it even nearer, and sat down. "May I?" At least they could talk without raising their voices.

"Mr. Moore?" She sat motionless, face expressionless, her hands folded over the leather blotter.

"Sorry about that, but it's a legitimate use of the name. I wouldn't be here if it were not for Alvin Moore."

Her eyes appraised him. "He sent you?"

"Indirectly. My name is Renwick."

There was a brief moment of astonishment but enough to reassure Renwick that no recognizable photograph of him was in circulation. In that case, he could face Brimmer if necessary.

He said, "I've some news—for your ears only." He pointed to the wall that separated them from Brimmer. "In? Or out?"

She hesitated, perhaps wondering which answer would be to her advantage.

"We've no time to waste. Is he in?"

"Out."

"For how long?"

"Until later today—he has been in Maine with his children for a week's vacation."

Renwick relaxed. "Has any message yet arrived from Klingfeld?"

Her face was unreadable. She shook her head. Her hands tightened.

"You would have seen it?"

"Of course." She paused. "What kind of message? Or don't you know?"

"I know."

"Well—what is it?"

"First, I'd like copies of three pages of Brimmer's illegal transactions." Then, as she remained silent, her eyes blankly innocent, he added, "Al called you from London, told you we needed these three pages as hard evidence. Didn't he?"

"Yes."

"You've photocopied them, haven't you? If not, I'll wait here until you do. Come on, Lorna, you're wasting time, and you haven't much of it left."

That startled her. "Why haven't I—"

"You haven't," he said grimly.

She rose, went over to the filing cabinet, selected a thick folder marked *Receipts for Office Expenditures*. From the middle of its numerous pages she extracted three. "I was going to mail these to you in London," she said diffidently as she handed them to Renwick.

"I also suggested a sample of Brimmer's profits—the ones he doesn't declare to Internal Revenue."

"I haven't had time to make a copy of that."

She doesn't intend to, he thought. Because she also hasn't paid taxes on excess earnings? No IRS investigators descending on this office until she has left and is beyond their reach?

"I'll mail it next week," she said as she turned away to replace the folder in the cabinet. Unlocked, Renwick noted. Clever girl: Brimmer would never look in a moribund file of simple expenses. The safe behind the painting was of more likely interest to anyone searching this office. And that safe, he was willing to bet, would contain nothing dangerous like the pages he held in his hand. They were authentic, all right. A quick scan down their entries shocked even him. She came back to the desk, studied him as he read.

"Next week," he said as he folded the three pages and slipped them into an inside pocket, "you will be with Al."

"No! I don't leave until—" She tightened her lips as if to keep any other revelation from slipping out. She eyed him warily. "Why should I be with Al next week?"

"Because Brimmer's luck has run out. The message from Klingfeld will give him the bad news."

Her hands, folded once more on the leather blotter, suddenly spread rigid. "How bad?"

"The crates shipped by Exports Consolidated to Djibouti were opened on the dock. By the French."

She must have known the contents of the crates, for she asked for no details, no reason why a search by the French spelled complete disaster. Now she was too preoccupied—with her own plans for escape, Renwick guessed—even to answer him.

"So," he went on, "Brimmer's day is over. All he can do, when he gets Klingfeld's message, is to skip the country. But unless you leave ahead of him, you'll be in trouble. Deep trouble."

"How?" she challenged.

"If he finds that his little black book with that Plus List is missing . . . ." Renwick shrugged, didn't need to finish his prediction.

The prospect didn't seem to alarm her.

"You think you can just walk off with it tucked into your handbag? But you're the first suspect—the only one: Brimmer and you shared its secrets. You and Al will be marked. Hunted down."

"By whom? By you? Brimmer can't—not now."

"By Klingfeld. The man in control there must know about Brimmer's Plus List. He may even have contributed some names of his own. He has been using Brimmer as cover, hasn't he? Why not in illicit payments, too?"

The idea disturbed her. Renwick pressed on. "That man in charge of Klingfeld and Sons has a long reach. In Djibouti, he had one man murdered—a French security officer—and another man attacked; two men who could possibly link him with the arms that Exports Consolidated sold."

"He arranged the sales," she said indignantly.

"He finds buyers abroad for Brimmer's exports—is that it?" A market made to order... "A name, Lorna. Give me his name."

She hesitated. "Would Interintell search for him? Find him?"

"Find him? That's the business we're in. He's arranging sales of arms to terrorists. He's providing instructors for these weapons—with Brimmer recruiting them as well as supplying the military and technological equipment. Brimmer must be making a couple of million dollars a year. Or more, Lorna?" And you, he thought, have had your nice little share of it.

She dropped her eyes. "It wasn't always like this," she said defensively, as if to excuse her own complicity. "Once, we—"

"Do you want to be rid of this man or don't you?"

Her voice lowered almost to a whisper. "Klaus. He ends his Telex messages with the name Klaus. That's all I know."

"Telex? Then the messages are in code."

"Only Mitch—Mr. Brimmer—knows how to read it. Even the name is coded. I wouldn't have heard it except that Mitch let it drop one day when he was angry. Klaus had sent a message, some suggestions that Mitch didn't like."

"But he followed them."

"There was no choice left." She sighed. "How much time have I got? A few days?"

"A few hours. There will be a Telex for Brimmer by the time he gets back here."

She opened the leather blotter and lifted a sheet of thin paper. "Then we had better destroy that message. I found it waiting on the Telex in Mitch's office this morning. No one else has seen it. I was here before anyone."

"Anyone? Are you sure?" The message was in no code he could recognize, but the key to it—part of the key at least— could be found in the name Klaus if that *was* the signature used. At least, we do have a name. Renwick drew a deep breath, folded the sheet carefully.

"Except for the supply-room clerk and an office boy," she replied. "What are you doing with that?" She pointed to the Telex, now disappearing into Renwick's pocket. "Destroy it!"

"Why not you?"

She looked most innocent. "How can I? I know nothing about it."

He could imagine the indignant protests if she were questioned: never saw it, you can search my room, I didn't destroy it, it must have been someone else on this floor. Just a girl who liked to have one truth in her story to bolster her confidence and make others believe in her sincerity. Renwick shook his head in amusement, rose to his feet.

"I said destroy it."

"Don't worry. I'll destroy it." When it had served its purpose: Interintell's deciphering machines would soon rip its secrets apart. "But I would worry, if I were you, about getting the hell out."

"I'm safe enough, for a few days at least. No Telex!" Then she added, "The FBI won't appear until they've gone through all the procedures to get a search warrant. And the French—well, they can't invade the office to arrest Mitch Brimmer."

"What about Klaus? One of his agents could have been inserted here—just keeping an eye on Brimmer's staff."

That was a possibility that had escaped her smart little mind. She stared at him.

"Has anyone come to work here since Klingfeld and Sons joined forces with Exports Consolidated?"

Her face whitened. "The clerk for the supply room."

"Where is that?"

She looked at the wall where the painting was displayed. "Next office—a small room," she said faintly.

"Keep talking," Renwick said and moved to the door. "Talk!" he told her as he opened it and left.

A man, young, with a windblown hair style and heavy glasses, a clipboard under one arm, a pencil stuck behind his ear, had just come out of the supply room. He was a friendly type who gave a nod and a "Hi, there!" as he paused to light a cigarette. Renwick had his handkerchief out and stopped a sudden sneeze, his face hidden as the man's lighter flicked. And failed to catch. And flicked again. By that time, Renwick had passed him. The young man walked on. "Hi, there, yourself," said Renwick as he entered the supply room.

It was cramped in floor space, its walls lined with deep shelving on which were stacked masses of envelopes, paper, every kind of replacement for office work from boxes of rubber bands and clips to a couple of spare typewriters. His eyes searched the dividing wall between this room and Lorna's. Here, the shelves had rows of filing boxes drawn up like soldiers on parade. And then he noticed the step-ladder, abandoned quickly, left in a precarious tilt against a column of boxes. Quickly, he scanned that column; the neighboring one, too. And *there* was something—a box well above his reach that broke the rigid pattern, retreated half an inch from the line-up. Replaced too hurriedly?

He pulled the ladder into position, climbed two-thirds of its height to stand on eye level with the filing box. It was of cardboard, not so light as it looked but easily pulled out by the leather tongue on its spine. Placing it on the top step of the ladder, he leaned forward to look through a hole drilled neatly into the wall. Judging from where he stood, the peephole must lie just above the painting next door.

He had a limited view of Lorna, sitting at her desk, sufficiently recovered from her paralysis to speak into a Dictaphone. He could hear nothing. He pulled out the next box; there was no mark of any listening device on the wall behind it. But this one was lighter in weight, much lighter. He replaced it exactly, opened the first box. Inside, fixed in position by a leather band—no slipping, no rattling when the box was lifted—was a cup-shaped item with a small earphone attached by a tube. An imitation stethoscope. It worked on the same principle, too. With the rim of its cup pressed against the wall, the earphone gave Renwick the clear sound of Lorna's dictation. He listened to only three words before everything was being replaced in its proper place and he could leave.

He opened Lorna's door, locked it behind him. She looked up at him, switched off the Dictaphone.

"Get out," he told her. "Leave now. As soon as you can, get out of New York. He could partly see us, and he certainly could hear us once he got his listening device working."

Her eyes showed fear. "Leave now? But there's no plane until this evening."

"Then get lost in New York until your flight leaves."

"He really saw us through that wall?" She could scarcely believe it.

Renwick walked over to the painting. It had been centered,

logically enough, in a column of gray roses. They were shaded, lifelike except in color. Leaves sprayed out from their stalks, all carefully shaded, too, but darker than the flowers. One leaf seemed almost black, a deep shadow nestling so innocently among the intertwining foliage. That could be it, he thought, and pulled the picture to swing open on its hinges. The gilded frame with its antique curves no longer distracted the eye. The blackened leaf was definitely a hole. He pointed to it, then closed the picture over the safe. He heard Lorna's gasp. He chose that vulnerable moment to say, casually, "If you're heading for Europe, you'd better start packing."

"Yes, yes." She rose, distracted. "I never looked up when I opened that safe."

"No one does." One looked at a safe, not above it.

She reached for the telephone, told the receptionist, "No calls, no visitors. I'm going to see my doctor—a bad migraine. I'll be back here tomorrow." She replaced the receiver, opened a drawer, began pulling out its contents, jamming them into her shoulder bag. "You don't have to wait. I'll be out of here in ten minutes." Like her words, her movements were rapid. She brushed past Renwick, pulled the painting wide, and opened the safe. She reached for a neat stack of dollar bills. "What's delaying you?" Her tone was brusque. She had recovered.

"Curiosity. I'd have thought you would have made a bee-line for Brimmer's safe. Or," he added, "have you already taken that little book with its Plus List?"

"It's secure. Beyond anyone's reach."

"Risky. What if he had opened his safe and found it missing?"

"A small black diary is easy to substitute. Two ninety-five in any stationery store." She closed the safe, then the picture.

"But inside"—Renwick persisted if only to hear her confirm his guess—"blank pages? A complete giveaway."

"Not so blank." She was much amused.

"I see. Brilliant. Names and dates and amounts of money— no relation to the real thing, of course." How long had she been preparing for this escape? The diary—and that was another detail for an estimate of its size—must have taken several weeks of careful imitation.

"Of course," she said mockingly, as she added the dollar bills to a zipped pocket in her handbag. "But good enough for any glance inside." She began filling a briefcase with a few folders from the filing cabinet, selecting them with care.

Beyond anyone's reach . . . So Brimmer's Plus List was not anywhere in her apartment but some place far from New York where she could collect it without fear of discovery. Some place, also, where she'd find more money: the dollars from the safe would pay her fare to Europe, would keep her for a week or two. On the run, no one risked leaving a trail with traveler's checks or a charge card: it was cash, nicely anonymous cash, all the way.

She closed the briefcase. "For God's sake, why don't you leave? You've scared me enough for one morning. What's keeping you?"

"A last piece of advice. I would avoid Switzerland. Klingfeld and Sons have offices in Geneva."

"Thank you for your concern, but Geneva wouldn't attract me." She was condescending, quite certain she had defeated him.

"Zurich could be safer. I hear it is a good banking town, too." That ended her assurance. "When you see Al Moore, give him a kind word from me." He will need it, poor guy.

"I'll do that. If I see him." She opened the door. Her voice sharpened. "Do I go first? Or you?"

"Ladies always first." He stood aside.

"Don't follow me!"

Renwick shook his head. But others might, he thought.

Should he warn her: another word of advice? The wind-blown-hair boy must have had time to contact a backup—if he had one. "Lorna—"

But she had left. Handbag strapped over her shoulder, briefcase in hand, pleated skirt swinging above excellent legs, three-inch heels clacking briskly on the tiled floor, she marched along the corridor, didn't look back.

Renwick followed slowly, gave her time to take the elevator before he passed the reception desk. He was still troubled by her last phrase about Al Moore. *If I see him*. Not when; if. Moore had served his purpose, so now . . . ? The money she intended to screw out of the men on Brimmer's Plus List would go twice as far if she were alone. Money . . . she had grown accustomed to its taste. There were two curses in life: money and politics. But no one—except the hermit in his cave—could live without them.

He stepped into a crowded elevator. No one edged near him; no one paid him any attention. He relaxed. But the sooner he emptied the inside pocket of his jacket, the better. For him as well as for those four pieces of paper.

10

By THE TIME RENWICK REACHED THE LOBBY, STEPPED INTO A whirl of people eddying around the elevators, Lorna Upwood had vanished. Almost half past eleven, he noted; he would be on time for his noon appointment with Joe Neill—Park Avenue and the Drake Hotel were only three blocks away. It would be a relief to talk with someone who was honest, straightforward, and with no avarice, either. How much did he make—twenty-five thousand a year? Everything was out of whack: Joe was worth more than any rock-and-roll singer or movie star in terms of the future of this country. But who thought much about the future? Me me me only thought about now now now. Renwick shook off the effects of his talk with Lorna Upwood and concentrated on reaching the entrance to this enormous building. The desk and its uniformed guard were just ahead. And there, too, was the supply-room clerk.

The man was alone, standing apart from the stream of people, watching. He had seen Renwick. He was either a fool or ill-trained: he wasn't even trying to melt into the background. At this hour the lobby was far from empty, yet this gas-head couldn't be missed, with his windblown hair and heavy glasses, posted as he was near the desk. Posted? A warning bell sent off its small alarm inside Renwick's head.

Quickly, he side-stepped behind two businessmen, ignored a friendly wave and a cheerful "Hi, there!" And where was the fellow's backup, ready to tail Renwick once identification was made? Renwick didn't wait to see. He turned on his heel, joined three lawyers arguing about torts on their way to the elevators, and broke into a short sprint to reach a closing door before it shut tight. He got out at the second floor, used the fire-exit staircase to lead him all the way down to a vast underground garage.

He had just managed it, but barely; no one could have had time to follow. This interest in him was to be expected. Inside his securely buttoned jacket there were four documents for which Mr. Klaus of Klingfeld & Sons would willingly murder. The clerk—and not such an idiot, Renwick admitted wryly—had seen him receive them from Lorna Upwood, had heard talk about illegal transactions and Telex messages in code. But the man hadn't stayed to hear a discussion about Brimmer's Plus List or Lorna's admission that she had taken it. Or, thank God, to hear Renwick leading her into the subject of Switzerland.

Plenty of problems, he thought as he made his way through row after row of cars—must have been hundreds of them parked here: the building was almost a small city in itself—but the immediate problem was a clean exit from this garage. Far ahead he could see a sloping ramp that led up to a wide mouth gaping into a busy street. He headed toward it. Waste no time, he told himself.

At the foot of the ramp's slope, a private ambulance was drawn close to a side wall. Door left open, waiting. But no one guarding it. Renwick halted, stepped instinctively behind a blue Chevrolet. A garage attendant had noted him, came forward at a leisurely pace.

"I was to meet my wife here," Renwick told him and forestalled any question. "But I don't see any sign of her—or her car."

"What make?"

"A Chevy. Blue. Like this one."

"Plenty of them around." The attendant was young, his voice not unfriendly. The glum look on his face was probably normal.

"An accident?" Renwick nodded toward the ambulance.

"Just an emergency in the lobby upstairs. Some guy had a

heart attack. They'll be bringing him out any minute. They'd better. Can't have them parked here for long."

"Why not in the street?" Renwick was sympathetic.

"Couldn't find space." The attendant shrugged. "So what can you do? Turn away an ambulance?" He stared at the ramp where two men came hurrying down from the street. "What— no heart attack? Perhaps the guy's dead." He didn't seem to find it remarkable that the men wore no white coats, carried no stretcher. Or perhaps it had been explained to him and the other attendants, still engrossed in a heated discussion near the ramp: no stretcher required, the driver would take the ambulance to the building's entrance, the sick man could be helped to walk that short distance from the lobby.

Now the driver climbed into his seat, the other man about to enter. He paused—heavily built, round-faced, with a genial look and thick dark hair—and gave a friendly wave to the three garage attendants. "False alarm," he called as they approached him.

"Wouldn't you know?" the young man beside Renwick said in disgust, and left to get his share of the tip now being handed out.

Yet another figure had appeared, waiting at the head of the ramp until the ambulance would stop and pick him up. He no longer wore glasses, but he hadn't changed his hair style or seersucker jacket. Renwick bent to tie his shoelace, straightened up when the ambulance's motor merged with the traffic outside.

So the supply-room clerk had a mini-transceiver among his other little gadgets. When had he called for support? As soon as he saw me enter Lorna Upwood's office at ten o'clock? Or perhaps five minutes later, when he had started listening in? The ambulance was stolen temporarily, no doubt. It wasn't intended for Lorna Upwood—they must know her apartment in Beekman Terrace, could pick her up any time. So you're the candidate, he told himself as he walked toward the street level, leaving behind an argument resumed: who was to blame— owners or baseball players?

He hailed a taxi, directed it to First Avenue and Sixty-third Street. There, he walked three blocks back to Sixtieth Street, making sure Klaus's long arm was no longer reaching after him. Another cab took him west to Park Avenue. He left it one street away from the Drake. A small evasion, but he had little time for anything more elaborate. He was already ten minutes late for Joe Neill.

Neill was making his glass of beer last and beginning to worry. Renwick was always punctual. Then he saw him enter and quietly raised a hand to attract Renwick's attention to his table against the wall. One signal was all it took. Renwick sat down to face him. The room was dark and cool, the tables half empty at this hour. By one o'clock the place would be packed.

"Traffic heavy?" Neill asked, noticing Renwick's tight face.

"Complicated." Renwick ordered an ice-cold beer, suggested a couple of quick chef's salads, and let Neill make light conversation until they were served.

Neill had been waiting for that moment, too. He switched to a lower and more serious tone, asked, "What's the problem, Bob?"

"How do you get a healthy man into an ambulance—take him from a crowded lobby with few people noticing one goddamn thing?"

Neill said, "You know the answer to that." But his interest had been aroused.

"Yes," said Renwick, his voice intense even if it was held low. "A needle in his wrist, or a sting at the back of his neck. Sudden collapse, unable to talk, but possibly still able to walk enough—propped up by a friendly medic and a couple of ambulance attendants who just happened to be there."

Neill studied Renwick's face. "You? They tried it on you?" For once, his usual calm deserted him.

"They planned it. But I managed to keep a couple of steps ahead of them."

"Where did this happen? When?"

"In a highly respectable building in the smart business center of Manhattan. One hour ago."

Neill recovered. "You should stay in London. You always find trouble when you come over here. I've never known whether you go looking for it or whether it meets you."

"A little of both, perhaps."

"How bad is it this time?"

"Bad enough, and getting worse."

"Need some help?" Neill frowned, wondering how much

involvement was necessary. He liked Renwick personally, admired him professionally, but there were limits to what could be done. Rules and regulations were rules and regulations.

"I think," said Renwick almost inaudibly, "that we both need each other's help. If you could prevent three Americans from being assassinated and—"

"What?"

"No exaggeration. Actually, there's a fourth on that death list—me, to be exact. But if you help me reach the other three, I'd be grateful. I've a copy of the list for you."

"My God," said Neill. A forkful of ham and cheese was poised in midair. "Do they live here?"

Renwick almost smiled. Regulations, regulations . . . "Houston, Palo Alto, Washington."

Neill nodded, went on eating. After a few minutes he said, "There was an 'if' in your last sentence. If we can help you, then what?"

"I can help you. About another matter. Highly sensitive. But immediate." For the last half hour Renwick had been trying to decide how much he could tell Neill—he couldn't hand over Brimmer's illegal accounts until he had made copies of them for Interintell's files in London. Tell Neill about them today, promise them for tomorrow? Not altogether satisfactory: evidence was best handed over with the facts. Yet, it was a pretty fair deal. He—and Claudel in Djibouti—had done all the groundwork on Exports Consolidated. "It would give you a head start on the others who'll be crowding into this case. A scoop, Joe, as our newspaper friends say." He pushed aside his half-eaten salad, looked around for the waiter. "The check is mine. Let's get the hell out. Some place where we can talk."

"My office?" Neill asked tentatively and wondered if Renwick would accept.

But Renwick did. "Not every day I get an escort from the Bureau," he said as they came out into the blinding light of the street and signaled for a cab.

He was back to his old form, thought Neill: finding a small joke in everything. In the Drake Room he had been as serious and intent as Neill had ever seen him. The information that Renwick could give must be a blockbuster. Neill's interest doubled. He noticed Renwick's glance at his watch as a taxi drew up. "We haven't far to go."

"Good." It had been a quick lunch. Now, it was only five past one. Renwick could catch Gilman in London at the end of his working day, alert him to expect a full report coming later tonight. "I have one phone call to make. I'll keep it brief," he said as they got into the cab.

A tactful hint. Neill grinned. "You can do that from my office. I won't listen. And I wouldn't understand a word of it anyway."

"I hope not." Renwick gave an answering smile. It broadened as another idea struck him. "By the way, how's your copying machine working?"

"It was fine this morning." Neill's amusement grew. "Taking over my office?"

"Just want to leave you with three interesting pages. Saves time—yours and mine."

As urgent as that? Neill settled back with his own thoughts. Renwick fell silent, too, calculating the tight schedule ahead. His visit to Joe Neill's office wouldn't take long. The bare facts about Brimmer, complete with hard evidence, were ready to hand over. Also a full description of the supply-room clerk at Exports Consolidated and of his two accomplices. Also a mention of Klingfeld & Sons, whose agents they were. That was definitely FBI business. But details of Klingfeld and Klaus were unnecessary: they were based in Europe. That was Interintell's affair. So was Lorna Upwood's possession of Brimmer's Plus List, now in a safe-deposit box somewhere in Switzerland. And after his discussion with Neill about the best approach to the other three American names on that death list— what then? Some concentrated work on his report for London, every scrap of today's information made crisp and clear and then encoded for transmission this evening. He would send it out by six o'clock, six-thirty at latest, the Klaus Telex included.

And after that? Nina . . . Her safety, now with Klingfeld's agents in New York, was the biggest problem of all. If they couldn't get him, they would make a try to kidnap Nina; a hostage to hold and use as blackmail, force him to— He cut off those thoughts. Keep her safe, he told himself, keep her safe.

"Let's skip that movie tonight," Renwick said as they ended dinner at the little Italian restaurant not far from the house on

Sixty-first Street. "Do you mind, Nina? I'm not much in a mood for it."

"I didn't think you'd be." She looked at him worriedly. He had been working in the top-floor study when she came back from shopping this afternoon, stayed there until after seven o'clock, and since then she had been making most of the conversation. He had listened, yes. Even joked with her over her first day's adventures in New York. But he had brought some problem to dinner with him—unusual. And instead of lessening, it had increased. Something I've done? she wondered, and her own anxiety grew.

Suddenly, watching her, he seemed to make up his mind. "Back to the house, darling. We'll put our feet up and talk. And tomorrow we pack."

That really startled her. She said nothing, only nodded. But, she thought in dismay, I was just beginning to settle down in New York. There's so much to see, and I'll never see it now. And as they left the restaurant, she glanced around the busy avenue—noisy, bustling, filled with a mixture of faces and clothes, everyone out for another evening of fun and pleasure—and repressed a sigh.

On the hall table there was a note, written in a large scrawl, waiting for Renwick. "Chet Danford," he told Nina, who was already halfway up the staircase on its climb to the living room. "He phoned us at eight-fifteen. Will call back later." Renwick frowned, wondering. At eight-fifteen, Danford must be phoning from somewhere outside his office. Then Renwick told himself, You're too much on edge: yesterday you wouldn't have sensed anything wrong about the placing of that call, felt any emergency. There probably wasn't.

Nina had noticed his frown, his slow step as he mounted the stairs. She glanced over the white banister at the kitchen door, which was ajar. "These shoes are a hideous mistake. They're far too narrow." She slid her feet out from them. "Now *that* feels good. This carpet is divine." Have I given a good excuse for our early return? It sounds vapid enough: the kind of remark Mrs. Whosis on the ground floor would expect from me. Why is it that strangers believe, if you're blond and twenty-three and wear a black chiffon nightgown, that you are a nitwit? "Do you think we should get a red carpet like this one? I rather like it. Of course, we'd then have to have a white staircase, too."

Renwick, having followed her glance, made no comment as he climbed after his barefoot wife. In the living room—two rooms, actually, knocked into one giant—Nina had chosen a central couch. He closed the door, said, "Has she been inquisitive?"

"No. Just a little critical—a slight sniff when she came to collect the breakfast tray and found I was still in bed. But I suppose she must wonder who we are and where we come from. Only natural, isn't it?"

Yes, it was only natural. He came over to sit beside her, slipped his arm around her, then disengaged it. "Can't think straight," he told her as he kissed her and rose. He pulled forward a small chair, faced her. "Hard to know where to begin. Look, honey—tomorrow morning, early, we'll leave for Washington. No, I don't know how long we'll be there. But my business in New York is finished. And there could be trouble if we stay."

She was about to speak. He leaned forward, kissed her lips lightly. "Hear me out, darling. Yes, I could be in some danger—and there was an attempt to waylay me today. No, no, nothing much. Just a warning—which I'm taking seriously. Because if I'm threatened at all, then the danger could spread to you. An unpleasant type, I'm up against. He has a long reach. Tried to have Claudel killed in Djibouti."

"Pierre?" She was aghast. "Was he hurt?"

"Not badly. A knife wound."

Nina drew a deep breath. "Will you be safe in Washington?"

The question was, would she be safe? "We'll have no contact with anyone linked to the O'Connell name, no one linked to the Renwick name, either. We'll call ourselves something original—like Smith."

"Where will we stay—in another friend's house? Or a hotel?"

"A motel to start with. Some place anonymous, where you won't run into any of your father's friends."

She said slowly, "Would it be better for you if I just cleared out? Went back to London?"

"No. Not that!" He quietened his voice. "The unpleasant type I mentioned—well, he knows about Interintell. You see, there's an informer connected with our outfit—no, honey, not in the London office, somewhere else. Don't worry, we'll find him." He took her hands in his. "Don't worry," he repeated, "or else I'll regret telling you all this."

"Don't, please don't. I wanted to be told—yesterday I pestered you with questions until you shut me up completely."

"I what?" He tried to laugh. "I must be worse than I thought."

"No, no. It wasn't you; it was what you said. About Austria four years ago, about the . . ." Her voice trailed off. About the girl who was killed there. And Bob, she saw, knew perfectly well what she had almost said aloud. She gathered her wits. "Well—if I can't go back to London, what about Connecticut? Aunt Eunice is there—mother's sister—so there's no O'Connell in her name. Besides, she's Mrs. Williams now."

"And there are three sons and a host of friends. How are you going to keep Renwick unmentioned? They'll never introduce you around as Mrs. John Smith, will they?"

She remembered her cousins. "Not without a wink or a nudge or a mysterious look," she admitted. "I'd be lucky if they didn't go off into a fit of wild jokes. The trouble is— they've never had to face anything like the dangers you face. Or Pierre. Or Ron Gilman. They just can't imagine—"

"Got it! I know someone who'd help us in Washington," he said, and then added more slowly, "if he's there at this time of year. He goes off to Europe in summer, looking at paintings—possible acquisitions. He's a museum director." Yes, Colin Grant had known threats and hidden danger and the grief they could bring.

"Museum?" That caught Nina's interest.

"Quite near Washington. Look, darling, let me telephone him—find out if he's around." Renwick had risen, was halfway to the door. "I'll use an outside line."

Nina made no comment about that. "Perhaps he won't want us."

"If he's there, he will." Renwick hesitated, then decided. "He was in Vienna four years ago—buying a painting. He wasn't Intelligence. Purely amateur standing. But with his help, we uncovered a secret funding for terrorists. He met the girl who was working on that case with me. They fell in love, were going to be married. She was killed."

The girl Bob had recruited . . . "So he won't joke when we use the name Smith," Nina said softly.

Renwick shook his head. "He will keep you safe," he said, and left.

Nina rose, walked around the room, and tried to divert her mind from Bob's last words. She concentrated on the outside call. Why use a public telephone near the corner of the avenue? There was nothing doubtful about Mrs. Whosis downstairs, except her natural curiosity. Or did Bob think the house phones could be tapped? Wanted his request for Washington Directory to be unheard by anyone? And a call to Washington tonight, followed by a hurried departure tomorrow, might—just might—give away their destination. Was that Bob's reason? Nina wondered. And with that, his last sentence came sliding back into her mind. *He will keep you safe.*

That could mean only one thing. Bob must be faced with the possibility of leaving her with someone he trusted while he traveled. A job that had to be done, and too dangerous for her to share. Or was she—as Gemma Gilman would say in her precise English voice—just a bloody nuisance?

Yes, Nina decided, I could be just that. There are times when I'm a total handicap. And having reduced herself to tears, she went upstairs to begin packing.

11

HALF AN HOUR LATER, RENWICK RETURNED. "I HAD TO FIND enough change, first," he told Nina. He was relaxed and natural once more. "So I went back to that Italian restaurant and got it."

"And your museum friend was at home. Not traveling?" Nina seemed equally relaxed. She snapped the locks on her suitcase. All ready to go, she thought, but where?

"Not until August."

"And he had no objections to having a lone female landed on him for three weeks?"

"Darling..." Renwick drew her away from the suitcase and with his arm around her waist led her to the chaise longue. "There, Madame Récamier," he said and settled her comfortably. He sat down facing her, his hands on her knees. "He had no objections at all. In fact, when I told him we were coming to Washington, he insisted we should stay with him. Plenty of room, he said. So we'll have lunch with him tomorrow, and I'll look the place over."

"Married?"

"No. He's alone except for a housekeeper."

"How old is he?"

"About a couple of years older than I am—forty-three, I'd

125

guess." Renwick smiled. "Better looking, too. He's quite a guy. I'll tell you more about him on our way to the Basset Hill Museum. It stands in acres of gardens just outside Washington. And"—this pleased him—"it is well guarded. Valuable collection of paintings: seventeenth century, with French Impressionists in a new gallery he opened. You'll have plenty of beauty around you—inside the museum, outside in the woodlands. And—" he paused to emphasize his next words—"I shan't be away for three weeks, Nina. Three days perhaps, or ten at the outside. I may not have to leave you at all, and I won't unless—well, let's see how everything breaks. I'll be with you for the first day, at least. Some meetings in Washington."

She tried to keep her voice light. "How many problems left, darling? Only that man? The unpleasant type, you called him."

Klaus of Klingfeld & Sons. "He's the main one." There was Klingfeld's informant, too; the mole who had burrowed deep into Interintell. We'll have to unearth him first, Renwick thought, end his threat to us all: that should help to defang Klaus as far as information about Interintell is concerned. And there was also a third problem. Lorna Upwood and the black diary she had stolen from Brimmer. That little notebook, Brimmer's Plus List, could be the biggest challenge of all.

"Let's give the unpleasant type a name," Nina suggested. "One word. Something easy for me to memorize."

"Snake."

"That was quick. A snake in the grass, is that what he is?"

"A snake in long grass who needs defanging. But we'll just call him 'the opposition,' I think; keep the drama out of it."

Suddenly, she was upset. "And you—"

"I'm not alone in the search,"he told her. "There's Interintell. And there are the intelligence agencies of at least twelve countries backing us up. We're in constant contact. Keep that in mind, will you?"

"And you direct the traffic."

He looked at her in surprise. "You overestimate your husband, my love."

No, she thought, I don't. Pierre's words—she had quoted him directly.

"Business over for the day," Renwick was saying, his arms

around her. "Remember what George Bernard Shaw's girl friend said?"

"How much of a girl friend?"

"Never could tell with old G. B. S. Mrs. Patrick Campbell—yes, that was her name. Now, where does this come undone?" He opened her blouse.

"Bob—you'll tear it. My best—"

"All in a good cause." He unfastened her skirt, pulled it off.

"What did Mrs. Campbell say?"

"Can't recall the direct quote." Who could, he thought, at a moment like this? "Something about the marriage bed being so peaceful after the hurly-burly of the chaise longue." He threw aside the rest of her clothes, stood looking down at her. God, he thought, she's the most beautiful woman. He was about to tell her that as he bent down to take her in his arms. The telephone rang.

Renwick straightened up, swore softly. It rang again.

It was Chet Danford, speaking against a vague background of voices and laughter. "Sorry about this. One moment—I'll get the door closed." There was a short struggle; the noise diminished. "That better? A man came to my office late today—just as I was leaving. Knew Frank Cooper had been one of my partners and thought I must know you as another of Cooper's close friends. He had heard you were in town, wanted to meet you again, and where were you staying? He sounded quite sincere. Most plausible. Except that he hadn't seen you since your last visit to New York three years back. You weren't in New York then, were you?"

"No."

"Then thank God I had some doubts. Told him I hadn't seen you for the last two years, and if you were in New York— well, you hadn't called me. Sent him away convinced I was telling the truth. As I was."

"What was his name? His appearance?"

"Josh Grable. Medium height, thin, brown hair—a lot of hair. Heavy glasses. Seersucker suit. Late twenties, I'd guess, or early thirties. Ever met him?"

"This morning. He didn't know me, thought I was someone else." Until Al Moore's name had been questioned and Klaus had decided the description he had been given fitted me. "Just a try-on for size. Glad you didn't make it fit."

"Anything I can do?"

"No. We're about to take off, tomorrow. Sorry our stay has been so short. It was most comfortable."

"If you're anywhere near Washington, remember that Rosen is now heading our office there."

Wallace Rosen, another of Frank Cooper's partners and friends. Might be too much of a connection there, too. "Have you told him I'm here?"

"Not yet. I'll call him to—"

"Don't. I'll get in touch with him myself."

"Fine. Have to go—the intermission is just about over. Wish the play were, too: another clunker. Take care."

"You, too. What about that little key—where do I leave it? In an envelope in the desk?"

"Oh, yes, I forgot about that. Or you could mail it to—" Danford had turned to speak to someone who had opened the booth's door. "Just coming, my dear." Then to Renwick again, "My wife. 'Bye."

Mail it where? Renwick wondered, and shook his head over wives who yanked husbands away from telephones. "That was Chet. He's as sharp as a carving knife, the kind of lawyer I wouldn't like against me in court, but why the hell did he mention Washington and Rosen on a phone in a theater lobby?"

"He must have thought it safe enough. We can't be suspicious of everything."

"No," he agreed. "Not suspicious of everything. Just careful. There's a big difference."

"Bad news?" she asked, watching his face.

"A confirmation, actually. The opposition is trying to find out where I am in New York." Messages from Klaus to his informant in The Hague must have been frantic this afternoon. "At least I don't feel my hunch was so damned stupid about getting us the hell out."

"When do we leave?"

"About eight o'clock. We'll breakfast somewhere, then take a shuttle flight to Washington."

She looked down at the chiffon negligee she had bought this morning. Bob hadn't even noticed it. "When I was in Bloomingdale's today, I saw..."

He was thinking about The Hague. Yes, he decided, that has to be our first objective.

"Bob . . ." She had caught his attention. "Let's leave at eight, take a cab to a place where we can have breakfast at leisure, take another cab back in this direction—to Bloomingdale's. I'll only be a few minutes inside. The store can't be busy when it's opening. I won't delay us, really I won't. It's just something I didn't remember to buy today. And there are lots of flights to Washington, aren't there?"

He was amazed but he only said, "Okay—if it's important to you. As long as we leave this house early enough."

"Leave at seven? Just drive around the park? That would be fun."

That would be safe, too. "Okay," he said again. "Couldn't refuse you anything in that getup. New, isn't it?"

The telephone rang. "Shall I?" asked Nina. "You weren't expecting any more calls, were you?"

He shook his head. It couldn't be Danford: the theater wasn't over yet.

Nina lifted the receiver. "Yes?" Then she broke into a relieved sigh, handed the phone to Bob. "It's from London—Ron Gilman's voice."

Thank God, thought Renwick and took the phone. "Glad to hear from you. I was wondering if I could haul you out of bed."

"I've just finished reading your letter."

Pretty quick work. Renwick's report had been sent out just before seven this evening; Gilman receiving it around midnight in London, decoding, reading, and now able to make some comment. "Interesting, wasn't it?"

"I'd like to hear more as soon as possible."

"Working late? You sound tired."

"An all-night job, I fear."

So Gilman was in his office, and communication would be easy. "I'll write you at once. Good-bye for now." Renwick cut off the call.

He turned to Nina. "Sorry, darling. I've got to go up to the study, discuss some business. Ron is still in the office."

At half past three in the morning, London time? Nina's eyes opened wide. But she nodded, said, "We'll be here when you get back."

"We?" he asked as he kissed her.

"My new negligee and me." That sent him off with a broad smile on his face. Well, thought Nina, wives may be a bloody nuisance some of the time, but not always. With that comforting thought, she lay back on the bed and wondered about tomorrow.

Gilman was waiting for Renwick's call. They used voice code where necessary, but their fifteen-minute talk decided several things. It began with the serious problem of Klingfeld's informant.

Like it or not, Renwick insisted, they had to start with Johan Vroom at The Hague. First of all, Gilman had to find out if there was any close assistant to Vroom—one who might know about Vroom's association with Interintell; better still, one who had even been sent on a special mission to London. "Let's hope that is what we're looking for," Renwick said. "But if not..."

Then, like it or not, they had to make inquiries about Vroom himself. Was he in debt—had he received any large sums of money recently? Or was it a woman? An affair that could wreck his home life with wife and children if Klaus made it public? Or some photographs taken in a Rotterdam brothel, an unwitting connection with a Soviet agent that would ruin his career? "Either he's being blackmailed or—and I hope this is true—he has an aide who is milking him of information," Renwick concluded.

Gilman said unhappily, "I hope so. He is really a very decent man. Devoted to his family."

"Where else do we start?" Renwick asked bluntly. "Believe me, I've been thinking about it ever since we received that information on The Hague. There's no other solution."

"I'll begin a check right away."

"We haven't much time."

"Yes, I felt that when I read your latest report. In fact, that is what I wanted to discuss with you now. I'm concerned—"

"Don't be. We'll be leaving tomorrow." And Gilman knew his next stop after New York. "I've made safe arrangements for Beautiful." Nina, of course.

"Thank God for that. The present climate isn't exactly healthy, is it? Don't forget to pay a visit to my aunt. She's expecting you."

"Always a pleasure." Gilman's aunt in Washington was an elderly gentleman with an upstairs room as nicely arranged as this study.

"Also," Gilman went on, "about those accounts you found today—you gave three copies to Federal Insurance?"

"It saved time."

"What about your own copies?"

"I'll leave them with your aunt." And Gilman could have them picked up and sent over to London in a diplomatic bag.

"Good. But frankly I wish you'd return with them and stay here—you could direct things from the office. We could assign someone else to—"

"Forget it." Waste valuable time putting a new man in the picture? "I've been in on this from the first. I know the full story—all the particulars."

"I know, I know. Still—"

"No delays. We're at the stage when every hour counts. How's our friend's arm, by the way? Fit enough to join me?"

"He's been talking about that."

"Okay. Set it up. We'll meet in his old stamping ground." That was Paris, Claudel's home town. "I'll call you again—before I take off—arrange time and location."

"You're in a hurry, aren't you?"

"Our competition is setting the pace. He moves damn fast. And that reminds me—I'm looking for a good watchdog to guard the household while I'm away. I was thinking of an Airedale, like the one you liked in Ottawa." That was Tim MacEwan, one of the early recruits to Interintell, a Canadian who commuted between Ottawa and Washington. Nina knew him but hadn't met him in the last twenty months—a safe-enough time lapse for any contact between them in Washington.

Gilman was surprised into a laugh. Mac's bristling reddish hair was indeed reminiscent of an Airedale. "Easily arranged. You'll find him at my aunt's. Anything more?"

"Bright Eyes." Yes, what about Erik, little by little?

He was still on board the freighter, its rate of travel slowed by a faulty boiler, and wouldn't reach the canal for a few more days. The captain had been instructed to search the ship. One seaman was missing. No sign of Bright Eyes. The crew knew nothing. Could be a payoff, made by his very old and very rich friend.

"We could damn well question the friend as soon as we can board the ship." That would be at Suez, just as the *Spaarndam* was being cleared for passage through the canal.

"But we were told he isn't our business," Gilman said. "A quid pro quo. Remember?"

"Yes," Renwick said curtly, repressing his anger. Worry was causing it; deep worry. If Erik slipped away from the *Spaarndam* at the port of Suez, he could head easily for Cairo. And Cairo's sprawling airport, a vast stretch of complete confusion, was just made for Erik's talents. Once through there, he could be in Europe and practically home free. Renwick said, "I'll be in touch day after tomorrow. The usual time," he added and signed off.

His anger surged back. It had been Vroom, dealing with a Dutch ship, who had instructed that goddamn captain to make a quiet search of his *Spaarndam*. Why the hell hadn't he put the fear of demotion into the captain, made sure he really stirred his fat stumps? No doubt the man had assumed this was just another stowaway, what was all the fuss about? Stowaways were plentiful—a headache that could be expected. "Vroom," Renwick said aloud, "your mind just wasn't fully on your job. Was it? And why?"

His anger subsided as he concentrated on routine, restoring the room to complete neatness, remembering to remove his cipher list from safekeeping in the metal cabinet before he locked its doors securely. He hesitated in front of the gun rack, then lifted down the Biretta, slipping it into his belt. In the drawer below the rack, he found an extra clip of ammunition. He still hesitated. Danford would notice the small gap left by the borrowed pistol. So he went over to the desk and wrote a brief note to keep the housekeeper clear of any suspicion: *Something borrowed, something new. To be returned unused, I hope.* He placed the key to the cabinet inside the folded note, sealed them in a Manila envelope with wax and Scotch tape, addressed it in block letters, and left it with its edge tucked securely into the desk blotter. As satisfied as he could be, he went downstairs with the cold touch of the Biretta against his waist.

Nina had fallen into a light sleep. She stirred, said, "You, darling?"

"Soon be with you." Quickly, he packed his small suitcase. The Biretta and its refill went into a sock; the cipher list in between two pages of Frost's lyrics. As he stripped, he looked down at Nina. Then he stared. "Oh, no!" he said. She had cut her hair. It no longer fell to her shoulders, just to her ear level. "Oh, Nina!"

She half awakened. He slid in beside her. "Why, Nina? Why?"

"Too hot. It will grow," she said drowsily and fell completely asleep inside the curve of his arm.

Next morning, Nina kept her promise: she was less than ten minutes inside Bloomingdale's, hurrying out to the waiting taxi with a small shopping bag under her arm. She didn't explain a thing. Otherwise, Renwick had to admit, she seemed perfectly normal. He concentrated on making the short flight to Washington as easy and pleasant as possible. He didn't mention her hair.

Once they had arrived, there was a short delay. "Just five minutes," Nina pleaded, and left him at a newspaper stand while she hurried to the ladies' room. When she returned, she was wearing a silk scarf in turban style around her head and not a blond curl showing. Her lips were altered, too: pink had given way to coral.

"Look, Nina—" he began.

"I know. Silly, isn't it?"

In the taxi, she waited until they had left the airport well behind them. Then she drew the scarf carefully away, shook her head and let a smooth sweep of dark-brown hair fall to her shoulders. "Do you like it?" she asked, showing her first touch of uncertainty.

"You're incredible. But you're taking this too seriously. No need to—"

"Isn't there? Father has a lot of friends in this town."

True. It was also true that Nina's blond hair and blue eyes were memorable. But so was Nina transformed into a brunette. Unrecognizable, however, unless you looked into her eyes and noticed their intense blue. "What about contact lenses?" he teased her. "And a cane to hobble with?" Then he kissed her gently. "As ravishable as ever, Mrs. Smith."

"Thank you, John."

"Not at all, Samantha."

She took out her sunglasses and put them on. "Better?"

He nodded. The transformation was complete. Best of all was her confidence: no sign of misgivings, of nervousness, of dejection. That could have been the case, he realized, and a wave of relief swept over him. "Incredible in every way," he said as he directed the cab to draw up at a pleasant-looking motel halfway to Basset Hill, and Nina didn't even ask one question. Not even one when he paid for two nights in advance, signed the register with "Jimson, Philadelphia," and they found themselves in a small sterile bungalow with a rented car waiting at its side.

"How?" Renwick asked the question for her. "Colin Grant booked the room and car this morning. We'll stay ten minutes. Next stop, Basset Hill."

"Are you sure his standing *is* purely amateur?"

"Quite sure. But he catches on damned quick—like you, my pet."

I've just had a medal pinned on me, thought Nina. She looked in the mirror and adjusted her new dark-brown wig. "Tell me about the museum," she said.

It had once been the late Victor Basset's eastern residence, a vast mansion standing on top of a gentle slope with nothing but parkland and trees surrounding its gardens. Four years ago its interior had been gutted and transformed into modern picture galleries, no expense spared in proper lighting and ventilation, a suitable place for the display of the valuable collection of paintings that Basset had gathered during his lifetime. He had lived to see his museum opened, to feel its future—handsomely endowed—was assured, and to know that his millions had been well spent. Fortunately for Basset now, he couldn't see the sprawl of a city forever creeping outward, turning countryside into bedroom annex. Basset Hill still stood apart in its twenty acres on the Virginia border—but it was only fifteen miles from Washington. Another few years and the tide of new housing would be lapping at its massive gates.

"Gates! But where are their walls?" Nina could only see thick high bushes leading out in a wide curve on either side.

"High iron fence disguised. Basset combined the practical with the aesthetic. It has an alarm system, too. There's valuable art inside that big house."

Nina studied it. An imposing entrance in the center of two

outspread wings, built of silver-gray stone, decorative yet simple—if huge size could ever qualify for simplicity. "Big? It's enormous. And where does Colin Grant live? On the premises?"

"At the back." Renwick followed Grant's instructions, took the driveway as far as the museum and then branched off to his right. Up here, there were flower beds and two gardeners at work. Nina glanced over her shoulder, down the long slope of grass with its small islands of trees ending in the wall of high bushes. Even the trees, she thought, had been carefully chosen for shape and size, perfection in color and balance. "Basset had taste."

"And expert advisers," Renwick said. Not to speak of a billion or so in cash. "Here we are." Within its own wall and gate stood a neat house, built of stone, good architecture, with two small wings, nothing to detract from the overall scheme. Renwick studied it as he angled the car over a short driveway to reach the attached garage. There were some trees, but not close to the house. And the wall kept any visitors to the museum—there were many, judging by the parking area on its other side—from wandering into private territory. There had been an attendant on duty at the cars, a guard at the museum's front steps, and a guard down at the front gates. Yes, he thought, I could leave Nina safely here. "What do you think? Like it?"

"Yes. I just hope he likes me." She was looking at Colin Grant, who had come out to meet them. Tall, with dark hair turning gray, a friendly face, and—after a slight look of surprise as he saw her—a warm greeting. There was little doubt that he was a friend, a very good friend, of Bob's. But why be surprised about me? she wondered. She took off her glasses and shook hands.

Grant laughed. "Bob wrote me he had married a blonde," he said. "But the eyes have it. Come in. What do I call you? You're my cousin, you know—can't go around saying Mrs. Smith."

"Samantha," said Renwick, hauling the suitcases out of the car.

"No," said Nina. "Sue. Susan Smith is a very nice name."

Grant raised an eyebrow as Renwick accepted that, then took hold of a suitcase and led the way indoors. "We've twenty minutes before lunch," he said after he introduced the housekeeper—Mrs. Trout, white-haired and bustling—to his cousin,

Mrs. Smith, and her husband. "Mrs. Trout can show you the house, Sue. I'll borrow your husband and let him see my own point eight nine four of an acre."

Outside, Grant said, "Now, Bob—put me in the picture. As you used to say, there's a need to know. God, how I used to bristle at that phrase."

They paced around the grass and trees while Renwick talked and Grant listened. "Sure," Grant said when Renwick brought up the subject of Tim MacEwan, "we can fit him in. He can be one of those foreign art experts who stay over in the guest cottage just beyond those trees—" he pointed to a roof near them—"whenever they come visiting the museum."

"Except that Mac knows little about art."

Grant thought over that. "Twice in the last eighteen months we had a scare about burglary. Each time we had an expert in security staying with us for about a week—he went over the alarm system, got to know the guards, the general layout. Is that more in Mac's line?"

"Much more."

"He can stay at the cottage. Or would he rather have a couple of rooms over the garage?"

"Whatever raises no eyebrows. Mac's probably the best judge of that," Renwick suggested. "I'll see him in the morning."

"When do you leave?"

"Tomorrow night, possibly. And I don't know how long I'll be away."

"Don't worry. We'll take care of Nina—Sue. Better keep calling her 'Sue.' She has a mind of her own," Grant added with a smile. "Did you have a hard time persuading her to wear a wig?"

"Her idea. She's like you, Colin: the inspired amateur. But don't let her get too inspired, will you?" Yes, he thought, everything will be all right. After lunch I'll take a walk over this whole stretch of land while Nina explores the museum. Best not to be seen with me in public. Tonight we can stroll around the park—our last night together. "What about lunch?" he asked. "And you can tell us about the museum. It looks pretty impressive to me."

"A fine place to work. Strange—" Grant paused—"I wouldn't have accepted this job if you hadn't pushed me into it. You know—I really meant what I said back in Austria—

about joining you, fighting those bastards from undercover—
but you wouldn't recruit me, and so here I am."

"In your own right setting," Renwick said. "But you tempted
me, Colin. You'd have been one hell of a smart intelligence
officer."

"We made a pretty good team," Grant said slowly. However
indirect, it was a reference charged with sudden emotion, a
tribute to the girl who had fought along with them and had
died. Avril . . .

They both fell silent, walked back to the house.

12

By SEVEN O'CLOCK ON A WARM MIST-HEAVY MORNING, REN-
wick was ready to leave Basset Hill. He stood at the side of
their bed looking down at Nina as she lay asleep. A last memory
to carry him through . . . Then he roused himself and kissed her
awake.

"So soon?" she asked.

"The sooner I leave, the earlier I'll return."

"I'm coming down—"

"No, darling. I never like long good-byes. And I'll be back
before you know it. I'll send you messages through Mac. Tim
MacEwan, remember him? He'll be around to keep an eye on
everything. And tell Colin I'll leave the car at Statler Garage—
it's near the hotel. He can have it picked up there."

And after that? she wondered, but asked no questions. She
slipped out of bed, threw her arms around him.

"You make it damn hard," he said, holding the soft lithe
body tightly against him. A long kiss and he released her. He
picked up the dark wig from the bedpost where he had tossed
it the night before and clamped it on her short blond hair at an
angle.

"Oh, Bob!" She was trying to straighten it.

That's how parting should be, he thought: a laugh shared.

Without delay, he reached the door. "I love you," he told her as he closed it behind him.

Renwick timed his visit to Gilman's Aunt Chris for half past eight. Christopher Menlo, an Anglo-American who had spent early years in his native England and the remainder in Washington where he had served his new country well, was in his dressing gown finishing breakfast, tut-tutting as usual over the morning paper. White-haired, pink-cheeked, tall, and thin but now rounding substantially at his waistline since his retirement from the CIA ten years ago, he showed little surprise when Renwick arrived.

"I expected you," he said as he shook hands and returned to his bacon and eggs. He picked up his newspaper again. "Hardly as early as this, I must say. Breakfast? You'll find all the makings in the kitchen." He gestured across the small living room, a disorder of books and papers, to an open door showing a kitchen in equal disarray. Chris lived alone and—in between working on his book about the wars and politics of the seventeenth century—pottered. His word. He pottered around his small rose garden, he pottered with his large stamp collection, and he pottered with his electronic equipment in the spare room upstairs.

"Later perhaps," Renwick said. "But Gilman should be in his office by two o'clock. His time. I'd like to chat with him. Is that all right with you, Chris?"

"Of course. You know the way." Chris was relieved now he could finish breakfast in peace—a sacred hour. He eased his dressing gown more comfortably around him, went back to shaking his head over the news from Lebanon.

It was a small house with a strip of garden at the back: living room and den below, two rooms above. Halfway up the narrow stairs, Renwick halted as Chris called to him, "Your friend Mac got into Washington last night. He phoned me to say he'd be here around ten."

"I'll be downstairs by then."

"Oh—and another thing. Farley wanted to see you. He'll be here at noon. That's all right, is it?"

Maurice Farley was attached to operations at the CIA. "I'd like to see him, too." So Farley decided to accept my invitation, thought Renwick. Why? Yesterday afternoon, when I phoned him, he expected to have committee meetings all of today. "He's a friend of yours, isn't he?"

"Yes, yes. Drops in here whenever he wants to pick my old brains." Silence followed, broken only by the rustle of a newspaper.

End of conversation, Renwick decided, and mounted the remaining steps. He had twenty minutes to get his suggestions in good order before he made contact with Interintell at nine o'clock.

First, there was the problem of Erik. He might be able to disappear at Suez or in Cairo, but his movements could be traced. Through the fake Englishman, William Haversfield. And Haversfield's identity, past and present, was also traceable: an early supporter of Erik's Direct Action (and that meant in 1973 or 1974), a wealthy greeting-card manufacturer in West Berlin, where Erik had organized his anarchist group. Yes, Richard Diehl, of West German Intelligence, could start digging in the security files and discover Haversfield's real name and political connections. Gilman in London could start some digging, too: if Haversfield could afford to travel around the world, Haversfield had an income and must file a tax return. (People such as he, living under false pretenses, would most certainly obey the law and run no risk of arrest or inquiry.) The income-tax boys had his address, his business or profession, and his source of income. Enough, thought Renwick, to track down Haversfield, who could lead us to Erik.

Secondly, there was the problem of Klingfeld & Sons. Several problems, in fact, but these lesser ones could be better gauged once he and Pierre Claudel had a face-to-face talk about the events in Djibouti. However adequate a coded report was, it lacked the small details that could round out the picture, bring it into complete focus. The major question about Klingfeld & Sons was simply this: how had they known about Frank Cooper's connection with Interintell, his friendship with Renwick? That was the excuse offered by the supply-room clerk, Klingfeld's undercover agent in the offices of Exports Consolidated, when he asked Chet Danford about Renwick's visit to New York.

Renwick thought he knew the answer to that question. Apart from the Interintell group—Gilman, MacEwan, himself—who had been working with Cooper at the time of his death, there were only three others—and they had belonged to East German Intelligence—who had known about Cooper's connections. Two of them had engineered his death on orders from the third man; and he had been more than an East German Intelligence officer: he was KGB. And that, Renwick guessed, could be the source of Klingfeld's information.

An unpleasant deduction, but it could damn well be true. In the last few years the Soviets had become past masters in the art of remote control: never visibly present, working most effectively from the far background. Renwick could hear Gilman's groan when he heard about this new possibility in the Klingfeld puzzle. What? Gilman would say. Not them again? Which reminded Renwick to set Chris's transceiver on Gilman's wavelength and get ready for a dialogue in code. A blasted nuisance, he thought; but here in Washington he was in KGB intercept-territory. Their elaborate listening aids, set up quite blatantly on their embassy's roof, were part of the landscape.

At nine o'clock exactly he heard Gilman's voice, and the strange, seemingly nonsensical interchange began.

It went more or less as he had expected, even to Gilman's groan. There were initial objections, of course, to his interest in tracking down William Haversfield. ("Not our business, we've been told," Gilman reminded him.) But Renwick had his justification ready. "We won't touch him. Just use him to reach Bright Eyes. We'll leave him entirely to Pete's girl friend."

Gilman had agreed to that, even suggested that he could have some results of his inquiries by tomorrow. "See you then?" he had asked.

"No, better not. I'll go straight to Pete's home, meet him there. Same old place, same old time." And the same old place was one of the bookstalls along the left bank of the Seine. The time would be that of his last meeting there with Claudel.

Satisfactory, Renwick thought as he went downstairs and joined Chris, now with his last cup of tea and his first pipe of the day. The old boy was rustling his way through a second newspaper: he was an avid reader of small paragraphs, searching them out even among the shipping news, convinced—from years of experience—that many an important little item got lost in the back pages.

"Nothing remarkable today," he reported, "except that a

man was found murdered in the Seychelles. He was an ex-Green Beret, which sounds strange. You'd have thought he would have known how to take care of himself."

Renwick, returning from the kitchen with a hastily brewed cup of instant coffee, looked at Chris sharply. "What was he doing in the Seychelles anyway? Snorkeling, skin-diving, or just lazing on the beach?"

"Doesn't sound much like the Green Berets I've met," Chris observed. "He was going to retire there, had just bought a house."

Renwick laid the coffee cup on the nearest piece of free space. "Let me see that, Chris, would you?"

Chris folded the paper to the proper column of print, pointed out the exact spot. "Really odd," he remarked. "Found dead in his bed. Throat slit. Was he drunk at the time?"

"Must have been." Renwick read the details, the more lurid of them already given by Chris. The man's name was Al Jones. Mystery around him was hinted at, but tactfully. He had bought the house on a secluded beach with a check drawn on a Swiss bank account immediately after his arrival on the island of Mahé only ten days ago. He was expecting his wife to join him in a few weeks. The authorities so far had not been able to find Mrs. Jones at the address on her husband's passport, which showed he had traveled by air to London and Zurich before he reached the Seychelles. Further inquiries were being made.

And they'll find the passport was false. Alvin Moore—is that where you ended, soldier of fortune, in bed with your throat slashed? You backed out from your contract with Brimmer, but you didn't handle it as neatly as you thought. You knew too much. Mr. Klaus of Klingfeld & Sons doesn't tolerate that. Where did they pick up your trail? At the airport in London when you were leaving, or in Zurich as you arrived? Or at the Zurich bank itself? Brimmer could have opened an account for you there—the usual procedure when payoffs were high.

Chris said, "You look thoughtful, Robert. Why? Did I miss something?" He took back the paper, scanned it again.

"Just a damned awful way to die," Renwick said. He drank his coffee and began talking about George Washington's victory at Yorktown, where the British were allowed to march in good order to their ships, their arms reversed, their band playing

"The World Turned Upside Down." Gallows humor, wry and cocky. "Typically English, I'd say."

"And not lost on old George, either. He was born an Englishman." Chris beamed. "I've always taken consolation from that when some Idaho character called me 'an ersatz American.' The fact is, Robert, if the Americans and British don't hold together, the West will become unglued. Churchill believed that and so do—" The front doorbell sounded. "Ten o'clock. That will be our Scots-Canadian. D'you know what I like about your Interintell?" Chris was talking over his shoulder as he went to open the door for Tim MacEwan. "Your care for the West. Much too good a civilization to be thrown away. Come in, Mac, come in." He watched approvingly as MacEwan and Renwick met with real, if properly restrained, affection. "And now I must potter around my roses," Chris said. "Quite useless to work with them when the sun gets hot. Robert, tell one of your bright boys to invent an exterior air-conditioning unit; he'd make a fortune in Washington." He closed the living-room door and went upstairs to change into his work clothes.

Mac hadn't altered much in the twenty months since Renwick had met him face to face, still the same cheerful pessimist, the romantic realist; but aren't we all? thought Renwick. He wasted no time on general chitchat but plunged into a complete rundown on Exports Consolidated's tie-up with Klingfeld & Sons and all it had entailed.

At the end of the briefing, Mac's square-set jaw was grimly serious. He hadn't even cracked one small pawky remark. He said, "What about Nina? Klaus is just the type to go after her if he can't get you."

So Renwick explained about Basset Hill and Colin Grant and Mac's role around the museum. "Okay?" Renwick asked.

"Sounds good," Mac said thoughtfully. "How long will you be away?"

"As short a time as possible."

"I'm on a two-week vacation. Got to be back in Ottawa by the twenty-second. Do you think you can finish your job by that time? It's complicated, Bob, damned complicated." And hellish dangerous. But there was no need to mention that. Bob knew.

"Oh, I'll just tie up some loose ends and then fade out."

"Like the way we tied them up in Sawyer Springs?" Mac

asked with evident enjoyment. "Crawling on our bellies over a rough hillside, scouting around a terrorist camp in sunny California?" He spent a few moments remembering that foray, every minute a threat from danger. "Wish I were going with you," he admitted frankly. "Too much desk work nowadays."

"The price of promotion."

Mac smoothed his red hair, patted a waistline that was still firm. "Got to jog a couple of miles each morning. You look fine, Bob. How do you keep in shape? Karate? Running? Bend and stretch?"

"A little of everything. By the way, you didn't smuggle a revolver over the border, did you?"

Mac shook his head. "Hasn't Grant got a spare?"

"I don't believe he has any. So take this—it's Chet Danford's. You can return it to his office on your way home." Renwick drew the Biretta out from his belt and the extra clip from his pocket. "The guards at Basset Hill wouldn't think much of a security expert who didn't pack a pistol."

"But this leaves you short."

"Don't like smuggling any more than you do. If necessary, Pierre Claudel will provide."

Mac stowed away pistol and ammunition. They were a sign for him to leave, he decided. "I'll phone Chris each day, find out if he has any message from you for Nina."

"And you send Gilman a daily report about Nina. She's calling herself 'Sue—Susan Smith—Mrs. John Smith.' And don't be surprised when you meet her. She's a brunette."

"What?"

"Just temporarily."

"Your idea?"

"Hers."

"How much does she know?" That's the trouble with marriage, thought the dedicated bachelor; you never can judge where to draw the line.

"Only the reason why I want her out of the picture."

"Enough," agreed Mac. "I'll drive out to the museum after I've spent an hour dodging around town. I won't see you there this afternoon?"

Renwick shook his head. "I'll leave here by the first flight available."

And the farther away he travels, the less attention will be

paid by Klaus to Basset Hill—was that it? Yes, Mac thought, that's his hope. He shook hands warmly, clapped Renwick's shoulder. "Don't worry about Nina."

"I'll see you when I get back."

"No fancy footwork, Bob. Stay safe." And with an encouraging grin once more in place, MacEwan headed for the small plot of roses and a last brief word with Chris.

There was half an hour to wait for Maurice Farley's noon visit. Renwick decided to give Chris a hand, cleared the window table of its breakfast dishes and picked up the scattered pages of newspapers. Chris didn't even notice the improvement when he popped his head around the door to announce he was going upstairs to listen to news bulletins from the Middle East. "Got Lebanon yesterday. Keeps my Arabic freshened."

Small wonder that Chris with all his side interests never mananged to finish his book. Or perhaps he didn't want to bring it to a conclusion. Renwick glanced at the pile of loose manuscript on the writing desk, at the scattering of notes lying beside it. Is this what we come to when we retire? he wondered. Pottering? Then he shook his head: not with Nina around.

Maurice Farley was punctual and as crumpled as ever in a gabardine suit that hadn't stood up to this morning's humidity. He was Renwick's age, thin and balding, pleasant expression in place, a tall man who tried to disguise his height with a slight stoop. Black socks and brown shoes—a preppy touch like his narrow-shouldered jacket. But his voice still had traces of the bright boy from Kansas who had made it all the way into the sacred groves of Langley. The new breed, Chris Menlo called him, as sharp and quick as the brown eyes that were now covertly studying Renwick. New breed or old breed, thought Renwick, they both shared the same deceptive air of complete disinterest.

"Glad you could make it," Renwick said.

"My lunchtime, actually. Meetings all morning and again this afternoon."

"Another flap?"

"Aren't there always?"

"You've had your share recently."

"Inherited mostly." The polite sparring ended. They had been friends, after all, for almost ten years: military intelligence dealing with Soviet capabilities, before Farley had left for the CIA and Renwick had joined NATO. Farley relaxed into a genuine smile. "You wanted to see me," he prompted.

"Interintell needs a little information. Oh, quite harmless. No state secrets implicated."

"That's reassuring. You know, Bob, we're really sympathetic with Interintell's work. Just takes some convincing of the old boys before they agree to let you into our files. Come to think of it, you are rather aggressive, could try to take over a lot of our business."

"A case of a very small tail wagging a very large dog?"

"Files *are* sacrosanct, Bob. Hard won, hard kept."

"No interest in your files, Morry. Just in a little co-operation when it can do each of us most good and the opposition most harm. Reasonable?"

Farley nodded. "As I said, we're not unfriendly. What information are you hunting?"

"Was it one of your operatives who passed a warning message to an Interintell agent in Djibouti?"

Farley froze. "Isn't that asking too much?"

"No. For one thing, we don't want to complicate any of your investigations in progress. For another thing, if that operative—a woman—was yours, we'd like to thank you. She alerted Claudel and perhaps saved his life."

"Now what makes you think that she belongs to us?" Farley was amused.

"If not to you, then to either Swedish or Swiss Intelligence. I can make some inquiries there, but I thought you'd prefer not to have talk about Djibouti or the freighter *Spaarndam* become general gossip, if—" Renwick paused—"if you were interested in one of the *Spaarndam*'s passengers."

"Either Swedish or Swiss or us? How the hell did you pick on these three? Why not the French? Djibouti is their problem. And a big one, judging from the flack they've been sending."

"That's to be expected after what was discovered at the port last Monday—crates of arms and ammunition, some for Ethiopia, some for a secret cache in Djibouti itself. You know the map of that area. Djibouti is Ethiopia's one outlet to the sea. What could be more tempting than to possess that port? Especially if you have a political ally—Communist Yemen—just a few miles across the entrance to the Red Sea. That could really lock and bar the door to Suez, couldn't it?" As for his reasoning about the woman who had passed the warning to Claudel—that was best left unexplained. For her sake. She had said too much, just a small friendly remark: her people were sympathetic, might even join Interintell someday. The Swiss and Swedish were neutrals, didn't talk of possible affiliation with Interintell. As for other nations outside the West, those who were sympathetic were already co-operating. It had to be the CIA.

"What exactly in arms and ammunition? The French haven't been altogether forthcoming."

"Understandable. Illegal exports from America. Yes, illegal in every way. The French could be wondering how much that involves you."

That aroused Farley. "We're involved with nothing at Djibouti! Believe me, Bob."

"I believe you."

"What export firm?"

"You probably know it—if that *was* your agent contacting Claudel. She made an excellent job of it, I hear. Was she yours, Morry? Just don't want to foul up her mission."

Farley's eyes showed surprise. "I believe you mean it," he said slowly.

"I do. We have parallel interests in the problem of Mr. William Haversfield. Let's not have them tangle."

There was a slight stiffening in Farley's shoulders. "She's one of ours."

"Then Interintell thanks you. And in return I'll give you the name of the American firm that was smuggling illegal weapons through the port of Djibouti. Exports Consolidated."

Farley said softly. "So that explains it."

"Explains what?"

"You'll hear it on the evening news. Their offices in New York and Washington were raided yesterday by the FBI."

"Oh? Was Brimmer still there or had he taken off?"

"He was found dead. Heart attack."

"Where?"

"In the New York office."

"And his files?"

"Not mentioned on any news reports."

"Come on, Morry," Renwick said urgently, "did the FBI get his files?"

"As far as we've heard, the files were—innocuous."

"Then whoever killed him removed anything incriminating." And, in particular, anything that could involve Klingfeld & Sons.

"Killed him?" Farley pretended disbelief.

"When was he found? In the morning? Had his body been there all night?" That would give the supply-room clerk and his two friends enough time to search Brimmer's files.

"Now," asked Farley gently, "what makes you imagine he was eliminated?"

"He was no longer useful. In fact, he was a danger."

"To whom?"

"Now," said Renwick, equally gentle in tone, "what makes you imagine he wasn't a danger to someone?"

"To whom?"

So Farley didn't know as yet about the close connection between Brimmer and Klaus. "Is there anyone missing from Brimmer's office?"

"A private secretary, I heard. And some junior clerk. Both on vacation, possibly. The FBI isn't explaining. Your friend Joe Neill led the raid and—" Farley broke off. "Seen him recently?" he asked suddenly. "You're a wily character, Bob. Why didn't you come to me?"

"Brimmer's office is in the United States," Renwick reminded him. "And don't underestimate Neill—he moved as quickly as he could." In spite of red tape and regulations. "But didn't you have any information about Brimmer's illegal activities?"

"Rumors only." Farley was tight-lipped.

"No investigation of him when he went around claiming he was CIA?"

"Half the crooks are doing that nowadays," Farley said in a surge of anger. "Yes, there was an investigation started. We're now trying to find out where it got sidetracked. Well"—he rose—"time to move off."

He hadn't mentioned Klingfeld & Sons. Yet it was the CIA that had intercepted Klingfeld's message to its informer in The Hague requesting details about Claudel in Djibouti. A lucky accident, a chance interception? Not likely. More possible that all messages from Klingfeld's Paris office were being monitored. And the reason for CIA interest in Klingfeld & Sons? Something beyond any connection with Exports Consolidated. "Thank you, again," Renwick said. "Whose idea was it to warn Claudel in Djibouti? Yours?"

"Nothing at all. Glad it paid off. We're on the same side, aren't we? Can't go losing good men."

Renwick agreed with a warm handshake. "You know, Brimmer had partners abroad."

Farley's face became expressionless. "No doubt. Good-bye, Bob. And good luck with your terrorists."

The keep-off-the-grass sign was out: Farley had definitely a very special interest in Klingfeld. Renwick said, "One of them—Erik—but you know about him, of course."

That stopped Farley at the door. "I've heard several things. What should I know in particular?"

"He's on the *Spaarndam*. Courtesy of William Haversfield. Well hidden, too. Your girl on board could be in trouble."

There was a brief silence. "Now it's my turn to thank you," Farley said quietly, and left.

Chris Menlo heard the front door close behind Farley and took the cue to come downstairs and say good-bye to Renwick.

"Farley had to leave for a meeting," Renwick apologized.

Chris waved that aside. "He'll be around here any day. We don't stand on ceremony. Very decent fellow, actually, even if his friends edged me out. It was time, perhaps. Everything changes, as Bergson said. And when do I see you again, Robert? Or shouldn't I ask?"

"I really don't know," Renwick said frankly. "But I'll drop in whenever I can. And thank you, Chris, for—"

"Not at all, not at all. Always a pleasure. When you meet Gilman, give him my best. We *are* related, you know." The blue eyes had an amused twinkle. "Rather distantly. Not closely enough to be traced. Security, security. It's always with us— like the opposition, alas. Do you know a cure for blackspot, Robert?"

Accustomed as he was to Chris's conversational jumps,

Renwick was nonplused. Chris was delighted. "Roses, Robert, roses. I've tried everything, but the damned spots won't out."

You and Lady Macbeth, thought Renwick, and left the old boy pottering happily through a garden encyclopedia.

13

THE FIRST AVAILABLE FLIGHT TO PARIS WAS AT SIX-TWENTY-five. Renwick put in the waiting time as inconspicuously as possible: a fast-food eating place where no one he knew in Washington would choose to lunch, a visit to an out-of-the-way bank to cash traveler's checks, and enough time left to pick up his suitcase from a locker in a bus station.

By nine o'clock next morning he was in a quiet back room at a little hotel on the Rue Racine, unpacked and everything paid in advance, apparently settled for the next week. Must bring Nina here someday, he thought as he shaved and tried a telephone shower in the bathtub. The room was worth a visit— giant pink and purple peonies, reminding him of Bombay, climbing all over the wall behind a bright brass bedstead with green pillows. But even if the interior decoration raised an eyebrow, the place was neat and clean. There was sunlight, too, easing in through French windows from a small and peaceful courtyard, and the *café au lait* was excellent.

He stepped into the street just before eleven o'clock, glad to be back in tweed-jacket weather. Sunny but cool. He had always liked this section of the Left Bank, with its tight rows of ancient houses lining the narrow streets. At a steady pace, keeping his route complicated enough to discourage anyone trying to follow him, glancing at the small shops that edged the strips of sidewalk—ceramics, primitive masks, hand-fashioned silver ornaments, Greek sculpture, surrealist imaginings—he reached the Seine five minutes ahead of time. Claudel wasn't in sight.

Renwick slowed down, strolled a short distance along the *quai*, his attention seemingly held by one of the excursion boats now passing under the Pont Neuf. There, the river branched around the Ile de la Cité—an island well worth a long look: the delicate spires of La Sainte Chapelle opposing the massive towers of Notre Dame. Nina, he began thinking—and cut off the thought. The sooner you finish this goddamned job, he told himself, the quicker you'll be back to a normal life. The job? It had to be done. Period.

He retraced his steps and paused naturally enough at a bookstall, with its overload of volumes, old and second-hand, that would attract any bibliophile in search of treasure trove. Claudel was there, exactly on time, burrowing through a stack of dusty tomes, looking for a collector's item. Renwick chose to examine a pile of early maps, each of them to be slipped out and held up for a closer view. Claudel, still checking the bruised and battered books, drifted nearer.

Renwick studied a map of Paris in 1860. Voice low, he said, "Call Vroom at The Hague. Tell him I'm flying into Amsterdam today. I'll meet him at Schlee's Rare Books. Four o'clock."

"In the Bruna Building?"

Renwick nodded, apparently over a detail of the Louvre.

That, thought Claudel, will revive a lot of sad memories. It was in the Bruna Building that Jake Crefeld, Vroom's onetime boss, had been assassinated two years ago. Vroom had taken over Crefeld's job in intelligence at The Hague, and—as a matter of course—Crefeld's unobtusive office in Amsterdam. Claudel picked out a likely book, began turning its pages. "Like me to fly you in?"

"If you can pilot with one arm." Renwick rejected the map, riffled through a few others, selected one that showed the River Loire.

"I could do it using one foot. The arm's mending, anyway." Dammit, Bob noticed the bandage bulging my sleeve. But at least he wants me along. Two could be needed. "And when Vroom asks where you are now—you aren't in Paris?"

"Right."

"See you at Orly, one-thirty." Claudel moved away, bought the book—a history of Montmartre when it was a village, apple orchards and all, before girlie shows and tourists had taken over. Then he set off along the *quai* to cross over the bridge onto the Ile de la Cité. Not only were there churches on the island but café-bars and small restaurants. Plenty of phones from which to choose.

Renwick put aside the maps, examined a collection of old magazines, bought a decrepit copy of *transition*, 1932. Those were the days when e. e. cummings declared all capital letters unnécessary, Renwick remembered—and then was astonished by the bits and pieces of nonsensical information that his mind had stored away. Like black spots on rose leaves. Still, they afforded some light relief on this somber day: the visit to Amsterdam would be grim. But if there was any setting that could make Vroom recall the decency and honesty of Jake Crefeld, it was the Schlee office in the Bruna Building. If he was Interintell's traitor, surely his load of guilt must double, make him more vulnerable to questioning when he faced Renwick across Jake's old desk. God, thought Renwick in sudden dejection, let it not be Johan Vroom.

He made his way to the nearest Métro, took a train that would drop him in the direction of Orly, and passed the journey by reading *transition*. So this was the magazine my father enthused over years before I was born, he thought in amazement. Strange sides to the old boy, always something new to discover about him. But he was glad his father couldn't see this sad copy: half its pages torn, a coffee stain blotting out a poem's lack of capital letters, a crude *"Merde!"* scrawled over some impassioned prose on the purity of art. He propped it on a seat as he left the subway and took a taxi for the remainder of his journey.

Claudel was infatuated by airplanes. He had flown since he was eighteen. Renwick could relax, with the aid of a new hard-crusted roll filled with pink Normandy ham and his share of the bottle of Châteauneuf-du-Pape that Claudel had provided. His light plane, a twin-piston-engined craft, was kept well below ten thousand feet. "Flat as a pancake," he said of the country below them. "No need to climb."

Renwick had no objections. The neat squares of green and golden fields, the darker green of trees and forests, were stitched together by the wandering streams and rivers into a patchwork quilt. Even the man-made blobs of villages and towns looked pleasing from this height. "When do we arrive? Three o'clock?" We live with watches inside our heads, he thought, watches and maps, times and distances. Their cruising speed was being held to two hundred miles an hour; the distance between Paris and Amsterdam was two hundred and fifty-seven miles. "Want me to take over? I've done some flying, you know."

"My arm's okay." Not all that much okay; but no one, not even Bob, handles this little darling. "About forty minutes to go before we put down at Amsterdam's old airport."

"Then we talk. You can stop looking for your Djibouti friend, Pierre."

"How the devil did you know I was doing that?"

"You would. I found out who she is. She isn't working for the Swiss."

"No? She's Swiss-American. Mother lives in Brooklyn. Father in Basel."

"She's with the CIA."

"Jean Zinner? You're sure?"

"Maurice Farley admitted it. Reluctantly. In return, I tipped him off about Erik on board the *Spaarndam*."

"Thank God you did. She isn't there to keep an eye on Erik. We know that. But Erik doesn't." One small slip by Jean Zinner, and Erik would think he was her target. "She's in double danger."

"Farley is warning her, will probably get her to stay on board at Suez when Erik and Haversfield leave."

"Will they?"

"Wouldn't you if you were Erik? When does the *Spaarndam* reach Suez?"

"Should be there tonight."

"A cloak of darkness—that's all Erik needs." That was all Erik ever needed, not just for tonight's escape but for concealment in his world of conspiracy. Men like Erik, fit for treasons, stratagems, and spoils, cloaked their lives in darkness.

"Why is the CIA so interested in Haversfield? He's a small fish."

"Perhaps bigger than we think. What has Gilman found out?"

"Haversfield lives in Chelsea, London. Semi-retired. That lets him travel—he's fond of Paris, it seems. And he pays his taxes."

"Semi-retired from what?"

"A large stationery business."

"Office supplies? Such as typewriters? An agent for Klingfeld and Sons, typewriter exporters? Visits their Paris office?"

Claudel looked at him. "Now you're stretching a point, Bob."

"Except that the CIA is interested in Klingfeld and Sons."

"Did Farley tell you that?" Claudel was amazed.

"He wouldn't even let their name cross his tightly buttoned lips. I bet the CIA guys were onto Haversfield as a dedicated Communist in Berlin. So they wondered about his frequent visits to Paris, set up surveillance, and were led to Klingfeld's office. That's why they monitored the messages being sent from there."

"You could win that bet. What if the CIA had discovered Haversfield was more than a dedicated Communist—a KGB agent? That would interest it, all right." Claudel shook his head. "But does Erik know that he's being KGB-controlled? He had a fight with the Communists in Aden—so Moore said."

"He had a fight with two Cuban Communists. The KGB may have decided they handled him badly. So—its old rule: change of tactics. He's a valuable piece of property to those who plan trouble for the West."

"But will he go along with them?"

"If and when it suits him. It's suiting him right now."

"Alvin Moore said he'd never make it."

"Alvin Moore's political judgment was never very good. He didn't make it himself."

"What?"

"Throat slashed. In his Seychelles hideout."

Claudel was silent. Then he said, "Nearly forgot—Gilman sent you this." He reached into the pocket of his flying jacket, handed over Renwick's Biretta. "You brought your papers with you?"

Renwick nodded. There would be no difficulties at customs. "What about Moore's girl?"

"Lorna got away. She's probably in Switzerland right now."

"Has she heard, do you think?" *Throat slashed, my God. Klingfeld plays rough.*

"She isn't worrying about Al Moore, just about her money and Brimmer's little black book."

"Fasten up! We're going in," said Claudel, ditching his thoughts about Klingfeld & Sons.

It was almost four o'clock before they approached the Prinsengracht, a street of gabled houses as ancient as the canal that ran down its middle. The building where Bruna Imports conducted its trade in pepper and coffee had been restored like its neighbors and now looked prosperous but restrained. Its fourth floor, a glorified attic, was unused by Bruna except for storage of outdated records, and Crefeld, Vroom's predecessor, had secured the front room for his more private and confidential business with Intelligence friends and contacts.

Renwick entered first. Claudel followed two minutes later to join Renwick waiting for him inside the very small elevator that took them directly and slowly to the fourth floor. They stepped out into a short corridor and reached the heavy wooden door where a small sign read: J. SCHLEE / RARE BOOKS / BY APPOINTMENT ONLY.

Renwick knocked, and as they waited he pointed to the cutout centered in a wooden rosette that was part of the door's carved decoration. *So that's the peephole,* Claudel thought, *and we're now being checked. Johan Vroom was taking no chances.*

The door swung open and Vroom, dark-haired and tall, impeccably dressed, was welcoming them into a paneled room. It was new to Claudel. He studied it covertly: a large desk, comfortable chairs, good lighting, three telephones, a filing cabinet, two long and narrow windows whose panels of diamond-shaped panes had been opened wide. *Much the same as ever,* thought Renwick, and took a chair to face Vroom, now seated at the desk. Claudel remained standing, keeping near the windows as if he were more interested in watching the canal traffic below than in any conversation.

Vroom was as voluble as ever, his American accent adopted

at Georgetown University, where he had once been a student. He was slightly nervous, breaking into complete details about the search for Erik on the *Spaarndam* and its negative results. "We'll board the ship at Suez, of course."

Renwick nodded, said nothing.

Vroom hurried on. "I've sent two good men to make a thorough search of the *Spaarndam* there. I assure you, Bob, everything is being done."

"I'm sure it is."

"How was Djibouti?" Vroom asked Claudel, veering away from the *Spaarndam*.

"Hot. In every way." Claudel turned from the windows to look at Vroom. "When did you hear about Erik?"

"When we got Interintell's request to get in touch with the ship. Tuesday, I believe. It had already sailed." Vroom noticed the exchange of glances between Renwick and Claudel. "Something wrong?"

"Yes," said Renwick. "Are you sure you heard nothing about Claudel's visit before then?"

"Claudel's visit? Oh, is that what you were talking about? Yes, Gilman told me he was on his way to Djibouti—a highly sensitive matter, he said. So I didn't mention it to the rest of my department although my guess was Erik."

"Not even to your chief assistant?"

"To Van Dam? Of course not. There was no need for him to know."

Claudel asked grimly, "Did Gilman mention where I was staying?"

Vroom said impatiently, "He didn't have to tell me. I assumed it was at that Greek's hotel—l'Univers—the one where you stayed last year. You told me about it. We joked about the name when we had dinner together in Athens."

Did I talk about it? Claudel wondered. He couldn't remember much of that evening—he and Vroom had been celebrating a small triumph they had just shared. He fell silent, thoroughly embarrassed.

Vroom felt he had won a point. "What's this all about?" he demanded.

Renwick decided on brutal frankness. "There have been serious leaks of information in Interintell. We have an informant among us."

"And you come asking *me* questions?" Vroom was furious.

"Yes," said Renwick, "we are asking you questions, and we want some answers. Because last week a secret message was sent to The Hague from a firm in Paris. It requested details about Claudel's mission there, mentioned Erik by name. So, Johan, who else at The Hague knew about Claudel in Djibouti? Knew he was trying to discover Erik's trail? Who knew about Erik himself?"

Vroom's face became taut, his features sharpening. He said nothing.

"Who is in your confidence? Van Dam?"

Vroom's voice had thickened. "He would never betray us. Never! I trust him implicitly."

"Someone else in your department?"

"No." The word exploded like a bullet. Vroom's anger increased. "And I am not having an affair with a woman. Nor am I homosexual. I am not being blackmailed into betraying—" He stopped short, compressed his lips, suddenly avoided Renwick's eyes. "Nor," he continued bitterly, "do I have any surplus money. You can examine my bank accounts. No doubt you already have."

Claudel said, "Your wife seems to have some extra cash—"

"That was a legacy from an aunt in Virginia. Not much— just enough to pay Annabel's expenses—she likes to ski so she visits Chamonix for a long weekend just every now and again." Vroom was talking too much, his usual sign of nervousness. "I tried a visit there last winter, but I don't ski. Mountains upset me; I'm not accustomed to them. Annabel, of course, finds Holland too flat." There was a forced smile on Vroom's lips. "The girl from Virginia, you know—grew up with hills all around her."

Renwick's gray eyes were thoughtful. "You skate, don't you? Surely you could have done that when Annabel was out on the slopes."

"Skate in a rink? Nothing more boring. I'm a long-distance man."

On the frozen canals, of course. Renwick nodded. "But you let her go alone to Chamonix?" That didn't make so much sense: Vroom was devoted to his wife.

"Perfectly safe. She has friends there."

"What about the children—don't they go with her?"

"They're away at school." Vroom's voice was abrupt.

So Annabel was restless, too little to do, and went off to Mont Blanc when the mood seized her. "Well," Renwick said, "your wife won't be leaving you for weekends at Chamonix now."

Vroom looked at him.

"No skiing," Renwick said quietly. Unless, of course, she was so proficient that she could tackle Mont Blanc's peak.

"She likes the mountains. The air does her good."

"She's still going there, in summer?"

"Not *every* weekend," Vroom reminded him.

Now what have we here? Renwick wondered. "No doubt she likes to go shopping in Geneva—it isn't far from Chamonix." Forty miles, perhaps even less.

Vroom stared at Renwick. "You are speaking too much about my wife. Why? You didn't come here to discuss—"

"No," agreed Renwick. "But now I do think we had better discuss Annabel. You talk with her a lot, don't you? Don't get angry! We all talk with our wives. And they ask questions."

"I resent this, Renwick, and I'll ask you to—"

"Do you tell Annabel much? Or leave your special notebook of very private addresses on the night table beside your bed? Along with your keys, or anything valuable?"

"Look"—Vroom was on his feet—"leave Annabel out of this! If I'm under suspicion—"

"We are all under suspicion," Claudel broke in. "All of us. Except Bob here."

"Why except him? Does he think that he's above—"

"His name is on a death list." Claudel controlled his rising temper. "He is marked for assassination along with eight other men—a list that the Paris firm has drawn up. The same firm, Vroom, that gets its information from The Hague."

"There are a thousand people it could contact in Den Haag. All the embassies. Or gossipmongers—professional spies— plenty of them."

"But," said Renwick, "how many among that thousand have their own private two-way transmitters that can reach Paris? Or Geneva, for that matter? You have one in your house, don't you? For emergencies? For your own convenience? Right?" Vroom was a man who liked his comforts.

Vroom nodded. He was no longer angry, just deeply troubled.

"What's more," said Claudel, pressing the sudden advantage, "who in The Hague could possibly know about Bob's telephone number at Merriman's? Or his old address in London? Or the names of certain restaurants where he gave you dinner? Or the pub where you've met—the Red Lion? Yes, Vroom, they are all noted down on that death list."

"Oh, God—" Vroom groped for his chair, sat down. With an effort, he said, "What's the name of this Paris firm?"

Renwick said, "Klingfeld and Sons. Offices in Paris, Rome, and Geneva."

Vroom shook his head. "Don't know it."

"Once it dealt in office supplies: typewriters, desk computers, copying machines. Now it's an arms broker. Illegal arms. It keeps in the background. Tries to pretend it is still the same old reputable dealer in office equipment."

Vroom asked quickly, "KGB control?"

Claudel said under his breath, "Careful, Bob, careful," and turned back to the window.

"Possibly," said Renwick, watching Vroom. "Its headman has several names, no doubt. But he uses one for very convenient cover." He paused, still watching. "Klaus."

"Klaus?" Vroom brushed that aside. "A common name. I must have met three or four of them—"

"Recently? Within the last six months?"

Vroom stared down at the desk. "One," he said, "one was seven months ago. In Chamonix. The weekend when I was there. Just one of Annabel's friends."

Renwick said gently, "Johan, why did you go to Chamonix when you didn't intend to ski or skate? Something was troubling you. Annabel?"

"Yes." With difficulty, Vroom added, "There was a ski instructor. I went there to—" He couldn't finish.

"Throw him down one of Mont Blanc's glaciers?" Renwick suggested. "I'd have done that with pleasure."

Vroom recovered himself. "But he wasn't there. Had gone. I thought the—the affair was over. Annabel swore to me that it was. Bob, she loves me. She loves the children. Believe me."

But there were photographs, thought Renwick sadly, of

Annabel and her ski instructor teaching her new tricks in bed. Photographs, threats of exposure and scandal; then her acquiescence in supplying small pieces of information that seemed harmless enough. After that, bribery—just to make doubly sure of Annabel. Tactfully done, of course: expenses paid, pleasure weekends, and some extra spending money on the side. It was the old pattern, and Vroom hadn't even guessed what was happening. Or had he some vague suspicion, tried to ignore it? Silence it?

"Believe me," Vroom repeated. He took out his handkerchief and wiped his brow.

"I believe one thing. You've got to deal with her. At once!"

Vroom stared at Renwick. Then he panicked. "How?"

"Use your brains for a change. Feed her false information, try to trace her control—the man who pulls the strings and makes her jump." Brutal, Renwick knew, but his words acted like a bucket of ice water dumped over Vroom's perspiring forehead.

He blurted out, "Klaus. It could be Klaus."

"Second name?"

"Sounded like Sanuk or Sunek—I only heard it once. Annabel just calls him 'Klaus.' They are all first-name people—Klaus and Willi and Celeste and Pieter and Barney and Magda. Never met any of them separately. Klaus picks up the dinner checks, the bar bills. He drives a gray Ferrari; has a black one, too, for his friends. He's older than they are—almost fifty. But I didn't think he was important. I paid him little attention."

"What? Your wife stayed for weekends at his house and you didn't check?"

"I had other worries on my mind," said Vroom, and his lips tightened.

The ski instructor. "Where did all those first-name people stay?"

"With Klaus. But the weekend I went there"—the words were being dragged out—"Annabel and I stayed down in the town. There was no room at the chalet, and I thanked God for that."

"What chalet?"

"The Chalet Ruskin. It stands above—"

"Bob! Quick! Over here!" Claudel called out. "There are a couple of men in that building directly opposite. Fourth-floor attic. See?" He stepped to the side of the windows. Renwick kept out of view, too, and looked across the canal. Vroom joined them hurriedly. "They've been watching me for the last five minutes," Claudel said.

"Did you install a couple of men over there?" Renwick asked Vroom.

"No one."

Claudel's voice was tight with anger. "Who knew we were meeting you here? Your wife? Was she with you when I called at noon?"

"No. I—" Vroom turned on his heel, walked back to his desk. "I don't believe this. It can't be. It can't!" He crashed his fist down on the heavy mahogany top, sending a large glass ashtray splintering on the wooden floor. "All right, all right. I took Claudel's call at my office. I went home to see Annabel for lunch, explained I couldn't drive her to the airport this afternoon. A meeting, I said. Important. In Amsterdam. Four o'clock. Just couldn't drive her to the plane, she'd have to take a taxi or stay at home. She—she had her driving license suspended a month ago—a silly accident—not her fault really." He was picking up the fragments of ashtray, dropping them one by one into a wastebasket.

"You named us?" Renwick's eyes were watching the window across the canal. The two men—or was it just one man?—weren't visible now. But the window was still open wide.

"Not that way. No. Indirectly. Annabel asked if I couldn't postpone the meeting until later this evening. I said, 'Impossible—Renwick is already on his way, flying in from London.' And then, as I was about to leave after lunch, there was a phone call for Annabel. She took it in the library. I heard her say, 'Klaus?' Then she started explaining she might be late in arriving." Vroom straightened his back, threw the cigar stubs and some burned-out matches on top of the broken pieces of glass, looked with distaste at the white ashes left on the floor. "I didn't listen. It was talk about the weekend at Chamonix, I supposed. Well"—he looked at Renwick, who had turned to face him—"I was wrong. I'll resign from Interintell of course."

"What makes you think Klaus asks questions only about Interintell? Your own department in The Hague is of vital importance."

Vroom slumped, half seated on the edge of the desk.

Claudel was asking, "What's that? At the window. A telescope? Or some kind of rifle? You're the armaments expert, Bob."

Renwick swung around to look. Too heavy for a rifle. "Even heavier than a shotgun." And aimed right at these windows. He yelled to Vroom, "Get away from that desk! Move!" The three of them made a dive for the safest corner of the room, reached its shelter as a bullet exploded on the desk. A second followed. That was all.

"A shotgun never did that," said Claudel, looking toward the debris of a desk. The two chairs that once had faced each other were now tilted drunkenly on broken frames, the remains of their backs torn by shrapnel.

"Keep out of sight from the window," Renwick warned Vroom. "And do your telephoning downstairs. None of these on your desk could possibly work anyway. Come on, Pierre, we'll try to flush them out." They left at a run, using the staircase for speed, and descended through two floors of startled clerks and bookkeepers to reach the hall.

"Whatever that weapon was," Renwick said as they took shelter for a moment in the small crowd at the Bruna Building's front door, "it's too valuable to leave. They'll be dismantling it."

"We're dead anyway," Pierre said. "You and Vroom at the desk, me at the window. They won't expect us."

A voice said from the crowd, "What happened up there? Just look at that smoke. A fire?"

"Not smoke. Dust," Pierre said. "An explosion."

"Gas?"

Pierre's Dutch failed him. So he looked ignorant, and eased himself through the knot of people to join Renwick.

"We'll approach separately," Renwick said. "You take the bridge on our right, I'll use the one on our left. We'll meet inside the hall." Then, as he eyed the house across the canal— it looked abandoned, a candidate either for demolition or for complete restoration—he shook his head, restrained Pierre from leaving with a hand on his arm. A thin straggle of people had been walking along the opposite side of the canal, some carrying children, some carrying rolled-up bedding. Squatters. They were standing now at the door of the deserted house, a tall, long-haired young man urging them inside as if he were leading a charge over the barricades. "The police will soon be here," Renwick said with a sudden smile, "and our friends with the popgun won't like it one bit. Not one bit. Let's join the fun."

There was no need to separate. In the continual flux of movement and sound, they wouldn't be noticed. The squatters, about twenty of them, had already taken possession, the last of them entering the doorway. Except for the young man, who was addressing a group of worried citizens with flights of high rhetoric. Renwick and Claudel reached the center of the small crowd, kept watching the entrance to the house.

"Still inside?" Claudel murmured.

"Unless they left their weapon behind them—made a run for it as soon as they thought their mission was completed." But I doubt that: the gun is something they'll take to pieces, pack away, carry out. "Look for someone carrying a heavy suitcase."

"They'll never get it out through that little mob," Claudel predicted. "The staircase will be jammed."

"They can't wait in the attic, either. The police will search every floor." Interesting, thought Renwick. He shook the remaining dust from his jacket, smoothed back his hair. "We could both use a wash and a brushup," he said. "At least we don't look like a couple of cops," he added as two men, neatly dressed, were hustled out of the building in the grip of four squatters. A large suitcase was hurled after them.

The orator halted his impassioned plea, yelled, *"Agents provocateurs!"* He seized the suitcase, darted with it around the crowd just as a squad of police arrived, reached the canal railing, and heaved it over. It fell into the gray, still waters and sank.

"Too bad," said Renwick. "Okay, Pierre. The show's over."

They left, a fight and loud arguments starting up behind them. "You marked their faces?" Claudel asked.

"Got a firsthand view." But the two men might be out of circulation for some time. Policemen had seized them along with their four escorts, and they were trying to struggle free. A mistake. Resisting arrest. A bad mistake, Renwick thought as one of the men landed a punch. The orator, of course, had vanished completely.

Once out of the narrow street and away from Old Amsterdam's encircling canals, they could find a taxi to take them back to the airport. "We'll clean up there," Renwick suggested, "while you get the tank filled."

"We've enough fuel left to reach Paris."

"What about Geneva?"

"Tonight?"

"We'll get there for dinner. Four hundred miles away, isn't it?"

"Roughly. I'd better get the plane tanked up. Enough cash?"

"Yes. Passport and papers legitimate, too. You?"

"All in order. Transmitter and the travel kit that Bernie prepared. You know, Bob, our mad scientist at Merriman's might have heard of that gun. What the devil was it? Any guess?"

"I've none—needed a closer look." Exploding bullets? Some kind of high-caliber rifle? "It was damned accurate anyway. And the clinching argument as far as Vroom is concerned."

"Do you know Annabel?" The girl whose small pieces of harmless information led to murder and mayhem.

"By sight. She was at one of Jake Crefeld's parties three years ago." Black hair, roving brown eyes, long legs, and a noticeable figure. "She won't remember me—too many men around her." Men who were serious in face and in talk, men who didn't have much time for skiing and dancing. Poor old Vroom, thought Renwick.

Conversation became innocuous until they had left the taxi at the old airport in Amsterdam. Claudel was still thinking about Annabel. "She must use a private plane, too. Or else she'd have to take a flight from Schiphol Airport to Zurich— a long way round for a weekend at Chamonix. Does Klaus send his plane for her, I wonder?"

"No doubt. Part of her expense account."

"She's valuable property. Meanwhile. Until Vroom resigns from all intelligence work. Then she's useless. If he resigns, of course," added Claudel. "Will he?"

"End his career? But what kind of intelligence job would he get with Annabel still on his back?" Renwick shook his head. "He never deserved all this."

"It's the undeserving who often get clobbered. Yet I just

can't imagine him teaching her how to use his transmitter. In fact, she wouldn't have risked asking him."

"Klaus probably gave her a lesson or two. It's not too difficult to master."

"And there was easy access to Vroom's study. He's only there for occasional meals and bed." Claudel fell silent for almost a minute. "How will he handle her?"

Renwick just shook his head.

"His problem," Claudel agreed.

And what did a man do when faced with that? "God help him." Renwick said under his breath.

14

They left Claudel's plane drawn up in its alloted space at the airport outside Geneva. Claudel, before locking up, had activated its alarm system: anyone attempting to enter it would set off a blast of sound that would bring out the fire truck itself. He had left behind his flying jacket, after removing a lighter that could photograph, a pair of eyeglasses that could amplify conversation from fifty feet away, a cigarette pack that could communicate within a three-mile radius. He was now wearing his tweed jacket that could take his neat automatic without bulging a pocket. His good arm carried Bernie's light-weight bag. (Duplicates of lighter, glasses, cigarette pack; a hairbrush whose back slid open to hold useful cipher lists; a talcum-powder tin that held spare film; and ordinary toilet articles such as toothpaste and brushes and shaving kit, useful for emergency stopovers. Also, infrared binoculars that could be used by night, a similar mini-telescope, and—of course— a book on bird-watching.)

Renwick was carrying the radio in its leather case, cut out in front to show an honest face, a portable that would keep a traveler abreast of the news and relax him with music. But remove the leather case and open the back of the radio, and

169

there was a transmitter that could reach approximately a thousand miles—double the distance needed for communication with London. Its antenna, a thin wire minutely coiled and packed under the vinyl lining of the case, was easily strung around a room or dangled down the outside of a window.

If, thought Renwick as they reached the checkpoints for customs and passport control, by any son-of-a-bitching chance we are questioned here, I'll call Duval in Geneva or even Keppler in Bern. Keppler was one of Swiss Security's top men, a big wheel. Duval was an inspector of police. They knew him, had co-operated fully when he was tracking down a numbered bank account in Geneva four years ago—money reeking of conspiracy, theft, and murder—destined for international terrorists. He had been with NATO Intelligence, then, but Keppler and Duval knew about Interintell. Renwick believed in keeping allies informed, even those who were usually neutral except, of course, when Swiss serenity was threatened. And Klingfeld & Sons, with a flourishing office in Geneva, was definitely a real threat. Chamonix was across the frontier in French territory, but it was possible that Inspector Duval could provide some useful advice, if not unobtrusive assistance. After all, he must have contacts there: Geneva and Chamonix were neighbors, both French-speaking, both sharing the same problem—Klaus.

"Nothing to declare," Renwick said. Except a ton weight of worry. They passed through customs. Then passports were examined: two representatives of Merriman & Co., advisers on construction engineering. Business or pleasure? "Pleasure," said Claudel—no one ever asked what kind of pleasure. With a polite nod, they were waved on.

Renwick relaxed. Suddenly he decided: I'll phone them both, Keppler and Duval, tomorrow morning before we leave for Chamonix. But now, a room near the airport, and while Claudel rents a car, I'll make contact with London. A quick report on Vroom and Annabel, information on our destination, and what news from Basset Hill.

The Swiss are larks, up with the break of day. There was no difficulty in reaching Johann Keppler in his office in Bern by eight o'clock, Duval in Geneva at eight-thirty. Renwick gave only a strong hint of serious trouble connecting Geneva and Chamonix, together with an assurance that Keppler and Duval would be kept informed and a promise that the final action in Geneva would be theirs. This was, Renwick emphasized, a matter both for police and for Intelligence. Interintell could need help and would be much obliged.

Both men listened. Renwick was not someone to sound an alert based on flimsy suspicion. Duval even offered the name of a young police inspector in Chamonix whom he knew well—he would contact him right away. Renwick, he suggested, might use the code name Victor for use in any identification there.

"Victor," Claudel said as they left Geneva, and glanced with amusement at Renwick who was driving the Audi he had rented. He was in good fettle this morning: his arm now rested in a sling after being freshly dressed by a Swiss doctor. He had, of course, objected to all that, but Renwick had insisted, and Claudel must admit the result was bliss. So far, at least. "Victor . . ." Claudel joked. "Flattering."

"I doubt that. Duval's a sardonic type."

"Where's your own sense of humor this morning? Come on, Bob. Just look at these buses rolling toward Chamonix. Two of them loaded to the gunwales with Japanese. What draws them to Mont Blanc? The fellow at the garage said none of them miss visiting it—almost a kind of pilgrimage. The highest mountain in Europe, is that it?" But Renwick only nodded. He's worried about that report he got from London last night, Claudel thought. "Look, Bob, it doesn't mean a thing that the supply-room clerk—what's his name? Grable?—turned up at Cooper's old law firm in Washington and tried the same dodge on Rosen that he pulled on Danford in New York. He got nowhere once again."

"Unless someone in the Washington office heard Rosen telephoning Danford about that visit, or Danford's subsequent call to Gilman—" Renwick broke off, passed another busload of tourists, a truck, and two cars.

"A telephone tapped? Even so, you've got Nina well hidden."

But Renwick, eyes on the busy highway—the scenery so far was unremarkable—was worried. "Could there have been some link between Colin Grant and me that I forgot?"

"Not likely. Your memory is too damned tenacious. I know

what's bothering you. It's having Grable snoop around Washington. But Nina wouldn't telephone her father, would she? Or visit him?"

"No. Not at present."

"Then let's start worrying about some real trouble. Erik, for instance."

Yes, he's still with us, thought Renwick. The *Spaarndam* had reached Suez ten hours ahead of expectations. Before Vroom's two men had arrived to search the ship, Erik had slipped away. Three hours later the bogus Englishman, Haversfield, had stepped with his luggage onto a launch and headed for shore. But he, at least, had been seen at the airport in Cairo. The Egyptians had reported yesterday he had taken a night flight to Rome. "They won't be far apart," Renwick predicted. "Haversfield needs to keep an eye on Erik, and Erik needs cash to get back to Berlin." Cash and false papers and changes of clothing; and a safe house, too, where he can hide while his identity is changed. "Terrorists don't travel far without a lot of help."

"I bet he learned that lesson in Djibouti when he found he had only enough money left to hire him a dhow as far as the nearest fishing village. Anyway, Bob, we've got the details on Haversfield, and that's something."

It was a considerable something, Renwick had to admit. West German Intelligence had come up with Haversfield's identity along with a photograph taken eight years ago, before he had vanished from Berlin. Its likeness compared nicely with the one on his British passport. And as a bonus to all this, Gilman had discovered the firms with which Haversfield's stationery business dealt. At the head of the list for office equipment was the name Klingfeld & Sons.

Suddenly, the highway shook off the octopus clutch of gas stations, cafés, small factories, same-looking neat houses, and began to climb. Hills heightened into savage peaks. Fir trees mounted the lower slopes, edging the fields and pasture lands in the valley, where a rush of water poured through its broad flat stretch. Above the tree line were precipices and giant ravines and the long gray rivers of ice that crept down from frozen mountaintops.

Claudel pointed to the glaciers. "They are white in winter.

Snow covers all the debris they carry along with them—rocks, stones, trees—everything that gets in their way."

"Like Klaus." And what was his second name? Vroom, you left your brains behind when you came into these mountains and met Annabel's friends.

Claudel nodded. First, the killing of Georges Duhamel in Djibouti. Then Alvin Moore. Then Brimmer. Everyone who got in his way. "Who's next?" Claudel asked, trying to keep his voice light. "And where the devil do we find this Chalet Ruskin? Ruskin, Ruskin—that's a strange name for a French alpine village. Who was Ruskin? Anyone at all? Or is it a place far away?"

"He was an Englishman—a pundit on art, architecture, and moral values. Totally nineteenth century." Then Renwick smiled, his first real touch of amusement today. "Ever visited Oxford? There's a college built after his favorite style. My irreverent friends call it 'Ruskin Gothic': red brick, imitation of early Italian, the kind you see in medieval churches around Milan. But what red-brick Ruskin Gothic has got to do with a wooden chalet in Chamonix..." Renwick gave up.

And this is the man who worried all morning about a lapse of memory, Claudel thought. "Could Ruskin have ever been here?"

"It's possible. He traveled. A lot of well-heeled English writers did in those days—looking at monuments, looking at mountains." Renwick slowed the car, glanced at Mont Blanc hidden by mists. "Byron was here. Shelley, too. He wrote about that beautiful monster. Called all these mountains around it 'a desert, peopled by the storms alone.' Oh, Shelley—if you could see what we see now." Renwick looked at the row of huge buses, drawn up in neat arrangement before a sprawling inn. Its front garden, complete with long tables and benches, was ready to welcome the avalanche of tourists now pouring in for an eleven-thirty lunch. There was a car park, too, at the side of the inn. "A good idea?" he asked Claudel as he edged the Audi into a free space.

"As long as we don't pretend we're Japanese." But there was plenty of cover available in the Italian, British, German, Dutch, Swedish visitors, even in the few French looking lost in their own homeland.

"Wonder if we could find a room here?" Renwick said. The

inn was on the outskirts of Chamonix, but it was a place where they would never be noticed. "Scout around, Pierre. Just see if anything is available—one with good walls where no ears can overhear." And if we're in luck, he thought as he watched Claudel thread his way through the mixture of foreign faces and voices, I can make contact with London before we walk into Chamonix for lunch and a general look-around. Ruskin. Why name a chalet after him? If he had been here, where did he stay? That could be a good angle to follow, however wild it seemed.

His mind branched off into Shelley's poem about Mont Blanc. It was twenty years since Renwick had read it, memorized parts of it. Now, odd lines came back to him, and trying to recapture them was one way to ease the worries that kept nagging at him. *The wilderness*—he remembered, and paused. Yes, the lines began with wilderness. And then?

The wilderness has a mysterious tongue
which teaches awful doubt, or faith so mild
—that man may be
in such a faith with nature reconciled.
Thou hast a voice, great Mountain—not understood
by all, but which the wise, and great, and good
interpret, or made felt, or deeply feel.

He had lost some phrases there, a rhyme, too. But that was the gist of it. And it had worked. He was less tense, less troubled. He watched the garden, with its colored light bulbs strung among the trees, listened to a babble of languages mixed with the clanking of plates and cutlery. No one was hearing the great Mountain's voice. But, from this sheltered spot, no one could even see Mont Blanc.

"Where do we get a view of Mont Blanc?" he asked as Claudel returned. "From the hills opposite. Right?"

Claudel looked at him in astonishment. "Right. And what brought that on?"

"Shelley. He didn't sit under trees in a garden when he felt that poem. And if Ruskin was here—he wasn't the type to miss a view, either."

Claudel broke into a fit of laughter.

"What's so damned funny?"

Claudel recovered, produced three postcards. "Bought these while I was waiting at the concierge's desk. We have a room, too. Not much to look at, but it's on the back corner, top floor, and the walls seem adequate. I booked us for a long weekend— three nights—until Tuesday. Not many people stay here. Day tourists mostly. We're just ten minutes, walking, from the center of town. Okay?"

"Very much okay." Renwick glanced briefly at the first two postcards. One was of the Mer de Glace, the sea of ice on Mont Blanc, where the glaciers began; the other showed a statue of the local doctor who had been the first to climb the mountain in 1786. At the third postcard, he stopped. Surprise, followed by delight, spread over his face. It was a view from a high hillside, from a small, flat stretch of grass overlooking the crests of descending fir trees. Below them, the valley. Beyond it, Mont Blanc's white peak soaring into a very blue heaven. But it was on the stretch of grass that Renwick's eyes were fixed. At one side was a giant boulder, beneath which the caption read: *Ruskin's Chair.*

He turned over the card, found an elucidation printed in four languages: *The famous English nineteenth-century critic, John Ruskin, spent many happy hours here each day admiring the beauties of Mont Blanc. Come to lovely Chamonix! All winter and summer sports!*

"Well," said Renwick, "what about that?"

Claudel enjoyed a small moment of triumph. Then, "Come on, Bob. Let's have a look at the room. Its door has a strong lock. Also the wardrobe. We French like security, even on holiday. We can leave our baggage safely there when we step into town. Don't worry about our transmitter. Anyone who doesn't know how to open it is in for a nasty shock. Literally."

The room was as described: nothing much to look at inside; outside, a vegetable garden with trees behind it. "Couldn't be better," Renwick said, and began setting up communications with London.

There was a favorable report from the Washington scene. Nothing more on Rome, as yet. "Love to my girl. Tell her all is well," Renwick ended, and signed off.

"Lunch in the busy metropolis?" Claudel suggested.

"We'll aim for a central café, and then we'll wander as tourists do."

"Wonder if Ruskin's Chair will be any help. If he was a local celebrity a hundred years ago, his name could be popping up all over the place."

"Hope not." Renwick's depression of this morning had been routed. Even if Haversfield—and Erik—were arriving in Rome right now, Renwick's spirits were rising. No worrying news from Washington: Nina was safe.

Right in the heart of the little town, neat streets, neat shops and houses—no Tyrolean decorations here—they found a café with a rushing stream outside its door and a large statue of Dr. Paccard, the first to scale Mont Blanc, pointing triumphantly to its distant peak. He also blotted out any possible view of the mountain from the café's picture window.

No one seemed to mind. The people crowding the well-spaced tables were not day tourists; or local inhabitants. Weekend visitors and summer residents, young for the most part, some in jeans, some in tennis clothes, others in well-cut blazers or smart cardigans. "Strange," Renwick said, "how there's always one café in any tourist town where the well heeled and carefree gather. A kind of homing instinct. How's it done? By word of mouth or telepathy?"

"By the prices." Claudel was studying a scant menu. "They're enough to chase any busload away. I'll have an omelette, cheese, salad, and a carafe of white wine."

"The same." They were speaking in French, and with their tweed jackets, ties already removed, and collars unbuttoned, they were casual enough to fit into the scene. Renwick looked for a waitress, took the opportunity to glance around the room. He laid the menu aside, lit a cigarette, looked out the window at Dr. Paccard's coattails, and let Claudel do the ordering.

He has spotted someone, Claudel thought, and resisted looking around at the far corner of the room. From a table there, somewhere near the small bar, he could hear voices speaking in English. The words came in snatches. A mixed group: men with German or Slavonic accents, a woman's voice with a definite French intonation, another woman's voice. American? Slightly Southern in its soft drawl? "She's here," he said very softly.

Renwick nodded. Annabel Vroom, dressed for tennis, was holding court.

"Her protector?"

"Not here." Klaus—so Vroom had said—was around fifty. The men at Annabel's table were her age mostly, late twenties, early thirties. "Let's eat and clear out." And start our search. There must be several hundred chalets tucked into the hillsides around the town. At least we know the view from Ruskin's Chair, and that's a start. But we can't sit here in dead silence. "I'd have thought Chamonix would have been built closer to Mont Blanc," he tried.

Claudel caught on and started a long explanation. The town had once been farther along the valley, near the approach to the mountain. Then the glaciers disintegrated.

"How?"

"Never could understand that myself. But the valley below them—all the houses, all the farms—was completely destroyed."

"So the people took the hint. Rebuilt at a safe distance."

"Exactly. Now over near Zermatt, the danger is from avalanches." The talk went on about the hazards of mountains, about the men who climbed them, and lasted nicely through omelette and Roquefort cheese.

As they rose to leave, Claudel could risk a casual glance around the room. Four men and two women at the corner table. Dark hair, he noted, on the girl in tennis clothes—she was listening intently to a blond man similarly dressed, a possessive type, and athletic. Partners for the day or for the night? Had the ski instructor returned for the summer season? Claudel followed Renwick toward the door. And then Renwick surprised him, turning his head to speak as a man paused just inside the entrance.

"Who's the smaller figure on the Paccard monument—looking up admiringly at the doctor?"

"Ballat—" Claudel began and was interrupted by a surprised shout from the corner table: "Hey, Barney! When did you get in?"

Barney gave a wave of his hand and a cheerful greeting. "Hey there, yourself!" he called back and passed Renwick and Claudel, who was now explaining that Ballat was Paccard's porter, had trundled the heavy ropes all the way to the top of the peak, and some said he had climbed it ahead of the good doctor.

And then they were out, leaving a lot of handshaking and backslapping and general welcoming behind them, stepping into the heady mixture of warm sunshine and crisp air. They paused, as good mountaineering enthusiasts would, to read the inscription at the statue's base.

There was a delighted look on Renwick's face. "That was the guy I saw in New York handing out a tip to garage attendants before he drove away in a borrowed ambulance."

"That was on Tuesday—just after your visit to Exports Consolidated. Time enough for Barney to be called back to Chamonix. As a reinforcement?"

"Or to deliver any documents he filched from Brimmer's office. When the FBI visited it, nothing incriminating was found."

"Nothing to connect Klingfeld and Sons with Brimmer," Claudel said. "Clever boys. They move fast."

"Why d'you think we've been breaking our necks?" Renwick asked. "Yes, they move fast. We just have to be faster."

"Barney gave us a sharp look—not that he could see much of your face. Would he recognize you?"

"Don't think so. I kept well behind a blue Chevy." But it had been Barney, all right: same round cheeks and broad smile, same wave of the hand, same voice. A threatened abduction was one moment you didn't forget: smallest details were stamped into your mind. "Okay, Pierre, let's start our search."

They strolled through the crowded street, veering—once they were out of sight from the café—toward the hillside that rose on their right hand. Judging from the postcard, its viewpoint was somewhere up there. "Could be several roads up that hill," Claudel said. And chalets dotted around each of them. Couldn't ask directions, either: Klaus was bound to have a couple of informers planted here as a safeguard. No easy way to trace his chalet, yet it had to be found. It was the surest chance of seeing him. Without that, no surveillance would be possible. "It will be a long hot afternoon," he predicted gloomily.

"Can't imagine any of those chalet dwellers walking all the way down to a café and then climbing back uphill. We'll have a look at the parked cars. A black Ferrari is what we need."

"You don't expect Klaus's gray one?"

"Later. If Klaus were in Chamonix now, I don't think Barney would have time to relax with the gang." He must have a report to make—details of his successes in New York, plausible excuses for his failures. It was nice to be one of these, Renwick thought.

"It looked as if he had just arrived, found no one at home, dropped down to the old hangout for lunch. Quite a welcome he got."

From dupes and dopes, thought Renwick. "He's one of the three who murdered Brimmer. Possibly by a cyanide pistol. Heart failure as usual."

"A team of three? Is that a fact or a guess?"

"A little of both. I saw three of them working together: Barney, the man who drove the ambulance, and of course Grable. As the clerk in charge of supplies, he knew the floor plan of the office and could smuggle the others inside. He also could talk his way into Brimmer's office, get its door unlocked. It took more than one man to kill Brimmer and go through all of the files, yet leave them in good order as if nothing had been touched. Otherwise, Brimmer's death might have raised questions."

"Will the other two turn up in Chamonix?" Pierre speculated.

"I wish they would," Renwick said. Then Grable would be out of Washington, with no lead to Nina discovered. "I wish they would," Renwick repeated, and began searching for a black Ferrari.

15

T HEY FOUND THE FERRARI PARKED AMONG A GROUP OF seven cars at the foot of a quiet road leading off the busy main street. The road was unpaved, broad at its start, narrowing as it climbed. There had been a row of simple houses at its beginning, with a woman hanging out some family wash and another beating a rug even if this was the start of a Saturday afternoon. Farther uphill, only trees and bushes edged the road. There were no chalets in sight.

There had to be some, thought Claudel: too many cars at the bottom of this road; or had the Ferrari been left there simply because of good parking space? A discouraging notion. He stopped, eased his arm in its sling, and waited for Renwick, who was picking up a small wooden sign that had toppled on its face along with its support. Renwick held it out, and Claudel looked. The lettering was faded but it was still legible: RUSKIN'S CHAIR. And the arrow that followed the two words had once pointed uphill.

Renwick replaced the sign among grass and wild flowers, exactly as he had found it. Someone hadn't wanted this hillside too easily identified. Either that or poor old Ruskin was now a defunct celebrity. Certainly this route was little traveled nowadays by anyone on foot, but on the flatter stretches of the road, where the earth soaked by recent rains had turned into half-dried mud, there were traces of several cars.

"Must be a dozen houses up this way," Claudel said, examining the crisscross of tread marks. "I bet you one thing: Klaus won't have any nameplate displayed at his gate." He looked around at the bushes and trees. "Houses, where are you?"

"Playing hide-and-seek behind clumps of firs. We've only walked about half a mile. Can't expect Klaus to choose a chalet so near the town." Or could we? With a man like Klaus, you could never guess.

But as they turned the very next curve, they saw a chalet lying quite openly on the right-hand side of the road with only a few bushes clustered around it. "Too small," Renwick said, and became more interested in a knee-high sign-post on the left side of the road.

"Too small and too exposed." Claudel studied it. "And no signs of life. All windows shuttered. But it's in good repair. Possibly used for winters only. Skiers?"

"Look at this," Renwick said and waved a hand toward the sign. It contained no name, nothing except a definite arrow pointing uphill. In size, age, and weathering, it matched the previous signpost they had seen, but this one stood straight and firm. Six feet beyond it, a definite footpath branched off to the left, climbing through thick bushes into a heavy fringe of fir trees. Surely that was the original direction of the arrow. Renwick was thoughtful as he looked at the sign. Yes, the arrow now pointed directly uphill. But that view on the postcard wasn't seen from any roadside.

"I spot two more chalets—over there, to the right—a short distance above the first one. Lots of trees around them. But," Claudel decided with regret as he pulled out his mini-telescope and focused on their rooftops, "not big enough to sleep Klaus's guests."

"Let's try this path," Renwick said.

In a few minutes they emerged onto a small stretch of grass that lay at the edge of a wooded cliff dropping down to the valley. And there, occupying most of this space, was a giant boulder. The view from it was identical with the one on the postcard. Renwick leaned against Ruskin's Chair, looked across the valley at a mass of soaring precipices and ice-filled ravines. But swirls of soft gray mist had started to circle around Mont Blanc's peak, blotting out its thrust into a sky of white clouds. "Will we ever see that mountain?" Renwick asked softly. Then he turned his head to glance behind him, noted the continuing hill that was thick with giant trees. "Could it be . . ." he began. Improbable yet possible. Yes, possible . . .

Claudel said impatiently, "Come on, Bob. We didn't climb up here to look at a view. Let's get back to the road, start searching—"

"There's an easier way to find Klaus's chalet. Safer, too."

"How?"

"Just answer me two questions, Pierre. Why was that arrow pointed uphill? It was meant to mark the path. But it pointed straight up that road."

"Someone angled it, fixed it firmly in place."

"To alert any visitor—anyone who is a stranger to that road—who is driving up to Klaus's chalet."

"A direction post? Warning him to be ready for the next opening he sees?" Claudel's voice had quickened.

"Next opening on his left," Renwick said.

"Why on his left? The next driveway could be on his right."

"Could be—except for the second question. How was Vroom going to end the sentence you interrupted, when you called us over to the window in his office?"

Claudel concentrated. Two men at a fourth-floor window opposite the Bruna Building, myself watching, Renwick and Vroom talking. "I heard Vroom name Klaus and then the Chalet Ruskin. As I called to you, he was saying, 'It stands above—' Right?"

"That's what I heard." Nice to be confirmed, Renwick thought. "Stands above—what?"

"The town."

"I thought so, too, until we came up here." Renwick patted the boulder against which his shoulder still leaned.

"Stands above Ruskin's Chair?" Claudel's voice quickened. "Could be, could be. The first driveway on the left would lead to a house just up there—above where we are standing now." He looked at the rise of land behind Ruskin's favorite perch. "Nicely wooded. Good protection for a chalet."

"And good cover for us. Let's have a look."

The climb might be steep, but it would have been easy enough if they hadn't been wearing leather-soled shoes. Underfoot, a heavy layer of dried-out pine needles coated the soft earth. It will be hell coming down, Renwick thought as they stepped into the wood; we'll be glissading all the way. Trees could be avoided; they were spaced enough, but there were scattered outcrops of rock. Pierre's wounded arm? We'll damn well have to take care, Renwick told himself: no headlong rush to lower and perhaps safer ground.

Suddenly, the dead silence was broken by a car at full throttle. They halted, concentrated on tracking its progress. It was traveling uphill, drawing nearer. And then it must have swung into a driveway just above these trees. It stopped abruptly. Claudel pointed straight up the slope in front of them. Renwick nodded: there was definitely some chalet ahead of them. In spite of the pine needles, their pace increased. Five minutes more and they were reaching the last of the trees, and beyond them a fence. Not a wall, thought Renwick in surprise: just an eight-foot fence of thin iron railings, blocking nothing from sight.

They took cover behind the drooping branches of a larch and studied the house. Everything lay open, totally innocent. Three chalets joined together and modernized with wide picture windows, rising above a terrace fronted by a narrow garden; below that, a broad sweep of alpine grass and wild flowers reaching down to the fence. At the side of this converted group of chalets was a garage where the driveway ended. The four-doored garage was open and empty except for a small yellow car—could be a jeep, Renwick judged—while a black Ferrari stood outside, carelessly parked. At the other end of the house there was a tennis court; behind it, a screen of well-trimmed bushes. It must shelter a pool: sounds of splashing, of diving, of applause and merriment, and the excited barking of small dogs joining in the fun. Yes, thought Renwick again, everything open and totally innocent. Look at me, the house said, I've nothing to hide. He signed to Claudel. Carefully they backed away, made a safe retreat down through the wood.

Renwick went first, insisting that Claudel grasp his shoulder in case of a slip. "Sure, you're indestructible," Renwick told him once they were out of earshot from the house, "but just hang on to me, will you?" Claudel's annoyance was showing, partly due to his arm in that confounded sling—he'd get rid of the damned thing before tonight—but mostly because of his disappointment over the chalet. How do we get near enough to the place with all those picture windows? Bright lights in every room, no doubt, and a collection of yapping poodles who might not prowl around like Dobermans or German shepherds but who'd start barking at the slightest shadow. Renwick felt the same way: no more words were exchanged until they came out into the clearing. There they paused for some estimation of the scene.

"It's so goddamn innocent," said Renwick. "Something is strange about that whole setup. We'll get a closer look tonight."

"Not too close, I hope."

"Just enough to let us see Klaus. He wouldn't have invited these guests if he didn't mean to be there."

"What about an alarm system? I could see nothing."

"None around the fence as far as I could make out."

"Just barbed wire laced neatly along the top. How do we get over that?" We're traveling light, thought Claudel, we haven't got the equipment for any assault.

"A small mattress." Renwick had walked over to the edge of the clearing. Its drop was steep but not impossible. But by night? And with Pierre's arm out of real commission? "The local kids probably climb it every Sunday afternoon."

"We're not local. We're not young mountain goats, either. And Sunday afternoon is not full of black shadows. Tonight, we'll have to use the road again." And damn this arm.

"Let's get back to it now. We'll have to do some shopping in town." Rubber-soled sneakers, for one thing; dark sweaters and jeans, for another. Night work would leave tweed jackets and flannels looking fit only for scarecrows.

They had almost reached the road. They stopped abruptly as they heard the sound of cars coming uphill. "Two?" Renwick asked.

"Two," Claudel agreed. "Both high-powered."

Quickly, they chose the largest bush with a view of the road, stretched out under its cover.

"Look at that, will you?" Renwick said softly, his eyes on the small chalet opposite. Its shutters were still firmly closed but its door had opened. A woman stood waiting just inside the threshold and half emerged as the first car reached the path that led to the house. It drew up expertly—a silver-gray Ferrari. Its driver stepped out, looking around him, checking the road, and then signaled to the Mercedes that had stopped behind him. Tall, fair hair neatly cut, tanned face, strong features, decided movements. Klaus? Could be, thought Renwick. But we are not close enough to make sure of his age. From here he looks younger than fifty.

Renwick's attention swung away to the second car. Its door was open, but there was a delay. Why? Then he understood. Someone was being lifted out of the Mercedes by the driver and another man, someone wrapped in a concealing blanket. No movement at all. The still shape was being carried quickly up the path and into the chalet. One minute passed; almost another. Too distant a shot for his lighter's little camera, Renwick judged, and concentrated on photographing the face and build of the Ferrari's driver in his memory. Beside him, Claudel was doing the same thing, his brown eyes gleaming with excitement. He had his heavy-rimmed eyeglasses out, ready to slip in place as soon as the men reappeared and possibly started to talk.

But only one man came out, hurrying down the path to stop at the Ferrari. He reported briefly, was given in turn several instructions. Then the man—definitely young, strong-shouldered, quick in his movements—hastened to the Mercedes while the other slipped back behind the wheel of the Ferrari. The Mercedes made a precarious but competent reverse on the narrow road, drove downhill, almost grazing the bank on which Renwick and Claudel lay. The Ferrari's engine had started as the other car completed its bold turn and was about to continue its ascent. And at that moment a woman came racing wildly down the road. "Klaus! Klaus!"

The Ferrari braked. The driver stepped out, caught her wrist. "What's wrong?"

"I had to see you alone. Oh, Klaus, he knows! He telephoned! He said—" But whatever had been said on the telephone was silenced as Klaus shoved her into the car, took his seat, began driving. The Ferrari roared uphill, turned left within seconds, and soon came to a stop.

Claudel rolled onto his back, pushed aside some leaves from his face as he removed his glasses. "I got both car numbers. But couldn't hear one mumbling word of those instructions.

Too far away." He pocketed the glasses carefully. "Didn't need anything to hear Annabel, did we? My God, she was terrified— hysterical. Wonder what Vroom did say on the phone." He sat up, drew a long breath. "What's next?"

"For us or for Annabel?"

To avoid being noticed by someone in the chalet opposite them, Renwick and Claudel had two choices. They could wait until darkness fell—possibly three or more hours—before they stepped onto the road. Or they could cut over the rough ground on the bank where they lay, reach the road a short distance downhill. "We've seen enough now," Renwick said softly, watching the chalet, which looked completely deserted once more. "Tonight we can risk a closer look." For that was where the real action was. The big house was a front, a cover, where Klaus played the country gentleman to a pack of informers and sycophants. But that woman at the chalet's door had looked more than a caretaker: as tall and strong as the man who had stayed with her.

With some difficulty, they made the scramble through the bushes, taking extreme care not to start any branches shaking. Soon they reached the curve that hid the chalet and could step down from the bank onto the road. They set out briskly.

Renwick was thinking about plain board shutters, no louvers, everything inside lit by electricity. Ventilation? Possibly at night when the back windows could be safely opened. "No dogs at least." No car visible, no bicycle, either; nothing to give the show away.

"Thank God," said Claudel. "Either they attack or they yap. Bloody nuisance. What shall we find in there? Two people on their feet, someone bundled in a blanket. But perhaps that third person is on his feet, too, now that he has been smuggled safely inside. What d'you think?"

"It's worth finding out." Renwick looked at his watch, slackened their quick stride to a more normal stroll. It was just after four o'clock. Ahead of them the road began to broaden. A little distance farther downhill, there was a cluster of parked cars, and then the busy main street.

"Well," Claudel said, "we can at last put a face to the name Klaus."

"We still need his second name. And not garbled this time."

"What about a visit to the local cop—get his help with that?"

"Later. We've plenty of suspicions, but Inspector Marchand will need more than them." So would Duval, his friend and mine, back in Geneva. So would Keppler in Bern. "Might be an idea to call Duval at once, get him to run a check on the gray Ferrari. You got its number—Geneva, wasn't it?"

"Yes. But the Mercedes had a Zurich plate."

Renwick raised an eyebrow.

"That doesn't mean it drove from Zurich today," Claudel reminded him.

"No. But it had collected more dust than the Ferrari." There had been mud spatters, too, above the wheels.

"Hate to spoil a good assumption. A black car does show more dust than a gray one."

Renwick's attention switched to the group of parked cars which they were now approaching. Against a white Renault, a man was leaning, watching them. He was of medium height, well proportioned, a neat figure in a tweed jacket, corduroy trousers, and turtleneck sweater. A cigarette was held in one hand while the other smoothed back a thick crop of black hair as he stepped away from his car and intercepted them. Dark eyes, quick and observant, studied them. Then he nodded.

"I'm Marchand," he said. "I've been expecting you since our friend Inspector Duval called from Geneva this morning. His description of you," he told Renwick, "was accurate. I don't think we need to use the word 'Victor,' Colonel Renwick." He bowed slightly. "Major Claudel."

"We don't use rank, either," Renwick said, keeping his voice friendly, repressing both surprise and annoyance.

"Nor I," agreed Marchand. "I hope I'm not not interrupting your plans." He paused, his eyes watchful.

You know damn well you are, Renwick thought.

"But," Marchand went on, "I am curious why you're here. We have no terrorists in Chamonix."

Claudel said, "Let's walk while we talk. I feel naked just standing around. Perhaps a drink somewhere? After all, you're out of uniform." But always on duty, he thought.

"Saturday," Marchand said as if that explanation was enough, and opened the Renault's doors. "It is quite comfortable," he told them, noticing a slight hesitation. "No abduction, I assure you," he added. "I'll drive you to the inn where you are staying and save you a little walk. You've had enough exercise for one afternoon."

Smooth, thought Renwick, smooth; and he probably is a cop. With a telescope trying to follow us ever since we started up this damned road? "Thank you, but we've some shopping to do in town. Didn't bring a change of clothes with us."

"I think you'll find what you need at a place I know."

Claudel climbed into the back seat; Renwick sat beside Marchand. That way—if Marchand weren't Duval's friend, if he did try to drive them to some remote house—they'd be able to control him more easily. Marchand just nodded at this small maneuver, as if he himself would have done the same thing. The shop he had chosen for them was excellent: a small establishment that sold ski clothes in winter, climbing and hiking outfits in summer; and the sign over its door was ETIENNE MARCHAND. "My uncle," Marchand said as he noted Renwick's eyes on the name.

He waited in the car tactfully while they selected two warm outfits, both dark blue in color, and made sure that there were deep pockets. Navy-blue sneakers came next. "Glad we don't have to carry out a rolled-up mattress, even cot-size," Claudel murmured, remembering the project of climbing over an eight-foot fence laced with barbed wire. No need for that now. They had seen Klaus, could identify him. The chalet with the shuttered windows took priority. Always the way, he thought: you plan one thing, and then something else pops up. Like Inspector Marchand.

Renwick added a couple of lightweight turtleneck sweaters to their purchases, one navy and one black.

"Will the expense account stretch enough?" Claudel asked slyly.

"Barely—after your extravagance today. Three postcards when we needed only one."

"Couldn't draw attention to—" Claudel began, and then realized Renwick was joshing. That's a good sign, he thought. "Decided to trust our friend in the car?"

Renwick nodded. "What else?" As a friend Marchand would be helpful. As an opponent, difficult. The man was no fool; no small-town lackadaisical cop taking everything with a genial shrug, well that's the way life is today, what can you do about it?

Marchand had the doors open for them, ready to drive away. He didn't ask any questions about the packages, but he didn't need to. He can easily find out what we bought, Renwick thought in amusement, when he picks up a phone and talks with his uncle.

The distance to the inn was short. Marchand had only time enough to say that he had heard about Interintell, in fact had discussed it with Inspector Duval. They had worked with Interpol, of course—a matter of dealing with criminals smuggling stolen diamonds out of Geneva into Chamonix.

"Why Chamonix?" Renwick asked. But at that moment they arrived at the inn. The garden was empty—too early yet for dinner to be served—just three thin waiters wandering around like stray ghosts as they laid out the place settings. Renwick saw one table near the trees, a sheltered spot, still bare of forks and knives and paper napkins tucked into thick tumblers. "Have you time for a drink?"

"Why not?" Marchand stepped quickly out of the car.

"What brings diamond thieves to Chamonix?" Renwick asked when three beers had been placed before them.

"A choice of exits." Marchand hesitated, said, "Perhaps we should speak in English, no? I was a student in London —and later in America." He broke into English. "Our talk would go quicker. Right?"

Renwick, who had thought he was coping pretty well with Marchand's French, only nodded. But he wondered if the use of English was to encourage him to talk more. "A choice of exits from Chamonix?" he prompted.

"To the west you can reach Lyons, and south from there Marseilles. Or, if you go north from Lyons, quick access to Paris. If you prefer Italy, then the Mont Blanc Tunnel takes you east and you arrive in Milan. From there, Genoa or Rome. The roads are excellent and more difficult to watch than airports or railway stations. So many car changes are possible—wayside garages that can't be observed all the time." Marchand's English was precise. Claudel was impressed. A good student, he thought, and glanced at Renwick. But Renwick's mind wasn't on accents or vocabulary at this moment.

A choice of exits meant a choice of entries, too. Take Rome, for instance, as the starting point for a journey to this part of France. By air, Rome to Milan was a three-hundred-mile flight. Then by car from Milan to the Mont Blanc Tunnel? Not as difficult as it sounded—trucks used that route all the time. The tunnel itself, right through the giant massif of Mont Blanc, was about seven miles long. A total, perhaps, from Milan to Chamonix of just over two hundred miles—not much more. And almost a third of that distance was on the plains of Lombardy where the giant highway from Milan would let a car stay within the speed limit at eighty miles an hour. In fact, thought Renwick, I've traveled that *autostrada* at ninety miles an hour. "Interesting," he said.

Claudel was watching Renwick. Now what is he calculating this time? he wondered.

More waiters were arriving. Marchand waved away two who hovered near the table. "Later," he told them, "later." He turned again to Renwick. "Tell me one thing—why are you interested in Ruskin's Chair? Or, rather, why did you explore the woods behind it?"

"Your telescope couldn't follow us in there?" Renwick asked blandly.

"Unfortunately, no. Is there something I should learn about the Chalet Ruskin?"

"There is. But, first, tell us about its owner. What do you know of him? Klaus—what's his name?" Renwick looked vaguely at Claudel, whose memory also seemed to have lapsed.

"Sudak," said Marchand.

"Sudak?" Claudel repeated. "Where does he come from?" It sounded Czech, Polish, even Hungarian.

"Originally from Paris." Marchand hesitated. Then he said, "A professor I know at Grenoble University—a specialist in Russian history—tells me there is a small village called Sudak on the Black Sea. Not far from Yalta."

"Was he born there?" Renwick asked.

"I've never heard even a whisper of Russia. He is a French citizen, resident in Switzerland and completely neutral. Also, a most successful businessman. Now tell me why you are interested in his chalet. Or are you interested in Monsieur Sudak?"

"Yes," Renwick said frankly. "Interested in him and in the

firm he now controls—Klingfeld and Sons. Head office in Geneva, I think."

"That's well known."

"Branch offices in Paris and Rome."

"Oh? Klingfeld and Sons are an old established business, of course. No doubt their market is widespread."

"Very widespread. Recently, Klaus Sudak has merged Klingfeld with an American firm, but secretly. He controls it, too."

"Oh?" Marchand asked again but added no comment this time.

"That firm, Exports Consolidated, is now under investigation by the FBI. Also, I suspect, by several other federal agencies. Its business has been the illegal export of armaments. Recently, since its amalgamation with Klingfeld and Sons, it has been supplying weapons—and instructors—for international terrorists in certain Communist training camps."

Marchand's dark eyes stared at Renwick, then at Claudel.

"Yes," Claudel said, "we have every reason to be interested in Klaus Sudak. And in his Chalet Ruskin. And in—" He hesitated, glanced at Renwick. Are we spilling too much? he seemed to be asking.

"And," Renwick finished the sentence for Claudel, "in the little chalet opposite the path to Ruskin's Chair. It's apparently closed."

"It is. It was bought recently by an Englishman, but he isn't taking up residence until the winter season starts."

"Klaus Sudak is occupying it."

"Sudak?"

"We saw his Ferrari arrive there, along with a black Mercedes. There was a woman, a caretaker perhaps, who opened the chalet door for two men from the Mercedes. They carried a bundle of some kind. Klaus Sudak waited until one of the men returned. They spoke. The Mercedes headed downhill. Sudak then drove to his house. The small chalet is still shuttered, looks completely closed and empty."

"But what—how—"

"We don't know as yet. But we'll keep you informed. If arrests are necessary, we'll need your men."

"You may need them before any arrests are made."

Meaning what? Renwick wondered. Marchand offering to

help in our search, or Marchand giving a polite warning that we don't break the law? Suddenly the little colored bulbs above their heads were turned on although daylight was as yet strong. "We can take a hint," Renwick said, playing on words, and rose.

They walked back to the Renault to pick up their packages. Renwick said, "I needn't add that all this is definitely in strictest confidence. We aren't the only intelligence agency that has become interested in Klingfeld and Sons."

"Strictest confidence," Marchand agreed. "But I should inform Duval."

"Agreed. But inform him quietly. Very quietly."

"We do exchange top-secret information." Marchand's serious face relaxed into a small smile. "About jewel thieves. Not about terrorists." The smile faded. He stared again at Renwick, then at Claudel. "Can all this be possible? A reputable businessman like Sudak?"

"Not only possible but true. Tell me one thing. Why did he use the name Ruskin for his chalet?"

The question was so unexpected that Marchand actually showed astonishment. "It's always been used—ever since the first chalet was built there, one hundred and thirty years ago. It burned down, was replaced. That one also burned. Then three adjoining chalets were grouped on that site. The name has always remained the same. In fact, when Sudak bought the chalets three years ago and had them converted for his use, the people here would have been scandalized if he had not kept the Chalet Ruskin name. It's part of the history of that hillside. Sudak understood that."

"He was told? Politely, of course."

"Yes. And he listened. He wishes to please, shall we say?"

Which made it all the more difficult for a young police inspector to deal with this situation, Renwick thought as he shook hands and thanked Marchand for his patience. Claudel put it more bluntly but in his admirable French accent it sounded almost diplomatic. "We'll be glad of any assistance you can render us, direct or indirect."

Marchand nodded, looked at the packages they carried, and reached into the glove compartment of his car. He produced a hand-size transmitter. "This will find me wherever I am. Within five miles, of course. It's set on the wavelength I use."

"We'll keep it there," Renwick assured him.

"Remember, any difficulty at all, any problem . . ." Marchand shrugged, got into his car.

"We'll remember."

Claudel had taken out his notebook and pencil, was scribbling rapidly. He tore the page loose, gave it to Marchand. "Number of black Mercedes. Zurich registration." Marchand raised an eyebrow, but he slipped the page into his pocket. The car left.

Early diners, footsore and cold, were trickling into the garden. On the road outside, a line of excursion buses moved into place, reminding those on a package deal they would be leaving within the hour. There was a blare of rock-and-roll from hidden louspeakers, a dazzle of little lights strung among the trees.

"Wild night life," Claudel said as they approached the inn. "We'll bribe a waiter to bring us hot food in the dining room. Chilly out there." And it would be colder on the hillside. "Wonder if we'll be alone tonight," he speculated once they had reached the privacy of their room. Everything, he noted, was in place; nothing disturbed.

"Marchand won't be far off." Renwick was busy setting up communication with London.

"We surprised him. He didn't expect to be told so much. Too much?" That worried Claudel.

"We need his help, and he needed to know. Don't believe in treating an ally as if he were the enemy."

"You're trusting him a lot, Bob."

"He's trusting us." Renwick pointed to Marchand's neat little transmitter, all set and ready to go, now lying on top of the bureau.

"He must have known we had a couple of our own," Claudel speculated, then added, "But not on his wavelength." He left to take a shower in the bathroom at the end of the hall. Renwick was already in contact with London.

"Good report?" Claudel asked when he at last came back into the room. "No shower. I soaked in the tub instead, with one arm held high." He had removed its sling.

Renwick finished packing the transceiver into its leather case. "Mixed."

Something's wrong, Claudel worried. "You had plenty to tell them."

"That, yes."

"Any news of Erik?"

"Reported seen in Rome, in Naples, in Milan. Take your pick."

"And William Haversfield?"

"In Rome. Under surveillance for two hours. He dodged it."

Expert, thought Claudel: we're dealing with a real professional here. "Then Erik was in Rome, too. Disguised as a priest. Or perhaps a nun?"

Even that didn't raise any response from Renwick.

"How's Washington?" Claudel's voice was as casual as possible.

"Grable is hanging around."

The supply-room clerk . . . "Where?"

"The FBI spotted him. Lost him. In Georgetown—near O'Connell's house."

"Nina's father isn't there, is he?"

"No. In Maryland. Grable probably tried that, too."

"When was he seen in Georgetown?"

"This morning." Then Renwick roused himself. "I'll have that tub. Won't take long."

So the search for Nina was on. Claudel swore softly as he opened the parcels and began examining the clothes for tonight's job of work.

16

At half past eight they were ready to leave. They made a rear exit through the inn's vegetable garden to reach the car park. It was deep in shadow. The buses had left, but over at the tables there were still a few determined romantics, local people with the sense to be well bundled up against the night air, drinking red wine by the light of colored bulbs, listening to a selection from Gounod. Overhead, the crescent moon was swimming through a sea of white clouds. Lucky for us, thought Renwick as he took the driver's seat: five days later and we'd have run into a full moon.

He eased the Audi into the road, took the direct route to town. Beside him, Claudel was in high spirits, his sling abandoned, his left arm free and less noticeable. Like old times, he was thinking, the two of us setting out, not knowing what we'll meet. Initial plans had been discussed, of course, over dinner in a dark and empty dining room with one small lamp to let them see what they were eating. As Renwick had said, "All we can do is to plan our first moves, but once we're up at the chalet, we'll play it by ear. There's always something you don't expect." The Audi would be left at the foot of Ruskin's road—what else did you call it when it wasn't even named on the town map that Claudel had picked up at the concierge's desk? From there they would use the road itself—probably unlighted—and be ready to dive for rough ground if they heard any car approaching. The silence of the hills would give them ample warning.

"Almost there," said Renwick as they came through the town, two figures in dark clothes that weren't noticeable. (On foot, Renwick had said, they'd make a weird sight: two joggers in the main street at this hour? Pockets filled with equipment, too?) A left turn and they were into the small parking space at the foot of the road. "What the hell's going on?" He had expected to find a couple of cars at this time in the evening. There were seven, and three of them almost blocked the Audi's way. Renwick edged through them, stopped just ahead of the leading car in the group. It was, of course, a small white Renault. He turned off the lights, switched off the engine. Marchand hadn't come out of his car to greet them, hadn't even looked at them as they had passed.

"Cool," said Renwick. "We'll play it cool, too." Without one backward glance, they started uphill past the row of houses with faint lights and sounds of television coming from their windows.

"Did you notice the two men standing at the car behind Marchand?" Claudel asked. "And the two inside the car behind them? No uniforms." The men, who had let themselves be clearly seen, had worn checked shirts, sweaters, britches, heavy stockings, and boots.

"One of them sold us our tennis shoes today. Marchand has drafted his cousins." And he is hedging his bets: tonight may not be police business, but in case of action—then Marchand will be there. "They look as if they know their way around a rough hillside."

"He didn't give a damn if we noticed him or his troops."

"I like his style. He's reminding us to remember."

"But will you?"

"I'll try hard."

By the time they cut away from the road and traveled over a field of grass, small boulders, and bushes to reach the blacked-out chalet, their eyes were accustomed to the broken darkness. The moon in its first quarter was muted by passing clouds: now and again, a bright beam; then, just as suddenly, deep shadow.

They moved carefully, taking cover behind a bush or beside a boulder whenever the half-moon's spotlight was turned on.

The structure of the chalet was simple. The first floor was raised slightly above ground level by squat supports; therefore, no cellar. No terrace; no garden, either. Just a pair of windows on either side of a front door reached by three steps. On the upper floor there was a balcony with three long windows under the overhanging roof. Two chimneys, but not even a trickle of smoke. The house was exactly as they had seen it that afternoon: shuttered tight. A desolate place.

They separated. Remembering the lie of the land, they would circle around the chalet and meet at the first line of trees some fifty feet on the slope behind it. Sparse trees, thin and small, but with enough cover to let them study the back of the house. Claudel, a few minutes late in reaching Renwick, was much entertained by something.

"Side windows?" Renwick asked softly.

"Two above, two below; all boarded up. No balcony."

"Same as my side." Nothing original about this place. Its rear view had three windows above, two below with a narrow door between them.

"Just over there"—Claudel repressed a laugh, pointed back to a group of bushes—"I nearly stumbled into their garbage dump."

Of course, thought Renwick, the people in the chalet might do without heat even on a cool night, but they needed food, and food meant garbage. "Small or large?"

"Only three bags, all neatly tied. They'll dig it in when they're good and ready. Not this evening, I hope."

Perhaps when the next delivery of food arrived—a night-time job, obviously. "I hope not," Renwick agreed fervently, his eyes studying the house once more. No balcony here, either, where it could have been useful, for this side of the chalet was in deep shade. "They must be suffocating in there," he added as he scanned the five shuttered windows, heavy black rectangles set into dimly white stucco walls. Then, "These bottom windows—something different . . ." And he unzipped a pocket to pull out his mini-telescope, and pressed its infrared release button. Claudel drew out his small binoculars and got them functioning for night work.

The two windows changed from dense black to the color of

bleached blood. Every line on the board shutters was shown as a dark seam. And at the center there was a very broad seam—an opening, a definite opening. But it revealed nothing beyond, only a blank smooth surface, the same ghastly color in infrared as the shutters themselves.

Renwick and Claudel exchanged a glance, pocketed their pint-sized instruments. Quickly, they crossed over the rough ground—grass with some outcrops of rock—and reached the dark shadows of the chalet. Claudel took one window, Renwick the other.

And there his question about ventilation was answered. A black blind, opaque, covered the glass panes, but from the outside. Concealed behind it, the window could be opened wide. As it was now. There were voices.

He signaled to Claudel, who came hurrying to join him. Renwick held up two fingers, raised an eyebrow. Claudel nodded: two people were talking, a man and a woman. Not clearly heard, only an occasional word recognizable, as if the speakers were at the far side of the room. Renwick and Claudel drew out their heavily rimmed glasses, put them on, pressing the frames close above their ears. The words became as clear as if the man and woman had been standing beside them.

Words spoken in some small argument, complaining, bickering, using German—probably as a common language: the woman's accent showed traces of French, the man's was heavily Slavonic. She was saying, "Stop searching! And sit down. There's no more beer. You've drunk it all."

"What there was of it." Footsteps wandered over a wooden floor. "They send you plenty of food and nothing to drink."

"Nothing? You drank six—"

"Six bottles of nothing. Where d'you keep the cigarettes? They sent cigarettes, didn't they?"

"No. You had two packs."

"They're finished. Empty."

"Oh, sit down!"

"Can't even phone." The footsteps stopped. "Why shouldn't I try to—"

The woman's voice rose. "No phoning! Orders."

"Stupid orders."

"You're stupid. The calls go through the town exchange. Do you want someone down there asking who is up here?"

"The two-way radio doesn't go through the exchange. I'll call, tell them we need some real booze and cigarettes—it's a long night ahead."

"No! Only to be used in an emergency. Only then!"

A chair scraped on the floor. "Think I'll have a breath of fresh air."

"The car could arrive—"

"He won't arrive until midnight. Or later. It's a long haul."

"What about her? Don't leave me—"

"She'll give you no trouble. She's out cold."

"Do we keep her quiet until he leaves tomorrow?"

"He's in the big room; she's upstairs. And gagged. Who's to hear her? No one did today. If you ask me—it's a damn stupid mistake having them in this house at the same time."

"I'm not asking you. And it isn't a mistake. It wasn't planned. It just happened. She is—"

"She's a damned nuisance."

"An important nuisance. Remember that! Where are you going, Stefan?"

"Out." Heavy footsteps were crossing the room.

"Where?" she insisted.

"Up to the big house—get cigarettes and something to drink, find out what's new. You clean up here, have the place looking good for our visitor. Who is he? Did they say?"

"No. And tell them she isn't talking, won't speak. Yes, better tell them that."

"I'll tell them it would be easy to make her talk if they didn't want her kept alive. And how long will that be, anyway?" There was a grunt, short and contemptuous. "Switch off the light. Can't open the door until you've got that light turned off. Move it!"

Renwick and Claudel didn't wait for the light to go out. They raced to the nearest tree, glasses safely in their pockets, their rubber-soled shoes both sure and soundless on the grass, and slid behind its shelter. Propped on their elbows, they watched that back door. They were aware when it opened—in the stillness of the night, the turn of a heavy lock was audible. But it was only when Stefan stepped out from the house's shadow that they realized the door had closed. Not locked again, thought Renwick. Why?

They watched the tall, heavy figure in its dark clothes

plodding slowly toward the road. Stefan stopped twice, looked around. Perhaps he really was enjoying the air. Perhaps he was checking to make sure everything was as peaceful as it should be.

And in the house he had left? The woman busy tidying the kitchen; someone in a room overhead, gagged and unconscious—a bad combination, thought Renwick. She could be smothered to death—orders or no orders from Klaus Sudak.

Stefan had reached the road, was lost from view as he turned to follow it uphill. "How much time?" Claudel asked. "Ten minutes to the big chalet. Fifteen minutes for supplies and some talk—and ten minutes back here. Give him half an hour?"

Renwick nodded. "The door wasn't locked. An invitation to enter, I'd say. Let's accept it."

"Marchand?"

"We'll scout around first. Time enough to call when—" Renwick, about to rise, broke off both words and movement. The door must have opened. The woman came out of the shadows, almost invisible in the dark cloak she had thrown around her. A shoulder tilted as she walked toward them. Carrying something? A large black plastic bag that glistened in a ray of moonlight as it bulged out from under her cape. They let her pass, scarcely fifteen feet away from where they lay under the tree. She veered to her left, up toward the bushes that disguised the garbage dump.

Renwick rose, gestured to Claudel, and they followed. She was out of sight behind the screen of bushes. "Deal with her now?" Claudel whispered and stood to the side of the path the woman had taken through the shrubbery. Renwick faced it. She came out, saw him, stopped. Her mouth opened, but she didn't cry out. Claudel's karate chop caught the back of her neck. She pitched forward, lay still

"Sorry about that," Claudel told her, "but how else do we keep you quiet for the next half hour? Come on, Bob. Lend a hand. She's the weight of two men."

Together they pulled her heavy bulk near some stones, dropped her head beside the largest of them. If any of her friends came prowling around, they might think it was a fall in the dark and a case of concussion. "All right, all right," Renwick said. "Let's go!"

They raced down the slope, stepped into a darkened kitchen

with its door ajar. Renwick closed it, used his pen flashlight to find the switch and turn on a ceiling lamp. On the far wall was a narrow door. Quickly, they moved to open it: the woman's room—underclothes on a chair and a dress, smeared with blood, hooked onto a wall.

Back into the kitchen, out into the hall. A small place, stretching from back to front of the house, lit by a table lamp near the main entrance. Opposite them, a narrow staircase leading up the wall, beginning almost at the doorway to a back room. Stefan's room: city clothes dropped on the bed, a soiled towel on the floor near a washstand and a basin of red-tinged water. There was a front room, too, its door under the top rise of the stairs.

"Well," said Renwick as they entered it and switched on the lights, "all the comforts of home." It was larger, better furnished than the others, with even an adjoining bathroom. The wardrobe held a man's suit and overcoat—new, apparently unworn. New shirt, new underclothes, new shoes. A complete and natty outfit even to the dark-red tie. On the bureau, there was an innocent display of lace mat, brushes, and comb. Inside a drawer, at its back, lay a wallet packed with French francs and German marks. "Okay," said Renwick as he replaced it exactly and switched off the light.

They climbed the steep flight of wooden steps and reached the upper hall, lit by a lamp on a rickety table that stood almost at the head of the stairs. Hall? More like a corridor stretching the breadth of the house with a window at either end. Four doors here; and three of them half open, leading into unused rooms. The fourth was locked. With the key in place, Renwick saw in astonishment. But then, they hadn't expected any intruders and by habit had locked the door from the outside. Not that they had anything to fear from the inside: their prisoner couldn't have made even the feeblest attempt to escape. Renwick and Claudel paused at the threshold to the brightly lit room, stared at her in horror.

She was naked, bound with rope to a high-backed wooden chair, her body scored with vicious red slashes, one wrist broken, her legs covered with congealed blood. Her head fell sideways, as if she had tried in her last conscious moment to avoid the glare of light from a powerful lamp aimed at her face. Her mouth was

savagely bandaged with a broad swathe of adhesive tape that
stretched from ear to ear. Red hair, its loose tendrils lank and
matted, had been hacked off at the neck and lay scattered with
shreds of clothing thrown onto the bare floor.

Renwick thrust aside the lamp, began peeling the wide strip
of plaster away from her cheeks and lips. Claudel had his knife
out, was trying to judge where he could safely start cutting the
rope that had bitten into her waist.

She moaned, tried to open her eyes, could only see two
figures bending over her, didn't even hear Renwick's voice
saying, "It's all right, it's all right." He grimaced in sympathy
as he pulled the last shred of plaster away from her skin.
The moan became a strangled sound of abject fear. Renwick
looked at the white face now fully revealed. "God in heaven,"
he said. Quickly, he snapped his knife open, began freeing
her arms. This must hurt like hell, he thought. The least
touch is agony.

"No, no more—no more." She flinched away from the
hands that were helping her. "No more—please. I'll tell you."
Her eyes closed. "Zurich. Cathedral. Poste restante. Karen—
Karen Cross." The hoarse voice became a whimper that ended
in a strangled sob. Suddenly, it ended. Her head dropped, fell
motionless.

"Dead?" asked Claudel.

Renwick felt her pulse. "Barely alive."

The ropes were cut. They carried her over to a cot, laid her
on the gray blanket which had covered her on the journey here.

Claudel looked at Renwick's tight face. "You know her?"

"Lorna Upwood."

"Lorna?" Claudel stared at her. He drew a long breath. "And
how do we get her out of here? I'm afraid to touch her."

Renwick nodded and took out Marchand's transmitter. "Five-
mile radius, he said. I think I'd better find a way onto that
balcony." This is one report that I want to go out loud and
clear. "We can leave her here. You nip downstairs, Pierre, and
find that two-way radio they talked about. Put the lights out
of action, too." He locked the door behind them, pocketed the
key, and hurried to the hall's French window as Claudel raced
downstairs.

Renwick's exit onto the balcony was speed combined with
destruction. He forced the window so angrily that a pane

smashed, he slashed the opaque blind with his knife, he shouldered the shutters apart after a heavy kick at their lock. And now, his back close to the stucco wall, a wooden railing in front of him, he faced the view of the road as it wound its way down into town. He pressed the signal on the transmitter. Immediately, Marchand's voice said, "Identify!"

"Victor."

"About time. Where are you?"

"Inside."

"So that's where you went. Who welcomed you?"

"No one. The man left—"

"We saw him."

Saw? I ought to have guessed, Renwick thought: Marchand and his boys followed us up here. "Then you saw us, too."

"Until you vanished," Marchand admitted. "Anything interesting?"

"Police business now. We'll need a stretcher. Serious injuries."

"An ambulance?"

"Later. Can't alarm the neighborhood."

"Give us five minutes." Then Marchand's voice changed to a warning whisper. "Man coming down the road—another following, carrying a box."

Beer and cigarettes? "Better hurry."

"They'll be ahead of us." Marchand was worried.

"Bring flashlights," Renwick said and switched off communication. He stepped through the torn blind, found the hall now in darkness, and signaled Claudel with a whistle.

"Finished here," Claudel called as he left the ground floor.

"Fourteen steps," Renwick said softly as Claudel's flashlight pointed its beam on the stairs to bring him up at a run. "We've got company. Stefan and friend."

"You saw them?"

"Marchand did. He's out there somewhere—near enough."

"And the troops?"

"With him, I bet." Renwick raised a warning hand as the back door opened. Claudel switched off his flashlight. Footsteps entered the kitchen, stopped. Renwick glanced at the broad stream of moonbeams pouring through the hole he had slashed in the blind. He gestured to the head of the stairs and its wooden railing. Claudel nodded, took cover behind the balustrade. Renwick reached the window, leaned out through the torn blind to close the shutters. One of them balked. It would be easy enough to yank it forcefully if he could risk any noise. He altered his grip, pulled firmly. The shutter almost creaked. He stopped.

Downstairs, the voices sounded angry and baffled. One was American—Barney? The other was Stefan, his words more limited as he struggled with English. "Door unlocked! Magda, where are you? Magda!" He shouted upstairs, "Magda—you there?"

"Open the door, let's have some light in here," Barney said. Someone stumbled and dropped a heavy load. "Where's that goddamned switch? Got it!"

"She is not in her room. Outside, perhaps. I look."

"It doesn't work. A fuse? Where's your flashlight?"

"Two of them. Near radio. Beside stove."

Silence, while Barney searched and Stefan had his look outside. It was brief.

Too brief, thought Renwick, trying to persuade the shutter to swing inward. The blind hampered his movements, and he couldn't tear it fully apart without sending a warning down to the kitchen. Every sound seemed to travel in this tight little house. He tried another grip. Careful, he told himself, careful.

Barney swore steadily. "Won't work. Batteries are dead in both of them."

"We signal the house."

"That's what I'm trying to do, goddammit. I get nothing—nothing! The radio's useless. You telephone while I search this floor."

Renwick's silent battle with the shutter ended. He swung it steadily toward him. It tilted as he was about to close it—one hinge must have slipped when he had shouldered it open—and showed a gap, small but definite, a finger-wide streak of moonlight, bright against the hall's darkness. He tried to straighten it, force it even. And its good hinge, now bearing the shutter's weight, creaked loudly.

Instantly, footsteps hurried to the bottom of the stairs and stopped. From the kitchen, Stefan called, "Telephone out! Kaput."

Silence from Barney.

He's listening, thought Renwick and didn't even risk crossing the wooden floor to reach Claudel. Quickly, he drew himself to the side of the window. The table was near enough, a black shadow among shadows, flimsy protection but the only cover within reach. He stretched out his arm, ventured two careful steps, touched its corner. He felt the lamp tremble, steadied its base before it could topple. Then he crouched low at the side of the table, putting it between himself and the staircase.

Barney had started to climb the stairs, slowly, cautiously, trying to muffle the tread of his heavy shoes. Renwick counted the steps. One, two . . . He withdrew his hand from the lamp, tracing its cord to avoid tangling his heel and found that it ended at an outlet on the wall behind him. He eased the socket free. Then he took out his automatic. He was still counting. Eleven, twelve—and there Barney came to an abrupt halt.

There was no movement, no sound from Claudel or Renwick.

A minute passed. Barney relaxed. "Just the shutter. Lost its catch," he said over his shoulder, and took the last two steps in one stride. He flicked his lighter and held its flame high, his right hand grasping a revolver. He saw the slashed blind. "Someone *was* here!" he yelled, whirled around, stared at the man rising from the side of the table, and instinctively pointed his revolver.

Renwick hurled the lamp at his face, deflecting his aim. A bullet splintered the staircase wall behind Renwick as he fired, caught the man's right shoulder to send him spinning. His pistol dropped on the floor.

Barney regained his balance, threw his lighter at Renwick and missed, tried to pick up the revolver. One sharp blow from the side of Renwick's hand on the nape of his neck and Barney went down, lay motionless.

At the first shot, Stefan had bounded onto the landing with his pistol drawn and ready to aim at Renwick's spine. Claudel lunged at Stefan's legs with all his weight behind the tackle. It brought Stefan crashing down on his face. Claudel rose, stamped hard on the hand that still held the revolver, kept it pinned under his foot. He drew his automatic, pressed it into the back of Stefan's head. "One move," Claudel said softly, "just one move."

Suddenly, a blaze of lights. Powerful beams flooded into

the dark hall from the staircase. Men's heavy footsteps clattered up the steps. And Marchand, reaching the landing, was looking at the splintered wall above his head, then at the two men on the floor, then at Renwick and Claudel. "Explanations!" Marchand said, his voice tight with anger.

Renwick walked over to the room where Lorna Upwood lay. He unlocked the door, threw it open. "In here," he said, and stood aside.

Marchand signed to two of his men to follow, and entered the room. He didn't stay long. He came out, visibly shaken. He even did some explaining himself. "We brought a stretcher. That was what delayed us." He looked at Stefan, at Barney. His voice hardened. "Are these the men responsible?"

"This one." Claudel released Stefan to the grip of two husky fellows. "And a woman. You'll find her on the hill behind the house."

"We found her. Are you positive she was part of this . . ." Marchand didn't finish, glanced back at the room. He couldn't believe it.

"Quite positive," Renwick said. "If it's evidence you need, you'll find a bloodstained dress in her room. Its blood will match the victim's."

Marchand nodded. "What about that one?" He looked at Barney.

"His revolver." Renwick offered it. "His bullet." He pointed to the wall.

Marchand signed to two men in police uniform. "Arrest all three. You know the arrangements."

One of the policemen was examining Barney. "This one can hardly walk."

"Make him!"

Renwick drew Marchand out of earshot. "The house must be cleared. Quickly. They are expecting a visitor to stay overnight."

"Who?"

"We don't know. But he's important. You'll find a complete change of clothes waiting for him in the front bedroom. Also a stack of money in the bureau's top drawer."

Marchand looked at Renwick. "You can leave police business to me," he said with a touch of acid in his voice. "We shall have the house cleared. Quickly. My men are quite capable, I assure you. But next time they'd prefer more action and less cleaning up."

Renwick accepted that rebuke with a nod.

"And what are your plans now, my friend? Sit out on a hillside and wait until this important but unknown visitor arrives?"

"Why don't you join us?" There was a smile in Renwick's eyes.

Marchand gave him another sharp look, began detailing his men.

Renwick followed Claudel downstairs, passed through a crowded kitchen where the woman sat handcuffed to a chair. "Quite capable," Claudel quoted. "And more of them, too."

Renwick nodded. "How's the arm?"

"Just beginning to remember it." Strange: he had forgotten the pain when he lunged at Stefan. There was nothing like real danger to distract the mind.

For a few moments they stood outside the closed door, breathed deeply of the cool clean air. Then, in silence, they started up the slope to the trees behind the chalet.

Renwick looked at his watch. Ten-fifteen. Almost two hours to wait . . . In Washington, another afternoon would be ending. And Nina? If only, he thought, I could get back to the inn, set up the transmitter, ask London what they've heard. But this is where I stay, wait out an arrival—it could come before midnight—nothing can be taken for granted—nothing. Not even Nina's safety.

Claudel halted at a group of firs where they would be protected from the sharp breeze and sporadic moonlight. "Okay?" he asked.

Renwick dropped onto the ground, his back against a tree trunk, his eyes on the path below them that led from the road to the chalet. "Okay," he said. But his face was taut. He tried to forget what had happened to Lorna Upwood, forced himself to concentrate on the Plus List she had hidden in a poste restante at Zurich. He should have felt excitement, even elation. All he could feel was exhaustion and worry. Worry about Basset Hill. About Nina. He had seen one hideous sample of what Klaus could do to someone he had abducted. I'll get him, he vowed. Before he wreaks any more harm, I'll get him.

17

In Washington, it had been another hot Saturday afternoon. Nina had spent most of it in the shaded porch of Colin Grant's house, working at her easel, trying to imitate the simple lines and delicate colors of the Dutch exteriors which had fascinated her in the Basset Museum.

At half past four she put aside brushes and palette—they had been supplied, like the easel, by Grant. Her interest in painting had delighted him, had created a sudden and warm friendship between them. The three days here would have been relaxed and pleasant if only she could stop worrying about Bob, if only she could telephone him, write to him. Tim MacEwan, looking the part of the security expert who was checking the museum's precautions against thieves, had brought her two reports from London. Bob was well. Bob sent his love. But, she wondered now as she went upstairs to change from her smock into something clean and cool for her daily visit to the museum, where *was* Bob? London never told her that. And if Tom MacEwan knew, he wasn't telling, either.

Quickly, she washed and dressed. She brushed her blond hair, left it loose for a few minutes. Then she replaced the dark-brown wig, added fresh coral lipstick, and put on her renovated sunglasses. Mac had brought them from Washington yesterday: dark lenses had been exchanged for a light color, enough to dim blue eyes but less faddish when worn indoors. Mac, she told herself, was—in some ways—much like Bob: he thought of everything. So did Pierre. A special breed—careful, watchful. Yet that didn't mean they could escape danger. Look at Pierre, for instance, with that knife wound in his arm. Of course, if he hadn't trained himself to be careful and watchful, he could have been killed.

"Don't even think of that!" she warned herself. "Don't!" She stared at herself in the mirror, forced her mind away from danger and death, concentrated on the girl who looked back at her. Not bad, she decided, just a little too serious at this moment. The eyeglasses emphasized it, of course. But they did change her appearance; so did the dark hair. Reassured, Mrs. John Smith—here on a brief vacation while her husband finished some business in Pittsburgh—ran downstairs.

She didn't use the front entrance. Mac had suggested that the back door, leading to the drying yard behind the garage and then through Mrs. Trout's vegetable patch, made a less noticeable exit. From there she reached the narrow gate on the boundary line of Grant's small property and entered the nursery, where a gardener worked on rows of seedlings and tender plants to replace, eventually, any wilting flowers in the museum's gardens and hallway. Today it was Jim's turn to be there at five o'clock—by arrangement with Mac, of course. They exchanged cheerful good days and a sentence about the weather. Then she skirted the side of the museum to reach its impressive portico.

The guard, standing at the top of its steps, gave a friendly greeting. So did the two guards on duty inside the main hall. She was accepted, she thought, and was even more reassured. Mr. Grant's cousin, the art student, who paid her daily visit around five o'clock when the crowd of visitors had thinned. The sketchbook and pencils she carried weren't questioned. Neither was her habit of sitting before certain paintings, nor the notes and sketches she made.

She entered the gallery where the Dutch masters were displayed. Large, cool, perfectly lit, with elegant benches covered in green velvet, it attracted most visitors to the museum. Several were still here, slowly wandering, stopping, sitting. Voices were hushed, footsteps were soft. Watching this peaceful scene, a guard stood at ease by the gallery's wide entrance.

Nina chose her favorite bench. Nothing ridiculous about coming here to memorize the curve of a line, the balance of a composition. If Matisse, when young, could visit the Louvre every day for ten years to study its paintings—even copied them at an easel, right there and then—who was to say it was ridiculous? Training his eye, teaching himself, admitting he was an apprentice. Well, thought Nina, I'll never be a Matisse but this is something I love. She was so engrossed that she didn't notice Mac, who came to have a word with the guard— his usual practice around five o'clock these last three days. She didn't even see Colin Grant making a quiet tour of inspection along with one of the museum's trustees.

But her concentration was broken when two girls sat down beside her. "I'm dead," said one. "My feet—these floors. Oh, this bench feels wonderful!"

Her friend, a pretty face with blond hair falling to her shoulders, looked at Nina's sketchbook and then at the painting hanging before her against an ivory wall. "Is that Vermeer?"

"No. Van Ruysdael."

"I thought the Vermeers were here."

"On the opposite wall—the Dutch interiors are over there. Here, these are the paintings of exteriors."

The blonde looked puzzled, glanced over her shoulder. Her friend said, "Just sit here for a few minutes, Peg. We've seen enough for one afternoon anyway."

"I've got it!" Peg said. "Some painted what they saw *in* a room, some painted what they saw *from* a room. Is that it?"

"Well—" began Nina, but Peg's interest had ended as quickly as it had begun. She was talking to her friend about plans for this evening, and Nina went back to sketching. Difficult to concentrate with Peg's voice, light and subdued though it was, chattering away about Jeff and the discothèque they had visited last night. Nina bent her head, tried to concentrate on a long, low, sweeping view of the Rhine.

A young man entered the gallery. His seersucker suit, freshly donned that morning, was crumpled with the heat and as forlorn as he was. He paused, looked down the length of the room. He was of medium height, slight in build, his face undistinguished, his appearance ordinary except for his hair. It was

thick and heavy. Uses a blower, thought the guard in disgust—
his own hair was cropped close. Then the guard remembered:
this guy had been here earlier today, gone through all the
museum. Why back again? He was beginning to walk along
one row of paintings—the Vermeers. Casing the gallery? The
man looked harmless enough, and yet art thieves were clever,
could send in a scout, someone to take notice and report. The
guard frowned, watching carefully.

Josh Grable noticed the girl with long blond hair who was
sitting across the hall between two others, a redhead and a
brunette. He continued past the Vermeers, halted at the end of
the gallery, gathered his thoughts.

For the last four days every lead he had been given had
ended in failure. First, the lawyer Danford in New York; then
the lawyer Rosen in Washington. Down to the Maryland shore:
no Renwick staying at her father's usual summer home; no
O'Connell, either—it was said he was lecturing in Boston. A
check at his house in Georgetown, just to make sure. But no
O'Connell or wife there, no Renwick, either. House closed for
the summer. Then last night, a long message from Geneva,
urgent enough to be delivered through the embassy. *Information from official files on Renwick show association, possibly
close relationship, with Colin Grant in Austria. Grant now
director of Basset Museum near Washington. CIA member known
to have met Renwick in Washington, Thursday. Renwick reported in Amsterdam, Friday. Nina Renwick not in Amsterdam,
not in London. Basset Hill? Investigate and report immediately.*

That message had troubled Grable. The amount of information given him by Geneva seemed to emphasize he had better
succeed this time. Yet to him it appeared to be a wild, a
ridiculous assignment, bound to lead to another failure. Only—
he had to admit—the reference to "official files" was impressive. Geneva obviously put heavy weight on that information.
Whose "official files" anyway? Straight from KGB? Better
make this last effort to trace the Renwick woman he had decided, even if he thought it was another false lead. So that
morning early he tracked down the museum and reached its
gates as it opened.

He had explored the museum, then its grounds, checked
every small building, told some inquisitive guards he was a
reporter writing an article on Basset Hill, was told in turn

(by a gardener) that Grant's house on the estate was occupied only by himself and his housekeeper. Grable had seen the housekeeper, an elderly white-haired woman, when he strolled around the wall that protected Grant's place from museum visitors. He had observed Grant himself in his office in the main building—door open to everyone. Grant's secretary was a woman, and so were two of his assistants. But none was near twenty-three years old or five feet four inches in height, or had long blond hair and blue eyes.

Now, on this final tour of the museum, Grable—tired, hungry, and thirsty—stood watching, wondering, waiting for the blonde sitting on the bench to turn her head, let him see her face. (The snapshot of Nina Renwick, given him in New York, was two years old, but it showed a vivacious girl with a bright smile.) Then he saw the museum director walking slowly down the gallery along with an elderly man, passing in front of the bench where the three girls sat, stopping just there to discuss one of the paintings on the wall. Colin Grant turned to look at the girls—definitely a friendly look. The blonde spoke to him, laughed as Grant nodded and walked on with the elderly man, stopping to examine another picture. That's it, thought Grable: the blonde knew him. (If Grable actually had been born and brought up in America, he might have been less certain: the spontaneous exchange between strangers was something beyond his experience.) That's it, he thought again. He began walking to the bench.

Tim MacEwan had finished his appointed round to make sure the guards had nothing further to report. There had been talk this early afternoon when he had returned from business in Washington about a journalist who had been spending the day at Basset Hill. But reporters did visit this estate, did wander around trying to dig up some story on old man Basset, whose millions had created the museum. Wealthy eccentrics made good copy, and safe copy, too, when they were dead. Once more, MacEwan was standing at the entrance to the Dutch masters' gallery, making his last check on Nina. The guard said, "He's back again. Casing the museum. Don't like it."

"Where?"

"Just crossing the floor. Seersucker suit. See? He's more interested in the layout than in the paintings. Been looking around him all day."

"I heard reports about him. A journalist—" MacEwan broke off. The man's face was clearly in view at last. It was almost similar to the composite drawing that had been shown MacEwan at the FBI building this morning. By God, it was Grable! Grable—stopping just behind the bench where Nina sat. "Don't let him out of the museum! Pass the word!" The guard left. MacEwan spoke into his small transmitter, reached the nursery gardener. "Take action! Tell Neill to bring a couple of men. Fast! We've got someone he's looking for." MacEwan pocketed the transmitter, began walking slowly toward Nina.

She had closed the sketchbook as Colin Grant reached her, was ready to exchange a word with him. But Peg, the irrepressible blonde with a quick eye for a good-looking man, assumed his glance was for her. "Isn't this place divine? I just love these Dutch exteriors, don't you?" It was a charming gush, a sweet come-on. Grant gave a polite nod, walked on. Peg laughed to cover her disappointment. She was not the type, thought Nina, to feel embarrassment. Peg began talking once more with her friend. "Who is he, d'you think? I told you we'd meet the most interesting people here. No, don't go yet. He's looking this way." And Colin Grant was indeed looking back— at the man who had ended his slow step at Nina's bench.

Nina was deciding to leave: it was obvious that Peg and her foot-weary friend were going to stay. Suddenly a voice behind her said, "Mrs. Renwick!"

Nina almost jerked around, caught herself in time, sat still, her eyes on van Ruysdael's Rhine.

"Mrs. Renwick—how are you?"

Peg turned with a swing of loose blond hair. "Just fine, thank you. But would some other name do?"

Grable stared into her large brown eyes, stepped back in confusion. "Excuse me," he said, and retreated. Anger surged. A fool's errand. I knew it, I knew it, he told Geneva silently. I didn't fail. You did. You and your reliable information from official files. The Renwick girl is nowhere near Basset Hill, nowhere.

A redhaired man caught his arm above the elbow. "This way, if you please," MacEwan said softly. "No, don't struggle. You wouldn't win." There were now three guards at the gallery entrance.

"But why—what have I—"

"Just routine." MacEwan led him with a firm grip into the main hall. Two of the guards walked on Grable's other side. Ahead was the museum's front door. "No, no, I wouldn't try that," the quiet Canadian's voice said. "The men outside have been alerted, too. In here!" They had stopped at the secretary's office, empty at this hour.

"But what have I done? I'm a reporter. I'm writing a story on—"

"Tell us the story. We're interested." MacEwan tightened his grasp, urged him over the threshold. "You can sit there." MacEwan pointed to a chair beside the desk, released Grable. The guards entered, closed the door. "I'm the security inspector. We've reason to believe that an attempted robbery of valuable paintings is being planned. Today you've been seen wandering around. Why?"

Grable's relief broke into a stream of words. "I told you— I'm researching a story about Basset and his museum."

"What newspaper?"

"I'm free-lance." Grable had recovered. His voice was normal. No more indignation, no more anger. "I write for magazines; trade papers, too."

"Tell us all about it," MacEwan said, his light-blue eyes expectant. "We have plenty of time." Plenty, he thought. Joe Neill would need forty-five minutes at least to arrive here.

Grable looked at his watch. "But I haven't. I have an important dinner engagement tonight. At seven o'clock. In Washington. So you start your questions, and I'll answer them. I must leave in fifteen minutes."

"Perhaps. Perhaps not."

"But you can't keep me here. You've no reason to—"

"A threatened robbery gives us every reason."

"Do you think one man could plan such a theft?" asked Grable sarcastically. Such idiots—overzealous fools.

"No. But one man could check out our security arrangements."

Grable was all innocence again. "Is that what you think I was doing? I was only walking around, getting the atmosphere of this place. All part of the story's background."

MacEwan and the two guards just looked at him.

Grable glanced again at his watch. "At this rate, I'll never keep that engagement. May I use the phone—or is that denied me?"

"Not at all." MacEwan even pushed the telephone across the desk.

"Thank you." Quickly, Grable began to dial.

Now what will he tell his contact? MacEwan wondered. That he still has suspicions? That someone else must make a second visit to Basset Hill? Or that he was following a false lead? MacEwan waited tensely.

Grable let the phone ring twice, cut it off. "Think I dialed a wrong number. Guess I was hurried. Better try again. Do you mind?"

So that had been the signal to alert his contact that a vital message was about to be sent. "Go ahead," said MacEwan, and again noted the numbers that were being dialed with exaggerated care. They were exactly the same as the ones used previously.

"Sam? Josh here. Can't make dinner tonight—got a bad migraine. A rotten day altogether. Found no story, nothing worth writing about. Tell my publisher to come up with a better idea next time. I'm calling it quits on this one. See you in New York." Grable replaced the receiver, looked blandly at MacEwan. "Sam's my agent, usually a bright guy, but this time..." He shook his head.

MacEwan looked disinterested. Thank God, he thought. The search for Nina was over. Basset Hill had been declared a complete failure. He said to one of the guards, "Tell the Director that everything is under control here." As the man left, MacEwan lifted away the telephone from Grable's reach. "Now, let's start with your name and address. Then your agent's. Then your publisher's."

Grable stared at him. "Is this some kind of inquisition?" But his voice was less assured, his eyes less confident.

"Not yet," said MacEwan, "not yet."

Nina hadn't moved. She stared at the van Ruysdael, saw only a blur of blues and greens. Mrs. Renwick... And she had almost turned around. So near to disaster, just one small swerve of her head. Would he have noticed her eyes, noticed the startled look on her face? Could he have suddenly realized that the color of her hair might have changed, but that her expression was too alarmed, too concerned? She bowed her head, wasn't even aware that Mac had taken the man out of the gallery, didn't even know that Colin Grant had bid the trustee a hasty good-bye and was now coming quickly toward her. She heard the blonde speaking as the girls rose and moved away. What chased them off? she wondered. And then in panic, Is the man back here again? She raised her head. I'll brazen it out, she thought. But it was Colin who was standing before her. He took her hand, sat down beside her.

"The man has gone," he told her. "Mac took him in charge. We'll find out who he is. What did he say? Did he threaten you?" Her hands were cold with fear.

"He said—'Mrs. Renwick!' And I nearly looked around. Oh, Colin, I almost did!"

"But you didn't."

"He wasn't speaking to me, of course. But I *thought* he was. And I was so startled . . ." Nina shook her head. "But how could he have traced me here? There was no connection between you and Bob—not openly, at least."

"That's what I thought." Grant was frowning, trying to recall any time in Austria when he and Renwick had been seen obviously together. "Once—" he said—"no, it couldn't have been that."

"Once what?"

"We were trying to enter a small cottage—three men inside, armed. A girl upstairs. Kidnapped. So we made a little assault. I set the barn on fire—"

"You did what?"

"—with a grenade. Didn't expect the place to go up in flames." Grant was smiling at the memory. "Bob was at the house door, got the men as they came out with their Lugers waving. Quite a moment." He glanced around the gallery, and laughed softly.

"Killed them?" It was self-defense, she told herself.

"No, no. He's a damn fine shot. Picks his target. He got them on shoulders and knee, put them out of commission."

She stared at him in wonder—the man who was devoted to art, who wanted people to view the best paintings in the best of surroundings. "Then they saw you both."

"Only Bob. He was alone at the door. I shoved past them to reach the staircase and get Avril out—the whole place was burning fast. They didn't see my face, couldn't have identified me—a moment of complete chaos. Soon, some of our friends arrived and helped Bob with his prisoners. I wasn't there. I was with—" He stopped abruptly. The first time in four years I've ever talked of this, he thought. He drew a deep breath. "With Avril. After that we got safely away by car." He stopped again. This time there was no emotion on his face—just a blank look of astonishment. "That's it," Grant said softly. "Avril and Bob and I and two of his agents—all in that car, making good our escape. One of those agents—like Bob, he worked with NATO Intelligence—turned out to be in the pay of the KGB."

"One of Bob's people? A man he trusted?"

"Trusted and liked. He was a refugee, an anti-Communist. Escaped from East Germany. A good agent, reliable, honest. And then—well, he was blackmailed, threatened with the safety of his wife and child, who had been trapped in Dresden. So he passed information to the KGB in Vienna. When he was caught, he swore he had only supplied them with worthless facts, nothing they could use."

"Bob believed him?"

"Gave him the benefit of the doubt. His past record had been blameless. But one thing's certain: he never worked for Bob or NATO Intelligence again."

What could anyone do when his wife and child were held hostage? Suddenly she thought, was that man here today to identify me, have me taken as hostage—tomorrow, the next day, someday when I walked across the gardens?

"Are you all right?" Grant asked quickly.

She nodded. "Then it is the KGB who knew about the link between you and Bob," she said controlling her voice better than her fears. "They're the opposition, aren't they? Behind all this?"

"Must be." How else had that little bastard come in here today, all primed about my connection with Bob Renwick? There was no other source of information except through the East German and his KGB control. "I'll brief Mac. He'll send the word. Bob can handle this. Nina, please—don't worry. Please!" The name had slipped out. "You see," he said wryly, "how easy it is to make a mistake? But you were superb today. You didn't make one. Not one."

The gallery was almost empty at last. Thank God, there had been no alarms, no outcry, no scene, no violence. Mac had led the man away with utmost discretion. And the guards, too, had— Here was one now. Bringing bad news? I'm as nervous as Nina, Grant thought as he watched the somber face approaching him. But the news was good. Everything was under control.

"You heard that message?" Grant asked as the guard left. "Couldn't be better. We're in the clear. Come on, Cousin Sue, let's have a drink to celebrate."

In spite of herself, Nina was smiling. "Just how did you read all that into one little message."

"A formula Mac and I arranged. The man hasn't a clue that you are actually here. But don't ask me how Mac found that out. He'll tell us at dinner." He took her sketchbook and pencils, pulled her up from the bench. He steadied her.

"Just a cramp in the legs," Nina said lightly, "sitting there so long."

Yes, sitting there petrified, thought Grant. He began talking about her sketches as he led her out of the gallery into the hall, past his secretary's office with its door firmly closed.

Nina noticed the guard standing there. Guards, too, at the front portico. Usually they would be going off duty at this hour. "Where is Bob now?" she asked and startled Grant. "Did Mac tell you?"

"In Europe. That's all he said."

In Europe. "Well, that's nearer than Asia." Then she said, "You know, I used to think that all these precautions were just a little—" She hesitated.

"Excessive?"

She nodded. "Which only proves how ignorant I was."

"I know. I've been down that road myself."

"I don't think we should let Bob know about today, do you?"

"Mac has to send a full report to London," Grant reminded her.

"That, yes. But not about the incident—it was small, so very small." It would upset Bob, she knew. He would start blaming himself somehow. "Bob is the world's champion worrier. No need for him to know—until he's home—and it's all over."

She's Renwick's girl, all right, Grant thought. "No need," he agreed gently. He looked around the placid gardens, quiet, undisturbed, not one intruder and he drew a deep breath of thankfulness.

18

MARCHAND WAS AS GOOD AS HIS WORD. THE CHALET WAS soon cleared, and most efficiently. Renwick watched the cortège leave by the back door: two men carrying the lightweight stretcher (how often had they carried it down a mountainside with its wrapped bundle strapped in place, just as now?); then four to guard a handcuffed trio—Marchand himself accompanying, with his hand close to his mouth. Using a transceiver, Renwick guessed, arranging his reception committee at the foot of the hill road. Which left two somewhere up here—he had counted six in the chalet in addition to a couple of police uniforms—to keep watch with us. Or to keep watch on us?

The slow procession took a shortcut downhill over the field. Darkness swallowed them. Claudel said, "Wouldn't be surprised if Marchand hasn't an ambulance halfway up the road as well as the van he mentioned. Hear that?" There was a distant sound of slow-moving engines. It ceased. "But even so," Claudel reasoned, "Marchand has a lot to do at headquarters. It's half past ten now. He'll never make it back here by midnight."

"He'll be back. He's curious."

"About us? That's nothing new."

"About Lorna. Why was she here? Did we know her?"

"And what do we say?"

"She was part of Exports Consolidated. Tried to quit."

Claudel listened intently. The low hum of engines had begun again, receded downhill. "Lorna," he said very softly. "Incredible, the way she hid that little black book with its Plus List. Not in a safe-deposit box in some big strong bank. Just in a private cubbyhole, guaranteed by a post office."

Karen Cross, Poste Restante, Cathedral, Zurich . . . The words couldn't even be spoken aloud; not here, not until I'm in Zurich, thought Renwick, and even then only to my old friend Keppler. He would be one man who could get at a poste restante box. Who would question a senior officer in Swiss Intelligence?

Claudel was saying, "You'd like to be opening that little box right now. Why don't you leave tomorrow? I'll hold the fort here if anything else develops."

"I'll stay. Wait. As if we had learned nothing tonight."

Claudel mulled over that. "Wise," he agreed. No one knew that Lorna had said anything, but some might begin to wonder if Renwick made a sudden dash to Zurich. After all, he thought, we were the ones who found her, had time alone with her. "Klaus Sudak—he's bound to have some ears and eyes down in Chamonix. How soon will they ferret out the story?"

"Marchand's men weren't a talkative bunch. Let's hope they keep their lips buttoned until midnight at least."

"Is Klaus just sitting up there in a comfortable room, ignorant of everything? Can't believe that. He's beginning to wonder now why Barney hasn't returned to the Chalet Ruskin."

"Unless Barney was expected to stay and make Lorna Upwood talk." And no more questions, Pierre: I'm depressed enough. Anything could go wrong at this stage; everything could slip away from us. "Take ten," he suggested. "Stretch your legs, keep the old muscles warm. But don't stumble over one of Marchand's men. Either they've slipped out by the front door and circled round to watch us, or they are still inside the chalet."

"Thought you said they were our allies." Claudel rose cautiously, straightened his back.

"Sure. The friendly adversary type. Competitive."

"Ten minutes and I'll be back here, let you wander around," Claudel said, his eyes now searching the trees behind him for adequate cover. "I can think of better ways to spend a Saturday night." He moved off, a silent shadow among shadows.

Ten minutes, thought Renwick, won't give him time to pay a visit to the Chalet Ruskin, try to see in his crazy way what is going on up there. I wouldn't mind having a look myself. Tempting. Klaus may be playing the genial host—bright lights, music, champagne, pretty girls and their handsome young men—but he is bound to be churning inside with worry. Too much at stake right here on this hillside: Lorna; the arrival of some overnight visitor; and don't forget Vroom's wife, Annabel—has he calmed her hysteria, solved the new problem she has given him? A very cool, capable customer is Klaus Sudak. Keeps apart. Gives his orders for Lorna's questioning, probably never even mentioned torture, just tells his thugs that her information is essential. He knows what they'll do—he chose his people, selected them carefully for just that type of work—and stays away. He won't even allow himself to be connected with this midnight visitor. Sure, he's giving him shelter, supplying him with new clothes, money. And that brings me to the question that has been nagging at me for the last half hour. Why doesn't he offer a room in his own house for an overnight stay? Either he doesn't want the man to be seen by any of his other guests, or he doesn't want the man to meet him. Whatever the answer is, one thing is certain: that man is not only important, he could be a danger to Klaus. In that case, why even hide him inside a shuttered chalet? On orders, perhaps: orders that even Klaus Sudak must take. This visitor is as valuable to them as that, is he?

Claudel returned. "Okay. All quiet up there," he said softly. "Just some lights from two small chalets above us." He grinned as he added, "And a lot of light from the Chalet Ruskin. Don't worry: I didn't risk that barbed wire. Hadn't time, anyway."

"Too bad," said Renwick and quietly left. When he returned, sat down beside Claudel, he said, "Pierre—try this on for size. We know that Erik has been traveling with William Haversfield. We know that Haversfield is linked with Klingfeld and Sons. We know that Klaus Sudak controls Klingfeld and Sons. We also know that Haversfield reached Rome from Cairo. He was seen, then slipped away after two hours from the men trailing him. Why did he lead them around for two hours? To draw them apart from Erik, let him get out of Rome safely?"

"I'd buy that," Claudel said. "But where would Erik go? He must have realized in Rome that they had been tracked down—the airport was under surveillance, that was obvious. So Erik wouldn't risk anything expected—such as taking a direct flight to Zurich or even Germany. All airports would be on the watch."

"Right. So what about a flight by private plane to Milan? With Haversfield meeting him there, also by private plane? From some small, out-of-the-way airfield?"

"Klingfeld has the money for that."

"Also an office in Rome—arrangements easily made."

Claudel nodded. "Milan? And from there? Not directly to Germany. Not by air. And a car—risky. He can expect the German and Swiss frontiers to be under tight surveillance."

"What about driving a hired car west? Leaving it at a gas station before the hill roads begin? Being met there? Brought into France?"

"By the Mont Blanc Tunnel?" Claudel stared at Renwick. "We are reaching, now," he said. "We've left our facts behind—they got us only as far as Rome." But he thought over Renwick's suppositions. Suddenly he said, "That wallet in the bureau drawer—francs and marks! Not Swiss currency for use in Zurich."

"Not Austrian schillings for a detour by Vienna. Not Italian lire for a freighter out of Genoa. That would take too long, anyway. He wants to get to West Germany fast. That's where the action is developing—anti-American feeling rising, protests against rockets and neutron bombs—Erik and his Direct Action terrorists would have their biggest chance in years. Might even be considered as fighting on the side of the angels."

"So that is why Klingfeld and Sons have gone along with him—not sent him into South America as they first planned." Then Claudel shook his head. "Bob—are you persuading me to believe that Erik will arrive *here*? Do you really expect him to step out of a car, all the way from Italy? What about the time factor—could he make it from Milan by midnight?"

"It could be done."

"You've calculated?"

"Roughly."

"You really are expecting him," Claudel said softly.

"Not expecting. Just thinking he's a good candidate for that big front room."

Erik was certainly that. The link with Klaus Sudak through Haversfield was a definite fact. And Erik never needed a safe house more than he did now. "All right. We don't expect. We just wait. And be ready." Erik—if it is Erik who steps into that chalet—will know there's something wrong the moment he opens the front door. He's too smart. He could take off like a shot. Where? By night, and darkness on this hillside for another four or five hours, Erik could disappear. He must have a pocket transceiver, could alert Klaus Sudak, be directed to safety. "We could lose him," Claudel said.

"Yes." Renwick smiled as he added, "If it is Eirk."

"Almost thou persuadest me," Claudel said softly. He began trying to calculate, from memory, the distance from Milan to the Italian slopes of the Mont Blanc massif—then the tunnel right through into France, landing almost at the back door to Chamonix. "It would need a first-rate driver, one who knew that route."

"And one who knows the little chalet."

Claudel was thoughtful. "I'll move down closer to the road. There's a clump of bushes near the path. See it?"

"Not much cover," Renwick said. And where were Marchand's men?

"Enough. Pity there couldn't be a roadblock just halfway to Klaus's entrance. The car will make its delivery at the path to this chalet, then go on uphill. What do you think?"

"I think you've got something there." The car wouldn't be left standing outside an apparently deserted house. And if it tried to turn to go down to Chamonix—that would be tricky. Even in daylight, a U-turn had almost ended stuck on the opposite bank. "A roadblock," Renwick said reflectively. He reached into his breast pocket, took out Marchand's transceiver. "Ten past eleven. He's just got time."

The connection was immediate. "Victor here," Renwick said as he identified Marchand's voice. "I have a suggestion. Could you borrow a couple of bicycles? Without delay? I saw several propped against a house wall near where I parked our car."

"Bicycles?"

"Yes. Two are needed. Three would be better. For a roadblock—just *above* where we are waiting. But not visible from the path. Got my meaning?"

"Yes. But you expect two men to pedal uphill?"

"No. Push. Mountaineers have pushed heavier loads than that up a steep slope. They could drop the bicycles across the road, make it look as if there had been an accident. That could let them stop the car's driver to ask for help to get back to town. But they'd have to work fast. Be here by eleven-thirty at latest."

There was silence from Marchand.

"Only a suggestion."

"Of course."

"By the way, where are the two men you left behind? We're moving our position—don't want to mess up things with them."

"Wait until I see you. Fifteen minutes. Details then."

"All is well?"

"So far." Marchand switched off.

"That is that," Renwick told Claudel and pocketed the transceiver.

"Will he take your suggestion?" Claudel had his doubts.

"We don't move from here anyway."

"He's got us pinpointed."

"Yes. I saw one of his men watching us from the back door when we came up the hill."

"So we wait, dammit." Claudel, like Renwick, kept an eye on his watch.

Five minutes passed. Suddenly, through the night silence, came the distant hum of an engine.

"Merde!" Claudel said, sat up straight. Then, listening, he relaxed. The motor had stopped halfway up the hill road.

Renwick, too, relaxed.

"Did he actually bring bicycles in that van of his?" Claudel asked as the engine started once more and retreated downhill. "And now they're being pushed the rest of the way," he said, amusement growing. "God, for a moment there I thought our visitor was arriving early." He reached for his binoculars and trained them on the road.

"Give them ten minutes more," Renwick said. "It's a steep push!"

Actually, it was eight minutes when two dark figures shoving bicycles uphill came around the road's lower curve and passed the path.

"Beautiful!" said Renwick. "Just hope these two can get the driver out of his car before he sends any warning to Klaus."

"They will," said Marchand, and he sat down beside them.

"You're good," Renwick told him, recovering from his surprise. His hands, ready to reach out and strike, relaxed again. Claudel closed his knife, slipped it back into his pocket. And where, wondered Renwick, did a country-town cop learn that covert trick?

"Now," Marchand said, a touch of acid once more in his voice, "what else do you have to suggest?"

Claudel, still angry, said, "I'm moving nearer the road—to the patch of bushes beside the path."

Marchand remembered his glimpse of Claudel's knife. "Then I'll alert my man who is stationed there to expect some friendly company." He pulled out his transceiver, and as he made contact and spoke he watched Claudel already on his way, choosing every shred of cover he could find. "He moves well," Marchand conceded when his instructions were over. He didn't stow away his little miracle machine, kept it ready. "I have two men posted at the foot of the road. We'll have good warning if a car drives uphill."

"And you've still got one man in the chalet?"

"He was there. Now he is under cover, near the front door. Quite a search he had for the fuses you hid in the garbage pail. Not a bad idea. I doubt if much garbage will be collected from that house in the next week or so."

"Claudel's idea. So the lights are working again."

"Not upstairs. We must keep the house looking blacked out. That blind you slashed would show light and might alarm the midnight visitor." Marchand paused and added, "You were in a very unpleasant mood when you went out onto that balcony. Because of the woman?"

"We had just found her." And now the questions about Lorna, Renwick thought. Marchand's lead-in had been clever, but expected.

"Do you know her?"

"Met her once. Lorna Upwood. Worked with Exports Consolidated. She tried to quit."

"Ah, yes—the firm that Klingfeld and Sons took over. Did she say anything?"

"She thought we were her captors. A few words, a lot of pain and terror. Then she passed out. Has she been able to talk—tell you where she was kidnapped?"

Marchand shook his head. "Now under heavy sedation. Fortunately, we have good medical facilities here."

"You'd need them—skiing and climbing accidents, I suppose." Thank God that the conversation had turned amiable, friendly.

Perhaps the mention of Exports Consolidated had reassured Marchand, had given him the reason why a woman had been abducted and tortured. He dropped the subject of Lorna. "Of course those other three have said nothing at all. I have a feeling they will remain silent. They're afraid they could incriminate themselves still further."

"They've plenty to hide."

Marchand nodded his agreement. "But what is unbelievable is any connection between those people and Sudak. If you hadn't seen him arriving this afternoon along with the Mercedes that brought the woman here— Are you positive it was Klaus Sudak who drove the Ferrari?"

Briefly, Renwick described him. "We also heard his name called—by one of his house guests who came running down the road to meet him."

"Did they speak?"

"He pulled her into the Ferrari and drove uphill."

"He was angry that she had seen him there," Marchand judged. Then he brightened. "She might talk to us."

"Perhaps."

"That's the problem, isn't it? No matter what we discover about that little house below us, we have nothing to connect any of its happenings with Monsieur Klaus Sudak up there on his hill."

"So far."

"Yet, he must keep in contact with the house. Especially when the Mercedes leaves here, after depositing this mysterious visitor, and never reaches the Chalet Ruskin. That, my friend, is one weakness of your roadblock."

"It's worth the risk. You'll have a car whose route you can trace and a driver who was seen bringing a visitor to a chalet, ostensibly empty, shuttered tight. If you can identify the driver, link him with Sudak, then you've got something to go on."

"That depends on who the visitor is," Marchand said drily.

"He sure isn't Sudak's long-lost uncle."

"No. But unless he has some criminal connection, we haven't—" Marchand broke off as his transceiver gave its signal. He listened intently. "A car has just come through the town, started up the road," he told Renwick, and began checking with his outposts to make sure they had heard the warning, too.

"What kind of car?" Renwick asked.

"A black Mercedes. Zurich plate. Hear it now?"

There was a distant hum, strengthening, drawing nearer.

"There was another car with it," Marchand said. "It drove to a house on the outskirts of—"

"I'm going down," Renwick said, and was gone, running toward the back of the chalet, skirting its far side to reach its front.

Marchand had just time to warn the policeman stationed there to expect the American before he saw the Mercedes come around the curve, its lights dimmed to parking level.

The bush was lopsided and stunted, but it was the nearest cover that Renwick could reach. His run ended in a slide onto the ground, green leaves above his head. He rolled over to lie on his stomach and study the path. At this end it stopped at the front door—about twenty feet away, he calculated. At the other end was the road. And a car that was now drawing up.

A soft bird call came from a larger bush over to his left, farther away from the corner of the house where he lay. Marchand's man, he thought, but didn't risk an answering whistle, his eyes fastened on the black shapes and shadows that formed and unformed as the moon's shrouded light played over them. The car, a hard, dark mass, was definite. He heard its door close, saw a black figure separate from its bulk and start slowly toward him. Slowly, carefully, although the path was even; stopping once, to listen and look. The moonlight strengthened briefly, was clouded over again. Enough to let Renwick see that this was an elderly man in a long black coat, white-haired, stooping slightly, walking with difficulty. So you guessed wrong,

Renwick told himself; all right, you win the booby prize. Too eager, too quick to play your hunches.

The Mercedes had waited, perhaps to make certain its passenger reached the house safely. He halted near its steps, faced the road, let one small beam flicker from his flashlight, and the car moved away. So he's satisfied everything is safe, Renwick thought, as the flashlight disappeared into the man's pocket and his hand came out empty. No key? Is he supposed to knock? If so, we've had it. He will get no answer, and he'll take off—he's been studying the lie of the land ever since he started up the path.

Then a change came over the man. With the car gone—and no one to see him as frail and old—he straightened his back, took the steps nimbly, tried the door handle.

Renwick's body tensed; he lifted himself into a crouch, his legs braced to move. God, he was thinking as the door was rattled again, was it supposed to be unlocked? Unlocked as soon as Stefan heard the Mercedes arrive, locked once more as the visitor slipped into the bedroom? Renwick drew a long breath.

The door opened.

Renwick's spine stiffened. Marchand—it could only be Marchand. Bloody fool, what does he think he's dealing with? An unarmed jewel thief? Now we'll have a goddamned shooting match, blast it to hell; and Klaus alerted—the last thing we wanted.

Marchand must have stepped aside to let the stranger enter. "Your room is over there," he was saying.

That does it. Stefan can't speak French. Just bad German and halting English as well as his native language. Renwick half rose, moved quietly to the side of the bush, freeing his legs from a grasping branch, and drew out his Biretta. Had the midnight visitor been briefed about Stefan? Surely, with all these exact preparations, he knew what to expect—must have been told. Well, thought Renwick as he straightened up, you just can't win them all. And to corroborate his words, at that very moment the moon chose to emerge from the clouds.

Yes, the man had been told. His hand went into his pocket, came out with his gun, and crashed it down like a bludgeon. He turned to run.

Renwick called out, "Don't try it. You're completely surrounded." Marchand's man—police uniform on this one—had risen from cover. From the other end of the path, two men loomed into view: Claudel with his automatic drawn, and a solid type with a rifle.

Renwick watched the man's right hand as it let the revolver droop—a powerful weapon made all the uglier by its silencer. Of course he'd use a silencer. This man was a planner, left nothing to chance. Tonight he had made no mistake; he had just stepped into the mistakes made by others.

For that long moment, he stood still. He seemed to have listened to Renwick's words. His eyes counted the odds against him, then his head bowed in acceptance. In a split second, his head raised and he fired, his body swerving around in a half circle as he aimed at each man. Four bullets in rapid succession: at Renwick, the policeman, the rifleman, Claudel.

Renwick had seen the man's right hand tighten and swing up, dodged sideways. The bullet aimed at his chest grazed the inside of his arm. The policeman, stepping forward to arrest the man, was not so lucky: he was knocked backward, lay motionless. The rifleman had dropped prone, taken a sight as the bullet intended for him whistled above his head. Claudel, too, had fallen flat on his face, raised his pistol. But before either he or Renwick could fire back, the rifle bullet had bored a hole through the man's heart.

In silence, Renwick and Claudel walked over to his body. It had been slammed backward against the steps, jolted so hard that the white wig had slipped. Renwick pulled it aside, shone his flashlight on the startled face that stared blankly at the sky above.

"Erik," said Claudel.

Renwick switched off the flashlight and entered the hall. Marchand was alive but unsteady on his feet. He had sensed the blow coming, tried to avoid it, and had almost succeeded. There was a savage weal across one cheek, a jaw beginning to swell, perhaps a collarbone smashed. Renwick helped him down the steps, past Erik's body, left him by the dead policeman to hear the rifleman's explanations.

Claudel closed the chalet's door and came over to join him. "I thought you had packed it in," he told Renwick. "You weren't hit, were you?"

Renwick raised his left arm, looked at the singed streak across its inner sleeve.

"Too close for comfort," Claudel said. "Where did he learn to shoot like that?"

"In a South Yemen training camp," Renwick said grimly.

"What now?" Claudel looked in the direction of the Chalet Ruskin. "He heard that shot."

"A rifle. It could be explained, perhaps." Renwick tried to think. "Accidental discharge by a—hunter or poacher—someone out on this hillside." Renwick made an effort. "Tell Marchand to phone Sudak and the neighboring chalets. Explain— reassure them all."

"Reassure Sudak?" Claudel was disbelieving.

"Try it, anyway. What else?" Renwick's voice was sharp. "If Marchand has a better idea, let him use it." Then he sat down, legs crossed, and stared out over the patchwork of faint light and dark shadow that covered the hillside. Behind him, Erik lay staring up at the stars.

19

MARCHAND WAS ANGRY, OBDURATE, AND IN PAIN. HE HAD lost a man, and nothing compensated for that. Not the Mercedes driven back downhill with bicycles and prisoner intact, an easy capture. (Its chauffeur—perhaps exhausted by a day of hard traveling, perhaps surprised by a totally unexpected danger almost at the entrance to the Chalet Ruskin—had been slow to resist.) Not the death of a murderer, the leader of a vicious gang of West German terrorists. Not even the fact that he, himself, had escaped that savage blow and remained alive. He had lost a man.

"Enough," Marchand said. He had rejected the idea of explaining the rifle shot to any chalet on this hillside. Instead, he had ordered his van partway up the road, and, with it, two stretchers. "Enough," he repeated. "Tonight we rest. I have a report to make. Tomorrow, early, we shall visit Sudak."

"We will lose him," Renwick said quietly.

"How? The roads ends above the Chalet Ruskin. If he tried to leave, he must drive downhill to the town. I have cars blocking the exit. He will be stopped. And what evidence do we have against him if the Mercedes' driver won't talk? A dead terrorist? He can't talk."

"He never would have."

"Sudak will claim total ignorance that the man was ever here. As for that guest—the hysterical female you saw today— what excuse could we offer to drag her out of bed at this time of night? No, tomorrow morning, early, we can prepare a reason, visit the chalet—"

"And why should we expect to find Sudak there?"

"I told you—"

"There's no way out by car except by this road." Renwick held down his impatience, kept his voice even. "But are there footpaths—through the trees—like the one we took today from Ruskin's Chair? A path that doesn't end in a cliff or a steep drop to the valley?"

Obviously, there was one. Marchand fell silent.

"What part of town does such a path reach?"

Marchand's eyes widened, then narrowed.

"You had a report about a second car—one that followed the Mercedes into Chamonix. It stopped at a house on the outskirts—isn't that what you said?"

"A wild guess, if you mean Sudak will try to reach that house."

So it did lie somewhere near the end of a path from the Chalet Ruskin. "Have you a map you could show us?"

"Haven't you one of your own?"

"Forgot to buy one today." The only map they had been able to find was one of the town with surrounding hills and mountains named, but with no details such as paths or trails. "We all make mistakes," Renwick added with considerable tact.

That admission was accepted with a nod. And a small confession followed, making a nice diversion from the subject of maps. "I thought we could trap that man—Erik?—inside the house. But"—Marchand shrugged—"there may have been an identification signal necessary. Yet, he gave no time for that. I invited him to enter, and he attacked."

Renwick refused to be diverted. "Have you a map you could show us?" he repeated. "One with ski trails and climbing paths clearly marked?"

"Not enough light to look at it here. You can study it in the van. Unless, of course—" Marchand's sardonic mood was back—"you insist on visiting the Chalet Ruskin now."

"No interest." The visit should have been made forty-five

minutes ago, just after the rifle had been fired. "By this time, Sudak—"

"Sudak will have sent someone to investigate this small chalet. But I have already ordered two men to keep watch around it. And two more near the Chalet Ruskin. Sudak will wait for a report, and when none reaches him—my men will take care of that—he will then assess the situation, and perhaps move. Or stay, to face us and play the complete innocent." Marchand nursed his jaw, now so swollen that even talking was difficult. But he persisted. "And we still have our problem. What connection between all this—" he tried to gesture to the house, flinched as his collarbone's pain sharpened—"and Sudak? He will send no one here whom we can identify. His men never were known in the town. If they appeared there, it was as tourists, day visitors."

Renwick nodded his agreement on that point. But he exchanged glances with Claudel, and they shared the same thought. Klaus Sudak wasn't the type to wait and assess any situation. His assessment would be done when he reached safety. He moved on instinct.

"The van has arrived," Marchand said, listening. He began walking rapidly to the road. "We'll take it down, send it back for the stretchers."

Renwick gave one last look at the chalet, tightly shuttered, deserted, a sad and lonely place, with two men lying still and another standing guard. And amid that silence, among the dark trees lost in shadows? Someone moving around, trying to guess what could have happened? If Sudak had even stayed this long to receive a report, then let him. This was one defeat he'd never repair.

In the van, they studied a detailed map. "Now, where's that house on the outskirts of town?" Renwick asked.

"There!" Marchand pointed to one of the neat small squares that were dotted over the layout of the valley like a scattered flock of sheep. "It was rented two weeks ago for the rest of the summer."

"Occupied?"

"Not until tonight, except for an occasional caretaker."

"What kind of car arrived there?"

"A white Fiat. Italian registration."

"Milan?" Claudel asked quickly.

Marchand looked at him, then at Renwick. "Perhaps my biggest problem is that I've been told so little. How did you know about Milan? Why didn't you tell me?"

Renwick finished memorizing the position of the house reached by the Fiat. It was among a cluster of five, the last group on the road from town. Fields around their sides, a wooded slope behind them. And the path that could lead from the Chalet Ruskin ended not too far away—close to a runoff stream from the hillside: a good marker, he thought, in a valley that was as flat as a billiard table.

"Why?" Marchand repeated, his lips tight.

"We didn't know," Renwick said. "Just another wild guess."

Marchand's look sharpened, but the American was rolling up the map, handing it over with a polite thank you.

"What color is the house?" Renwick asked.

"White. Blue shutters."

"Not tightly closed, I hope," said Claudel. He was feeling a delayed elation. Even if we win nothing more, he was thinking, we found Erik. We found him. And no sharpshooter in Marchand's outfit would have been there to get him if we hadn't flushed him out.

"Keep away from that house," Marchand told them. "There's no need for you to go near it. I have posted two men already. If anything develops, I'll know at once."

"So we just go to bed and enjoy sweet dreams?" Claudel asked.

"Yes. You're lucky. I have work to do."

"First," Renwick said, "have that shoulder looked at."

"Then what? You'll write my report for me?" Marchand's temper was fraying rapidly.

"Tomorrow, when there's a quiet moment, we'll sit down with you in a closed and very private room. We'll answer your questions if we can." Renwick looked at his watch as the van came to a halt.

Marchand opened its door. "If you can," he mocked, but he was partly mollified. "Tomorrow morning we meet here at the foot of the road. Six o'clock sharp. That will give us time to make our plans before we pay a visit to—" He broke off, staring uphill.

A small vehicle, headlights blazing through the darkness,

had swerved around the last turn on the steep slope. It was out of control, driving right at them with incredible speed, its horn blasting as its powerful beam swept over the group of men near the van and parked cars. Barely ten yards away, a violent twist of its steering wheel sent the yellow jeep careening over to the road's left side. It hit the low bank, leaped wildly, turned over, came to rest on its side in the field beyond.

Renwick and the van's driver reached it, Claudel and Marchand at their heels. "Light here!" Marchand yelled over his shoulder to the men at the roadblock, who had been standing as if paralyzed. It came on full strength.

The driver was dead, still held in position by a safety belt. His passenger had been thrown clear—a young woman, dark-haired, wrapped in a traveling coat. A suitcase was some distance away, its contents spilled onto the bank and field.

Claudel went over to her. "Alive," he called to Renwick, who was looking at the driver, partly unrecognizable. But he was the blond young man who had sat and joked with Annabel in the café that early afternoon. The ski instructor. Renwick had named him. Whoever he was, he had saved some people from injury, perhaps some lives, and lost his own.

"Annabel?" Renwick asked very quietly as Marchand and he reached Claudel.

Claudel nodded. "She's hurt but alive."

Annabel's eyes had opened. She said, "Oh! My leg! I can't move it."

"Don't," Renwick said. Her voice had been natural. Nothing too seriously wrong. A broken leg, perhaps. She would live. "Why were you leaving, Annabel?" he asked gently.

"Wait until we get her to the hospital," Marchand said, and turned away to direct the removal of the body from the jeep.

"Annabel," Renwick repeated, dropping on one knee beside her, "why were you leaving? At this hour?"

"He told me—told me to pack and leave. Oh, my leg!"

"Don't move it. Lie still. You'll be all right. When did Klaus tell you to leave? What time?"

Her voice was angry, indignant. "Midnight—after midnight. Didn't stay around to say good-bye, can you believe it?" She was suddenly worried. "Where's Jerri? Hurt, too?"

"What went wrong? Isn't Jerri a good driver?"

"The best. It was the jeep—the brakes." She struggled to

rise, cried out with pain. She began to weep. "Where is Jerri? Where is he?"

Renwick rose. "You handle this," he told Claudel and went over to the jeep, interrupting Marchand, who was ordering an ambulance. "Yes, again!" Marchand almost shouted into his transceiver. "Return here! At once!" He switched it off, looked at Renwick. "Brakes, did you say? Tampered with?"

"Get your best mechanic to find out how they were put out of commission, and you'll have a case of homicide against the Chalet Ruskin." Renwick was speaking rapidly, signaling Claudel to join him. "Who gave the order? Question them all. Jerri's death may loosen some tongues. The girl—name is Annabel Vroom—could be a good witness." And with that, Renwick moved quickly to his car.

He was already in the Audi, had its motor running, by the time Claudel reached it. "Slightly abrupt," was his comment on Renwick's speedy departure. "I suppose Marchand guessed why."

"He didn't try to stop us anyway." That was a relief: no more argument, no more wasted time.

"Now he will be warning his two men who are watching the house in the valley to expect a couple of lunatics in ten minutes."

"Five." The street was empty of traffic.

"Even at this hour there's still a speed limit." Claudel flinched at a sharp corner, added, "We'll enter for Le Mans next year." Then he turned serious. "Do you really think that Klaus Sudak is now climbing down a dark path over a rough hillside?"

"No. I think he is at the end of the path by this time. You saw the map."

Claudel nodded. The path would only take about an hour of walking, even by night. We may be too late, he thought as he looked at his watch. It was almost ten past one. If Klaus had set out as soon as Annabel had orders to leave, he could now be reaching the meadows at the foot of the hill. From there to the house with blue shutters was a short distance. "Let's hope he delayed."

"For what? For news that two people had been killed in a car crash? He believes they're dead. A jeep without brakes on that hill road at night? A disaster. But Jerri could drive." And with his hands gripping the wheel he hadn't a second to unbuckle his safety belt. "If there hadn't been a roadblock, he might have made it. He just might."

They took the road that lay on the right bank of a narrow river that ran through this broad, flat valley toward the town. Houses were now sparse, set down here and there, sometimes singly, sometimes in groups, square blobs of ghostly white, and all neat and solid and fast asleep.

"This might be it," Renwick said as he saw a cluster of houses ahead of him. He wasn't sure. They weren't the close group he had expected. Three seemed more or less together, fields at their sides and backs. Then two followed, slightly apart. Behind all the stretch of fields was definitely a dark hillside, heavily wooded. By daylight it would be easy to identify a path coming down from the hill; by night, impossible. "See any blue shutters?" he asked as they passed the first three houses at reduced speed.

"Can't tell color by this light." Claudel was depressed. No cover anywhere—just small gardens and rough hedges, shrubbery, no large sheltering trees. Then his voice quickened. "There's a white car—parked at the side of that last house."

"You're sure?" Renwick kept on driving for another fifty yards before he brought the Audi to a stop. Still no cover around them—flat fields reaching the hillside on his left, the River Arve flowing far to his right.

"The car was the same color as the house. Shutters looked gray. Could be blue by day. But I'm damned well not sure of anything at this moment. Do we risk it? Go in?" And if the car isn't pure white, if it is isn't a Fiat, we could be in trouble.

"We risk it," Renwick said. He was looking at the flat road just ahead of them. It rose slightly as if it were bridging some small tributary to the river. A man-made stream, a runoff for the torrents of spring from the hillside. His eyes followed its straight line, as far as they could see by the half-moon light. Yes, it ran toward the woods. "The path is just over there," he said, pointing to the hill. He switched off the car's lights, reversed, and drove back to the houses at low speed. "No sign of Marchand's men."

"They are keeping well out of sight."

"They know this territory. We don't."

"Where do we park?"

"Just beyond the house—near its neighbor. It's the best we

can do." And damn all this maneuvering: it was taking as much time as the drive through the town and its outskirts.

They passed the house where Claudel had glimpsed a possibly white car in the driveway. It was there, all right. The next house had no shutters, its upper windows open for air; no lights, everyone asleep; and the car at its side was black.

Renwick brought the Audi to a slow and soundless halt, drawing it close to a hedge. "The best we can do," he said again as he turned off the engine. "Now we check the car we saw. If it is a Fiat, you deal with it. I'll cover you."

"If Klaus did use the path to reach the house, why the hell did he delay? Why not take off in the Fiat?"

"Change of clothes, change in appearance."

Claudel nodded. "It would be too much to hope he had sprained an ankle coming down that hill."

"Or broken his neck," Renwick said grimly. "Let's move it. After the Fiat's dealt with, we'll have a close look at the house, see what's stirring. You take a look around the back. I'll watch the front. Then we meet. Okay?"

"Okay."

They left the Audi at a half-run, reached their target in a few seconds. The shutters were closed, but a streak of light came from the ground-floor rooms. So people were awake. And moving around; one room darkened, another lit up. How many of them? Klaus—if he were there; the man who had driven here tonight—alone or with a chauffeur? And possibly the caretaker. Not too many, thought Renwick. Still, Marchand's men would be useful. Were they both at the back of the house, keeping watch from the field or a vegetable patch? The front garden, small, was absolutely still.

Renwick and Claudel exchanged a nod, separating as they started up the short driveway, one on each side of it, crouching low behind a rosebush or shrub as they advanced cautiously toward the white car that was pointed toward the road. It was a Fiat.

Claudel bent down to check its plate: Milan. He signaled an okay to Renwick and opened the Fiat's hood. Renwick waited until Claudel had dealt with the distributor—taken off its cap, removed the roto inside and thrown it over the hedge, replaced the cap—and closed the hood again. In spite of Claudel's extreme caution, there was a small click. Renwick's hand went to his automatic, rested there. But no one in the house had heard anything. No door opened. Claudel signaled once more as he disappeared around the side of the house to reach its back, and Renwick relaxed. Now he could move to a bush that seemed a likely spot: larger than most, not too high but thick and heavy, a good piece of cover with a first-rate view of the front door.

He reached it, head and shoulders well down, and dropped into its shadow. His hand fell on a sleeve, a rough sweater, an arm that was still and lifeless. My God, he thought, my God . . . He had found one of Marchand's men.

For a moment, Renwick froze. Then he drew his Biretta. He glanced at the body lying beside him. Face down, it had been pulled or shoved under the spread of branches. To be got rid of later, when time was less pressing? Gingerly, he reached out to the man's back and felt a heavy dampness between the shoulder blades. The man had bled a lot, but the blood was cold. A knife wound.

He eased Marchand's transceiver out of his pocket. Risk it? He'd better. This house was more than suspect now. He looked around him, listened. Nothing stirred, only the dappled light of a moon struggling to free itself from the clouds. They thickened, grew. As the garden was plunged into darkness, he made contact with Marchand. All he said was, "Victor. Send help." And Marchand, after a second of shock, said, "Understood."

Renwick put away the transceiver. Marchand knew he was here. Marchand knew he wouldn't call for help if it weren't urgent. Marchand knew it was police business if he made such a call. Marchand, thought Renwick, must be cursing the day when Claudel and I arrived in town.

He had to move away from here. He tried to recall the layout of this patch of ground as he had seen it in the last burst of moonlight. The heavy clouds would last another two or three minutes. He rose and began a cautious approach in the temporary blackout over the ill-kempt grass to reach a dwarf tree that stood, all seven feet of it, in the corner of the garden. Its branches were thin, its leaves sparse, but they would blur any clear view of him when the moon came out of its cloud cover. From here he would be able to see one side and the front of the house. He looked at his watch. All this—the approach to the driveway, the Fiat, the body, and now a sheltering tree—

had taken only nine minutes. Yet up on the hill beside the chalet there had been almost two hours of waiting, and worrying and waiting. It was always the same: hurry up and wait. When the action did come, it could be counted in seconds—like a torrent bursting out from a breaking dam.

The cloud was passing, the moon reappearing. Renwick caught sight of a dark figure standing at the side wall of the house, right at its front corner, barley twenty yards away. Claudel? Yes, Claudel. He had taken his time; but there he was, every sense alert as he looked around. Renwick tried a hand signal, stretching his arm beyond a branch, holding it there briefly. It was enough. Claudel's quick eyes had seen it. He made a desperate dash before the moonlight strengthened, racing in his rubber-soled shoes to reach the thorn hedge that bounded the garden, and then the long grass beside Renwick. He fell prone, lay still, regained his breath.

Slowly, Renwick dropped to a kneeling position, keeping his body behind the trunk of the tree—however small, it gave some protection from the house. Something was wrong. Claudel wouldn't have come directly here if it weren't. Once he had noted Renwick's position, he should have chosen shelter farther away. And now they were breaking their second rule. Claudel was speaking. In a whisper. Renwick bent his head to catch the words. They were certainly less loud than any murmur into a transmitter—couldn't Claudel have risked even that?

"One of Marchand's men—looked dead. But he isn't. Still breathing."

"Where?"

"At the back of the house—near a truck. I dealt with it."

"How was he hurt?"

"A knife between the shoulder blades."

"The other one is dead. Knifed, too. I've called Marchand. Must have happened just after they got here, took their positions." Renwick paused. "A throwing knife, I'd guess."

Claudel thought over that. Then he said, "I think we'd better stay together."

"Back to back, if possible."

Claudel nodded. "I'll laugh at that tomorrow."

Renwick put a hand to his lips for silence. A light footstep had sounded. They turned their heads toward the house and watched the man who had emerged from its front door.

He looked young and trim, walked with a spring in his step. Like them, he wore dark clothes, and became barely visible as he reached the shadows of the bush where the dead man lay. He was checking, thought Renwick in a sudden rise of anger. Checking to make sure nothing was disturbed, everything just as he left it. Then Spring-heeled Jack walked on, starting a tour of inspection around the garden, pausing to look briefly at the road outside. It must have been empty—and where the hell is Marchand? Renwick asked himself—for he walked back, up the short driveway toward the Fiat. Once past it, he was lost to sight.

It was a quick tour of inspection. He reappeared from the back of the house, walking down its side, reaching the spot where Claudel had stood before his ten-yard dash to the hedge of thorn bushes. He stopped at the corner, looked around. Satisfied, he walked on. At the front door, he paused again and knocked twice. Then he stood aside, waiting.

The inspection tour was over—no more trouble had been expected, so no more trouble had been found. The signal had been given: it was safe to leave. Renwick reached for Claudel's shoulder, touched it. Claudel nodded, his eyes on the house, his automatic ready. Renwick released the safety catch of his Biretta. He glanced up at the sky—no clouds to cover the moon for another three or more minutes. We are in luck, he thought: enough light to see by. His attention switched back to the house. Its door had opened.

Two men stepped out, barely pausing to look around the garden before they hurried to the car. One was white-haired, stoutly built, wearing a suit that was silver gray in the moonlight. The other was tall, broad-shouldered, his hair hidden by a chauffeur's cap. He was appropriately dressed for the part he was playing: a white shirt under a dark-blue or black suit. At that moment, as they reached the Fiat, Renwick heard a distant hum—the sound of a car, two cars perhaps. Marchand? But the sound stopped.

Claudel was staring. "Haversfield," he whispered. That dear, sweet old Englishman in Djibouti. "He's mine."

Renwick nodded, still listening. Only silence from the road. Perhaps the cars had been bringing people home from a Saturday-night dance, he thought wryly.

Silence, too, from the Fiat. No response from its engine.

The chauffeur must be cursing it, but his voice was held too low to be heard. Just Haversfield in the back seat, his driver at the wheel, and a car that was dead.

Now? wondered Renwick but hesitated to move. Spring-heeled Jack was still standing by the house door. (One warning from him and the other two would be heading for the back field.) He was looking toward the Fiat, wondering why it wasn't moving. Then he ran to help.

"Now," said Renwick. Jack had his back turned, his head bent, as he argued with the driver. Yes, the car had been in good running condition all the way from Milan; Jack had checked it after he had dealt with the interlopers; Jack was sure. A quick command sent him hastening to the hood. He started raising it.

He caught sight of Renwick and Claudel, halfway across the garden, fanning out as they approached the car. He yelled a warning, his hand reaching toward the back of his neck. The gesture was unmistakable—a throwing knife. Renwick took no chances. He fired as the man's hand brought the knife out of its holster and threw it in one quick sweep of the arm. The blade sliced past Renwick's head as the man fell to the ground and doubled in pain.

Everything burst loose. At the sound of the shot, two men raced up from the road. The chauffeur was out of the car, running, firing at Renwick, then at Claudel, but unable to aim properly as he bolted toward the back of the house. He never reached either the field or the truck. Renwick's bullet caught his hip, sent him sprawling into the grip of two more men who had just burst through the hedge at the side of the driveway. Claudel, now at the Fiat, pulled Haversfield out. "Unarmed, unarmed! No weapon!" Haversfield was saying, his voice as high as the arms raised over his head. "Not worth the trouble," Claudel said in disgust, and handed over Haversfield to a newcomer.

Renwick slipped his automatic back into his pocket. Yes, he thought, everything happens at once: the dam broke and the torrent swept over us; danger counted in seconds. He turned to greet Marchand, who had appeared at his elbow.

Marchand's anger was against himself. "We parked farther along the road—wanted to give them no warning."

"You didn't. It was a good idea." And Renwick meant it.

If the cars had approached any nearer, all three men would have made a dash for the field. And Claudel and Renwick, over by the dwarf tree, couldn't have hit them. There would have been a chase after them, a scattering across the field into the woods. The Englishman, so-called, could have been taken, but the other two? Renwick looked at the chauffeur, lying on the ground a short distance away. That's the one we want, he thought; but first things came first. "You have a wounded man at the back of the house. He needs help—fast. Claudel will show your men the place."

"How? When?"

"Before we arrived. He was knifed." Renwick waited until Marchand had detailed two men to leave with Claudel and was, himself, about to follow. Renwick caught his arm, said very quietly, "Another over here. Come!" He led Marchand to the bush under which the body lay. "Knife in the back. There's the man who threw it." He pointed at Spring-heeled Jack, now moaning and clutching his groin.

Renwick left Marchand kneeling beside the body and went looking for the knife that had just missed him. The sky darkened—more of those damned clouds—he'd have to use his flashlight. A brief search, and he found the knife buried hilt-high in the earth. He handed it to Marchand. "Evidence," he said, and went back to the driveway and reached the fake chauffeur, still face down on the ground, two men pinning his arms and back. His leg was out of commission. "Turn him over!"

Renwick flashed his light on the man's face and pulled off the cap. The hair was blond, but it belonged to a young man. Up close, his resemblance to Klaus Sudak was superficial. Oh God, thought Renwick, and he felt suddenly exhausted, exhausted and sick. All this for nothing, and my fault. I was so damned sure. And I was wrong.

He turned away, walked toward the Fiat, leaned against it. The moonlight strengthened. He forced himself to watch as Marchand's man, barely alive, was carried away; as a body wrapped in a bag was taken out; as two wounded criminals were removed along with an elderly gentleman who had nothing to say but was almost smiling in silent triumph. Renwick noticed that smirk. His depression deepened.

Claudel, and then Marchand, joined him. "Let's go back to the inn," Claudel said.

Renwick nodded, straightened up, left the Fiat. All three walked slowly down the driveway.

"We've searched the house," Marchand said. "Klaus Sudak is not there." Never has been, said his eyes. "So tomorrow at eight I shall visit the Chalet Ruskin—as I originally planned."

Renwick's voice was flat, expressionless. "He won't be there."

"You still believe that?" Marchand was incredulous. Tactfully, he didn't add, "After tonight?"

"If you were Sudak, would you wait?"

"I'll telephone now. Speak with him. About the accident to the jeep."

"Someone else will answer and tell you that he can't be disturbed at this hour."

Marchand's anger broke. "If he isn't there, and he isn't down here, where *is* he?"

Renwick roused himself. "I don't know. But if you've watched the roads, checked the cars—"

"We have!"

"—then the path from the hillside down to this valley is his only escape route. Logical."

"Logical?" Marchand looked at Claudel for support, but Claudel was keeping silent. Besides, his arm had started acting up again: he couldn't ignore any longer that it was far from healing, had gone on a rampage of its own.

Renwick said, "Yes. And when he got to this house and heard that two men had been watching it, he wouldn't stay. Sure, they had been dealt with. But the fact that they were here proved the house was under suspicion. He'd take off within a couple of minutes."

"Where?" demanded Marchand. He held out his hand. "My transceiver," he reminded Renwick, and took it from him. "No more need for that!"

"Let's get back to the inn," Claudel said again. "We are dead on our feet."

"And I have another report to make," Marchand said grimly. Then he relented, put a hand on Renwick's shoulder. "Mistakes can be made. Don't be so hard on yourself. Tonight, we gained something. And lost something." But the biggest loss was in my two men. And Renwick knows that, he realized, watching the American's face. "Good night."

"A quarter to three." Claudel said when they reached their room. "Bed—and a long sleep—that's for me."

"I have to contact London," Renwick said wearily. He was too exhausted, physically, emotionally, to make out a detailed report of today's results and put it into code. That would have to be done tomorrow. Now he'd give the basic news, and briefly: about Erik; about Haversfield; about Klaus Sudak. And ask for the latest word—if any—from Washington. Nina... If something had gone wrong at Basset Hill, then I'm to blame for that, too. His depression turned into an agony of despair.

He began to set up the transceiver. Gilman, he told himself, would be sleeping on a cot in the office: standard procedure for a crisis situation. And the delay in sending this report was possibly keeping Gilman awake with anxiety.

He made contact. Gilman was there. Renwick, with an effort, tried a voice code. And Gilman's reaction was one of frank astonishment. "Splendid, splendid," he said and didn't even let the news about Klaus dampen his optimism. But much of that came from a report he had recieved only two hours ago from Washington. "All is well," he said. "The supply-room clerk has been arrested by the FBI. Everything is normal. Under control." And with that, he signed off.

Renwick's heart lifted. Nina was safe. Josh Grable was no longer searching. Nina was safe.

Claudel, unable to sleep, watched him. Bad news? Renwick's head was bowed, a hand over his eyes. He rose, began putting the equipment safely away. He glanced over at Claudel, saw he was still awake. "Everything is under control at Basset Hill." That was Mac's phrase—when he said "under control" he meant it. Then Renwick laughed, the first real laugh he had given in two days. "Nina's okay, Pierre. The FBI have caught Grable. She's safe." And Renwick laughed again.

20

Renwick was asleep as soon as his head hit the pillow. Claudel envied him. There was a throb in his arm that not only kept him awake, tired as he was, but worried him. For the first time he was admitting that he had better do as the doctors had told him. A six-inch cut in his arm—nothing to it, he had thought: in the past he had suffered more serious wounds than that and recovered quickly. But this time his body was being beaten. It troubled him and it angered him. He closed his eyes, tried to forget the London doctor who had said, "East Africa? You can pick up the worst infections there. You should have had stitches in that wound within hours of receiving it. Be careful!" And the Paris doctor had said much the same, adding with Gallic realism, "Be careful you don't lose that arm." As for the doctor in Geneva, he had prescribed two days in the hospital. Like hell I'll go there, Claudel thought. But the next three hours were misery.

Suddenly there was a shout from across the room. Renwick was sitting bolt upright in bed, totally awake within that split second. He looked over at Claudel, saw he wasn't asleep. "That house next door—the one without shutters—with the windows open for air. People sleeping inside. Why the hell didn't they wake up with those pistol shots? They didn't even stir." Ren-

251

wick was out of bed, grabbing a towel on his way to the bathroom.

"Didn't want to become involved," Claudel tried.

"Not one light turned on, dammit."

"There was hardly a light turned on anywhere."

"In the nearby house there were some." A few. But in the place right next door? Nothing. "Where were our eyes, blast them?" Renwick left.

Claudel struggled to rise. Our eyes were working, Bob, but our brains were scrambled with frustration. And disappointment. Disappointment? Too mild a word. We don't enjoy losing, Bob. And underneath all that exhaustion—God, were we tired! A long, long night. We had our own troubles, repressed, held down, until the job was over. Then they surfaced. Mine about this blasted arm, a small thing compared to Bob's. Deep inside him there was anxiety and fear—for Nina.

Claudel sat on the edge of his bed, made an effort to reach his clothes, began pulling on socks and trousers. He was trying to ease his arm into a shirt sleeve when Renwick returned.

Renwick dressed quickly, looked at Claudel. "No go," he said quietly. "I'm taking you to a doctor."

"I'm all right."

Renwick picked up the phone, had to wait for a slow answer from the lobby before he got the number of the police station. There, he ased for information about Marchand's home address. It wasn't needed. Marchand was at his desk. Poor old Marchand and his reports, thought Renwick as he heard a tired and irritated voice. "Yes," he told Marchand, "it's me again. Where's your hospital—or a clinic? Claudel's arm needs attention."

Marchand's annoyance vanished. "Was he hurt?"

"A knife wound on his arm—a week ago. Yesterday didn't help it."

"I'll send someone—"

"Just give me the directions. I'll get him there." A few seconds more, and Renwick could put down the phone.

"Look," began Claudel, "you may need me."

"I'll leave you at the clinic. Marchand uses it for himself. Good doctors. I'm only going to have a look at the next-door house anyway. Klaus—if he was there—has left by this time. But I'd just like to check. Okay?"

Claudel nodded. That's a bad sign, thought Renwick as he helped Claudel with his jacket: not one argument.

It was ten minutes to seven by the time Renwick had dropped Claudel at the hospital and could follow the right bank of the Arve, glacier gray and ice cold, into the flat spread of fields. By day, everything had changed. The surrounding hills, their peaks lost in last night's darkness, had become mountains piling up one beside another, flying buttresses to Mont Blanc's cathedral. Blue sky, cloudless, and the silence of Sunday spread over the valley. Few people were stirring either in the houses or on the highway.

Renwick's furious speed slackened as he approached the last two houses on the road. He hadn't been quite accurate when he had told Claudel he was coming here merely to look at the place. Klaus might be still around, using a two-way radio—communication was a necessity—to receive the last possible reports. He had never been alone here, never isolated. He must have installed one or two of his people in the town to keep him informed of any interesting newcomers or developments when he was absent in Geneva. Or in Paris. Or in Rome. Renwick could hope that no details of yesterday were being bruited in Chamonix, but even the best of Marchand's men—not knowing what was at stake, only what had actually happened—could let a few words slip. So could a nurse or a medic, and they had plenty to talk about. Impossible to seal all lips: curiosity, excitement, speculation made sure of that. Our one advantage was in speed, he decided. In one day we arrived and the action was begun. By tonight, even this afternoon, whispers will be circulating.

He passed the house without shutters. Its windows were open. And the car was gone. Too late, he thought, and drew the Audi into the driveway where the white Fiat still stood. Then he walked back to the neighboring house and strolled around it.

No signs of any caretaker, no movement or sound from the kitchen windows. The back door was locked and, although he dealt with that easily enough, it was also bolted from the inside. He would have to try his skill on the main entrance and hope that no early hikers were on the road.

Breaking and entering, he thought as he loosened the lock

on the front door; now what would Marchand say to that? He began looking into each room. All was in order, barely furnished, a light film of dust on the wooden surfaces, but nothing disturbed. No food in the kitchen, no signs of cooking, just the stale smell of disuse. And a two-way radio.

He mounted the narrow stairs, treading softly. The upper floor, thanks to the open windows, had fresh air circulatin that held the cool touch of night. Three small rooms were neat, unused. The fourth had been occupied: the bed was rumpled. Heavy clothes—flannel shirt, thick sweater, loden britches, wool stockings, strong boots—were dropped in one corner. So Klaus had come down from the hillside dressed like one of the local guides—except that all these items were dark in color. No white stockings, no yellow plaid shirt here. On a chair was a rucksack, empty. Last night he had backpacked a change of clothes down the hill path. Something to transform him into a gentleman of leisure? Or into a businessman in his town Sunday best?

Possibly the businessman, Renwick thought as he entered the bathroom. There was the scent of lemon and traces of lather in the basin. Inside the cabinet above it, a barely used tube of shaving cream and a discarded razor lay on one shelf beside a small bottle, half empty, of verbena toilet water. Trying to get rid of the smell of blood on his hands? But not all the perfumes of Arabia . . . Renwick went downstairs.

He was shaping last night's scenario in his mind. Klaus had reached the house next door safely and planned to change clothes there and use the Fiat. Which meant he had given Erik up as a total loss—perhaps had tried to reach the shuttered chalet by its two-way radio after he had heard a rifle shot: no response. And if he had risked a telephone call, there would only have been a dead line. More than enough to warn Haversfield and Spring-heeled Jack to expect him within the hour instead of Erik this early morning. He arrived. And left as soon as he heard two men had been watching the house. So he slipped over here, played possum, congratulating himself on always taking extra care, extra precautions: a neighboring house readied for any emergency. Possibly, thought Renwick, the bastard even had four hours of solid sleep—one more than I got. So he is now in that car—it looked either black or dark blue—and traveling. Where?

At that point the scenario ended. He opened the front door and faced Marchand.

"Good morning," Marchand said. He had discarded the stained windbreaker he had worn last night and was now back into his dapper tweed jacket, but he wasn't a pretty sight. He had an arm in a sling to take the pressure off his collarbone. The weal on his cheek was covered by a broad strip of plaster, the swollen jaw was turning black with jaundice-yellow undertones. His eyes were ringed and heavy from lack of sleep.

"Good morning," said Renwick with equal politeness.

Marchand's attempted smile was lopsided but friendly. "Claudel told me you were here."

"Talkative this morning, isn't he?"

"He was afraid you would run into danger." Marchand looked at the patch of fresh oil stain on the driveway. "You might have."

"Are you still watching the roads?"

"All of them. When did he leave, I wonder—just after we did?"

"As soon as he had rested—perhaps slept. He's cool, very cool. But why don't you have a look upstairs? You'll find it interesting. Front bedroom on your left." Renwick stood aside and watched Marchand climb the stairs. Tenacious—my little French bulldog, he thought, and sat down on the front doorstep to wait. The sun felt good. His eyes traveled up the mountain mass in front of him. He could actually see Mont Blanc's white-topped peak. It does exist, he told himself and laughed.

Marchand was back again, staring at him in amazement. The change in this man was startling: what had he to laugh at?

Renwick said, nodding toward the mountain, "Thought I'd have to leave without ever seeing it."

"You're leaving—when?" Marchand took a seat beside him.

"After I pack and pay the bill and visit Claudel. How is he, actually?"

"In bed."

"Strapped down? Better keep him there until the doctors clear up that arm. Not good, is it?" Renwick was serious now.

"Not good."

"But they got the arm in time?"

"Just in time, they think. Didn't you warn—"

"Sure, I tried to tell him. He wouldn't listen. Said he was okay. He's stubborn, you know."

"So are you, my friend. And now you are going after Sudak?"

"If I knew where a black car was traveling early this morning. Have you had any reports?"

"I'll check as soon as I get back to my office." Marchand rose, and Renwick with him. "I'll leave word for you at the hospital if there is any information. Might drop around again myself. The woman Upwood is on the critical list but conscious now. This morning she even managed a few words."

"Oh?" Renwick kept his impatience in check. He closed the door. The lock wasn't too badly damaged, he saw with relief. "Anything important?" he asked as they walked slowly toward the road.

"No, no. Just like a woman, she wanted to have her clothes fetched from her hotel in Zurich." Marchand was preoccupied. "By the way—" he began.

"What hotel?" Not only clothes but all her possessions were there.

Marchand eyed him, hesitated, then said, "The Bürkli."

"Where was she kidnapped?"

"As she left her hotel. Yesterday morning. Drugged and brought here." Marchand's voice sharpened. "Why are you so interested in Upwood?"

"Just wanted to complete the picture. I saw her arrival at the chalet and wondered where her journey began. Did she say why she was kidnapped?"

"She hadn't the strength for any more answers." Just her name, nationality, where she had been abducted and how. But she had pretended to sleep again when she was asked *Why?* "She may have known too much about Exports Consolidated." That seemed to remind Marchand of something, or perhaps his introduction of Lorna Upwood into the conversation had been leading up to this point. "By the way," he repeated, "there have been inquiries from Paris." He lowered his voice, although the road which they had now entered was still empty. "From French Intelligence."

"Sent to you?"

"No, no. Inquiries sent to my friend Inspector Duval in

Geneva. And to his friend Keppler in Bern. Do you know Keppler? He is with Swiss Intelligence."

"We've met. Four years ago."

"Keppler and Duval are now interested in Klingfeld and Sons. You see, French Intelligence has been investigating Exports Consolidated—a matter of weapons being smuggled into Djibouti."

And a matter of the murder in Djibouti of one of their own, Georges Duhamel. "So Paris has traced the connection between Exports Consolidated and Klingfeld and Sons?"

"Actually," said Marchand with appropriate modesty, "I mentioned that connection in my report to Duval yesterday evening."

Just after I had given him that information at the inn, thought Renwick. No objections. I expected it. "But why didn't French Intelligence ask Interintell's help directly? We've worked together before. Did they think this time there was no need to contact us? They could handle everything themselves? Or that we wouldn't move quickly enough?"

Marchand's face was expressionless. He changed the subject. "Keppler is with Duval right now."

"In Geneva?" That was surprising in a way. Keppler rarely traveled out of Bern nowadays. He must have decided that the case of Klingfeld & Sons needed special attention.

"Yes. They are meeting in Duval's office for a close consultation."

"Surely they don't expect to find Sudak in Geneva."

Marchand went further. "Switzerland is the last place he would visit."

Yesterday Renwick would have agreed. This morning he wasn't so sure. Not Geneva, certainly. But Zurich? Would Sudak risk that? If the stakes were high enough, the risk might be taken. And what greater prize than— Renwick shut off that thought. No more guesswork, he warned himself. At this moment he had nothing on which to base any sound deduction.

Marchand's car was parked near his. Renwick said, "I think I'll go to the hospital first."

"Anxious about your friend?"

"Wouldn't you be?"

"Yes. But he is in good hands."

"I'll have to persuade him to stay in them."

"I may see you there." Marchand looked back at the house they had just left. "But first I send two men out here. Fingerprints, of course, and a thorough search."

"And, of course," Renwick said blandly, "to detain the man or woman who comes to collect Sudak's clothes and remove all evidence."

"That, too," said Marchand, and climbed into his car with a smile that cost him considerable pain. What would have irritated him last night now seemed comic.

Not just a matter of sunshine and blue skies instead of night shadows under cold moonlight, thought Renwick as he backed out of the driveway. The reports Marchand had made yesterday would be enough to bring a smile to his lips even if his jaw had been broken. And the report he would send this morning? Marchand, you'll be the brown-eyed boy of French Intelligence.

Suddenly, Renwick was startled. French Intelligence? Well, well, well . . . He must try that idea on Claudel: nothing like a good joke to cheer up a hospital room.

Claudel was resisting sleep. "Hoped you would come," he told Renwick. "What did you find?"

"He was there overnight. He was gone this morning."

"And now?"

"I'm waiting for news of a black car. Marchand says he will tell us as soon as he hears anything." And if his superiors allow him, Renwick thought. "French Ingelligence is now in on the game."

"I half expected that. Do they know about Lorna and her—"

"Kidnapping?" Renwick's glance around the room was marked. He raised a warning hand: no talk about a poste restante in Zurich, it said. "They must have heard. They're in Geneva. Probably here, too. They've connected Exports Consolidated with Klingfeld and Sons."

"They may resent us being here."

"They're just friendly adversaries. You know the type."

Claudel's eyes widened. That had been Renwick's phrase yesterday for Marchand. And if he was connected with French Intelligence, this room was surely bugged.

"And why any resentment? We filled in the facts for them

about Klaus Sudak. And who gave them some brand-new leads and half a dozen arrests?"

"Marchand's damn smart," Claudel said. He was beginning to smile. "Knows his way around here."

"A natural for the job. Relatives, too, to help him out."

Claudel's grin was wide. "Visited his police station?"

"I haven't been invited. He was in his office there when I phoned this morning. One thing I admire: the co-operation here between police and Intelligence. Or vice versa," he added, suddenly seized by the imp of the perverse. "The name of Sudak, for instance. Traced by a professor at Grenoble. Doing research for French Intelligence?"

Claudel burst into a laugh.

"I thought that idea would cheer up the invalid."

"Shall we tell Marchand?" Claudel was enjoying himself.

We've already told him. Renwick said, "And destroy his faith in his professor? Perish the thought. How's the arm?"

"Forgot it in these last five minutes. You're better than any antibiotic." Claudel turned serious. "I'd like to leave right now with you. Don't like the idea of you taking off alone. Where are you going? Sudak—" He compressed his lips; he had almost said too much there, almost asked about Sudak. I'm half doped, Claudel thought; brain's not working.

Renwick said lightly, "First, some breakfast. Then I pack and pay the bill. Next, I'll drive to Geneva, see Inspector Duval. A matter of saying thanks. Marchand has sent full reports, of course, with more to follow." He paused, reflecting. He never had met any police officer who made so many reports within fifteen hours. "Of course, I'll only be repeating Marchand's information. We told him everything we knew. Inter-intell will think we've lost our marbles."

Claudel had stared in amazement as the unnecessary recital began. It wasn't Bob's usual style. Then Claudel understood and he relaxed. *We told him everything we knew*. Except about Zurich. "And now Klaus Sudak is on his way to East Germany." Claudel was all innocence.

Renwick was just as bland. "No doubt. But that's a problem for Geneva. And Paris. And Rome. Klingfeld's offices will need a thorough investigation. We've done our part, Pierre. So get some sleep. I'll push off, can't spend all day hanging around for Marchand. In fact, I think I'll drop in at the police

station and pay him a call. I'd like to hear where that black
car headed this morning. Always curious; you know me. Besides, it would complete my report on Chamonix."

"Wonder if Marchand will tell you."

"Why not? Unless, of course, he is working with French
Intelligence. They might think we are trying to muscle in on
their act."

"After Interintell completed their case against Sudak? They
didn't even know his connection with Exports Consolidated
until we—"

The telephone rang. It was Marchand speaking. He was still
in his office, a mountain of paperwork. But he had checked
on all cars leaving Chamonix this early morning. There were
only three that were black. One, a Fiat, had taken the road to
the Mont Blanc Tunnel into Italy. The second, a Porsche, had
traveled southwest to Grenoble. The third was a Citroën using
the Geneva route.

"Leaving when?"

"The Fiat at five-forty-five, the Porsche at six-twenty, the
Citroën at six-fifty-four. What do you think?"

"Anyone's guess."

"I agree. And where are you going?"

"Geneva, actually. I'll see Duval and thank him. And, of
course, I'll mention your invaluable help to Interintell's friends
in Paris." Then Renwick's formal voice changed to something
more natural. "Our thanks, Marchand. You're one helluva good
cop. *Au revoir.*"

And he was. Whatever Marchand really was, he made one
hell of a good cop.

Claudel was half asleep.

"I'll phone you. So will Gilman. Just to make sure you're
doing well."

Claudel nodded and closed his eyes. Renwick give up the
chase for Klaus Sudak? The man who had placed his name on
a death list, threatened Nina, too? "I should be with you. I'll
be out—soon—I'll . . ." His voice drifted. The antibiotics took
over. He fell asleep, didn't even hear Renwick leave.

21

Renwick HAD HOPED HE COULD COVER THE SHORT DISTANCE from Chamonix in sixty easy minutes. But Sunday drivers were already on the road by nine-thirty, and he didn't reach Geneva until amost eleven o'clock.

The delays didn't irk him. It was a more pleasant journey by far than the one he had made with Claudel yesterday morning. Then, the news he had received from Washington had him worried sick: Grable was on the prowl, circling round Nina's old home in Georgetown—too close to Basset Hill for any peace of mind. Now, Grable was safely under arrest; Basset Hill was not in danger; everything, according to watchdog Mac, was under control. Renwick's intense anxiety was lightened, and he could concentrate on Klaus Sudak. On Sudak and on a poste restante in Zurich.

Were they connected? Not quite. Not yet, at least. One thing was certain, though. When that little black book with Brimmer's Plus List had disappeared from his office just as his most private and confidential secretary had taken off for Zurich, Klaus Sudak was interested. Interested enough to have her traced, abducted, brought to a remote chalet in France, and put to torture. Her abject terror when Claudel and Renwick had been trying to cut her loose gave the answer to Sudak's

questions: Where was the book, where, where? Yes, Sudak
wanted that list of names.

Wanted it? Sudak needed it. It was his last chance.

His cover was blown; his network—with seven agents cap-
tured, seven and a half if you counted Annabel Vroom—was
fractured. Total failure, even in the loss of Erik, the prize
terrorist who was to have started raising hell for the West
Germans. It was a bleak and icy future for Sudak, unless he
could arrive in Moscow with that Plus List safely in hand. Its
value was incalculable: men of importance, all named and ready
for blackmail and manipulation. Brimmer's diary would give
him a reprieve; not a full pardon, not until he could reorganize
his network and have it functioning again. Klaus Sudak was
just brilliant enough to be given a last chance—if he could
deliver the Plus List.

He has to head for Zurich, Renwick decided: he has no other
choice. But what does he know?

Not the name of Karen Cross. Lorna's handbag was searched.
It didn't hold any false passport; otherwise Stefan and the
Godzilla woman wouldn't have ripped Lorna's clothes to pieces
in search of a note with a bank account number, a key to a
locker, anything at all that would give them some clue. Sudak
got nothing out of Lorna Upwood.

He does know her hotel. He will search her room there.
Thoroughly. Tear it apart if necessary, go over it inch by inch.
That takes time. And it's precarious—a forced entry could be
discovered. So will he try to search now, or wait until the hotel
is notified by Marchand that Lorna Upwood isn't returning?
Then he could engage the room himself. A hefty tip to the
reservations clerk could make sure of that.

And when do Marchand's friends in French Intelligence
enter the scene? Are they on their way to the Bürkli Hotel to
make their own search, trying to solve the question why Sudak
had ordered abduction and torture?

It would be tempting to let Sudak and the French have a
battle of wits all between themselves. What branch of French
Intelligence? wondered Renwick. Anyone I know?

Well, whatever they find in Lorna's room—the name Karen
Cross, the receipt for rental of a box in a poste restante—they
have two disadvantages to overcome. Just as I have. We are
all foreigners in Switzerland. And today is Sunday: a day of

rest, and official business closed. Monday morning could be a fascinating time when the post offices in Zurich open their doors.

Renwick gave up his thoughts for some skillful maneuvering of the Audi as he approached the city. He knew Geneva well—what avenues to follow, which of them to avoid for a quick run into its center. Eight years ago he had spent weeks here along with a NATO delegation to a disarmament conference with the Soviets. At that time his intelligence work had been directed at the military developments in the Warsaw Pact countries. Four years later he was back in Geneva, now concentrating on the spread of well-organized terrorism, the latest weapon in the Soviet secret arsenal. That was when he had met Duval and Keppler, who became as concerned as he was with a numbered account in a Geneva bank, millions of dollars culled by theft and murder in Vienna, a nicely anonymous source of income for international terrorists. Then almost two years ago he had returned here. With Nina. That memory brought a smile to his lips.

He skirted the head of the lake, crossed over a bridge where its waters poured into the beginning of the Rhône, and drove to the railway station. Duval had a small office not far from there, useful for his own special conferences; and if he was indeed spending his Sunday morning at work instead of boating on Lac Leman, that's where Renwick would reach him.

With the Audi legally parked and Claudel's air-travel bag safely at his feet, Renwick began dialing with zero two two and added Duval's private number. Automatically, he was through. Duval's voice answered.

Delighted to hear from Renwick, but only too sorry he couldn't manage to see anyone today—not even for lunch.

"Next visit, then," Renwick said, much relieved. This call to thank Duval was a necessary gesture. But he, himself, had an eye on his watch—eleven-forty-five now—and another idea in mind.

Duval was talking of Chamonix: a busy night they all seemed to have had, and congratulations to Renwick.

"Not yet," said Renwick. "Later perhaps. With luck. By the way, Marchand mentioned that Johann Keppler was in town."

"He's here," Duval said, "and wants to speak with you.

One moment, then. And, again, felicitations, my dear fellow."
With that, a dead silence followed.

His hand is over the mouthpiece, thought Renwick with
amusement. He and Keppler are discussing whether my words—
Not yet. Later, perhaps. With luck—mean I have more information to add to the reports they've been studying all morning.

The telephone came alive again with Keppler's deep-throated
voice. As usual, he was quick and direct. "I have a feeling we
should meet."

"So have I."

"Then twelve-fifteen in the café of the hotel where you and
your wife stayed. Suitable?"

"Perfect."

And the call ended.

The old boy actually remembered about Nina and me, Renwick thought with astonishment. But the fact that he had known
about their visit to Geneva was not surprising. It only reinforced
Renwick's belief that Keppler was the sharpest ear that Swiss
Security possessed.

Renwick left his bag in a locker at the station, safer there
than in the Audi's trunk. He could scarcely carry it into an
elegant café on the Place des Bergues and pop it under a table.
The well-drilled help would try to carry it off to the cloakroom,
where it belonged. And Keppler himself would wonder what
was so important in that bulging carryall. Just everything Claudel and Renwick had brought into Chamonix, with the addition
now of a Biretta wrapped inside Claudel's jogging outfit. There
had been no room for Renwick's clothes, not with the addition
of the radio transmitter in its leather case. Anyway, he had
been glad to get rid of his suit; that singe streak on its under-
sleeve kept reminding him he was damned lucky to be walking
around today.

As for the spot chosen by Keppler for this meeting, Renwick
wasn't enthusiastic. But Nina and he had never used the café,
or the restaurant. And with the constant turnover of visitors in
a hotel with two hundred bedrooms, it wasn't likely he would
be remembered. The only excuse he could find for Keppler's
choice was that his Swiss friend hadn't wanted to name either
a café or an exact street for their rendezvous. Certainly he had
kept it anonymous enough and guarded against anyone trailing

him. As Renwick had done. No one had been following him. He had made sure of that.

Avoiding the hotel lobby, he entered the café directly from the street. Keppler was already settled in a corner where the neighboring tables were as yet unoccupied. We'll have about half an hour to talk before the place fills up, Renwick decided; I'd better waste no time. He gave a warm greeting, a firm handshake, and took a seat with his back to the room.

For almost a minute they studied each other. Keppler was of medium height and solid build, his close-cropped hair now white. His features were strong—a well-defined nose, a long chin, a firm mouth. Heavy eyebrows, usually knitted in a small frown above clear blue eyes, eased slightly as he nodded his welcome. His promotion three years ago—but not all the way to the top, as his friends had expected; perhaps he was too near retirement age for that—had brought him definite prosperity. In his well-cut, dark-blue suit, he looked like a most respectable burgher who had spent the morning in church and was only contemplating a large Sunday dinner surrounded by grand-children.

A waitress arrived with two bottles of Spatenbräu, a beer Renwick had favored four years ago. The time was exactly twelve-fifteen. "You haven't lost your touch," Renwick said.

"And you haven't lost your knack of finding trouble. I thought you were safely upstairs in Merriman's head office." Keppler's English was good, its accent tinged with the German spoken in his canton.

"It was there, in my office, that the trouble began."

"When?"

"Thirteen days ago."

Keppler's eyebrows lost their frown, shot up. "Thirteen days? You move fast, Robert."

"The opposition set the pace. And it isn't over yet."

"No? I've read the Chamonix reports. They seem full, but there are gaps. Big gaps, I feel. Why don't you fill me in? Tell me how it all started."

"How much time do you have?"

"I am expected back in Bern by five o'clock."

Renwick said, "Unavoidable?" His disappointment showed.

"Where were you hoping I'd be?"

Renwick looked at the nearby tables: still empty, but he lowered his voice even more. "Zurich."

Keppler slowly drank some beer, lit a cigarette. "Tell me how it started," he said again.

"It will take half an hour at least," Renwick warned. "A brief rundown. But with all the essential facts."

Keppler noticed his second glance at the tables around them. "The weather is on our side. A warm Sunday in summer means picnics or open-air cafés. We won't be disturbed."

So Renwick began with the phone call to his office from Alvin Moore, the ex-Green Beret who had thought he could outwit and outrun both Exports Consolidated and Klingfeld & Sons. The essential facts, he had promised, and these he gave: Brimmer's lists, both Minus and Plus; the lead to Klingfeld & Sons, to Klaus Sudak, to Chamonix; the death of Erik. (Keppler knew who he was, had followed his career, and had put out an alert at Swiss frontiers in case Erik had tried to cross them.) Lorna Upwood, Renwick kept to the last—she was the natural lead into Zurich.

Keppler didn't speak, let him finish without interruption. Even then, Keppler remained silent for almost two minutes. At last he said, "Are there any Swiss names on Brimmer's Plus List?" His face was grim.

"There could be. It's international, I understand."

"And if you find that list? What will you do with it?"

"My first impulse was to burn it."

"You've changed your mind?" Keppler asked quickly.

"I'm not sure. If one of those names, American, belongs to a politician who hopes to run for president—" Renwick broke off, shrugged his shoulders.

"A problem," Keppler agreed. "You wouldn't want that kind of fellow in your White House." He lit another cigarette, his frown more intense than ever. "And we could have a similar problem if one of those names belonged to an ambitious Swiss politician. Particularly if . . ." He paused, then questioned, "Are you positive the KGB is involved?"

"Sudak had information that only their files could contain. And London confirmed it—at three this morning. I don't know how Interintell learned that fact, but they sent me a definite warning."

"You know that there are others who are trying to solve the mystery about Lorna Upwood?"

"The French. Naturally."

Keppler nodded. "Two of them were with Duval when you telephoned him."

Renwick raised an eyebrow. "They move fast, too." But let's get back to the question of Zurich. "What's the usual procedure for a foreigner collecting mail at a poste restante?"

"You produce your passport."

"No signature?"

"Not if the passport photo and physical description are identifiable."

"But if someone is ill, sends a friend?"

"The passport is still needed along with a written authorization."

"That could be faked."

"Penalties are heavy."

"If the fraud was discovered right then and there." And Klaus Sudak wouldn't delay one minute. He would be out of the post office at the first premonition of danger. "Couldn't it be possible," Renwick said, choosing his words carefully, "that the Zurich post offices be notified? Anyone trying to collect Upwood's mail must be refused unless he shows proof of authorization?"

"*All* the post offices?" Keppler prodded. "Did she not name one in particular?"

"Cathedral," Renwick admitted.

"Then," said Keppler, pleased with his small victory, "she was referring to Fraumünsterpost. It is the main post office, opposite the cathedral, which is called Fraumünster. Not far from her hotel. The Bürkli, I believe?"

Renwick nodded.

"So," Keppler went on smoothly, "you would like me to notify Fraumünsterpost. But how do you come into possession of her passport? Do you know where it is?"

"No."

"She was registered at the hotel under her own name, but I do not imagine she used it for the poste restante address. I suppose you must know her assumed name?"

So he's already been in touch with Zurich about Lorna Upwood, thought Renwick. Encouraged, he dodged an answer to Keppler's question and said, "If I do happen to find her fake passport, would you back me up when I present it at the Frau-münsterpost?"

"Say that you are her brother? Her lawyer?" Keppler was curt. His eyes were hard.

"No. A matter of national security, as it may well be. You could vouch for me at the post office. When I get that Plus List, you'll read it along with me." That was a fair-enough deal, but Keppler was still brooding over his glass of beer. What had got into him? Had he become the complete bureaucrat after all—afraid to take chances? Surely not Keppler...

Keppler said, "One difficulty. A telephone call from Cha-monix—a request from Marchand to Duval just before you phoned. He wants Duval to contact Zurich police and have them hold Upwood's possessions until he can have them col-lected tomorrow."

"Until his friends in French Intelligence collect them." Some people made it the easy way, Renwick thought bitterly. "They won't even know the importance of what they are taking. Dam-mit all, Marchand hadn't even heard the name Lorna Upwood until Claudel and I—" He stopped short. No use whining. Bellyaching was something you kept to yourself.

"Until you and Claudel . . . ?"

"Found her, cut her loose, dealt with three of Sudak's thugs." Renwick's voice was brusque.

Keppler said in surprise, "That wasn't in any of Marchand's reports. And you didn't mention it when you—"

"It wasn't part of the essential facts."

"Then you must tell me all about the unessentials when we meet again." Keppler was on his feet. "Order more beer. And some ham and cheese. We will keep our waitress happy—and have lunch, too. Don't worry if I'm delayed. I may be ten or fifteen minutes absent." He left their table, walking with his usual brisk light step through the half-empty café, and vanished into the hotel lobby.

Telephoning, thought Renwick; but he put all speculation aside. Enough to know that Keppler was interested. Keppler was still Keppler, and no bureaucrat. He had been right, too, about a warm Sunday in July: they had peace to talk in this most unlikely place for a serious meeting. Renwick glanced around at the green-and-gold room, pink-frilled lampshades on every elaborate panel, velvet-covered chairs, lace mats under glass on the spindle-legged tables. A change of scene. Sixteen, fifteen hours ago, he and Claudel had been entering a squalid room with one blinding light focused on a woman tied to a chair. In ten years of his work in intelligence he had seen many appalling sights. But that was the worst. The worst.

He pulled himself back into the present, signed to the pretty blond waitress, and had food and drink waiting on the table by the time Keppler returned.

They ate as they talked, and—conscious of the need for haste—had completed lunch and conversation by half past one. Keppler's news was encouraging. He had phoned Duval and suggested that—as a matter of national security—he, himself, would contact the Zurich police, and Duval had agreed. "I shall notify them at seven o'clock. I cannot delay beyond that. You understand?"

Renwick nodded. By seven-thirty, he could expect the police to seal off Lorna Upwood's room. "I'll take the first flight out."

"And are you staying overnight at the Bürkli Hotel?"

"If I can get a room at such short notice."

"You have one. I took the liberty of arranging for a room for you there. Talk with the manager when you arrive. Your name for your visit is Brown."

"That takes care of one big problem." Sudak had never seen him, but he knew the name of Renwick.

"You are on your own until tomorrow morning. I'll meet you at Fraumünsterpost when it opens. Seven-thirty."

Renwick nodded. "I'll be there. Can't thank you enough."

"Always a pleasure to work with Interintell."

Renwick pushed back his chair. "Do I leave first or do—"

Keppler stopped him with a gesture. "Some bad news. I kept it to the last. Duval has just received another call from Chamonix. About the hospital."

Renwick went tense. "Claudel?"

"No. Not Claudel. The woman Upwood—she's dead."

There was total silence.

Keppler said, "Marchand is blaming everyone. Fortunately, Claudel was asleep, and you were about to meet me here." Keppler enjoyed his little joke. "A priest visited the hospital

at noon. He came, so he explained, in place of the regular
parish priest, who was taken ill that morning."

"A priest? Or a man dressed as a priest?"

"Priests do visit the sick."

"And what about the nurse in Lorna's room?"

"He sent her away so that he could hear Upwood's confession. He left before the nurse returned fifteen minutes later."

"And found her patient dead."

"With her throat slit."

"Good God!"

Keppler said nothing.

If the nurse had believed confession was possible, then
Lorna must have been conscious and able to speak. So Klaus
Sudak's agent had found the information he needed, and made
certain—quickly, surely—that no one else would have it. Renwick said very quietly, "Sudak now knows."

Keppler nodded. "He will be in Zurich."

Renwick rose, shook hands, said nothing.

"Auf Wiedersehen!" said Keppler as Renwick left. *Auf
Wiedersehen?* Or was this a last good-bye? His frown deepened. Sudak was a dangerous man, too prone to violence.
Ruthless and merciless. Power had corrupted him completely.
Grim faced, Keppler watched Renwick enter the street, and
called for the bill.

"The gentleman paid everything," the waitress told him.

Independent young cuss, Keppler thought, relaxing into a
polite nod. Yes, he decided, definitely another phone call to
Zurich: Renwick going in alone, his partner hospitalized, needs
more help than he has requested. And he must stay alive until
he finds that Plus List: I can't be involved with that—not
directly. Besides, he never did mention Lorna Upwood's assumed name—not only an independent young man, but careful
too. I've always liked him; that's the difficulty. I'm risking a
lot in helping him. I'm risking everything. That's my problem.
How do I handle it?

Keppler rose and made his way into the hotel lobby toward
a public telephone. His movements were slow and heavy.

22

THERE HAD BEEN A MIXTURE OF GOOD AND BAD LUCK TODAY.
Good, when Renwick found a taxi leaving its fare at the door
of the Geneva café, persuaded it to wait for him while he picked
up his bag at Cornavin Station. Good luck, too, as they drove
past his parked Audi and saw a sharp-eyed man who had nothing much to do except lean against a neighboring car, his ankles
crossed, his arms folded, complete picture of innocence. Bad
luck this morning, though. If Claudel's arm hadn't acted up,
if Renwick hadn't taken him to the clinic, then Renwick would
have arrived at the house in the valley before Klaus Sudak left.
A matter of minutes—ten, perhaps fifteen at the most—and
Sudak, caught by surprise, a bullet in his knee as discourage-
ment, would now be under lock and key. And there would be
no need for this race to Zurich. But at least Claudel was worried
enough about his arm to listen to the doctors. He'd be all right.
And that was a major consolation.

Strange, thought Renwick as the taxi drove through broad
avenues with glistening shop windows, passed small parks of
trees and flowers, skirted wide sidewalks, I've always liked
this town, and yet today I barely noticed anything in it—had
no time to stop and look at any of its pleasing prospects. Next

visit, he told Geneva, I'll see you properly. Next visit? Would there be one? He blocked that question, kept it out of his mind.

At the airport he had a wait of twenty minutes. Five of these went in a telephone call to Claudel.

"Better by the hour," Claudel told him with his usual Gallic optimism. "I'm fine. What about you?"

"Fine."

"Where are you?"

"In honeymoon city and watching some fireflies. Not much of a show until their tails light up at night."

Claudel caught the allusion to Geneva's airport and laughed. Then his laugh ended abruptly. "Some bad news here."

"Yes. It travels fast. I heard."

"Marchand would like to know what you think. Could it have been Sudak himself? The priest was tall, fair-haired. Sudak might have stayed in town, got someone else to drive away by seven o'clock, and then left by another route in a different car."

"It wasn't Sudak—unless the priest used verbena toilet water," Renwick said. "Ask Marchand—he'll explain." And he slipped up on that one. "Where was he, anyway, when it happened?"

"Catching some sleep. He had been up all night."

"You lie down and do the same."

"I'll be out of this bed by tomorrow. Wait—will you?—until I can join you?"

"What—aren't the nurses pretty enough? I saw one that was a knockout." At least he had Claudel, now talking about the sparkling brunette who liked to ski, far away from the topic of joining him. "I'll call you tomorrow," he told Claudel and hung up the receiver.

The next five minutes were spent in a lavatory, typically Swiss in its neat cleanliness. There, he removed Claudel's outfit, rolled pants and shoes and tops into a tight bundle, jammed it into a trash bin. His Biretta was secured in his trouser belt. And space was now waiting for a few purchases: he'd buy a shirt and underclothes as soon as he had time and saw a likely shop. Not at this airport—in Zurich, if he had a few minutes to spare, where there were giant arcades and goods of all description for sale. He might not know Zurich, but he did know its airport. Which reminded him to stop briefly at the tourist information booth and pick up a couple of folders dealing with that town. One of them had a map of the streets, a complete layout with public buildings named. Just what the well-briefed intelligence officer needed. Renwick gave a wry smile over his present state of ignorance as he jammed the tourist folders into his pocket and made a dash for the plane.

Zurich and Geneva: two contrasts with much in common. They each lay at one end of a large lake from which waters poured to divide the town and begin giant rivers—the Rhine from Zurich, the Rhône from Geneva. Each had long histories of siege and war ever since their Roman days—plenty of courage and determination in those independent-minded cities. Even in religion, Geneva had its Calvin, Zurich its Zwingli. And both had bankers, boats on the lakes, boutiques and shops with enticing displays. But Geneva spoke French and Zurich German, and Geneva's broad avenues ran straight while Zurich's streets curved and twisted. Thank God for that tourist folder, thought Renwick.

First, he taxied to the railroad station as a simple precaution. A second taxi took him down the Bahnhofstrasse—the main thoroughfare—past fashionable shops and tramway junctions into a medieval city where the thirteenth-century cathedral, the Fraumünster, was faced by a giant twentieth-century post office. The Bürkli Platz lay just beyond, and there the street ended and Lake Zurich began.

The Bürkli Hotel was not, of course, on the plaza. That would have been too logical for this constantly surprising city. He left the taxi there—he hadn't wanted to drive up to the hotel door, in any case—and, turning away from the astonishing view of lake and hills, he started back into Bahnhofstrasse. Again he blessed the tourist folder with its list of hotels and their locations. The Bürkli was on a small street branching off to his left, and should be only a two-minute walk. It was, he noted as he reached it, a close neighbor to the national bank as well as the Fraumünster post office. Lorna Upwood had enjoyed convenience. She also had chosen a quiet, self-effacing, and wholly respectable hotel. Staying here, she must have felt secure.

He entered the Bürkli. No doorman at its well-polished entrance, and only one elderly bellboy—a porter, or both? At the reception desk, there was a young, dark-haired man poring over a heavy ledger. Clerk, concierge, and accountant? Not exactly overstaffed. Renwick crossed the immaculate floor, barely glancing at the scattering of guests—three men, two women, all separate, each in a comfortable armchair—and reached the desk. Only one of the men had paid him much attention. Okay, he thought, I'll know you again, too, buster. To the clerk he said briskly, "I believe you have a reservation for me. The name is Brown."

The young man came to life. He pressed a bell, trying to disguise the movement of his foot, and wherever it sounded, it wasn't in this lounge. Renwick studied the wall behind the desk, with its pigeonhole slots for keys and mail. Four floors, judging by the room numbers, and only ten of them to each floor: forty rooms, no more, in this hotel. Then his attention switched to the manager's door (designation and name—Wilhelm Goss—clearly printed) that lay adjacent to the pigeonholes. It had opened. A gray-haired man in a dark suit came forward; his features bore a marked resemblance to the clerk's, and his manner to that young man was definitely family. "I'll attend to this, Hans! Better finish these accounts." He turned to Renwick, gave him a quick but thorough inspection. "Welcome, Herr Brown. Glad to see you again." His voice had carried across the lounge.

Not bad, thought Renwick, not bad. He relaxed slightly. "Glad to be back."

"Formalities, formalities," Goss said and pushed the register toward Renwick, but he laid aside the pen it held and kept it under his hand. "Passport?"

Renwick, his back to the room, hiding any movement of signing or not signing, hesitated but reached into his breast pocket. He didn't like this one bit: no need for the name Renwick to be left at a reception desk.

"Thank you," Goss said, and turned away without waiting for the passport. He reached for a third-floor key, said, "Now, if you'll just follow me? We are short-handed today. One of my clerks was called up last week for military service, and my accountant is doing his annual two weeks back in the army. Next year, fortunately for us, he will be forty-nine and won't need to do any more military duty. Just keep his rifle and uniform, like me, and have shooting practice once a week."

Goss was talking too much, a sign of nervousness, but at least the flow of words got them out of the lounge and into the self-service elevator. At one side, Renwick noted, was a flight of stairs; at the other, an entrance to bar and restaurant. A compact place.

Silence broke out and lasted all the way upstairs and down a narrow corridor to its end—Room 305. "Thank you for your help," Renwick said as he took the key and unlocked the door.

But Goss followed him inside. Quickly he said, "You aren't staying here overnight—just passing through."

"Oh?" And where do I sleep tonight?

"Otherwise you would have to sign the register. And then—your passport?" Goss shrugged.

Yes, Renwick on the passport and Brown on the register would have been an embarrassment. "How did you know I was legitimate?"

"A good description of you and your clothes."

Keppler, thought Renwick, was thorough.

"I understand this is of national importance?" Goss queried.

"Of security."

Goss's face, usually placid, with its broad cheekbones and square-shaped jaw, was heavily creased with worry. "I haven't been told—except that this is an emergency measure. It won't last long?"

"Not long."

Goss lowered his voice. "There is a man from Bern—from Security—in the lounge."

"The man with reddish hair and a thin face?" Renwick asked quickly.

"No. That one is waiting for one of his friends. Your man is reading a newspaper."

"He hid well behind it. His description?"

"Dark hair but half bald. Eyeglasses. Medium height . . ." Goss floundered.

"That's enough," Renwick said reassuringly. "One other thing, Herr Goss. A friend of mine has been staying here—a Mrs. Upwood. What is her room number?"

"Frau Upwood? Room 201. She had stayed with us before—three weeks ago. And then returned last Wednesday. But she wasn't here last night, and that is strange. She was so quiet, regular in her habits, always back for dinner and the evening in her room. Oh, yes—that reminds me, Herr Brown. We aren't supplying room service on Sunday. Shortage of help. But what can one expect these days?" He was about to leave. He paused at the door. "If Frau Upwood isn't here tonight, I shall call the police tomorrow. Don't you think?"

"It wouldn't do any harm."

"Very difficult, very difficult. She may have spent the weekend with friends." Goss sighed, now concentrating on his own problems.

Renwick said nothing at all. The door closed quietly. He placed his bag inside the wardrobe and locked it, then looked around him. It was a small room, furnished simply, with one window overlooking a courtyard, all neat and clean, a place for an overflow of guests. But there was an adjoining bathroom fitted into cramped space, and a toilet that worked.

Almost five o'clock. Klaus Sudak must be installed in Zurich by now. Yet, even allowing for his seven o'clock start this morning—letting him cross the frontier before the alert went out—his journey here couldn't have been simple.

He would have to stop, once over the French-Swiss border, to get rid of the Citroën and rent another car. As he skirted Geneva, it must have angered him to know his own plane was parked at that airport. But he would avoid all airfields, all railway or bus stations: these were now under observation. Would he risk the main highways which would let him cross Switzerland at high speed? No, decided Renwick, he would calculate that they would be too easily watched. It would be safer to keep to the smaller roads where there was less chance of checkpoints. But on them he could only travel around sixty miles an hour with constant drops to thirty-five as he reached the villages. And there were plenty of villages. He would make sure he kept within the speed limits. Infringement brought instant arrest and fines: the Swiss took their traffic laws seriously. There were other delays, too, for Sudak. Sunday drivers and tourist buses.

So, thought Renwick, probably Sudak hadn't reached Zurich until midafternoon. There, at last in some apartment or house, he could safely make contact with his agent who had forced the name Karen Cross out of a terrified woman with a knife at her throat, then silenced her swiftly, permanently. Communications took time. His agent hadn't stayed around Cha-

monix to send an immediate report but would have made his
escape far to the west, where he'd find a safe house, secure
enough for his top-secret information to be transmitted in code.
(Karen Cross and her Zurich poste restante were not names to
be openly trusted to telephone or radio.) Sudak's planning
would need time, too, before he made his move. Or perhaps
he had already made it. Renwick locked his room door and set
out for the staircase.

The second floor had a wider corridor and higher ceilings,
a relic of the days before elevators were installed, when lower
rooms were considered superior and upper floors were only
engaged by those who had less money but stronger legs. In
keeping with the age of the building, there was a slight creaking
at each step, which even the crimson carpet couldn't quite
muffle. The rooms themselves were silenced by their old thick
walls: Renwick could hear no sound from any of them. There
was no maid around, either; the service door was firmly shut.
It was a somber corridor, wood-paneled like the entrance foyer
downstairs, decorated with carved heraldic emblems, lighted
by parchment-shaded bulbs fixed to the walls, a peaceful place
in a quiet hotel on a Sunday afternoon.

He tried his room key in the simple lock and—as he half
expected—it worked. No thieves were supposed to wander
around this family-run hotel. If Lorna Upwood had only known,
she'd have barricaded her door at night with table and chairs.
But no danger had touched her here. It was on a little street
just off a busy thoroughfare, with people all around her, that
she was in jeopardy. Had she been thinking how well she had
planned everything? The numbered account in a nearby bank,
growing in its tax shelter year by year; Brimmer's little black
book mailed to Karen Cross, Poste Restante, here in Zurich.
And why the hell hadn't she been content with an ill-gotten
million safely banked. Another possible million or two from
blackmail—had that been too big a lure for her greed?

Quickly, Renwick opened the door of Room 201, stepped
inside, locked it. A very pleasant place with two windows and
bright chintz and a large couch behind a coffee table at one
end of the room. Opposite, a double bed with nightstands. On
one side wall, a wardrobe and dressing table. On the other,
near the door, a small desk. Everything was in order. Yesterday's newspaper on the coffee table was neatly folded, and

beside it lay tourist brochures in a small stack close to a guide-book. Nothing looked disturbed, even to the perfume bottles and powder box that were precisely arranged along with brush and comb on the lace mat of the dressing table.

It would be a long search: too many drawers, too many shelves. He had a full hour of safety, perhaps an hour and a half with luck. From the Zurich police, he reminded himself. Not from Klaus Sudak—he could appear any minute.

Renwick set to work. By ten minutes to six he had completed the unpleasant task. He had not only examined the drawers but felt their undersides for a taped passport or envelope. The wardrobe had only a row of suits and dresses, with nothing pinned to their folds or deep in any pockets. The bed's covers and mattress hid nothing, the pillows were soft and innocent. Nothing inside the bathroom's cistern; and its cabinet's shelves contained only a few items that couldn't have concealed even the new-style U.S. passport, barely five by three inches. Nothing was taped behind two pictures of rustic Switzerland or behind the dressing-table mirror; and the hairbrush had a solid back, unremovable. The desk drawer was locked—a moment of expectation—but when opened it was only protecting Lorna Upwood's regular passport, a bankbook, a list of traveler's checks, a note of purchases made and of expenditures for meals and tips. The window-length cretonne curtains concealed nothing in their pleats. Not one thing under the coffee table. The couch was firm, tightly upholstered; so were its three cushions, with no side openings, no zippers. Under the couch? Too heavy; she could never have turned it over by herself. He reached under it as far as his arm could stretch, and found not even a hairpin.

He sat down on the edge of the couch, looked around him. Nothing. What had he missed?

An idea flashed into his mind and was almost dismissed as fantastic, even stupid. Yet, yet... He had been searching in every place where he, a man, might have hidden something. But—with all deference to equality of the sexes—Lorna Upwood was a woman. He remembered Nina's ingenious ploys: her solutions to a problem were always simple, seemingly ridiculous, but they worked. Nina, he asked silently, where would you have hidden a passport?

Quickly, he reached for the stack of travel folders and guide-

book. Nothing. The newspaper hadn't even been read. Then
he went over to the desk, where at one side was the usual hotel
literature: prices for laundry, dry cleaning, and breakfast
menus—all too thin and light to conceal a passport. There was
also a leather folder, well worn, containing a shopping guide
and advertisements. He had a moment of hope when he picked
it up but—like the desk blotter he had already examined along
with the underside of the telephone—it hid no secret. A leather
folder...

He glanced at the telephone on the other side of the writing
table. It sat on top of a local directory encased in a mock-
leather cardboard binder, faded, unremarkable. He set aside
the phone, opened the binder. The directory was secured by
two long, thin wires, attached at the top of the binder's spine,
that snapped down between the book's pages and divided them
into three sections. The first division held nothing. But spread-
eagled under the grip of the second wire was the passport.

He pulled it loose, shaking his head. Dammit all, you just
searched in the stupidest, most ridiculous place and you find
it in two seconds flat. No—not so stupid. Not ridiculous,
either. Just so simple that it couldn't even be suspected. The
passport seemed slimmer than usual: its twelve pages had been
reduced to eight by removal of its two center folds, carefully
done so that the stitching had been left intact. Who would
notice except a U.S. immigration inspector? Certainly not a
Swiss post office attendant.

He slipped the passport for Karen Cross of Wilmington,
Delaware, into the deep inside pocket of his jacket. The directory, with telephone on top, was replaced exactly. One glance
around the room: everything was just as he had found it.

Seven minutes past six. He was about to unlock the door.
Outside, he heard the creak of a floor, a tentative fumbling at
the keyhole. Police? They were prompt. Too prompt, unless
Keppler had called them earlier than he had promised.

Soundlessly, Renwick stepped well to the side of the door.
No escape by the window: no balcony, no ledge out there. The
bathroom? A trap.

The hall floor creaked again. A smothered curse. Then a
man called in German, "Room service!" There was a knock.

Renwick slipped his Biretta loose from his belt, held it
behind him.

"No one there," the voice said more quietly, and the lock was burst open. Two men entered. One was ferret-faced, with reddish hair, gaunt cheeks. The other—tall, hair now darkened, but with that unmistakable profile—was Klaus Sudak. He pushed the door shut, looked around the room, saw Renwick.

He stared, backed a few steps, kept his eyes fixed on Renwick. "What are you doing in my room?" he demanded, his hand slipping inside his jacket. Ferret-face, keeping parallel with Sudak, was quietly reaching for his gun, too. There was a fixed smile on his lips.

Renwick shot twice as two long-nosed pistols were whipped out and took aim. Their shots, muted by silencers, missed: Sudak fell even as he fired, the other man crumpling in pain as he pulled the trigger. But he would live.

Renwick kicked the red-haired man's pistol clear of his loosened grasp, sent it spinning across the room. There was no fight left in him anyway. And in Sudak? None at all. His hand still gripped the revolver, but he would never fire it again.

Renwick placed the Biretta in his pocket and closed the door behind him. Along the hall a man came running at full speed. Dark-haired, half bald, eyeglasses, medium height, well built. He couldn't have been waiting downstairs, must have posted himself on this floor. Renwick relaxed his grip on the Biretta, ignored the revolver in the other's hand. "You're Keppler's man?"

"Security," he answered abruptly, showing his identification as he replaced his gun in its holster. He turned his head to glare at two opening doors, answered a jumble of alarmed questions. "No need to worry," he called to them. "Just a car backfiring." And then to Renwick quietly, "One shot, it sounded like. One shot and an echo."

"Four shots. One in the chest, one through the heart, two in the wall behind where I stood."

"Who was killed?" The question was quick, angry.

A man who had listed nine men for assassination. "Klaus Sudak."

Keppler's agent stared. "Well, now—we've been searching for him."

"Better get your cleanup squad here—as fast as possible."

"Won't take long. We were expecting some trouble. And

where do you think you're going?" He stopped Renwick, who was about to leave. "Give me the facts. You saw them enter the room?"

Renwick nodded. "They broke the lock."

"So you were suspicious?"

"They could hardly be the Zurich police."

"They had their guns out?"

"You'll find one in Sudak's hand, the other is under the wardrobe."

"Who fired first?"

"Well, let's say they were just a split second too late." Gently, Renwick disengaged his arm from the restraining grip. "I'm going up to my room. You'll find me there if you have any more questions." He added impatiently as Keppler's agent still blocked his path, "Look—last night I had three hours of sleep. Today I've traveled across Switzerland. And five minutes ago it was kill or be killed."

The man nodded, walked quickly along the corridor toward Room 201. His transmitter was already out in his hand.

Renwick reached his room, sat down on the edge of the narrow bed. Suddenly, he was exhausted, so drained of physical energy that he couldn't move, couldn't even draw off his clothes to lie down and sleep. He sat there staring at the thin carpet at his feet. The first time he had ever had to kill a man.

Not planned. And no choice offered. A split-second reaction that had saved his own life. He had nearly packed it in. He drew a deep, long breath. Yes, a moment's hesitation and he would have been dead—as dead as if Brimmer's Minus List had been given the chance to become a reality.

The first time, he thought again as he drew out his Biretta. He looked at it. Then he threw it onto a chair across the room. The hell with it, and the hell with a report I should now be encoding to send to London; or this waiting for questions now from Bern Security; or with this room which I'm supposed to leave—pack up, get out, walk into a cold street. The hell with all of it.

But he remembered to take the passport out of his pocket and slip it under his pillow. He pulled off his clothes, fell into bed, and slept for ten hours.

23

THE EARLY LIGHT THAT FLOODED INTO THE ROOM AWAKENED Renwick. For a few moments he lay on the narrow bed staring at the plaster walls, wondering where the devil he was. The Bürkli... This was Monday. He thrust his hand under the pillow, relaxed as he found the passport there. It was ten minutes past five by his watch. And a lot to be done.

Briskly, he rose; showered, shaved, and washed in record time; and even had a change of shirt to make him feel still better. Before he set up the transmitter he began making notes. His last message to Gilman in London had been sent at three in the morning, yesterday. My God, he thought, how do I pack all that has happened since then into one brief report?

He solved that question by just giving basic facts. Elaborations and elucidations, words as tiresome as the processes they begat, could wait until he reached Paris. The emergency was over; danger, too. His relief—and the deep, unbroken sleep of last night—sharpened his wits. The coding of the information for Interintell went easily: Sudak dead, Upwood dead; necessary passport discovered, diary to be retrieved today, Keppler co-operating; Claudel in hospital but recovering. He ended with, "What news Washington? Immediate reply requested. About to leave."

It came within two minutes. No comment about the report he had just sent—that was still being decoded. But the reply to his question couldn't have been better. "Washington all clear. Nina safe and well."

That was a thought to keep him happy as he packed everything—including the Biretta—into Claudel's bag. By six-fifteen he was ready to leave. Time enough for a quick call to Chamonix and reassure Claudel.

"Can't talk much now. But all is well."

"The show is over?" Claudel's disappointment was clear in his voice.

"Mostly. Should be simple from here on out. So relax. I'll drop in to see you as soon as I can."

"No need." Claudel's voice became decisive. "I'm signing out."

"Too soon."

"The doctors have fixed the arm. So where do we meet? I mean it, Bob. I mean it. Now, where?"

"Where we arrived. Early afternoon, possibly. Say two o'clock?"

"We'll have to buy a couple of tickets. But don't talk me out of leaving! Meet you at two—or whenever you can. I'll wait."

There was no arguing with that mood, even if it belonged to a man whose arm wasn't fit enough to let him pilot his own plane. "Okay," said Renwick, ending his call. He understood what Claudel was feeling: if he had missed the action, then he damned well wanted to be the first to hear the details.

The telephone rang as Renwick was halfway to the door.

It was Keppler. And angry. "You should have kept this line open."

What has got into him? I was only on the phone for a couple of minutes. "Sorry."

"Did you find what you needed?"

"Yes."

"You will be met outside the Fraumünster at seven-twenty-five."

"The cathedral?" Renwick asked to make sure.

"Yes. Main door. It's only a few minutes to the Fraumünsterpost."

"Met—by whom?"

"You know him. He spoke to you yesterday evening. He will accompany you and see everything safely through."

"Won't you be there?"

"Later."

"When?" Renwick's voice sharpened.

And Keppler's voice eased. "As soon as I can get away from my office. There are several urgent problems."

So he was still in Bern. "I thought you wanted to see that list."

"I do. A little delay won't matter, provided the list is safe. It won't be in any danger now."

"I hope not."

"But you took care of our major problem last night. Most efficiently, I hear."

"There could be other interested people."

"As far as I can learn, you are way ahead of them." With that piece of encouragement, Keppler ended their talk.

And am I supposed to hang around Zurich until he can leave Bern? Then Renwick's annoyance subsided. He had asked for help, he had got it, and now—it was always the way—he would have to go along. Gracefully, he told himself. He picked up his bag and left the room.

As he started downstairs, he had other worrying thoughts. It could be that Keppler might have co-operated too willingly with Interintell and was now trying to pacify his chief in Bern or the Zurich police. But if Keppler was meeting difficulties, had overstepped his authority—well, whatever he learned from the names on the Plus List should get him out of that fix. And if no Swiss names were on that list?

Renwick paused at the second floor, looked down the corridor. A workman was busy at the door of Room 201. On impulse, Renwick strolled along. The man was installing a new lock, didn't even lift his head to glance at Renwick. The blood-stained rug had been removed. Another workman had filled two holes in the opposite wall with plaster and was now touching them up with cream-colored paint. A woman was packing Lorna Upwood's possessions into two suitcases while a young policeman watched her carefully. Renwick, at the threshold, didn't wait for any questioning. He left as quickly as he had appeared.

He felt the better for that brief visit. Keppler had taken care of everything. And if Keppler had any difficulties in Bern, he was capable of dealing with them, too. With that reassurance, Renwick could blame his attack of bad temper on the fact he needed a good solid breakfast.

In the empty lobby Manager Goss, even at this early hour, was busy at the reception desk. He was posting sealed envelopes—no stamps on them, no addresses, just names in large handwriting—one by one in each correct pigeonhole. Renwick said, "Good morning," and received a glare. Herr Goss placed the last bill in its allotted space and faced him.

Renwick laid his passport on the counter. "I think you need this. Temporarily. I'll be leaving as soon as I've had something to eat. And"—he drew the register toward him—"I should sign here." Not Unknown Brown, either, but Robert Renwick, London.

Goss stared blankly. His glum expression changed, first into surprise, then to relief. He took the passport, compared it with Renwick's signature, made a note of its number and address, returned it most politely. "I am afraid the dining room is closed, Herr Renwick—until seven o'clock."

"Then where is the nearest place where I can find something to eat?"

"Not near. It's early, you see."

And in less than an hour I've to meet Keppler's man— Losch or Lasch or Lesch. He flashed his identification so damned quick, or I was so damned tired, that I didn't read it properly. Karl was the first name. That I did see.

Goss was watching him. "Perhaps," he said slowly, "we could stretch our rules."

Considering the rules that had been already stretched, Renwick could only smile. "Very kind of you."

"You did not come down to dinner last night," Goss observed.

True, true. "I fell asleep."

"Yes. So we saw. This way, Herr Renwick. May I suggest you eat at my table? That would be the easiest place." He led the way through a small bar into a small dining room, and reached a corner table near the kitchen door. His son, finishing a last cup of coffee, rose to his feet, said, "Yes, Father, I'll attend to the desk" even before he heard the command, and hurried away.

And now, thought Renwick as he sat down and placed his bag close to the leg of his chair, I'll be questioned. Goss is curious, wants to talk. But I have a question of my own: who saw me asleep?

Goss fulfilled the prediction. He took an opposite chair, summoned his daughter from the kitchen (the family likeness was strong), and ordered a substantial breakfast for Herr Renwick. "So much happened last night," he began.

"Sorry I missed it."

Goss dropped his voice. "Two men—burglars, we think— attempted to rob one of our rooms. When they were intercepted, they fired their pistols. Yes, they were armed!"

Renwick shook his head in wonder.

"Fortunately, Inspector Lasch was there. He was with the military for several years—an expert marksman."

"Oh?" Renwick's interest was real.

But Herr Goss's information stopped short of one man dead, another wounded and arrested. Such things did not happen in his hotel. "You didn't hear anything last night? Nothing at all?"

"As you saw, I was asleep." Renwick tried to keep everything light and easy. "Were you actually in my room? I never heard a thing."

"Just for a moment. When Inspector Lasch saw you were so soundly sleeping, we left."

"Lasch was there?"

"This is the way it was. After the—disturbance, he was checking the rooms."

I bet he wasn't. Not rooms plural. Just mine. But why? "Of course," said Renwick.

Goss rushed on, feeling the need for an apology by way of an explanation. "He came to me for a key to your room. He hadn't been able to get any reply when he knocked at your door. Naturally, I insisted on going upstairs with him. No one enters a guest's room without his permission—or mine."

"So you stayed with Lasch when he entered my room?"

"Certainly. But you were deeply asleep. He couldn't ask you any questions. So we left."

An honest man, thought Renwick as he looked at Goss. Perhaps Lasch is honest, too: all he wanted to do was to ask me some questions for his report on the disturbance, as Goss had put it so eloquently. Perhaps. But I'll keep an eye on Inspector Lasch.

Yet why hadn't he broken the lock instead of trying to borrow a key? One answer could be that a broken lock would have had me tight with suspicions when I discovered it this morning. Or perhaps I'm in a doubting mood until I get something into my stomach.

Breakfast arrived. Herr Goss rose tactfully, prepared to go back to supervising his son. "I'll have your bill prepared for you when you leave."

"In half an hour. And, by the way, Herr Goss, could I trouble you for a strong envelope? I'll collect it when I pay the bill."

"An airmail envelope?"

"A Manila envelope, if possible. Heavy."

"Certainly, Herr Renwick." Goss didn't seem mystified. Guests make stranger requests than this one.

Renwick poured the coffee. Once he was in possession of that little black book, once Keppler had been shown its contents, as promised, he would mail it from the airport. He wasn't going to carry it around with him halfway across Europe, that was for damn sure.

He began eating. It was an excellent breakfast.

There was a fresh touch to early sunshine that invited a brisk walk along the lakeshore. But with regret Renwick turned north on Bahnhofstrasse. He passed Fraumünsterpost, an imposing edifice, lying just across a side street from the cathedral buildings. He reached the Fraumünster itself, ten minutes early.

So was Inspector Lasch. He looked friendly, even if his face was white and tired. He couldn't have had much rest last night. Yes, definitely friendly; and very correct. "Colonel Renwick—good morning!"

"Good morning, Inspector Lasch. Or should I say Colonel, too?"

Lasch's eyes wavered. "Perhaps it is better if we do not use rank."

He's a major, Renwick thought with amusement. "Much better. I prefer it. Shall we walk a little?" Or just stand here and look obvious.

They strolled around the cathedral's precincts. "Were you,"

asked Renwick, "with military intelligence before you joined Keppler's outfit?"

"Outfit?" Lasch's English, good, didn't stretch that far.

"Section—department—whatever he heads. He is chief of operations, isn't he?"

"Of his division, yes. But of the whole department—no. Last year when our new chief was appointed—" He broke off; he may have felt that his politeness had let him say too much. His voice changed. "These are matters we do not talk about."

"Sorry. You know my status. I'd like to know about yours. But if it's a state secret, then we'll drop the subject."

"Not a state secret. Just security."

"I don't think we are being overheard here. Do you?"

Lasch smiled too.

"So you are with Keppler's antiterrorist division, and not with the department. You couldn't have a better boss—probably the most capable man I've met in any intelligence service. Certainly, he carries a lot of clout."

"Clout?"

"Important, powerful."

"Yes, indeed."

"Why was he passed over last year?" The question seemed aimless.

"Never had any training in military intelligence," Lasch said abruptly.

"And that disqualifies him? Permanently?"

"No, no. With Inspector Keppler's record, that may be overlooked next time. Changes are happening. But he may reach retirement before that position is open again."

"That's a problem in all careers." The man who makes it to within touch of the top job, Renwick thought, and then is defeated by age. Retirement on what? Half pay? And a life of pottering around a small garden like Gilman's Aunt Chris in Washington. "He never married, did he? Lives with his sister, as far as I remember."

"She died last year. A long illness." Lasch shook his head in sympathy.

"Sorry to hear that. Well, I just hope Keppler gets that final promotion before he retires. But of course there will be other competitors for it, too. There's always a lot of infighting between various intelligence departments. That happens in every capital I've visited."

"Does Interintell suffer from that?"

"So far not, thank God. But we aren't large-scale; we are more concentrated. On terrorist activities. And we don't pull rank. We began as friends—people who knew each other— and we keep it that way."

"Interesting." Lasch liked the idea.

"I just hope that Interintell's request for help hasn't put Keppler in a difficult position. His competitors might—"

"Inspector Keppler can handle all difficulties." Lasch looked pointedly at his watch. "I think it is time."

Time to close a delicate conversation? "I believe it is," Renwick agreed. They retraced their steps and began to approach the Fraumünsterpost. "So you're my bodyguard, as it were," Renwick joked.

"There is nothing to guard. Just formalities."

"Do you know what I am collecting?" Renwick watched the man's face.

"An envelope. But it is of some importance, I understand."

He's telling the truth; he has no idea what the envelope contains. "It's damned important," Renwick said, and saw Lasch's eyes open in surprise. "Just keep a sharp lookout, will you?"

"There is nothing to worry about, I assure you."

But there he wasn't telling the truth. The sharp eyes were suddenly uneasy. The white face was strangely taut. "Good," said Renwick, "good." And as he seemed to forget any possible danger, Lasch relaxed also. One thing I did find out, thought Renwick: Keppler has enough power to handle any difficulties. If some quibbling is going on in Bern this morning, Keppler can take care of it. And thank God for that. If I had got him into some real trouble, I'd have had that on my conscience for a long, long time.

"Everything is arranged," Lasch was saying as he led the way into the post office. "You have also your own passport? Identification papers?"

"What about the authorization?"

"That has been given."

It sounded easy. Although there could have been complications from the current renovation of the Fraumünsterpost's interior, with scaffolding and work-in-progress around, Lasch knew exactly where to head for the poste restante section. The actual transaction was simple. Renwick and Lasch were expected, and at this early hour they had the place almost to themselves. Lasch flashed his identification, then turned everything over to Renwick, who showed Karen Cross's passport. Yes, he said, he was acting on behalf of Karen Cross, and signed a paper to that effect. Then there was his own passport to be examined briefly, and his signature compared with the one he wrote on the receipt. That over—a matter of minutes— he was in possession of an envelope, addressed to Miss Karen Cross at this poste restante in Zurich, and mailed in New York two weeks ago. "One moment!" he told Lasch and opened the envelope. It held a thin black notebook, four by three inches, no more, in size.

He riffled through some pages. This was it. The Plus List.

Suddenly, Lasch's arm shot out, his hand trying to grasp the book. Just as quickly, Renwick jammed it into his inside pocket. He stared at Lasch as he closed its zipper, made the pocket secure. "What the hell were you trying to do?"

"You are to give me the book."

"I what?"

Lasch gave a worried glance around the room. "No argument here, please. Keep your voice down. My instructions were that you give me the book."

Renwick walked on. He reached a long row of grilled windows now open for business and stopped abruptly. He dropped his bag at his feet, took his stand. He lowered his voice but spoke with a fury that startled Lasch. "Whose instructions? Whose?"

"We should leave. We talk outside."

"We talk in here. Whose instructions? The Chief of Intelligence? Or someone who wants Keppler's job?"

"No, no. Please. I can't tell you. You understand?"

Renwick was recovering. The book was still in his pocket. Lasch was armed—that formidable Swiss army pistol he had drawn last night was in its holster under his jacket—but he hadn't tried any threats with it to force Renwick to walk outside into a waiting car. Renwick's voice lost its intensity, became low but clear; and he didn't move from where he stood.

"No," he said, tight-lipped. "I don't understand. And you

don't understand, either. This book, which you tried to grab, was Interintell's discovery. We learned about it, we risked a lot for it—one helluva lot. Including yesterday evening. Do you think I enjoy having to fire to kill? Do you? If I hadn't, I would have been dead. Sudak would have searched my pockets, discovered the passport. And he would have found a way to get this book. Oh, yes, he would have. He must have had his plan all arranged: a woman who resembled Karen Cross, who'd pass muster. Easy enough."

Lasch only stared at him.

Renwick went on, "What is more, Major Lasch, I signed for this envelope. My name is on record. If there is an inquiry and I can't account for the contents, what then? I got it and I lost it, all within forty seconds. Is that what I say?"

"Inquiry?" That astonished Lasch, horrified him, too. "No need for any—"

"What do you expect if someone is trying to prevent Keppler's future promotion? Sure, there will be an investigation, an inquiry. So whose orders were you following? Your general in charge of operations who—"

"No." The sharp rebuttal was spontaneous, indignant.

"Then whose orders?" Renwick was curt, authoritative.

Lasch looked the unhappiest man in Zurich. "Inspector Keppler's. It was understood that you should get the book for him."

"It was not!"

"But—"

"Look," said Renwick, becoming the civilian again, "you must have misunderstood Keppler's instructions. He was to see the names in this book and act on them—if any of those names do belong to Swiss citizens. That was all. There was no talk whatsoever that the book was going to Bern." Then Renwick paused, said, "You haven't been told why these names are so important, have you? They belong to men of several nations—several. Not just Swiss. They took money to aid and abet the illegal business of Exports Consolidated and of Klingfeld and Sons. You've heard of them, haven't you?"

"Of them, yes." The tight control over Lasch's face was slipping. There was anxiety now, mixed with doubt and uncertainty.

A man who is loyal, obeys orders, but he's not stupid: if he let me talk, it was to find out what I could tell him. And he's listening. Renwick said, "When did you hear of Exports Consolidated? In the last few days? But not in the last two weeks when you should have heard."

Lasch looked at him sharply.

Renwick said, "Who could have smothered any report on Exports Consolidated? Who could have sidetracked its link with Klingfeld?"

There was a long silence. Lasch glanced at the hall's entrance. Two men had stationed themselves there, blocking its exit.

Renwick noticed the glance and the men.

Lasch said crisply, "You refuse to hand over that book to me?"

"Yes."

"And if you were to be threatened with arrest, with questions about the death of Klaus Sudak, you would still refuse?"

"Yes."

"For the reasons you have given me?"

"Yes." No other exit, thought Renwick. But the business day had begun: people moving around, lines forming in front of the grilled windows, stamps being bought, packages mailed. If he could mix with a group as they left, reach the street?

Quietly, with an abrupt hand sign, Lasch signaled to the two men. They moved away.

Dismissal. Renwick's breath came more easily.

Lasch said, "You wait here. I shall telephone Bern."

"And tell Keppler to stop playing hard-to-find. I promised to show him the names in the Plus List, and I'll keep that promise. Tell him also—"

"Plus List?"

"Exports Consolidated's list. The man who kept it had a peculiar sense of humor. Useful friends were a plus," Renwick explained patiently. "So when you call Keppler in Bern, tell him to get over to Zurich as fast as he can. I'll wait—until noon. That gives him four hours."

Lasch's eyes were hard. "Inspector Keppler is not in Bern."

"In Zurich? Has he an office here, too?" *As soon as I can get away from my office.* Keppler's words.

"No." Lasch turned and hurried toward the doorway.

Renwick's face tightened. He took out Brimmer's diary.

Thirty-eight names were on the Plus List, one to each page. There were only two Swiss names. One was Johann Keppler.

For a moment, Renwick felt paralyzed. He hadn't wanted to believe it. It couldn't be, he had told himself in those last few minutes, it couldn't be. But it was.

He snapped the book shut, picked up his bag, and reached a counter. There, with the bag safe at his feet, he pulled out the Bürkli envelope. Into this he slipped the Plus List, sealed and addressed it to J. P. Merriman & Co., with *Attention Ronald Gilman* across one corner of the envelope. He marked it *Luftpost—Par Avion—Airmail*. Then he had the envelope weighed and stamped and registered. He asked for special delivery. Contents? A personal diary. And so noted. And so mailed.

It was with mixed emotions that he let the envelope fall out of sight through a slot for delivery abroad. I'll rely on the Swiss, he thought as he walked back to the spot where Lasch had left him: their mails, like their trains, run on time. No sign yet of Lasch; or of any self-effacing men standing against a wall, watching.

How could Keppler have done it? Thirty years or more of honest service, and then this. What made him? Why? Disappointment over promotion? Savings vanished with the expenses of his sister's illness? Retirement on little money? But other men had faced these questions and hadn't answered with betrayal.

It was a recent involvement. The first payment came last October: fifty thousand deposited in a Nassau bank. A second deposit of fifty thousand in March. The third was made two weeks ago: seventy thousand. Peanuts compared to what some of Brimmer's helpers had been paid. Keppler would never know how cheaply he had been bought.

And then, in one last desperate hope, Renwick wondered if Keppler could have mounted a secret investigation of his own into Exports Consolidated and Klingfeld. Had he thought he could infiltrate, get proof of their bribery and corruption? Yet, that wasn't Keppler's style: he never took wild chances. Everything he did was calculated. One of the most capable and reliable men I've ever met, thought Renwick. He was all of that, four years ago, when we first worked together. What happened? Or did it happen? Am I condemning a friend who took a fantastic risk to furnish real evidence?

Heartsick, he stood motionless, scarcely heard Lasch's voice at this elbow. "Inspector Keppler will meet you at noon."

Renwick nodded.

"At the Belvoir Park, north entrance."

No park, thank you. Renwick shook his head. "At the airport. Twelve o'clock. I'll wait one hour. Then I leave."

"Where do you wait?"

"Inside the terminal—the corridor with the long stretch of shops." And plenty of people around. "There's a café at its far end."

"Which end?"

"If you stand looking out toward the runways, then it's to your right-hand side." Not brilliant, but the best he could do at this moment.

"I know the café." Lasch paused. His face was impassive, but his eyes were worried. "Did you look at the Plus List?"

"Yes."

"Were there names of Swiss citizens?"

"Two."

"Will you show the list to Inspector Keppler?"

"I will tell him."

"You promised—" Lasch began. And then, "So you don't trust us."

"At this moment I trust no one," Renwick said bitterly.

Lasch wasn't too surprised. "The list does concern our national security?" he persisted.

"Very much so. Interintell will keep your government fully informed."

"Then," said Lasch softly as he gestured in the direction of the poste restante where Renwick had received the envelope addressed to Karen Cross, "all that was of importance?"

"Of vital importance to Switzerland. And to six other countries."

Lasch's relief was transparent. "There will be no inquiry about this morning."

"Not concerning you and me, at least." Renwick picked up his bag, and they walked out together.

"May I give you a lift?" Lasch asked as they left the Fraumünsterpost.

Renwick looked at the olive-green car that waited by the curb. The two men inside it were those who had blocked the exit from the main hall. "Very kind of you, but I think I need some air. By the way, what changed your mind about giving me a lift earlier today?"

Lasch hesitated, seemed to take Renwick's measure, said very quietly, "Your questions: who smothered any reports on Exports Consolidated—who sidetracked its link with Klingfeld?" There was another hesitation. "That happened two weeks ago. But I thought it was a mistake in judgment, an error."

Seventy thousand dollars two weeks ago. Renwick's small hope grew fainter. "You have a phone call to make. I won't delay you any more. Good-bye, Major Lasch."

Lasch smiled, showed a small transmitter concealed in his hand. "No need to telephone. *Auf Wiedersehen*, Herr Renwick."

So Keppler isn't far away. He could have met me here and now. Grim-faced, Renwick made his way toward the crowded Hauptbahnstrasse.

24

I<small>T HAD BEEN A LONG MORNING OF WALKING, OF THINKING,</small> of trying not to think, but eventually Renwick took a taxi and reached the Zurich airport. He entered the café in the terminal building at twelve o'clock exactly.

It was almost filled. People waiting for planes, people spending time between connections, people concentrating on their own worries—schedules, safe transfer of luggage, delays. People everywhere, but no sign of Keppler. Renwick made sure of a table, vacated in near panic by an elderly couple as they heard their flight being called, by sitting down as the remains of their lunch were being cleared away. He ordered a pot of coffee.

By half past twelve he ordered more coffee and a sandwich as his pretext for occupying the table. Its position was too good to lose. He lit his fourth cigarette.

He had always liked his café, a pleasant place to relax in the middle of an airport's turmoil. It wasn't walled in; it needed no door, no windows. It was simply a large space roped off from the broad indoor avenue, lined with shops, that ran the length of this giant terminal. Its decorative plants didn't block the view of anyone walking outside its boundary; its tables were jammed together: Keppler would see him easily. And Renwick had taken a chair that let him have clear sight of anyone who stepped out of the crowd to enter this oasis.

So there he was, sitting in a place he usually liked and hating every minute of it. He stubbed out his ninth cigarette. It was one o'clock. He pushed aside the uneaten sandwich, looked no more at the entrance in front of him, began counting out Swiss francs to cover the bill and tip. Five past one. Keppler wasn't coming. No talk; no clarification. But, then, there was the old-time rule for intelligence officers: never apologize, never explain. If your friends couldn't take you on trust, they were no friends at all.

He reached for his bag—that goddamned bag filled with old Bernie's little goodies he had been lugging around Zurich as if it were Fort Knox in miniature. He sensed a movement toward his table, looked up sharply. It was Lasch who stood there, his face set and his arm stiff as he indicated the chair opposite Renwick. "May I?" he asked.

Renwick straightened his back. What now? A last-minute summons to a police station? Questions about the shooting of Klaus Sudak?

Lasch sat down. "I am glad I found you. I only heard half an hour ago. I came at once."

Renwick waited.

"He is dead."

"Dead?"

"Drove into a stone marker at the side of the road. He was traveling at high speed. It was a dangerous curve."

"On the highway to the airport?" Renwick could remember no sharp curves.

"No. On the road to Luzern. He must have left Zurich just after—just after I talked with him." There was a long pause. Then Lasch forced himself to say, "He knew that road well. He used to say he could drive it blindfolded."

Renwick's last shred of hope was gone. He felt stifled, couldn't speak.

"In Luzern—there was a woman. Very young. Forty years younger."

"Since when? In the last year?"

Lasch nodded. Again a pause. He said slowly, "Death was

instant. He made very sure. It was one solution. The only one perhaps?"

Yes, Renwick answered silently. For Keppler it was the only solution.

Lasch went on talking, but his voice was now brisk. "You said there were two Swiss names on the list of men who had taken bribes from Exports Consolidated."

Renwick nodded.

"You said that Interintell would send these names to my government. Will they?"

"Yes. I think that's the way Interintell must handle that list: names to each government of its citizens who have taken those bribes. The government concerned can keep an eye on their future ambitions—it won't want men like that running for public office or occupying positions of power and trust. But," Renwick added, "there would be no need for Interintell to send a dead man's name. He would no longer be a—" and this was difficult to say—"a security risk."

"I agree," Lasch said, and relaxed. He looked at the American's tight face, then at the heap of cigarette stubs and the uneaten food. "One more thing. It is important. To me."

"Yes?" Renwick had pushed back his chair, was about to leave.

"Yesterday evening—at the Bürkli—I had no idea you were in Upwood's room. No idea. I wasn't told you could be there."

Renwick stared at him.

Lasch rushed on. "In the lobby I saw the red-haired man keep looking at his watch. At six o'clock he rose and went through the bar into the restaurant. A tall man, dark-haired, arrived within a few minutes. They took the service stairs from there—without a word, moved quickly. I followed. Discreetly. When I reached the second floor, they were already at the door of the room. I was calling for my backup as they broke the lock and entered. I thought—I swear before God—that I would let them start searching, and then I would surprise them, hold them until my two men arrived. I did not know you could be in there—facing them—alone." Lasch's eyes hardened at that thought. "Believe me," he said, his first sign of anger showing against Keppler, "I wasn't told. That is not how I work."

"I believe you."

"My report reads that there was an exchange of shots. You

were standing to the left side of the door. Facing the men.
They had their backs to the couch at the window. Yes?"

"Yes."

"I knew it! The two bullet holes were in the wall of the
room, just behind you. The bullets we extracted were matched
with their revolvers. There will be no doubt that the two men
fired at you. But missed, *Gott sei Dank*. So, Herr Renwick"—
Lasch actually smiled—"as you were acting for Interintell,
there should be no difficulties, no unpleasantness for you. It
was self-defense, in the line of duty."

Then I'm free to leave, Renwick thought.

Lasch said, "More important, your actual name will not be
mentioned. There is no need to have it recorded for the benefit
of any KGB file."

"No need," Renwick agreed. "And thank you for that."

"The least we can do. You have done us a service."

"Not one of my choosing."

Lasch said quickly, "You didn't destroy him, Herr Renwick.
He destroyed himself."

Yes, last October, Keppler destroyed himself. "Good-bye,
then. I'm glad we talked." Renwick was rising to his feet. He
couldn't resist adding, "And thank you for letting me sleep last
night."

Lasch's white face flushed. "I entered your room to ask if
you had found the passport."

"And to persuade me to entrust it to you for safekeeping?"
Renwick asked gently.

"I was instructed—" Lasch broke off. "You understand?"

"Fully."

"Of course, if you hadn't found the passport, then all our
plans for this morning would have been changed. *Nicht wahr?*"

"True," Renwick agreed, and eased the look of embarrassment on Lasch's unhappy face. Plans would have been changed,
and Keppler would have been still alive, still undiscovered. He
would have searched for the passport, and when he had found
it, he'd make sure this time that Brimmer's Plus List would be
delivered into his hands. As it was meant to be, this morning.
Renwick resisted one final question. Why didn't you grab harder
at that little black book, Karl—or force me with a gun at my
ribs into your car? Instead, he put out his hand. "It was good

working with you, Karl. Fortunate for me, too." And that was the solid truth.

"A pleasure to work with Interintell." Lasch was on his feet, his hand crushingly strong in its firm grip.

"Good-bye."

"Auf Wiedersehen."

Renwick was three paces away. "Herr Renwick!" he heard. What now? he wondered as he turned around.

"You forgot your bag, Herr Renwick." Lasch handed it to him with a bow.

Renwick took it, shook his hand, and walked on, back into his thoughts about Keppler. Strange: they had talked about him for the last fifteen minutes and never once had they mentioned his name. Yet not so strange: Keppler, as they had known him, had died nine months ago.

Now, where was a telephone? In Washington it would be half past eight. He would waken Nina with the best news in his life: he was coming home.

25

In Zurich, Renwick hadn't been able to reach Nina. There was only the housekeeper's voice, cool and impersonal, telling him they had left Basset Hill. Yes, Mrs. Smith had left. And Mr. MacEwan. With Mr. Grant driving them in his car. No, she didn't know where they were going.

The short flight to Geneva became a long plunge back into frustration and anxiety. He had expected too much, he told himself, when he hoped to find Nina waiting by the phone for his call. Everything was all right, must be. But the last message from Basset Hill, relayed by London this morning, had been sent out from Washington last night. Anything could have happened in that time-lag. Anything.

At the Geneva airport, he found a cheerful Claudel with an arm heavily encased in bandages and a bright word of welcome. "I was delayed," Renwick said. "Sorry to be late."

"Nothing to it. Got here early." It didn't seem the right moment, judging from Renwick's face, to mention Claudel's own efficiency. He had put the hours of waiting to good use. His plane was tanked up, ready to soar. And for once he was going to allow someone else to take over the controls. Leave his sweet darling alone and abandoned at Geneva until he could come back to fly her out? No, thank you.

"How's the arm?" Renwick asked as they walked through the terminal.

No explanation given for the delay, no mention of what had happened in Zurich. Claudel controlled his impatience. He'd hear the details once they had taken off—another good reason for flying private. On a commercial flight there would be no serious talk. He began describing the wire cradle in which his forearm was resting, a neat piece of medical engineering to hold the wound together and let it mend naturally. "There will be a scar, of course, but the girls never object to that—intrigues them. It will cramp my style for a week or two. Can't move it around."

"You'll think of ways," Renwick told him. He was abstracted, his eyes searching for a phone booth.

"Gilman reached me this morning and—"

"Have you any spare Swiss francs? I'm running short."

"Sure. But—"

"I'm calling Washington. Where's the nearest phone, dammit?"

"No need, Bob. She's en route. To Paris."

Renwick's voice sharpened. "Alone?"

"Bob—the danger is over. Anyway, Mac is traveling with her. That is, if they made the shuttle to La Guardia in time to reach Kennedy by nine-fifteen. She's taking the Concorde. It doesn't fly from Washington on a Monday." Claudel laughed. "Nina decided it all—must have been studying timetables for days. Gilman was slightly astonished—especially by her last question. Couldn't understand it quite, but he said yes anyway. She asked, 'Then the snake has been scotched?' What the devil did she mean? Klaus Sudak?"

Renwick nodded, a first smile playing around his lips. "Thoroughly scotched." He calculated quickly. "Arriving at DeGaulle just before six. When's the first flight out of here?"

"We can do better than that. I've got my plane all ready to go. You can take her up, can't you?"

"You bet I will." Renwick was already moving off.

"Easy, easy," Claudel told him as he caught up. "Gilman has booked Nina into the George Cinq—he knows the management. He will be there himself tomorrow—he's eager to get the full details. Who isn't?"

"He'd better be back in Grace Street by the day after tomorrow. There's a registered envelope on its way from Zurich."

"You mailed Brimmer's Plus List?"

"Seemed the safest bet."

"Rough going this morning?" Claudel was astounded.

"Well—let's say it could have been."

"Didn't Keppler deliver?"

"He sold out."

"What?"

"Later, Pierre, later. When did Gilman call Nina?"

"Just after he got your report and had it decoded."

"At half past one in the morning?"

"A telephone call means good news." Bad news would have been sent in a message to MacEwan and let him break it, face to face. "Bob," Claudel said most seriously, "don't you know how worried we've all been?"

And there were moments when I was damned worried, too. Renwick said, "What's the best flying time we can make?"

"We could—with this good weather—reach Orly by five o'clock."

And then traffic delays. "We'll try for De Gaulle."

"Problems, Bob. I usually fly into—"

"You work them out."

"Well, well. Delegating authority, are you?"

"From now on there will be plenty of delegating."

"I think I've heard that before."

"This time I mean it." Renwick's face went taut.

Claudel looked at him quickly. I believe he does, Claudel thought. I really believe it. I didn't even have to tell him how near Nina was to danger. That news can wait, like the other items Gilman gave me on our double-talk over the phone this morning. Vroom, for instance: Vroom resigning from Dutch Intelligence as well as from Interintell, Vroom taking a job with Bruna Imports, leaving next month for Indonesia and the problems of the spice and coffee trade. Or perhaps I won't mention the threat to Nina, let Gilman do his diplomatic best with that. What Bob needs now is an hour in a decompression chamber. This time he went too far down below the surface. And he knows it. Goddammit, why did he go in alone? With such speed? But Claudel knew the answer: the only way to deal with Klaus Sudak was to be one jump ahead of him. "Okay," he said as they reached the plane. "Sure you won't strip her gears?"

They arrived at De Gaulle Airport, as Claudel had predicted, with time to spare. They even managed a very late twenty-minute lunch of sandwiches and beer, and still had half an hour to wait. Midway through the flight, Renwick had begun to talk. Back to normal or almost, thought Claudel, and thank heaven for that. Now it was he who began worrying. It was more than possible that Nina hadn't managed the distance between La Guardia and Kennedy airports before the Concorde lifted off. In that case, Claudel could see his own plans for tonight evaporating. Tomorrow morning he would be waiting again with Bob at this bloody airport for the arrival of an overnight flight from New York.

As they paced along the exits from customs and immigration, Renwick said, "No need for you to hang around, Pierre."

"No need," Claudel agreed cheerfully, but he stayed. No need? After all that he had heard this afternoon? But the decompression chamber was working: Bob was out on deck, breath normal, and it only needed Nina to complete the cure. My God, what if she didn't arrive? Quickly, Claudel began talking about next January. If he could manage it, he might be back in Chamonix for some skiing.

"The brunette nurse?"

"Yes, the knockout—the one that caught your roving eye."

But at that moment, Renwick's eyes were riveted. The first arrivals were beginning to appear.

Claudel said, "Give me that bag, and I'll see you tomorrow. In Gilman's room at the George Cinq. Around eleven?"

"Two o'clock." Renwick's eyes were searching.

"Gilman will be there by ten."

"You can start with Amsterdam and hold him with Chamonix. You've got plenty to tell—" Renwick broke off as his eyes found a girl with fair hair cut short and curling. Nina. Nina, more beautiful than ever, with her large eyes and the tilt of her head and the smile on her lips. She hadn't seen him yet as she walked—high-heeled sandals tapping lightly, cream shirt open at the neck, cream skirt slightly swinging at each step—beside a red-haired man, and listened to him talk. Mac, thought Renwick, I like you; I like you a lot, but you don't have to be so damned fascinating.

Mac, quick as ever, had seen them both and caught Claudel's high sign to follow him out.

Renwick didn't even notice. Nina had halted, her blue eyes widening as she stared at him in wonder. Renwick scarcely heard Mac say, as he dropped Nina's suitcase beside him, "All yours, now. Glad you're back, Bob."

Renwick put out his hands to grasp hers. For a long moment they stood looking at each other. Then he drew her into his arms, tightening them around her as they kissed. Soft lips, soft cheeks, soft silken hair against his mouth. Suddenly, he was alive again. He laughed with the joy of it. He released her, held her back from him to look at her once more. "Magic, you are pure magic, darling." He picked up her suitcase and slipped an arm around her waist as they began walking toward the street.

About the Author

HELEN MacINNES was born in Scotland, grew up there, was graduated from the University of Glasgow, and later studied at University College in London. After her marriage to the late Gilbert Highet, they lived in Oxford, where he was a don at St. John's College. In 1937 Mr. Highet was invited to lecture at Columbia University and, except during his distinguished war service as a high-level member of British Intelligence, the Highets made their home in New York. They became United States citizens in 1951.

Miss MacInnes started to write for publication in 1939. Her first novel, *Above Suspicion*, was an immediate success and launched her on a spectacular writing career that has made her an international favorite. Her previous nineteen novels have sold well over twenty million copies in America alone and have been translated into twenty-two languages. Each of her novels has been a best seller and a book-club selection. Several have been adapted as films.

Miss MacInnes is recognized as the creator of remarkably acute and supremely exciting novels set against a background of meaningful present-day events. In the genre of highly literate suspense, she is unrivaled.

L.H.